THE
DAZZLE
OF DAY

Also by Molly Gloss

MOLLY GLOSS

THE DAZZLE OF DAY

SAGA  PRESS

LONDON SYDNEY **NEW YORK** TORONTO NEW DELHI

SAGA PRESS
AN IMPRINT OF SIMON & SCHUSTER, INC.

1230 AVENUE OF THE AMERICAS, NEW YORK, NEW YORK 10020

Text copyright © 1997 by Molly Gloss

Cover illustration copyright © 2019 by Jeffrey Alan Love

For information about special discounts for bulk purchases, please contact Simon & Schuster Special Sales at 1-866-506-1949 or business@simonandschuster.com.

The Simon & Schuster Speakers Bureau can bring authors to your live event. For more information or to book an event, contact the Simon & Schuster Speakers Bureau at 1-866-248-3049 or visit our website at www.simonspeakers.com.

Also available in a Saga Press hardcover edition

Interior design by Vikki Sheatsley

The text for this book was set in Cormorant Garamond.

Manufactured in the United States of America

First Saga Press paperback edition March 2019

10 9 8 7 6 5 4 3 2 1

Library of Congress Cataloging-in-Publication Data

Names: Gloss, Molly, author.

Title: The dazzle of day / Molly Gloss.

Description: First Saga Press paperback edition. | London ; New York : Saga Press, 2019.

Identifiers: LCCN 2018022758 | ISBN 9781481498470 (paperback : alk. paper) | ISBN 9781481498487 (hardcover : alk. paper) | ISBN 9781481498494 (eBook)

Subjects: LCSH: Space colonies—Fiction. | GSAFD: Science fiction.

Classification: LCC PS3557.L65 D39 2019 | DDC 813/.54—dc23

LC record available at https://lccn.loc.gov/2018022758

For Ed
kamarado

AUTHOR'S NOTE

Esperanto is an artificial, international language favored by many Peace churches for its facility at clearing the way.

There are no silent letters; every word is pronounced as it is spelled.

Vowels are sounded ah, eh, ee, oh, oo—as in "Are there three or two?"

The semi-vowel ŭ is like the English w, and combines with a preceding vowel to form a diphthong:

aŭ = ow (landau)
eŭ = ew (euphemism)

Consonants are sounded as in English except for these:

c = ts (prince)
ĉ = ch (cello)
g always "hard" (goat)

ĝ *always "soft" (gypsy)*
j = y (hallelujah)
ĵ *= zh (Taj Mahal)*
r always trilled
s always sibilant (sensible)
ŝ *= sh (sugar)*
-j is the plural ending.

Among some Esperanto speakers, female children take the family name of the mother, and male children the family name of the father.

Questions asking whether a thing is true or not (yes/no questions) are formed by the use of the particle ĉu. Here, that usage is suggested by the colloquial English interrogative, "eh?"

Verano

Darest thou now O soul,
Walk out with me toward the unknown region,
Where neither ground is for the feet nor any path to
   follow?

MY FAMILY ONCE considered themselves Tico, but the old Hispanic tradition of community has so long ago disappeared from this continent, subsumed in the monoculture of the west, that I consider my only culture to be Quaker. Still, the Friends who are joining us in this migration have Japanese names, English, Norwegian—these *Friends* are strangers to me. Moreover I don't speak Esperanto very well, and maybe I'm too old to learn it better, or maybe too tired. Esperanto is a language without much grace: In the rainy season, who would want to give up saying *invierno*, which lies sweetly on the tongue, in trade for the crabbed little sound of *vintro*?

   I am sixty years old, and afraid the arthritis in my knees,

which is a new thing, may before long make me no use to anyone—or worse, an encumbrance, which would surely be a vaster problem in that young ship than here on this old land.

It might be, the matrix that's been used is too diminished after all for species survival. With the first of these toroids it was something like that, the one named *Crommelin*, built for the rich man, Jon Crommelin, a scrupulously beautiful, flauntingly private refuge put to circling the earth just above this poisoned sky, every grain of dirt disinfected, every person and object sterilized, unpleasant insects and reptiles shut out. In a year, less than a year, there was a collapse of the organic life, and the dead construct was abandoned. It was sects of the counterculture—Carsonites and bird-watchers and Rodale farmers, Quakers and Mennonites—who understood the microbial needs of a closed system, guessed the conceit that must have killed the life there, and joined in bargaining for the *Crommelin* and attempting its renascence, as a kind of public proof of the connectedness of all life.

A decade of seeding and reseeding, trials of species-packing and of minimalism, emending and remodeling the nexus, and now there is a modest proliferation of these small forged moons, these hollow wheels with their interior, tubular landscapes. I, for one, had thought every isolationist party from Aryan Nation to Doomwatchers would soon flock up to the sky, but what has been proven by these toroids is only the absolute unmindful benightedness of the greater part of the human race. The very difficulties and economics of a closed circle of recycle and reuse have kept the stations, against all expectation, in the hands of the patient and whole-minded; our *Miller* is the only one yet to make preparations for casting off moorings—setting sail for the farthest shore. What if, in ten years or twenty, when we are too far away to get back, all the trees and the birds begin to die?

The toroid takes its plain Quaker name, *Dusty Miller*, from the reflective sail's whitish aspect in the sun's transparent light, and I have lain awake and imagined it; the small circle of raft—the houseboat, as people are saying—at the center of its great circle of flimsy sailcloth, moving soundlessly across the blackness of space like a moth, a leaf, a little puff of pollen adrift on a solar wind, which is an image that sits well with me. But I shall not see it thus except in my mind's eye; I shall live within its ceiled and narrow view, in a circumscribed world lying under fields of lamps. Never to see the sky! The stars!

The closed circle of the hollow torus can be walked round in fifteen or twenty minutes, a bare two thousand meters from starting point round again to starting point. Big as some islands, people say, and they tell me of balance and proportion, scale and siting, the compact order of a Japanese garden. But other people have said there is a melancholy that gets into the soul of an island people—and, indeed, into the souls of migrants, for among the pilgrims of the *Mayflower*, and at Plymouth, there was black discouragement and suicide. There still are mornings in the Fourth Month rains when I get a yearning to tramp out to the horizon, a wanderlust so palpable it makes my breast ache. Where, on the *Dusty Miller*, would I tramp to?

Quaker people have endured on this old estancia on the Pacific slope of middle America for 240 years, steadfastly practicing love and faith in the midst of chaos and wars. My parents are buried in this soil, my sister, my sister's daughter, I always had thought I would one day be buried beside them.

Who would have thought it would come to this—sitting among the boxes of my possessions waiting to be taken up from this house, the house in which I have lived the whole of my life until now? Who would have thought I would one day be sitting on the floor of my house in the oppressive heat and drought of the *verano*, indulging myself in qualms and skittishness, thinking and now writing about the forepart of my life and the after, on this day that separates them?

I always have considered myself strong-minded, someone who would act on her feelings without faltering, and it has been a surprise to realize: I have been thinking of changing my mind, and hiding the thought from myself in this flurry of last-minute, agitated misgivings. Tonight, the last night for sleeping under this roof, I have been thinking of changing my mind, and looking for peace or clarity or certainty by trudging round in circles, sleepless, through the dusty night.

Tonight I walked along the cart road across the Rio Pardo and through the east-side fields and houses up onto the rocky ridge of the Ojo de la Luna, and home again by way of the goat-paths—a long looping tramp. The cart road is a rutted track; we have deliberately kept it poor and unpaved to discourage non-Quakers from coming onto the *estancia*, a tactic that has been only a little successful. There have been killings, crazy wildings, here as everywhere, but we have gone on using the road after dark on Quaker principles, bearing witness to peace, trusting in the unknowable justice of God. *What happens, happens,* people frequently say, meaning not only murder and rape on the roads but death by plague or by cancer, which seem in these days to be distilled from the very air and water. I went along the road through a breathless darkness, slapping my sandals down briskly in the dust.

My old house stands alone, but a little way up the road the houses of my neighbors stand in the manner of Friends, gathered up in a hamlet, and there I was kept company by the voices of people who know me, calling my name from their porches. Children were playing in the road in the still night, and some of them made me a little escort as far as the edge of the river where the road drops down in the rocky channel and begins to follow the low water. The air was darker there, cooler, more silent, a comfort of another kind: In the daylight the Rio Pardo is a grief, scummed yellow along its margins, but in the darkness tonight the sound it made was soft and easeful, and there was only the grayish bulk of the boulders against the colorless blackness of the water.

The heavy forest has been shorn from the steep slopes higher on the watershed, and in the flood season the river is every year more ravaging. Where a bridge had once spanned it, I waded across following the cart tracks between the old concrete footings, pushing my bare ankles through the dead and tepid water. Afterward, on my skin, the slime itched and stank, and finally I had to stoop and rub my sticky legs with handfuls of dust.

Where the track climbs from the gully of the river and turns east toward the rocky *arista*, the houses are scattered among their fields in the old Hispanic manner. People have been moving up to the *Miller* for months, and many houses are vacant, abandoned. Tonight even the occupied homes stood dark and mute, seeming to ghost the landscape. I imagined people lying inside their houses in the hot, torpid darkness, asleep or awake, measuring their breaths on the still night.

We are at the height of the dry season; no rain has fallen for weeks. The ground is fissured, the grasses brown, shrubbery stooped and withered. At this time of year, the *verano*, it is easy to imagine the death of the Earth, easy to believe in its imminence. Walking along the road, my sandals raised a fine pale powder that hung in the night, and I remembered suddenly, it had been in the *verano* the year before, when I had said I would go onto the *Dusty Miller*. It had been in the *verano* that I had become afraid I would live long enough to see the end of the world.

Species are extinguished by the hundred a day in the name of hungry people; wholesale obliteration of human cultures has been the history of the world for dozens of generations, in the name of human rights. By the time governments and corporations, those grindingly complex and malignant machines of human culture, have finally broken down under their own weight and can no longer deal destruction on the Earth, what of value will be left? It was in the *verano* that I began to dream the *Dusty Miller*'s dream of a world in which people respectfully take part in their landscape, and go on doing it generation after generation.

But tonight, walking up the road through the fields of empty houses, I thought: If I see the end of the Earth, I see it. And I wondered why I had been afraid. "Now I am clear. I am fully clear," the prophet George Fox was supposed to have said when he died. It might be, there is only so much that can be learned from life; perhaps then one has to wait for what will be exhibited by death.

I never have married, have no children to persuade me. Quite a few people I know are staying behind—some of them consider themselves too old for this change, and some are frightened. Some people see a moral imperative in standing against government oppression of the Peace churches. Or they say this emigration extends a frontier mythos whose legacy is destruction and exploitation. I haven't any compunction that way. Quaker principles have been proffered to the world for many hundreds of years, and indifferently spurned or actively expunged everywhere. I am weary of trying to live a moral and religious life against the persistent oppression of an immoral, irreligious world. It has become a terrible, exhausting struggle. How much longer can we few go on sustaining a society based on joy and authenticity—defining success as an internal process in a world that defines it by power and wealth? What is the mythos that propels the *Dusty Miller*, if not Wholeness?

No, my qualms are secular, personal, banal. This weather they have made to be inside the metal skin of the houseboat: Will there be the Fourth Month rains? What if I want to go on calling the dry season *verano* and not have to call it *somero*?

While I was turning over these worries in my mind, a shape reared up in the darkness alongside the road-cut, and my heart sprang against the cage of my ribs. I stood up straighter and made a swift plan for escaping through the taro field, back to the last lighted house. The person looked toward me and lifted both hands in a peaceful or inquiring gesture—there was something familiar in the way he stood. In a moment, I came on along the ruts.

"Arturo?"

"Dolores!"

"You gave me a start. Were you just sitting there by the road?"

"I been walking but my feet got hot. I need a drink, you got one?"

Arturo Remlinger is a slow-witted man whose mother died in the rainy season this past year. He frequently goes walking up and down the roads looking for her. He understands as much as a five-year-old, maybe, and what do five-year-olds understand of death? Oh my dear, what does anyone?

"No, I haven't got water, Arturo. But come on with me, we'll walk up the road and get you some." Arturo's brother has taken on his care. The brother's house wasn't far off; probably Arturo had padded out the door after everyone there had gone to bed.

I took his soft hand and led him. He has a big, doughy body, a round face without angles. He is prone to unpredictable storms of temper—he wheels his big arms and stomps his feet, rolls his head on his thick neck. The sounds that come out of him then are rageful and wordless, terrifying, heartbreaking. Neighbors come when they hear him, and help his brother as they used to help his mother, gently press him out-of-doors where he isn't as likely to hurt himself. The house his mother had lived in was bare of ornament; she had learned to give up breakable things. The brother has a wife who is a clay artist, and two young children. I wondered: What hangs on their walls, what sits on their tables now?

We walked along the road together. "What do you think? Is the dry season about finished?" I asked him. One of his interests is the weather. He likes to repeat and repeat the accounts he hears on the satellite radio stations, of weather in Lithuania and Botswana, Kampuchea, Greenland, Chile.

He swung his head back and forth heavily. "No. Not finished. But we'll get some rain someday, ha ha." He grinned softly and used the hand I was holding to gesture for both of us, vaguely overhead. "Rains every night, just about, on the house-boat. I like raining. Hey, Dolores, I'm going to live up there, how about you?"

I had been present when someone at a New World Planning Committee Meeting had wondered aloud: Should impaired and disabled people be kept from joining the emigration to the *Dusty Miller*? The way of Friends is to think quietly and to listen. We ask the question, we consider how the answer is made by different people, we ask again, answer again, change our minds; we reach an understanding. The Meeting evolves this way, not by shouting each other down, not by the weight of the majority, but by the capacity of individual human beings to comprehend one another. So there was a pondering silence and then someone stood and said, "What is impairment, I wonder. Is it arthritis? If one eye is blind but not the other, is that disabling?" People considered this. After a while someone else, a surgeon, said, "There won't be the resources to treat serious health problems. No microtechnology for prosthetics, for the metered administering of insulin, for synthetic laryngeal voicing."

People went on in this way for quite a while—not back and forth but circling around. There was a Japanese woman sitting at that Meeting, a young woman who had come over from Honshu to talk to our Farms Committee about the growing of kenaf and cilantro. This woman stood up after a long, listening silence and said what everyone there already knew—one of the four cardinal principles of the Religious Society of Friends: "Something of the inner light of God lives in every human being." I remember the precise pitch and cadence of her voice, her precisely correct Spanish, and the way the air felt at that moment, charged and vivid. And afterward there was no further questioning about the disabled.

"Yes, I'm going too," I said to Arturo Remlinger, before remembering I had been walking along the road doubting it.

"Hey!" Arturo said. "You know they got a hurricane in the Philippines, and floods killed 82,056?" He went on telling me about the weather—hailstorms in Azerbaijan, drought through-out Africa, tornadoes in the delta of the Mississippi River. He remembered or invented numbers of dead, rainfall statistics, the projected paths of storms. I walked beside him silently, holding his clammy, pulpy hand. I was thinking of what I had said to him, and considering whether I had told the truth. *I'm going too.* Well, if I didn't go, no one would be angry. No one would ask me for an explanation. The heavy lift launches always were deliberately overbooked, allowing for the five or six who could be counted on to draw back at the last minute. Some few people have even gone up and then come down again. There isn't any shame in it. No one would want people living on the *Dusty Miller* who weren't sure they wanted to be there.

"Here, you're home," I said softly to Arturo when I led him up on the porch of his brother's house. The door stood open; Arturo had left it ajar, going out, or the family had left it open to release the built-up heat from under their roof. I wouldn't have gone inside, I didn't want to frighten anyone who might wake and see me standing there, but Arturo kept stubborn hold of my hand and brought me with him into the dark front room, where there were shapes of things—cupboards and tables and low cushions—but no shapes of people, who must have been sleeping in the second room.

"I sure need a drink," Arturo repeated patiently.

"I haven't forgotten." I peered in the darkness for their cask of distilled water while Arturo went on holding my hand. I was groping with my other hand in the shadows along the shelves of a cupboard, hunting for something to pour the water into, when a barefoot woman came out from the sleeping room.

"Arturo, who is it with you?" the woman said with a loud, false boldness, and I immediately understood that her husband wasn't in the house.

"It's Dolores Negrete," I said. "Arturo was out on the road."

The woman's body released its stiffness. She said, "Arturo," and then tiredly, "He goes out after we're asleep."

Arturo released his grip from my fingers and, standing with his heavy legs planted, he swung from the waist toward his sister-in-law, and swung back, lifting his arms slightly. "Dolores'll get me a drink," he said.

I made a hand motion. "I can't find a cup."

The sister-in-law came across the dark room. She wore a thin cotton slip, white or ginger-colored, that seemed to move alone, luminous, through the darkness. The woman took a cup from a shelf and held it beneath the tap of the water cask. "Here, Arturo, here's your drink, but you know where the water is, and the cups. You could just help yourself."

Arturo drank the water swiftly down, holding the cup to his mouth with both big hands. His drinking was silent, neat. Afterward, lowering the cup, he said, "Thirsty," as an explanation.

"Go and pee and then go to bed," the woman said to him.

"I already peed. I did it on a tree." I could see the edge of his white teeth, the sly smiling.

"All right, then. Just go to bed."

"Hey, Barbara, Dolores wants to live in the houseboat and so do we." He swung toward me. "My mother isn't going," he told me.

"Go to bed now," Barbara said. She took the big man by the shoulders and turned him toward the door of the sleeping room. He came around with her slowly, his shoulders ahead of his hips and his feet.

"See you, Dolores," he said, twisting his head back.

"Good night, Arturo."

"They got a big storm in the Philippines today."

"Good night, Arturo."

"Okay, Dolores, see you."

He went out of the front room slowly. We could hear him in a moment, whispering loudly to someone in the bedroom, his words obscure. "Philippines," he whispered.

"Thank you for bringing him home," Barbara said. She stood with her thin arms folded across the front of her slip. She had a small face, short hair, there was no seeing her features in the darkness. I didn't know her except by her work—delicate clay pots painted with rigid, grimacing faces in dark colors of blood and jade and cobalt, and ornamented by bits of bone and feather. Burial pots, I think they are, and I have enjoyed the irony of their popularity at the souvenir shops, in the gambling casinos and whore houses along the coast.

"Your whole family is going up there? Up to the *Miller*?" I had to ask her. Other people's decisions in this matter seemed suddenly important to me—they might have considered things that had escaped my attention.

"We are, but Juan is on the Legal Committee and he wants

to stay until the expropriation appeals are all turned down."

As people leave the *estancia* for the *Dusty Miller*, and as the numbers of people here dwindle, there will be a government expropriation of "underutilized" land—this was something that was generally known. The tactic of the Legal Committee always was to exhaust every appeal.

There won't be a need for attorneys on the *Dusty Miller*, surely, nor perhaps artists, as some people say there won't be the resources. I wanted to ask her, *What will your husband do in that place? Will you give up your art?* Then Barbara said, as if I had spoken, "He'll be glad to be out of law, he never was happy in it. He wants to take up teaching, now that we'll be free of government constraints on our schools. He can keep Arturo with him. It's to be all home schooling and tutoring and apprenticing there, you know."

I nodded as if I did know, though I hadn't paid much attention to reports of things to do with children, or families.

"What will you do?" I asked Barbara, now that I'd been made to feel the subject was open.

Barbara's thin shoulders lifted slightly. "I'm a potter."

"Yes. I have seen your pots."

The woman made a soft sound, a laugh. "Oh, not those. Not there. Art is craft, anyway, at its pure heart. I'll make plates and bowls and ceramic parts for machinery. And tiles." She sounded satisfied, and there wasn't any way to see, in the darkness, if her face spoke another truth.

I said, shrugging, "I've always only farmed, myself. I guess the farming will be the same, there or here. That's what people say."

"Only the weather will be better." Barbara smiled slowly,

gesturing with one hand. "Arturo has been telling us everything about the weather up there."

"And in the Philippines."

She laughed again. "Yes. In the Philippines."

"Well, there won't be any hurricanes in that thing, I guess. And if they've thought it out right, the made-rain won't burn the trees."

There was a brief silence. Then Barbara asked me, "When is it you're going up?"

"I'm packed. A car will come for me in the morning, deliver me to the launch site." I thought of adding, *But I don't know if I'm going,* and discovered I had no wish, after all, to let anyone else look at my decision.

Barbara nodded. She shifted her weight silently, and it became clear she was waiting to go back to her bed.

I went to the open door. "Well, good night, then," I said in embarrassment. I would have kept on with our talk. I seemed to have this compulsion now, to discuss the environment of the *Dusty Miller*.

"Good night," Barbara said, without moving from where she stood, arms folded, in the middle of the front room. "Thank you for bringing Arturo home. We'll see each other up there."

"Maybe we will."

I went out again to the cart road and stood at the edge of the ruts and thought of breaking off for home; I thought of giving up this restless, useless night-wandering and taking my poor wayworn body home to bed. But then my feet went on up the track toward the rocky ridge of the Ojo de la Luna.

The air became thicker, freighted with smoke, and I fell to a plodding pace. I wished I had gotten a drink from Arturo's cup.

Wished I had brought him to the door and said goodnight and gone quickly away from the tired woman's house.

The cart road, when it had gained the ridge called the Eye of the Moon, turned south along the face of the limestone bluff, but I left the road and followed dimly worn trails northward along the backbone. From the high outlook, in the smoky night, the neat checkerwork of fields in the valley seemed fashioned of bronze, copper, umber, terracotta. The darkness was starless and feverish, the moon a smudged, brownish ellipse behind the dirty sky.

Where will the smoke go on the *Dusty Miller*? I wondered suddenly. People say the bodies of the dead will be burnt and the ashes turned in with the soil, but where will the smoke go in a closed world?

When I was young, still a girl, in certain months of the year the sun would come above the Ojo de la Luna in cool mornings and flood the sky with transparent light, and the atmosphere on such mornings was clear at least as far as the nearest summits of the *cordillera*. But even in those years, the farming populations all up and down the narrow highland spine of Middle America were burning their fields, the hillsides too stony or steep for plowing, and in the sowing months the burden of smoke in the air would shroud the peaks, the sun would rise red, a glare. Now the vast forests of the Amazon burn throughout the year, making way for fields of cattle, and there never are clear days now, not in the rainy season, not even in January, which has traditionally held the year's most pleasant weather. In the afternoons in every month the air is hot, murky, oppressive.

We grow a maize, a small old kind with a dark purple husk that fits the ear tightly and trails beyond it in a long stiff beard, tough husks that for the most part keep out the weevils that destroy so much stored grain in a climate prevailingly wet and warm, and we go on planting our maize as the Indians must have done on this same land before Columbus came, cutting the old stalks with machetes, dropping the seeds into holes made with pointed sticks, while elsewhere in this world people follow the pandemic, destructive impulse of technology: They plant larger and yet larger hybrids that outgrow their clothes, corn that keeps badly and has to be treated with pesticides, fungicides, formaldehyde. In the rest of the world, huge machines with glassed cabs roll across vast fields of played-out soil, and a bushel of corn is paid for in two bushels of topsoil, lifted to the sky in voluminous brown scrims of dust. In March, when the corporate farms are making ready to plant their fields, columns of smoke rise high above the tops of the ridges all around the *estancia*, and ash settles on the porches, the fields, the jacaranda trees.

If they want to put my ashes in the soil, there is a clarity to that, a circularity I like, but I don't want the smoke of my body to foul the air. *What if there are no Fourth Month rains, and the smoke from people's burned bodies is let out to darken the air?*

The goatpaths took me gradually down from the Ojo, northwest across a gravel wash and then westerly along the edges of terraced fields where a branch of the river had once flowed—a dusty channel now overgrown with shrubs and small trees. It was this same long-abandoned side channel that divided my own taro field from the maize, and finally, having decided nothing, I followed the troublous avenue of bare rocks in a long slow circling toward home.

My house is older than the Quaker settling of the land—built before The War, before the last several wars perhaps, a thick-walled *bahareque* with white-washed beams and an idiosyn-cratic placement: Its windowless back stands to the road, and the unglazed "front" windows look behind to a field dotted with orange trees, and a high-peaked shed roof that one time housed a sugar mill. When I came through the orange trees in the hot night, a Gray's thrush flew out from the *dulce* shed, and, looking, I saw she had built her nest high up in a dark corner of the metal roof.

I remember in the days of my childhood, my mother stand-ing with her forearms resting on the wide frame of the window, watching birds crack apart the leavings of corn in their horned beaks, and she would name for me the doves and shy woodrails, the toucans and quails attracted to the spillage. In those days there had been cinnamon-bellied squirrels as well, and a pair of blue tanagers who year after year made a small soft cup on the ridgepole in the very center of the high-peaked *dulce* shed. But no squirrels have been seen on this land in the last decade, and the tanagers have gone too, after yearly failing to hatch or raise a single nestling. The native birds are steadily more rare as their sheltering forests dwindle and coarser, more commonplace species take possession of the land. In the recent days since my corn was laded up to the sky, only grosbeaks have flocked into the yard to glean the spilled grain, and this Gray's thrush is the first I have seen in a year.

While I stood pondering the thrush's neat little nest, the poor bird waited in one of the orange trees, her eggs unde-fended. She will hatch them, if any of the eggs are viable, after I have moved to the *Miller*. And standing there in the hot dim-ness at the edge of my fields, I realized that this bird brooding in my shed might be the last Gray's thrush I would see in my lifetime.

The fields of the *Miller* are in the ancient Pennsylvania Quaker manner, every seventh acre set aside for forest, but the plantings are deliberately various, a subtropical pastiche. Among the few trees familiar to me—kapok and paperbark, breadfruit, candlenut—are to be *banyan, bamboo, litchi, camphor*: trees that seem to me as astonishingly exotic as cactus or the stunted pines of a tundra. And the greater part of the fauna have come from a little parcel of mountainous land that was willed to the Japanese Society of Friends by the Nature Conservancy. No carnivores have survived on that steep little woodland nor any of the big, wide-ranging herbivores; those are gone, all of them, gone for decades. But the Japanese Friends have succeeded in protecting a native biology, a few dozen species of formerly hundreds of tortoises, snakes, lizards, toads, frogs, newts, birds, insects; and these have formed the core of the *Miller*'s living and creeping things. Whether a Gray's thrush will make its life in that polyglot forest among that little multitude of Japanese birds, Japanese animals, is not known to me. What birds will nest in the farm sheds of the *Dusty Miller*?

At last I went into my house and waited in the darkness until the wary bird came back to the eggs. When I put on the light, there were—almost a kind of surprise—the waiting boxes, and the loose drifts of uncrated belongings, things to be handed over to my homebound neighbors. I ought to have gone to bed. The long, absurd walking had brought me no clarity, I thought—had been only wearing and dusty and maundering. I was tired and someone would be at my door early to take away my packing. But I sat down among the crates and then got up again suddenly, restless, and went among my things until I'd found the books.

In early Meetings, worries were raised, and laid to rest, about the technology in the *Miller*: People wanted to go on living plainly, in the manner of Friends, and after all there would not be the resources for repairing or replacing complicated machinery, problematic instruments and appliances. But the balance that has been struck is sometimes odd, incongruous. Books, which are the plainest of human tools, must be housed in a manner to keep them carefully from the wet and warmth, and the limited space in that sealed and air-conditioned place, set against the necessary compass of knowledge, means a vast library of microfiche and videos, and just a tiny library of bound volumes. There are, in the two rooms of this house, many hundreds of books that will remain behind, and a single crate of twenty-six books that will travel with me to the *Miller*. The size of the box, the bulk and weight that are permitted to me, have forced me to providence: I have kept Zardoya's translations of Whitman, but nothing of Calderon. Have put aside *Le Grand Meaulnes*, kept *Les Miserables*. Now I was inexplicably, suddenly, stricken with apprehension: had I put *Song of the Lark* in the stacks to be given away, or the box to be taken up? *Adios, Mr. Moxley? Sigrid Lavransdatter?* I sorted through the books, reading and rereading the indexing in a fever of suspicion. By what measure had I included *The Magic Mountain*, but not *Pajaros del Nuevo Mundo*?

The air remained thick, hot. I knelt painfully before the box, overcome with nostalgia and an indecipherable sorrow. How had I imagined I could live the balance of my life without holding the pages of Cesar Vallejos in my hands? What if the people who had promised to include *Beloved*, *Ficciones*, *Historie de ma Vie*, changed their minds or forgot their promises?

In my crate, one book is old, rare, has a value beyond words. Elizabeth Martin and her husband had been among the First Seventy who settled the old *estancia*, and her handwritten diary is a family treasure. The First Seventy had been members of Ohio or Iowa Yearly Meetings, had emigrated after one of the first World Wars—escaping militarism, as they thought—thus Elizabeth's diary is in English. I am even now making my slow way through it for the third time or the fourth, my English still as poor as my Esperanto. There is a rayon ribbon I use to mark my place in it, and the ribbon now lies among painful pages: She is waiting for the slow doctor, the slow lab, to say if she has a cancer. She kept the secret, the little hard bead in her breast, even from her husband, confided her dread only to the pages of her diary. It is an old anxiety, made edgeless by familiarity, and tonight when my hands brought that book up from the bottom of the box I suppose my sudden brief weeping had as much to do with birds and starless nights and the burned and buried bodies of the dead, as with the worn old sorrows of Elizabeth Martin's life.

I have wondered: When Elizabeth wrote her secrets, who were they meant to be read by? She always would identify people. "Mary (my mother)," she would say. Or, "Arthur, my aunt's second son." Did she know, then, that her private words would be read by strangers? Why else identify these people she well knew? Who did she imagine would take the trouble to work out her English words, her crabbed vertical hand? Who would need the benefit of such naming?

Many people are keeping diaries again. They want to record

the momentous events of these times, and their feelings—explanations, apologies, defense—addressed to children and grandchildren and the seven or eight generations afterward who must live out their lives within the hull of that houseboat until it fetches up on the distant rocks of Epsilon Eridani. I have no children, no one to whom I must apologize. I have wondered: What person would struggle to work out my spidery handwriting, my idiomatic Spanish, to read of arthritic joints, of the making of pottery and the growing of maize? For whom should I write?

But here, as you see, are the first pages of my diary.

Perhaps Elizabeth Martin imagined herself writing for a woman then unborn—for Dolores Negrete, who is only an old and childless woman descended from the Martins' family line, a Spanish-speaking woman who trudges through the night in order to circle round to the truth, a woman who sits on the floor of her house reading old painful confidences as she makes ready to begin her life again after sixty years. As I now imagine you, an Esperanto-speaking person unrelated to me, a person now unborn, who in 150 years, or two hundred, will be circling round again to the truth, beginning your life again. I imagine you sitting on the floor of your house reading my anxious musings about the smoke of burnt bodies and the leaving-behind of birds' nests, and as I am writing this, you are thinking of the forepart of your life and the after, in the days that separate them.

PART ONE

INSCRIPTIONS

1

Juko

And you O my soul where you stand,
Surrounded, detached, in measureless oceans of space,
Ceaselessly musing, venturing, throwing, seeking the
*   spheres to connect them,*
Till the bridge you will need be form'd, till the ductile
*   anchor hold,*
Till the gossamer thread you fling catch somewhere, O
*   my soul.*

ON THAT DAY, the go-down day, Juko Ohaśi stood at the head of the weathermast—stood with her feet on the spindly seven-yard and her arms spread wide in the windless glare—looking sunward for her husband.

People who had never gone aloft imagined they might climb to a masthead and see the compass of the windship spread below them, but there was no seeing the whole of it from anywhere on the rigging; this was something every sailmender knew. You had to go out in a small boat, get five or ten kilometers away from it, before it began to be possible to see the whole configuration, the sails entire: Seven carbon-fiber yards thin as thread ringing the torus in concentric circles a kilometer apart, as though the torus had been a pebble dropped in still water; twelve wire-fine spokes radiating from the center in a complex reticulum of torsional support, intersecting the ring-yards and branching, branching again, until the twelve masts were fifty; two hundred panes of reflective vilar—a crowd of sail—each infinitely more tenuous than a soap-bubble, each broader than a corn field, bridging the delicate webwork of yards and masts; myriad servos as fine as watch-work trimming the sails in a restless canting with respect to the horizontal axis; and all this immense diaphane supporting the small cumbrous payload of the inhabited torus, a thick-bodied, eight-spoked wheel lying at the center of the sails in a hammock of stays and shrouds along the elliptical plane, like a moon at the eye of its corona.

Among sailmenders, yes, there was a custom, a usual habit, of standing at the outermost tip of a spoke, but not, as other people thought, for a glimpse of the whole architecture turning in an elegant roundelay against the stars. From a boat, at ten kilometers' distance, or twelve, the *Dusty Miller* was a vast round mosaic of mirror, a great segmented disk rippling with light and movement; but from the seven-yard, standing up from the head of a mast, what you saw was a billowing field of sailcloth stretching wide and away beyond eye's reach, as the sea must have stretched away from the eye of the blue-water sailor, and the torus a small purplish atoll at the far horizon. Standing at the head of a mast, people looked, not for the whole, but for what must be the true aspect of a World: something larger than the eye could take in.

Juko Ohaśi, standing at the head of the weathermast, only looked for her husband.

She had meant to keep from it. In the sixty-nine days since Bjoro had sailed ahead of them in the *Ruby*, other people had daily looked sunward from the fields of sail seeking a glimpse of the far off boat, but Juko had not. She and her mother-in-law both were inclined to eat sporadically and to sleep at unlikely hours, and Bjoro inclined to push them toward more orderly habits, so there was a certain narrow pleasure and freedom in his absence, and she always had taken to heart the old axiom that you shouldn't expect your husband or your wife to carry too much of the weight of your happiness. For sixty-nine days she had felt very clear, very self-contained, unsentimental. She'd been comfortable not missing Bjoro at all, and had understood in a dim, restless way that looking for her husband, or toward him, she might be stricken suddenly with loneliness.

She knew, in any case: From the rigging even the world they steered for was indistinguishable—three hundred days across the measureless distance: a minute light circling the small orange sun amid a turning field of stars, and the little *Ruby*, circling the world, an infinitesimally small mote of dust. Foolish to look for it—she had not meant to look for it. Had not meant to stand along the weathermast finding a balance in the compass of space, opening her arms as if she were offering something to God or calling up a spell against the night; had not meant to put her feet along the outermost rim of the flut- tering array of sails and, spreading her arms to the black, wind- less firmament, to let in this fierce, this very precise longing for the smell of Bjoro's wet hair when he came from the bath, for the weight of his hands resting on her shoulders absently as he stood behind her in a crowd or in a queue.

It is the šimanas, she thought, and took a kind of mournful satisfaction in it. *All of us are gone a little mad these days.*

Her mother-in-law, Kristina Veberes, was apt to keep still about a worry until it was well past, and then she liked to complain to everyone how she'd lost sleep over it. She hadn't spoken a word of misgiving in the sixty-nine days, and wouldn't be wanting to complain yet with nothing known, no one safe; but Juko, standing at the head of the weathermast staring irresistibly, uselessly sunward, suddenly had in her mind that she and Kristina could get a little drunk tonight and comfort themselves with sarcasm, a habit they were both prone to. People believed the go-down day needed ceremony, and neighbors privately had given over to her two rare, small bottles of wine; she yearned suddenly to be sitting in the bath with her mother-in-law, drinking that wine, listing the son's, the husband's manifest faults.

They had an old, mother-daughter friendship, she and Kristina, years older than her marriage to Bjoro. Juko's own mother and Kristina had been childhood intimates, their families bound together in a tangle of distant kinship, of marriages several generations removed, and Juko had made a second mother of Kristina when her own mother was dead. She had been still married to Humberto in those days, but when their younger son had died and she and Humberto had divorced, she had moved her belongings into Kristina's house as a daughter returning to her mother's family. Much of that unmarried year was lost to her, a dull grayness, unremembered.

She remembered the Plum Rains—the haloes around the xenon lamps in the wet, humid nights. And Kristina's son, Bjoro, a man she had known only as a would-be cousin—she remembered his gravity, his tolerant look, and the way that look had become unburdening, a safehold. Before the Plum Rains had come round again, they were married. And their marriage had been knit to that old friendship between Juko and Kristina—an inextricable web of family and familiarity.

On a little release of breath, someone said, "Ha! I'm up-top," and Juko, who was standing up-top herself, looked round for the other. On the incom the voices always were burry, indistinguishable, and across the great distances of the diaphane the sailmenders were gnats against the burnished vilar, but they had named the two hundred fields of sail as farmers will name their fields of corn, and she recollected some part of the sail chart for this watch: There was Aric Engirt on the Weather-Beater, Al Poreda on the Square-Away, Orval Wyho on the Rock-Bottom. Someone was pulling swiftly out along the dark thread of the spankermast, no telling who that was. The one who was up-top, standing at the head of the skymast—Juko thought it was Marĉa Negro.

In the earpiece there was a little sound, a sort of grunting disgust, and the person crawling up the spankermast made a quick slow-down, going clockwise onto the sail named the Far-Cry: giving up a race.

"Who's racing? Is it Juko Ohaŝi? I seen Sonja go sprinting by me with her eyes fixed on her hands, but you beat her good, eh, Juko?"

Sonja Landsrud was twenty-three or four, quick as a snake, and it had been years since Juko had pulled out a mast on the race, fast enough to beat Sonja Landsrud. She laughed. "No, wasn't me," she said. "But I guess I'm not old, then, if somebody's thinking it could've been me."

"Could be you're still old, but fast," somebody said, and people laughed. Then Marča said, "It was me—Marča. I'm the one beat her. I beat Sonja," and she let a little flourish be in it. *I beat her!*

"I was one-armed," Sonja said, a squawk. "Hey, Marko, you saw me, eh? When I came out the hub? banged my wrist a hard one on that damned big fitting that sticks out beside the hatch."

"Get on, Sonja. Marča beat you, so don't whine." That was Marko, maybe, though hard telling on the vague incom.

Sonja said, surprised, "Whining's what I do," and that made people laugh again. It was an old aptness of Sonja's, become a joke she played to: She had always a particular reason for defeat.

Juko's ear became silent—they kept the incom mostly open for matters to do with the work, and for exigencies—and when the laughter had quieted, the weight of the silence carried her down past the moment of inertia and foolish yearning as she had stood at the vantage of the masthead. She fell softly onto the sail, the field called the Knock-Around, as softly as people, waking, fall back into the middle of their lives.

On the great sails there was silence, aloneness, as there never was in the crowded torus and maybe for this reason menders had a habit of coming together at the junctions where their fields joined—exercising their human connections. At the six-and-weather corner of her field she waited for Al Poreda, thinking he would come across the Square-Away in his usual steady plowman's pattern, lapping back and forth between the masts, monotonous, prosy. But maybe the *Lark* had brought his soul to poetry: He was covering the sail today with a loose, indecipherable chasing, a secret hieroglyphic. He kept at it, leaving out the corner, not seeing her there.

"Beauty," she said, her thumb on the incom, and that brought his head around slowly, looking for her. "Don't know what design you're making, but it has beauty," she told him.

There was distance between them, two or three hundred meters. He let himself come up from the undulating field, until his white exo was a small, drifting brilliance against the absolute blackness of the void. He opened his hands, a slow gesture, open-palmed, and brought his body around to her orientation. "Looking for a pattern," he said. "Not finding it." Al Poreda had a grimacing, intent smile, like a man placing himself between fire and the body of his child. The skull of his exo was opaque, but she imagined his mouth letting the words out through that smile.

"No corner in your design, eh? I guess I'll quit waiting for you."

He was silent, his arms still open. Then he said in a tender whisper, "Don't wait," and let himself down on the sail, on the winding, unknowable pattern. *We are all gone a little crazy.*

A little retractable ribbon had a house in the waist of her exo, and when she pushed off with her hands against the weathermast the tether trailed her, sliding soundless on its end-pin, following the curving track of the seven-yard. The *Miller* was braking, had been braking for forty years, and now they had come within the inner harbor of the new star their navigation had become an intricate, interminable equation of motion, a continuous contraposing of the outward stream of light, and of the solar wind, of the star's centripetal attraction, the perturbations of its four small planets, and the old momentum of the torus. The diaphane presented its face, like a blossom, always toward the sun, while the petals of shimmering sailcloth tilted their edges at shallow angles to the elliptical plane: finding their balance and then seeking a new one. Juko bobbled over the Knock-Around like a shorebird above a slow heaving sea.

Where there was a tangle in the halyard, she wrapped her legs over the yard's thin line and swayed there, picking the little knots in the fine carbon filament. Where an edge of sail was hung up in its rigging she pulled scrupulously at the jam until it was loose again, and with a flat-iron tool pressed out the creases in the cobwebby cloth. Where there was a hole in the sail she soldered the little breach—a dozen atoms expelled in a bead at the tip of the fine mending needle.

The mechanicals were ancient, deteriorating, the sailcloth and the rigging frayed and dilapidated. The *Dusty Miller* had borne sail for its first fifty years, gathering way in a stately, deliberate acceleration; but for eighty-five years, while the bare toroid coasted through the darkness between the old star and the new, the vast diaphane had been furled, its vanes contracted about the torus with some little hope the folds of mirrored cloth might shield them from the bombardment of cosmic rays. Then in Juko's childhood the great circle of sails was spread again for this long, difficult braking, and the Maintenance Committee blamed the poor condition of the old sails on the long closure, the reopening.

Juko had heard some people say they thought it was a decay of artistry as much as apparatus. She had learned the sail-mender's art, herself, from people who had, years before, gone up in the hub and hung a field of sail in that high-ceilinged space above the foundry and studied the servos for the spar devices, setting and resetting them, and watching the ways the little mechanical brain turned a halyard wrong or needed a hand to pull a yard down taut—setting and studying and resetting and watching again, figuring out the old art and then climbing out onto the black void, spreading the great sails for the long braking inward toward the new, the unnamed world. Most of those people were dead now, never had seen the new sun. Juko thought if you complained of lost artistry, probably you never had been out on the rigging; she thought people who had never been outside sometimes were inclined to criticize the people who had.

Where the jackmast joined the seven-yard, she went inward along it, girdling the big trapezoid of the Knock-Around, eleven hundred meters along the seven-yard, a thousand meters along the six. The Weather-Beater and the Knock-Around abutted one another along the six-yard and whenever the sail luffed under her, Juko saw Aric Engirt in the glimmering swale, working steadily toward her across the Weather-Beater. When he had made the corner where the jackmast crossed the six, he floated there with his legs wound round the thread of the yard, his face turned toward the little orange bud of the sun. Maybe he was keeping track of Juko from an edge of his eye: In the soundless sky, as she came down to him at the corners of their fields, he broke off his staring and let his body come around to her orientation.

"Phtt," he said, a wordless complaint, with his thumb shutting out the others on the incom so the sound of it was closed-up, a small-room sound. He made an exaggerated gesture with his shoulders, a slumping, and she remembered he had been sick lately, a cold or a cough, one of the nameless, catholic viruses.

She said, "You should have stayed home, kid, you look still down with the bug."

He gave her a grimace, a ducking boyish look. "Should've. Yeah." He lifted his gloved hands gently, numbering with his fingers. "There's six babies in our damn house. People kept wanting to put me to someone's breast. I've got this baby's face, Rita keeps telling me."

Juko laughed. It was true, his face was smooth, dimpled; inside the fiberglass skull of the exo, his hair hung down in a thick, childish forelock. "Six! You ought to tell Rita to let you alone." Juko had not much recollection of this wife—a small woman, dark hair? She remembered they had a new baby, maybe it was a boy, born in the dry season.

Aric grinned, showing his teeth in a leer. "Too bad we didn't make them all," he said. "Only one, and the rest are my brother's doing, and the neighbors'."

"Six in the same house?"

"Six! Born in the same year, in the same damn domaro! Maybe all the husbands laid down with their wives on the same night, and in the morning all the wives got up pregnant. Anyway, now one of the chicks is ailing with something, maybe it's what I've had—you know how a thing like that goes round a neighborhood—so people are carrying that baby back and forth and up and down, and a house with so many babies is prone to be in a kind of rush regardless, eh? things never still. Rita likes it. I guess I do, but this bug has made me surly." He grinned again. "No crying kids out here, anywise."

Juko thought he wanted this to be a joke, but his pallid face, grinning, drew up in a sort of pinch, suppressing a little dry cough. She said, "So you thought you'd find some other people to be surly with, besides your neighbors? Come out here and gripe at your friends?"

He laughed in a small way, looking at her shyly. "I guess I just wanted to come out. Couldn't lay in bed, you know." He moved his shoulders once more, eyeing her self-consciously from beneath the straight brow-cut of his hair. "The *Lark*, you know. I wanted to come out."

She didn't know why she skirted her eyes away from him. Maybe she had caught from him a kind of embarrassment. *Both of us are crazy then, I looked for it myself.*

Twice a day or three times, the radio people had been sending someone around to neighborhoods with copies of the *Ruby*'s voice logs, everybody wanting to know what was being said, even if the only talk going on was pointless and sentimental. *This from Arda*, the word had come down today. *We have a window thirteen o'clock for the go-down. Hans and me will stay on the* Ruby. *On the* Lark *there'll be Luza, Bjoro, Peder, Isuma. They'll mean to call again when land is made but they'll be busy so maybe not. Don't worry! Hans or me will call when we hear up from them. Now we'll have a real look-see!*

Not Bjoro's words—this was something Juko would have known without Arda naming herself. Bjoro was inclined to be methodical, mathematical; he'd have been more formal and more precise. Arda had a deep, loose alto, she always would say important things in an offhand, exclaiming way. *So at the window, will launch the* Lark!

For years, while the *Dusty Miller* had gone on making its slow and slower approach, they'd been slinging little scoutboats out ahead to learn what could be learned from brief robotic flybys of the sun and its small system, but now they had come inside the orbit of the star's outermost planet, and the slow old *Miller* was within a year of parking round the sun's second planet, its one livable world, and so they had sent six people in the fast motorboat *Ruby* sprinting ahead across the inner compass of the solar system for a first human glimpse. The *Ruby* had had a sixty-day traverse, and now for nine days had been orbiting the new world while they sent down the first two dozen tropospheric survey balloons; and today, finally, the *Ruby*'s tiny go-down boat, the heavy-lift launch the *Lark*, was cast off from the *Ruby*; and the four people in it—*Bjoro!*—must even now be making their quick, narrow crossing to close with the land.

"So you've had your look at the boat," she said to Aric Engirt with a tender grimace, "and maybe you should go in now. There's no babies in my damn house, and I've got a small family, eh? and Bjoro gone. My mother-in-law will leave you alone if you want to roll out my bed and sleep on it. When I come off, I'll send you home to Rita."

He made a slight, sheepish hand sign, a sort of pushing away. "No. Not that sick. Anyhow, I've just got started. I ought to get the cross done so I don't lose track of what I've done." Menders had each their own style of working a field, few of them crawled the same sail in just the same way. It was Aric's habit to run up a mast then down on the diagonal, go across the yard and upward diagonal again, cutting the field into diamonds. "I'll quit when I've run the ex." And then, beginning to smile, "It must be this damn baby's face, eh? You're aiming to mother me, now your own has grown up and flown away from you."

He meant Ĉejo, seventeen. He would not know—would

have been a child then himself—one of her babies had flown away from her by dying. She hunched one shoulder up, deflecting the little irritation, if that was what it was. "Go on, then, if you want," she said, and made a mouth, a smiling frown. She lifted her hand in a quick, half-peevish good-bye, and pulled out along the six-yard, taking herself off swiftly until Aric had fallen out of sight across the luff of his field and she was alone again.

She had an old, leathery callus that protected her in such moments, but he had got by it a little. She never had been inclined to mother anything sick, that was the sore point. It had been Humberto who had clasped their first son to his breast in the first colicky weeks, muttering useless wordless sounds of comfort, walking round the room and round in his flat bare feet, while Juko sat on the floor making wicker, or peeling oranges. She had liked Ĉejo rather better at three and four, thin sweaty arms wrapped round her neck, solemn kisses pressed on her lips. But by then she and Humberto had made a second son, and sometimes in those days she had gone on lying in her bed with the heels of her hands against her ears while that son was crying, crying, and other people had brought Vilef to her breast, brought him to lie over her unmoving heart, and it was only afterward, when he was dead, that she had felt the slow beating behind the bone.

People liked to say romantic love was a childish sentiment, something you ought to get over with in your green years. *To marry a lover is fatal,* people said. Everyone knew, the relationship of lovers was transient, electrical, while marriage above other things must be a durable partnering, a system of mutual reliance, a friendship. Family and neighbors were expected to indemnify a marriage by anchoring it in patience, affection, and support; and Juko's family had mostly followed that charge. She had been given, in Humberto, a husband who was melancholy, passive, prone to chronic physical complaints—but someone of tolerance and stillness, someone disposed to agree with her values and judgments, an undistinguished, predictably tender sexual partner, a conscientious father to their sons. The Senlima Clearness Committee had admired the tying of their wedding knot. And counseled its unraveling. People had blamed that divorce on Vilef's unhappy birth, but she and Humberto, both of them, always had understood: It was Vilef's death, not his birth, that was to blame. Humberto never had been able to forgive her for receiving her son's death as a gift, and she unable to forgive him for his unequivocal, stubborn devotion to grief.

Now her marriage with Bjoro, without children at its center, but tied to Kristina in a complicated gyre of mother-son, husband-wife, daughter-mother, was altogether unsentimental; everything between them was arguable, everything sufficient, abiding. She had, as she thought, reinvented marriage, and it had been years since she had thought of the Plum Rains at the end of her old divorce. But she was adrift, today, in the wake of a vague resonance. The narrow, explicit lonesomeness that had come up in her body when she had stood at the head of the weathermast had become a kind of homesickness, a bleary unfocused pining.

Her own pattern of mending was to circle a field at the yards and masts, repairing the halyards and smoothing the tangles, and then to drift inward slightly and inward again, spiraling toward midsail, looking for tears. While her body rose and fell on the slow breath of the sail, she made the wide smooth circle around the field and then around again, a chip of wood borne in on the eddy, circling. The silvery web of sails wheeled languidly, the star field turning with it. She kept from looking starward but she felt herself turning with the sails, felt the small orange sun holding steady in the vast blackness, and gradually she began to feel the muddy mood suspended about her like the depthless sky. She began to work well, to work habitually, not thinking of Bjoro finally nor the *Lark*, nor even of old marriages and dead children.

Someone said "Hans!" in a sudden yell drawn out long on a fading note. There was a small silence, a surprised dumbness among them all. Finally someone said, "Hey, Sonja. What?" for Sonja and Hans were cousins—one of them had an aunt who had married the other's uncle—and everybody knew Hans was orbiting in the *Ruby*, waiting with Arda while the *Lark* carried the other four down to landfall.

Sonja laughed. There was not much timidness in that woman anywhere. "Oh hell. I can't hardly believe I did that. Oh hell. I guess I was just sending him a sort of kiss or a marker buoy or something. I'm up the head of the spanker and from here you can see forever or what passes for it, and I all at once had to send his name out on the wind, eh?" Juko, looking, made out the tiny thread-end trailing from the tip of the spankermast, Sonja Landsrud standing as Juko earlier had done, at the rim of the sail staring sunward. *We are all gone a little mad these days.*

There was only a brief silence and then it was Orval Wyho who said, flat and short, "The śimanas, I guess. It's put you over the edge." Orval always had a crabbed way of speaking; you knew his voice on the obscuring incom. Some of them laughed, making an indistinguishable noise.

"Hey, Juko, you'd better leave a word for Bjoro too!" There followed a smacking sound, wet, a loud kiss.

"Who's to yell for Arda, then, and Peder? They'll be lost."

"Arda! Here's for you, dear!" "Luza!" "Hey, Isuma!"

"H-A-L-L-O-O-O the *Ruby!*" "Hey, *Lark!*"

Juko had no impulse to call to Bjoro, but she had liked Sonja hailing the boat that way, girlish, not grown too staid yet nor too reasonable. So on the little momentum of the other voices, she yelled once too, "Bjoro!" hearing it come out stiff and fierce-sounding.

There was a lot of laughter, a choppy noise. Then Romeo Thorkildsen, from the sailchart desk in the hub, sounded through it with his steady voice, unamused. "Can't hear a damn thing, you know, mid that racket," and made them subside. In the short silence afterward, it seemed to Juko that their little stopped-up breaths, their sighing restlessness, must be the sound of the *Dusty Miller*, sails and torus all, falling light as a milkweed seed inward toward the sun. Then Romeo said, a closed sound only for her ear, "You see Alberto there, Juko, from where you are?"

Her eyes followed the black edge of shadow slipping smoothly clockwise, the luff of her own field casting its umbra across the Square-Away. "No. What."

"He's clockwise of you. On the Square-Away."

"Sure, but he's hid in the dark." Looking for him, waiting for the ebb of the shadow, she said, "Al?" and then, "Hey, Al."

She had known Alberto Poreda a long time, been a child with him in the Senlima śiro, been a little in love with Al once, when she was eleven. In Senlima, in that neighborhood of their childhood, the Ring River cut two shallow channels, and the footings of the Fiddle-Spoke rose straight up from the gravelly island to pierce the high ceiling. When she had been eleven, she had sat on the island in the shadow of the spoke with a boy whose name she no longer remembered, and she'd let that boy touch her flat brown nipples. She had told this to Al afterward, without knowing why she had wanted him to know, but she remembered the reddened look his face had taken on, and that he had kept away from her for weeks—maybe it was from panic. Why was she remembering that now? All this looking backward.

"Juko," Romeo said, "he's gone offline is all, see if you can get him to answer up, wave his hand or something."

She made a reply, wordless, and left the center of her field for the weathermast, sculling across the open sail without hurrying, and then coming in along the mast beginning to pull swiftly hand over hand. There was no wind, only the steady small light of the little sun, and the star field skipping a dim shine off the facets of sail. In the absence of windrush, Juko heard the beating of her own blood in her ears.

She and Al had used to sail tetherless, all bravado and foolishness when they were young, twenty, sweeping across the face of a field in long, heart-stopping glissades, imagining other sailmenders watching them must be struck with envy and respect. People who were twenty still sometimes went onto the sails without a tie. *Young, stupid, reckless,* Juko thought now. She knew, though, why they were doing it—remembered her own body's voiceless yearning to belong to a larger, a less coherent pattern. She hadn't loosed herself from a sail tether in years, she and Al both having become more careful after their children were born.

And she remembered suddenly: Where Al's son should have had a hand there was a smooth rounded nub, very pink. She could not remember the child's face at all, but very clearly the look of that nubbin, and the use he made of it, deft, delicate. Or she was remembering her own son Vilef, the single finger of his ill-formed hand climbing her chin.

When the mechanism of the sail drew the edge of shadow back smoothly across the Square-Away, she could see Al's small dark shape on the shivering field of vilar, and another little beetle, it would be Aric Engirt over there on the Weather-Beater, pulling slowly out along the six-yard.

She said, "Al," and no one answered, but then Romeo said something, not to her, and she heard several voices but not the words, and then Romeo again, the others falling silent as he spoke. He was a balding little man with a big voice. "Juko," he said. "I guess you'd better go on in to him. Aric, you go too, eh? until you can see him? what he's up to? One of you get an answer out of him, so we don't worry."

"Going," she said—for Romeo, an answer—and then heard Al's soft word, the echo unexpectedly in her ear, "Going."

In the small silence afterward there rose in Juko an uneasy remembrance of Al Poreda's dark narrow face, the line of his white teeth below the edge of his burning smile. And then in her ear the little hissing as in a closed room, as if he had put his body in the fire at last. She was struck by a preposterous fear, something to do with Al sailing tetherless across his field as they had used to in the old days, all bravado and foolishness. And now she was crossing over the long bright sail to him, dropping like a bird, a bead of rain, a stone into his open hands, when she saw the sudden stiff spreadeagle puff of his exo, and the shape he made bobbing on the tether like a New Year's kite, bright cloth on a wire frame standing out stiff in the windless cold.

"Oh!" Aric Engirt said, in a surprised, childish voice, and Juko saw that he had checked his momentum, had hooked his legs around the rigging of the Weather-Beater. She went on a moment longer, falling toward Al, the mast passing swiftly under her in a thin blurred thread, and then she tripped the dragline with her thumb and when her body had ceased moving she felt something still moving within her, a jittery excitement in her chest.

"What," Romeo said, steady and gentle.

"He's breached his exo," Aric Engirt said, still filled with astonishment.

The silence had its own quality of surprise. "He's dead, then?" Romeo said, dumbfounded, without truly asking anyone anything. In a moment he said to someone else, not to any of them out on the sail—perhaps turning to tell the others gathering behind him there in the hub—"Alberto Poreda has got himself killed." Juko thought she ought to say something to Aric or to Romeo on the incom, but what she felt, still felt, was that breathless flutter, and no words came.

She had bathed her mother's body when the soul went out of it, had watched or helped other people do the same for their own family members—she wasn't afraid of looking at someone who was dead. But the tumid body seemed not Al's, seemed only ambiguously human. She waited, looking, from a hundred meters, and then went on slowly out to the end of Al's tether, and in a little while Aric Engirt came on too.

Al was bobbing above an edge of field that had tangled hard

in the lines. The exo had a glossy look, solid; there was a long straight rift in the left forearm of the exo, and a distended blip of Al's arm was extruded into it, an egg-shape, taut and shiny, bruise-colored. The knife was still in the fist of his right glove. Juko fixed her eyes on his closed hand, the narrow serrated knife, and kept from looking at the clear skull of the exo, the fierce grin in the blood-swollen face.

"He's cut through his exo," Aric said, whispering this as if it might be a secret other people weren't listening to.

Romeo Thorkildsen, his voice going on being surprised, said, "Oh! My dear God!" Then, becoming steady again, "Well, you'd better bring him in, eh? Aric? You and Juko bring him in."

Aric Engirt looked to her in alarm. The soft pouches below his eyes were dark, the way Ĉejo's had used to be when he was needing sleep or coming down feverish. Baby's face. Something moved again in Juko: It was her jumpy heart contracting, tightening. "Yes," she said. Then she put her hand out deliberately and took hold of Al's big wrist. There wasn't any feel of a limb inside an exo. The thing she had hold of had a smooth slick softness, rubbery. She opened Al's hand and took the knife from it and folded the knife and put it away in her own tool belt. Then she took a better hold of his wrist, and the old marks of her fingers remained impressed in the exo.

Aric watched her, or he watched Al, not coming up to take hold of the other wrist. His need not to touch the body made her feel obscurely admirable. She didn't speak to him—what would she say?—but then a few murmuring words spoke themselves, not for Aric's sake. "It's still Al. He's just got himself killed, is all."

She sculled gently, starting down along the mast, bringing

Al's body by the one arm. It twisted slightly, trailing behind her as a stubborn child twists to have a hand let go. Aric opened his mouth to let a breath in, and the air going down in his body made a little sound in her ear, a sigh. Finally he came and took a gingerly hold on the other arm. They went slowly inward, both of them, with Al Poreda carried buoyant between them.

People were waiting at the ring-yards. Without speaking, they fell in behind, a few and then a few more, until it had become a sort of cortege.

"He has that father sick and set to die," someone said.

Someone else made a small answering sound, a sort of clucking of the tongue.

"What," said Orval in his flat, recognizable tone. "I don't know about that."

"A cancer," someone said. "He's not old yet. Maybe he's sixty, sixty-five."

Juko cast around for something to say. She had learned from that dying old man, Al's father, how to roll sweet brigadeiros in cinnamon and the zest of an orange; should she say that? She found that she had got used to the feel of the body. After a while she took a new, firmer grip, and looked down with mournful curiosity to see the old marks of her fingers where they remained imprinted on the exo.

"It was the simanas, eh?" someone asked them all tenderly.

It was a sort of madness, an exquisite pain of utter and unspeakable aloneness. Their own. It was not a small thing. In Juko's memory, perhaps a dozen people had killed themselves to end unbearable, unspeakable alienation; and when the clerk read the names of the dead at Yearly Meeting, these suicides seemed to lie at the center of all their lives, a heart of inexplicable grief. But they had all got to calling any least sadness or fear by its name. *It is the śimanas,* they said, blaming that mind-sickness for quarrels and forlornness and names cast like bottles into the void. Maybe they meant to enfeeble it, giving its name to other, slighter insanities. It was plain, though, that this question was asked in the old way, true and narrow. *Has he gone crazy, then? killed himself?*

Juko's eyes sprang with tears, a short stinging that was not grief, she thought, but tiredness and an obscure fear, something to do with madness, with bad weather, or the Plum Rains. She didn't look at anyone.

"He maybe meant to cut the halyard," Aric said, low and sick, a boy's voice. "There was a big snarl. Maybe the field swung up and put him off his balance."

It was Orval Wyho who said, "I never have tried it, but I expect you'd have to saw quite a bit to cut through an exo." On the incom his voice had that crabbed sound, grumping.

Juko had known people to die on the sails—three, now four, in twenty years—but it was not those people she thought of. She was remembering poor Tual Mendoza, who had gone mad one day and cut his tether, had folded out his thin sailmender's knife and carefully, neatly, sawed through the cord and kicked himself adrift. Juko had been in the tugboat that had taken him in afterward. She remembered how he had stared at them all with great child's eyes, bewildered, terrorized, inarticulate.

At Meetings for Business, people every day were reporting the bleak particulars gathered up from the balloons, the first real details of weather and landforms, the discouraging measurements and jargon of glaciation, of vulcanism, of storms. What Juko had felt on hearing all this bad news, these bad reports, was just a failure of her imagination. Maybe she never had believed it would one day come to this—people standing on the new world. *A hundred and seventy-five years. And now people standing on the land.* She remembered how, in the tug, looking for Tual Mendoza in the black depths, all the grandness of the sails was shrunk to triviality: From a thousand kilometers, the *Miller* was a silver bead on a dark starred field.

Things began sliding around in her head, a random disconnectedness, none of it to do with death, now, none of it to do with Alberto Poreda. She was thinking of a long rattan table she had in mind to build; of asking Leo Furuso for the necessary bundles of reed; of getting some smaller works of hers finished before the big table could be started. Leo Furuso was one of those who'd made her a gift of wine, straw-colored, distilled from the skins of mandarin oranges, or mangoes—she wasn't able to remember which, and fretted over this in a useless way. *I don't like waking alone in bed,* she thought, as if in defense of herself, as if this fact was to blame for the earlier, bluesy pining for her husband. *People shouldn't expect their husband or their wife to hold up too much of the weight of their happiness.*

The torus gradually took on size and effect. It had a quick gravitational turning, and at its circumference it lapped the slower diaphane of sails with a tireless constancy. From the one-yard, the periphery of the torus rose from the horizon in a long, lustrous, reeling palisade, with the globe-shaped hub at the axis seeming to stand unmoving behind it like the inner keep of a castle. A small confusion of cupolas and knobby spires projected north and south from the hub, and these poles spun swift or slow or not at all, according to their uses. People climbed out to the sails or back from them along the cat's cradle of lines between the one-yard of the diaphane and the docking ports at the north pole. It was the usual thing to trip a dragline and leap over the thwarts of the torus in one long splendid planing: In that one moment, the gray fastness of the wheel became the nucleus about which and for which those two hundred fields of silver-gilt sail were spread. But now, having Al Poreda's swollen body in their hands, they climbed the hawser with deliberateness, with gravity; and the torus, revealing itself incrementally beneath them, seemed unrevealed, flat, jejune.

There were long apertures chasing the inner circumference of the wheel. The apertures had been baffled against the dizzying turn of the starfield—there was no seeing in or out of them. There had been mirrors once, corresponding to the apertures, for letting the light of the old sun into the world, but they had been disassembled early on and the mirrors sold off, and it had been a myriad of xenon fixtures that had brought them ersatz daylight in the long years between suns. There was a spangle of lights at the hub, in the few small windows and defining the docking ports, but the wheel and its spokes were dark, windowless, arcane. Juko, looking down on it through the architecture of Al Poreda's stiff, spreadeagled legs, felt bitterly its lack of a human reference.

She thought all at once, inexplicably, of the big, yellowing camphor tree standing on the high side of her house. The altejo aqueduct ran in a narrow channel up there, but where the roots of the old tree shouldered it to one side, the water spread out shallow and slow. It was a favored place for birds to come, drinking and bathing, though the water was brown and there were bits of twig and dead leaves in it. The camphor tree was inborn, but old for all that, a crown ten meters high, shedding leaves now in great dry drifts, the limbs displaying themselves against the ceiling. People in the śiro had had the young forester to look at the sick old tree, but it occurred to Juko now: The camphor might be dead before her husband had gotten home again. He'd be four days, five, surveying on the ground, then thirty days sailing back here in the *Ruby*—at least that. *Al Poreda is dead,* she thought, as if that ought to keep the death of the camphor tree from surprising her.

2

Ĉejo

To think that the sun rose in the east—that men and
women were flexible, real, alive—that everything
was alive,
To think that you and I did not see, feel, think, nor bear
our part,
To think that we are now here and bear our part.

IN THE LIFT, Ĉejo stood with a woman who was mournful and silent—he thought he remembered she was a relative of Al Poreda's. He didn't know if he should speak to the woman—he was in an agony of fear—but finally he said, "Are you Ina's sister?" She was fair-skinned, narrow-eyed like Al's wife, Ina; they had the same stoopy shoulders on a long torso.

The woman's face was red in a blotchy way, but if she'd been weeping she was done with it for now. She nodded gravely. "You're Humberto Indergard's son. You look his image. Your mother works the sail with Alberto. Is she Juko Ohaŝi?"

"Yes."

She nodded again. "Do you know about Al? He got killed just now. I'm sent to meet the body."

The bad news, which had been vague, became at once more specific. He felt a quick, excruciating relief: *Alberto Poreda*.

One of Ĉejo's cousins had spent his green years with Al and his wife. Ĉejo had used to spend a little time there too, with his cousin, when he had been nine, ten. He had gotten from Al and Ina a short-lived, very fierce interest in Jesus Christ. But when the word had come round the neighborhood, *someone on the sail was killed*, his heart had turned over; he had thought it was his mother.

Ĉejo and Al Poreda's sister-in-law came gradually buoyant in the lift, turning round to new positions relative to the floor, the door. The exit opened in what had been the ceiling. At the egress of the lift there was a corridor yoked to other corridors looping out to the docks and into the warren of labs and manufactory. Ĉejo didn't know the way. He followed the sister-in-law, who went ahead of him slowly in a long, drifting stride. It was cold in the hub. He rolled down the sleeves of his shirt.

Against the bright-green field of the curving wall were mahogany-colored people, yellow lions, stilt-legged white birds, all dancing long-limbed with their teeth bared, their feet turned out; then he passed a row of peak-roofed brick houses standing with shoulders adjoining, women sitting in bunches on the steps before the cherry-red doors; and a person in yellow trousers walking along a dry road beside a tile-and-plaster wall, beside trees arrayed high-crowned against a vivid blue firmament. On the long, windowless passageways of the hub, without an orientation to ceiling, to floor, people had painted a kaleidoscope of murals. Ĉejo had painted here, himself, two or three times. There were thousands of meters of intersecting corridors, no lack of surfaces. People had been painting on these walls since the beginning of life in the *Miller* and the murals beside the lifts were very old—maybe they were the work of people who had been dead for a hundred years.

When he and the sister-in-law came out to the periphery of the north pole, windows were set at rare intervals, letting on the docking ports. The ports had been meant to receive the big heavy-lift vehicles that had used to come up from Earth launches. They were used now chiefly by individual sailmenders entering and leaving the hub, for which use they seemed cavernous, out of scale. There were strands of lights framing each of the portals, a frame for wheeling stars, but within them was blackness, hugeness. In one, finally, Ĉejo saw a lit torch and shapes drifting inward seeking the human-scale hatch in the deep darkness of the interior wall. Their shadows fell away long and utterly black in several directions at once, jumping up the walls, the ceiling, down to the floor, in the great cave of the docking port. He put his face to the glass, looking for his mother.

"Is that Al they're bringing in there?" the sister-in-law asked him, coming to look also. There was no telling yet. He saw tiny shapes, five or six, in the bright white of exos.

"I don't know," he said.

But it must have been. When they followed the curve of the corridor, they saw other people had got there ahead of them, crowding the space in front of the hatch. Ĉejo knew most of them, by face at least; they worked the sailchart room or the sail, were friends of his mother and of Al. Some he didn't know.

One was dark like Al, an old man, his skin close to his bones. The sister-in-law didn't speak to the old man but took hold of his arm as she came alongside him.

Ĉejo thought he should wait out of the way, at the edge of the group. Someone he knew, a sailcharter named Anĝelo Jutaka, held a wall strap away from the others. When he was next to him, Ĉejo said, "Do you remember me? I'm Juko's son."

Anĝelo nodded without smiling. "You're grown up. I remember you, a little child. Did you hear about Al Poreda?"

"Yes."

"It's Juko who's bringing in his body."

Ĉejo looked toward the door. There was a small round window set in it, letting on the pressure chamber. From where he was, he could see nothing through the glass. He waited, imagining his mother and the others crowded into the little room with Al Poreda's body, their white exos bumping silently together in the whispering room.

"They've let the *Lark* down, did you hear?" Anĝelo Jutaka leaned closer to him, speaking the words softly next to his ear, a solemn whisper. "Nobody should be surprised if it was the ŝimanas killed Al—it's the anxiousness does it, that's my feeling, and these are anxious times, no denying."

Ĉejo didn't know what he should say to that. He had been wild with restlessness earlier in the day, feeling on the cusp of great change. Now his anxiousness had an immediacy he didn't think Anĝelo was meaning—he wanted his mother to come out of the hatch. He wanted to see her face, let her see his.

"Isn't that Ina's sister?" Anĝelo asked him, murmuring into his ear. "Isn't her name Ajlina?" He bent his head toward the sister-in-law.

Ĉejo had not remembered the woman's name until now. "Yes. She's come to meet the body."

"Well I don't know him, but I guess the other, the old man, must be from Al's family too. He looks like Al, eh? Dark and short like that."

The hatch door released a little breath and then swung slowly inward so the people next to it had to move out of the way, some of them pressing their backs against an old wall painting: the graying spines of books in untidy rows and stacks among oddments and keepsakes. It was Orval Wyho who had opened the hatch, but he didn't come all the way out of the chamber. He unfastened the skull of his exo and drifted to one side, bareheaded, solemn, waiting for the body to be taken ahead of him into the corridor. Ĉejo's mother and a man named Aric Engirt guided Al by the elbows as if he were a child or an old man with frail legs, but the shape in the exo was unliving, sufflated, the image behind the clear faceplate tumid and black.

The old man of Al's family slid his look gently over Al's poor face, shook his head, said "Ah, ah" in a sorrowful way. The woman, Ajlina, when she saw Al, expelled her breath in a sound loud and clipped as a bark. "Oh! God! Who can believe this?" She began a harsh moan, and the old man embraced her, his own lament become a condolence, "Ah, ah, ah." Ĉejo could see it was a pantomime of grief for his mother: She and Aric, while they went on holding Al's wrists, his puffy elbows, were shut inside their hardhats, not able to get out of them one-handed. People came together around the body, supporting the father, the sister-in-law, and in the narrow, crowded space Ĉejo lost his view of Juko. She had not seen him, hadn't looked toward him.

It was Ajlina, suddenly, who gave up her hold on the old man and took Al's hands deliberately in her own. Her face was stiff, tearless, she was abruptly finished with her outcry. "They have got a bier waiting at the foot of Esperplena, eh?" She said this to no one specifically, but looking around at them all hopefully. Then she gave over one of Al's hands to the old man, who touched it to his lips and said "Gift of God" in a trembling voice. The two of them led some of the other people in a little procession down the corridor. They were tenderly guiding Al's buoyant corpse between them, as if he were a blind man.

Then Ĉejo could see his mother. She had at last unfastened her headpiece and was holding it in the crook of one arm like a parcel. Her face was pale, mournful, her hair sticking up in a ridge along the crown of her head. When she saw him, she grimaced silently. She said something to Aric Engirt, a few low words, and spoke to others as she made a way through them slowly to where Ĉejo waited with Anĝelo Jutaka. "I guess it was the ŝimanas, eh?" people said to her anxiously, and she shrugged a shoulder.

"Juko," Anĝelo said.

She touched Ĉejo's arm lightly, but she looked at Anĝelo, said to him, "What did Romeo hear, do you know, Anĝelo?"

Anĝelo looked away. "I guess he said a word, 'going,' or something like that. That's all Romeo heard."

She shook her head. "Before that, eh? What made Romeo think there was trouble?"

Anĝelo shrugged. "Just a little sound is all. Maybe it was the air going out the hole, or the knife against the exo, sawing. He hears everything, Romeo does." He looked at her. "Al never said anything to him, if that's what you were meaning."

"I guess it was."

"No, he never said anything." He shook his head. "He never said a word. Not on the incom, anyway. It was the šimanas, eh?"

Juko grimaced, lifting her shoulder again.

"Do you have to log out?" Ĉejo asked her.

She squeezed his hand. "Yes. You don't need to come. Will you wait for me?"

"Don't get started talking to people." He wanted Anĝelo Jutaka, hearing him say it, to help her go in and out quickly from the sailchart room.

"I won't. A little while. Wait for me."

She and Anĝelo and other sailmenders went off without him and he found the long, complicated way around to the gallery of the spokes. He waited. When she finally came, she was free of the exo, wore an undyed flaxen shirt and the kenaf trousers she favored, the ones dyed red. He liked the trousers himself, but not the shirt: The yellow at her throat made her skin look sallow.

She made a face, screwing up her mouth again. "People wanted to talk."

"It's okay," he said. In the hub of the *Miller* the fluorescent lights were garish, equivocal. He had waited alone, in the cold lights, the cold air. What time was it? You had to go outward to find the day, the night.

They held on to the wall silently, waiting for the lift, their bodies insistently adrift. After a while she said, complaining, "I'm tired, I want to sit. There's no sitting up here."

He said, "No."

She looked toward him. Then she put her arm out, reaching

for him, and let her head rest against his ear. Ĉejo's eyes sprang unexpectedly with tears. "I thought it was you," he said, his voice breaking helplessly, and she made a sound of distress, wordless, without lifting her head.

They went down from the hub silently, heavily, in the lift of the eightspoke. People liked to name every mechanical thing, and they had named this spoke the Way-Around: At its foot on the east side, the Ring River completed its circling of the world and went under the ground, where a pump lifted the river to its beginning again on the spoke's west side, and released it in the short steep cataract of the Falls From Grace. When Ĉejo and his mother came out from the lift into the high, upcurving vault of the torus—out into the damp heat and yellowish light of afternoon—the clamor of the falls was a sudden steady noise, obscurely comforting.

The earth in the *Miller* was impounded on the slopes— terraces and steps that followed the long curving geometry of the torus. People in his mother's ŝiro, the Pacema, lived on the high banks, the altejo, their houses built along the curve of the walls, near the bones of the ceiling. In the rainy season, Pacema houses stood above the fog, looking out through the tops of trees to houses and fields on the other side of the short arc, sixty-five meters across, or down the long, narrow, embowed vista to the houses of Bonveno ŝiro, westward, or the footings of the sevenspoke, the Violin String, which stood at the top of the rise to the east.

People in the terraced fields were weeding the flax or tying up the seed pods of onions with little sacks to catch the seeds as they dried and dropped off, but as Ĉejo and Juko went by them on the little path between the river and the maltejo fields, they stood up from their work and spoke to Juko anxiously, wanting to know if it was true that someone on the sail had been killed, or wanting to know who was dead, or asking if it was the śimanas that had killed him. Ĉejo's mother nodded or shrugged, answering people impatiently without speaking, walking with her hands pushed down in the pockets of her red pants. Ĉejo wanted to say something to console her, but didn't know what it ought to be.

"I came up in the lift with Al's sister-in-law," he said uselessly.

His mother, with her eyes fixed on her sandals, said, "Do you know Armando? The old man who was there with Ajlina? I think you met him once at Yearly Meeting." She made a dismissive gesture with her hand. "Well, it was a long time ago." Then she told him, "Al is the old man's son."

"I can see it. They have the same look," Ĉejo said.

"I guess they do. People say that, anyway." She looked at Ĉejo. "People say you look like Humberto."

This was something he always had refused. From habit, he made a grimacing face. "I don't look like him. I don't know why people always say that."

In a moment, another old habit, she said to him, "You're prettier," and gave him a sliding look, a little smile. She brought one hand out of her pocket and reached for his. They walked up the footway between the fields, their clasp of hands connecting them.

People trained vines to go up the posts of arbors but often kiwi and ĉejote had a habit of ranging out, unruly; in Alaŭdo fields, where Ĉejo lived and farmed with his father, he had been tying up the blind vines, helping them find the poles. No one in Pacema was doing this, or they had fallen behind in the work.

Where ĉejote had come snaking out in the path, Ĉejo stooped and pushed back the tender stems. He felt his mother watching him. She was still getting over her surprise at seeing him a farmer. Her look made him feel proprietary, adult.

"Are you solidly moved in?" she asked him.

He had only lately come back to live with Humberto. He had spent his green years in his mother's brother's household in Senlima, but when he had made up his mind to farm, he'd come back to his father's house.

"Yes. I'm in. We've got the loom moved, that was the worst thing. Four of us carried it."

"Who all is in that apartment now?"

"Leona and Petro"—these were his father's parents, Ĉejo's grandparents—"and Heza Barfor." When Juko looked toward him, he added, "She's a divorced woman without children. She was living in her sister-in-law's house but they didn't get along. Alfhilda, too, she's living with us now."

Juko looked at him again. "Alfhilda's twelve, then? She's a good girl. She and her mother were always my favorites in that family."

Children, when they were twelve, moved out of their parents' home to spend their green years with other people—uncles or grandparents or the parents of friends—and Alfhilda, who was a cousin of Ĉejo's, was as new to the house as he was. He had been fond of her, himself, when they'd both been children, but he had left the green years now, and imagined he ought to put a distance between himself and twelve-year-olds. "She leaves things where they land, never picks up," he said.

Juko maybe wasn't listening to his complaint about Alfhilda. "It's a small house," she told him, murmuring.

"It's all right. We get along, all of us."

She nodded. "Yes." There was something in her face, a look; maybe she was feeling shut out.

"You get along with your household, too," he said, without knowing how it could help her mood.

She nodded again. "Yes." He didn't know if she was thinking of Al Poreda.

The weight of their bodies fell off a little, going up the steep way onto the slope, but Juko went up the easeful climb slowly, looking into the darkness beneath the crowded houses. Houses were built to stand on poles, to let the air flow from below, let the heat and the damp out; the sutaǧo, the underneath, was used for a threshing floor, and chickens sometimes roosted there. Under one house some children were scratching something in the cool dirt, squatting with their sticks, whispering, and that made Ĉejo think of something he had forgotten.

He never had lived in the house his mother lived in now, but from his childhood Kristina Veberes had been an auntie to him, a third grandmother, and before his mother had moved her belongings into Kristina's house, before she had married Kristina's son, Ĉejo often had slept, played, visited in the two rooms of that apartment.

He remembered suddenly, there was a little low-roofed alcove in the front room that borrowed its space from under the stair of the sadaŭ, and he had played and slept in that odd little cranny with Kristina's grandchildren, who had been as cousins to him. Ĉejo had not paid much attention to Bjoro in those days—a man his mother's age, the father to one or two of Kristina's grandchildren. But Bjoro's wife had died, and Ĉejo's brother; and his mother and father had ended their marriage.

Now the alcove Ĉejo had slept in, the little cave where he had scratched his name in the floorboards, was Kristina Veberes's sleeping place; and Ĉejo's mother slept with Kristina's son in a room that looked out on the incurvature of the world.

When Ĉejo led his mother up the ladder of her house, neighbors were standing there on the loĝio with Kristina. Four or five families divided up the long U of a house, and people liked to bring their handwork out of their apartments and make the common middle, the loĝio, a place for gossiping and arguing, for coming together to visit with their neighbors, and for children playing. Now they had made it a place for waiting to hear bad news.

Ĉejo's father was there, too, a surprise. He turned and looked at Ĉejo coming up the ladder, and Kristina's look followed his, white and stiff, and other people turned, and then they saw Juko coming behind him, and there was a loosening, a relief. One woman said, "There! Not Juko, eh?" Kristina pursed her mouth and then opened it silently.

The divorce of Ĉejo's parents was old, the edge worn from it, and Humberto had kept up a quiet friendship with his once-wife, and with Kristina, but Ĉejo was surprised to see his father's eyes fill with tears; he was surprised when Humberto put out his hand and touched the crown of Kristina's head, stroking the old woman's hair, and she put her hand up, too, and patted his fingers.

In a moment she said, "Who is dead then?" and Juko said quietly, "Al Poreda. It is Al Poreda."

The people who knew Al began to shake their heads, to make small sounds of regret. Some people cried. Ĉejo cried a little himself, a guilty sorrow: He was glad it was Al who had died, and not his mother. Kristina put her hand out and drew him in, wiped his eyes on her shirtsleeve. "Well, I'm sorry for his family," she said flatly. "But I didn't want it to be my daughter-in-law."

Someone said mournfully to Juko, "It was the śimanas, eh?" and she looked away in irritation, not answering. Then she went into the little apartment, leaving her neighbors and her family standing out in the loĝio. Ĉejo went in too, feeling still a helpless wish to comfort her. Humberto and Kristina went on standing out there a little longer, speaking together in a murmur Ĉejo couldn't hear, but finally they came in too, and Kristina slid the wall closed to keep out the neighbors.

Juko had filled a kettle for tea and plugged it in, had begun to measure the leaves. Kristina unfolded a repozo but she wouldn't sit against it herself; she brought out little cups for each of them and sat down with hers in the middle of the rug. Then Juko left the tea kettle unfinished and sat down against the unused repozo, her legs folded under her. She let her head fall back against the wicker rest and shut her eyes. Ĉejo sat too. It was Humberto who went to stand in the corner of the room, the little galley, to wait for the kettle to get done with heating itself.

The daylight through the open casement was yellowish, warm, stirred by a small draft. Ĉejo closed his eyes as his mother had done. A brief dark dream was imprinted behind his eyelids: Al Poreda's broad brown face swelling suddenly and blackening, eyes widening to let fear swiftly out, and his mother's face contracting, taking the fear in through her open mouth, the holes of her eyes.

"I should go and see Ina," Juko said, in a tired, flat voice.

Probably she was waiting for someone to forgive her for not going. Ĉejo looked at her.

"Her family and her neighbors will be there," Kristina said. "You don't have to go right now."

Juko made a small, indeterminate sound. In a moment, Humberto brought the pot of fragrant tea. When he was pouring for Ĉejo he lifted his brows in a vaguely questioning way, nothing to do with the tea. Maybe, like the others, he was asking, *Was it the śimanas then?* Ĉejo shrugged his shoulders. He only half remembered the last time there had been an accident on the sail: A woman named Ĵulia? Ĵunio? had suffered an embolism, something to do with her air mix, a faulty exo. He remembered someone's words, "Choked for breath," but then he realized: He didn't know if these words had to do with Julia, or if they had been spoken to explain the death of his brother, Vilef.

Juko and Kristina began to talk quietly about Al's wife and son, Juko telling and Kristina asking tedious particulars to do with that family, and both of them relating anecdotes about Al's distant relatives, people Ĉejo didn't know. They went on with it for a while and then fell silent. Ĉejo sipped his tea, looking down in the little cup. All at once he began to hear the slight, distant rush of the Falls From Grace, and then in other apartments two women talking, and the scraping of a table leg or a cane against the floor, and children calling to one another, and chickens fighting, and birds vocalizing in a multitude of languages.

He had recognized in himself, for a long time now, a deeply morbid curiosity to do with the rare violent deaths, and gradually it became too difficult not to ask his mother: "Will you say how Al was killed?"

She looked at the vertical poles of the wall, or through the casement to the dry crown of a tree framed there. Ĉejo looked too. Above the lineaments of the tree, he glimpsed a delicate cluster of xenon lights in the arching scaffold of the ceiling. "Maybe he was looking for the *Ruby*," she said, sighing. "We all were, I think, but maybe it was too far off for him, eh?"

In a moment Ĉejo said, "Yes," though she may not have meant to ask anyone anything. She had brought him out on the sails once, pulling along the hawser from the hub of the torus to the one yard, and then out the gallantmast the long distance toward the masthead. They had seemed to float on the vast array of sheets, rocking, below an infinite field of wheeling stars. His mother had warned him: "Don't look at the stars," but how could he not? He had vomited inside the exo, sailsick, and they had had to turn back at the three-yard without reaching the head of the mast. All the way back, he had kept staring out at the dizzying turn of the starfield, and the undulating, unimaginably distant horizon of the sail. *It was too far off.* He thought he knew what that meant.

"There was a cut in his exo," she said after a moment. She said it in such a way, tiredly, that Ĉejo felt a quick waxing of his guilt. But at a certain age—eleven, twelve—he had liked to imagine the effect of vacuum on the human body. He had not thought, then, that the swelling corpse maybe would seal a hole in an exo. He used to imagine a body freely dilating to the point of dispersal of the atoms, keeping a human shape with infinitely widening interstices until, like the universe, its form became too vast to perceive.

"He cut it himself," Juko said, and Ĉejo found a brief, terrible appeal in imagining Al Poreda cutting at his exo, trying to let his shape out upon the stars. After a brief silence, low-voiced, she said, "But maybe it wasn't meant. He might have slipped, cutting the tangle out of a halyard."

Kristina Veberes made a small, chaffing sound, *shuh*. Ĉejo saw the look that went between his mother and her mother-in-law. Kristina and Juko's friendship was old, they got along with few words. This was something to do with Al's death, but he was excluded from its meaning.

"Do you remember Karlina Remlinger?" Humberto said. He had been silent until now. Ĉejo looked at him, but he had been asking Juko. She rolled her head slightly against the head of the repozo.

"You know her. She repairs electrical things. She carries around her tools in that high-sided red cart with the rope handles." He waited for Juko's face to tell him she remembered. Then he said, "She has a theory to do with persons whose ancestry is equatorial, being more prone to ŝimanas than other people. She thinks racial memory or something, a tolerance of artificial daylight, is on the side of the Norse line, the English." Ĉejo saw him glance sideward at Juko. "She's doing a compiling. Maybe she'll ask people about Al's family line, and whether he is from Costa Rican people. If it was the ŝimanas killed him."

Juko moved restlessly. She set her tea on the boards of the floor, pulled her feet up under her and sat on her toes, sideways. "Where does this theory come from, eh? She might be wrong about this, about a racial tolerance. People who lived in those winter-lands, they were known for unhappiness, I thought." But then she said unhappily, "He's Costa Rican, I think. His father, Armando, is dark, anyway, his name is Poreda. I don't remember Al's mother. Do you know her family?" She looked at Kristina.

Kristina's old face gathered. "Linda Florencio," she said. She made that abrading sound again, *shuh*, and looked at each of them. Her hair was white and long; she habitually pulled it back and tied it with a bright piece of yarn or a ribbon, but it was coarse, frizzy, the unruly ends stuck out in a halo. "There's been endless intermarrying, eh? There can't be many families who are mostly of one line, do you think? Anyway, hardly any records are kept. Do you know Armando's parents, or Linda's? How can Karlina know they weren't Norse, eh? or English?"

"She has found some old disks," Humberto said. "They kept better records early on, I heard. She asks the old people, makes family trees. I don't know how many families she has found that are mostly one ancestry." He had a habit of smiling crookedly while squeezing his brows up high above the bridge of his nose: a quizzical look, unconfident. He was prone to use it when he thought he'd be disputed. It had a childishness that vaguely irritated Cejo. For a couple of years, he had been watching himself for that look, in case it might be inherited. Now, when his father made that face, Cejo studied him. He had straight black hair, long eyes, slightly folded lids, though his family name was Norwegian. Juko was Juko Ohaśi, though he thought there was less Japanese in her family than in Humberto Indergard's— her hair was brown and fine, her eyes were blue. Cejo usually didn't see his father's face in mirrors; he was more than half serious about that. Only sometimes, unexpectedly, he glimpsed Humberto's long eyes looking back on him from the glass. He had not thought of them as Japanese eyes until now.

"Why's she doing it?" he asked his father. "Nothing's to

be done, only we'd worry about everybody we knew who was Costa Rican, and they'd worry about themselves."

Humberto said, "Well, we're worrying anyway, I guess. It might not hurt to know who we should worry about." He still kept his little smiling frown.

Ĉejo shook his head, unpersuaded. "I think it would just push them over the edge, anybody who was leaning that way." He felt a sudden indisputable certainty. "If I was prone to ŝimanas, I wouldn't want to know."

Humberto shrugged softly. "Some people would want to know. How can some know and some not?"

Ĉejo was impatient with this reasoning but not able quickly to rebut it. He was a slow thinker, he felt; he would realize his answer tonight or tomorrow, too late.

"Maybe Karlina is thinking about the long run," Juko said. "She might be thinking to keep equatorial peoples from parenting with each other."

"People should marry whomever they choose," Ĉejo said fiercely. He made ready to argue this conviction if his mother took the usual view. Families and neighbors liked to arrange marriages, but he had lately fallen in love for what he felt sure would be the last time, and his feelings ran high on the subject. A small look passed between his parents but there was no telling what it meant, whether it was something to do with him, or with their own marriage, the finish of it, or the beginning.

"No one would stop anyone from marrying," Humberto said. "But people would know, if this theory of Karlina's is true, that a person who was Costa Rican should try to marry someone from another line, a northern line. If you were looking for a good husband or a wife for someone in your family, you wouldn't suggest that a Costa Rican marry another Costa Rican. It would just become a known thing."

Ĉejo said nothing. He didn't know why he felt boxed off, defeated. It hadn't been an argument. Helplessly, he began to worry whether this girl he loved, Katrin Amundsen, might be equatorial.

The others were silent as well. It had begun to be dusk, and in the lowered light they sat on the floor without touching, without looking at one another. Humberto still held the little cup of tea in the hollow of his hand, and he looked into it. Juko, with her head pressed against the repozo, watched the slow darkening of the ceiling, the rafters that were the floor of the sadaŭ.

"What can be grown in that cold," she said after a while. She said it flatly, not a question.

Humberto looked at her with his brows squeezed up, that quizzical look. "There is some native flora," he said. "Woody plants, mosses, lichens, small trees in the stream valleys."

"Can you grow kiwi fruit? Ĉejote?" she asked him irritably. "What will you eat? The woody plants? The mosses?"

In the next year they must settle on a way of going. They must swing around the sun to get up speed for leaving—for going on fifty years to the next likely world—or iris the sail and make an anchorage around this one—settle on this world now and forever. Ĉejo felt a thrill of fear, that his mother might have made up her mind already, on a question that was so momentous.

Humberto drank down the little bit of cold tea and examined the inside of the cup. "Nils Truhijo and many others are drafting designs for plantodomo. There is a library of frozen agricultural cells; people are looking for species suited to a tundra. Or there may be more temperate zones—where the balloons failed, eh? in the southwestern islands, the eastern midlatitudes." He glanced toward Juko, perhaps gauging the quality of her discouragement. "For twenty years we've known there was not much hope of a mesothermal climate," he said, watching her.

Ĉejo looked at Juko too. "You haven't made up your mind, have you? How can you find the sense of a Meeting if your mind is made up?"

Juko shook her head angrily. "No. My mind isn't made up. I only want to be gloomy today. Let me cry over my ĉejote and kiwis, and tomorrow you can tell me about greenhouses and temperate zones." Suddenly she did cry a little, putting her fist to her cheek, and a few tears ran down the path between her curled fingers. Ĉejo stared at her in surprise. He could not remember when he had seen his mother cry. Not even on the occasion of his brother's death.

Humberto looked at her too. "There are some hardy kiwis, I think," he said in astonishment. "But you can cry for the ĉejote."

Kristina, without speaking of Juko's tears, stood suddenly and picked up people's cups from the floor. "I have some tortillas. I'll find something to put in them. Ĉejo, maybe you would come and slice things."

She put on the little light in the galley and brought things out of the cold box: bits of pepper and mushroom and steamed rice left from another meal, cilantro, peanuts, sprouts of lemongrass. On the narrow pocket table, Ĉejo cut the peanuts and the cilantro with a knife. The tortillas were dark, Kristina liked to make them from breadnut; she built upon them slowly, arraying the food on the flat rounds, while Humberto and Juko went on talking quietly, asking and answering things to do with Juko's now-husband, Bjoro, and the go-down boat, the *Lark*.

"She was crying for Al Poreda," Ĉejo whispered to Kristina when he had thought it through.

She didn't look up from what she was doing. "I don't know," she said. There was a distant quality in the sound of her voice, and Ĉejo felt suddenly excluded from something. He was afraid, while they all had been sitting together drinking orange-scented tea and speaking of tundra plants and closed minds, the others had experienced a different conversation.

They sat around the low table and Kristina, with a look, encouraged them all in a brief, religious silence: gratitude for the meal. Then while they ate, they talked of the health of several people they knew, and slightly sordid hearsay about a woman who was an old enemy of Kristina's, and gossip about Humberto's cousin's daughter who was marrying a man none of them knew. When the table was cleared they might, on another night, have played Obsession, or got out the chess board—it was rare for Ĉejo to have his mother and father in one place, under one roof. But there was Al Poreda, and the cold tundra planet, and his mother's mood was dark. He kissed Kristina's dry cheek and Juko's, and received their kisses, while Humberto stood watching, shifting his feet. Then he and his father walked home from Pacema in the darkness.

The daylights had been extinguished. In the narrow lanes between the houses, light fell out of casements and made the air visible, but in the farmed land the darkness was whole, uncompromised. Humberto went ahead of Ĉejo, finding the way carefully on the beaten tracks. He was silent. Only when they had got at the edge of the Alaŭdo śiro he said suddenly, murmuring, "Is there soul in a plant, do you think? Why do you suppose we honor the food by a silent grace?" with the end of it dropping so it became less a question. He had a habit of doing this, brooding on small mysteries, but when Ĉejo looked at him he looked back squinting, as if he were surprised to have asked it, and he said quickly, "I don't know," as if it might have been his own answer, or the unfinished beginning of something. Then he put his hand to the back of his head and ruffled his own hair fiercely. In a moment he began to lay out the next day's work tying up the ĉejote vines, harvesting leaves and flower buds from some of the doan gwa melons, repairing the runoff piping under a bed of radishes and en-kai, and it wasn't as if he had asked Ĉejo anything.

Ĉejo's grandmother and her friend Heza Barfor sat together under the lamp in the front room of the apartment. Leona sat against a repozo with both her feet extended in front of her. She was a little lame from an old accident, a bone broken when a pipe had fallen on her; she was a sewage engineer. Her lap was full of milkweed and she was picking it clean with swift skill, the seeds raining in her bowl with a tiny, steady patter. Heza sat on her hips and heels on a cushion and knitted.

"She is only a couple of years older than us," Heza was saying, "but look at the difference. If she wasn't so cross-grained, I ought to feel sorry for her."

Since Heza had come to live in Leona's house, she had complained ceaselessly about her sister-in-law, using always the indefinite "she," as if the woman's name was a sour fruit she didn't want in her mouth. Ĉejo didn't know the sister-in-law, and had got swiftly tired of Heza's complaining. If his grandmother was tired of it, she didn't say; she would listen and nod while Heza let her bitterness stream out. Leona's tolerance was storied.

She lifted her head to Cejo and Humberto and said over Heza's complaint, "Do you know? a sail mender was killed today, but I heard it wasn't Juko, eh?" Her eyes narrowed, looking at them.

Cejo's father crouched down on the floor beside her and busied his hands with the milkweed. "It was Alberto Poreda, panja. It was Juko who brought in the body." He glanced at his mother. "We went to her house and stayed a while. We ate our supper with Juko and Kristina Veberes."

Leona looked away. "Well, Juko takes a death without much trouble, eh?" She had a long-standing bitterness toward Juko, and her bottom lip curled on it.

These were matters that weren't spoken of except left-handedly, but Cejo understood that the anger between his mother and his grandmother had to do with Vilef's death, which had also been the beginning of the end of his parents' marriage, and not an occasion for Leona's tolerance. Because no one had told him an unambiguous account, Cejo had no position, and tried to hold back every malign outbreak. "My mother has an old friendship with Al Poreda," he said in defense of his mother, and then, "She was crying, eh?" because his grandmother was prone to complain of Juko's insufficient tears. Leona looked sideward at her son but not at Cejo, and did not speak. In a moment, Cejo deliberately sat down at his loom and took up the half-finished stringing of the warp on his warping board.

His grandfather wandered into the apartment with a handful of figs in his hand. He said, with his mouth chewing, "I heard somebody killed himself on the sail. Was that it? The śimanas?"

Leona said without bitterness, "If he was a religious man, God knows where his faith was when he let this happen."

"It's not so easy as that," Humberto said to her, but he made no effort to untangle it.

"Nothing, not even God, is greater to a person than their own self is." Heza pronounced these words solemnly without lifting her eyes from her knitting needles. All of them looked at her. Heza had a well known habit of stating things without seeming to connect them to what other people were saying. Ĉejo wasn't sure if her declaration had anything at all to do with Al Poreda's death.

Leona answered as if it did. "I would have said he didn't value himself enough," she said sorrowfully, an abrogation.

Ĉejo's father and his grandparents and Heza got gradually round to their old argument about Alfhilda, who was spending a night in her parents' house. She was like Leona, a science-minded person, and she'd lately taken an apprenticeship to Anejlisa Revfiem, the plant geneticist. The whole family liked to argue mildly between them whether this was a field one could learn well without first having farmed. Ĉejo thought Leona's and Alfhilda's understanding of hybridizing and cloning was abstract, not rooted in the soil as his was, or Humberto's, and he had brought this up before. But he kept out of the argument now, absorbed in the unvoiced counting of the warp ends; and when he got up from the loom, he went out to use the toilet and brush his teeth. Then he unfolded his bed in the room he shared with his father and his grandfather. He was in a mood for thinking about dying.

Against the darkness, lying on his shoulder and hip on the

mat, he saw Al Poreda's tumescent face, swollen black with blood. Once, lying waiting for sleep, he had experienced a kind of flashing intimation, had glimpsed the absolute and unending loss of himself that must be death. He had thought that he believed in the enduring of souls, but at that moment, and while the streaking white afterimage still burned behind his eyes, he had believed in nothingness. Now he lay deliberately remembering that moment of meteoric fear and astonishment, but not able to reproduce it. He turned death over and over in his mind, listening morosely to his own heartbeat and imagining carefully that men and women would be real and alive, continuing to take a great interest in food and sickness, stringing a loom, love, when he, Ĉejo, would be dead. He imagined Katrin Amundsen grieving for him, but then his mind led him away from there.

He followed Katrin to a hidden place she knew of up the ladder of her domaro into the rafters of the sadaŭ, behind baskets and a stored piece of a split bamboo wall. It was dim and dusty, a narrow triangle of space with the sloping bamboo making a sort of low roof. They sat down close together on the sadaŭ floor, facing one another. Ĉejo was anxious, filled with heat and longing, and he whispered to her, *I love you*, and put his mouth on her throat, his hands at her waist, at the neat fold of her hips. She arched her head back, lengthening her throat for him, rocking her hips toward him. Katrin was twenty, had a woman's rich lust and experience. She pulled her shirt loose from the waist of her trousers and he slid his hands along the skin of her ribs, kissed her throat and her hair, her ears, her eyelids. *I love you*, he whispered, and helped her take her shirt off, then his. She was thin, her breasts small neat cones, the nipples very dark and peaked. He cupped them tenderly in his hands. She took a shuddering breath, arching her back, pushing her breasts into his palms. They stroked each other, her fingertips tracing his ribs and nipples, twisting the few wiry hairs in the hollows under his arms; his thumbs scribed her breasts as his hands closed slowly, fondling her. She lay back with a low sound. He kissed her throat and shoulders, the soft inner flesh of her arms, held one of her nipples lightly in his mouth, the areole springing under his tongue. She cradled his head, and her hips stirred against him. They took down each other's trousers, and when she touched him, held him gently, a yearning fire ran under his skin. He said *Katrin,* whispering and urgent. She pulled his head down against the delicate skin of her belly, and he moved his mouth over her, into the heat and darkness of her opening legs. Her whole body moved to him, shuddering, a kind of wildness in the pent sound of her moaning, *ah, ah,* and later when she sat on him, clasping his hips between her thighs, when she put him inside her and rocked, he deliberately tried to make that same sound, *ah, ah, ah,* wildly whispering, moaning, as he pushed up to her in a sweetly aching undulation, but his body filled with the roar of his own blood and he sank into the red booming and wasn't able to remember afterward if he had made any sound at all.

A door slid quietly and his father said something, a few words, and his grandmother answered, or Heza, soft words, shapeless, who knew what they said? After quite a while he heard the rain beginning to fall on the roof and the trees, the earth, a sound as alive as the streaming of blood.

3

Bjoro

I see, just see skyward, great cloud-masses,
Mournfully slowly they roll, silently swelling and mixing,
With at times a half-dimm'd, sadden'd far-off star,
Appearing and disappearing.
(Some parturition rather, some solemn immortal birth;
On the frontiers to eyes impenetrable,
Some soul is passing over.)

BJORO REALIZED HE had made a sound, dreaming. When he opened his eyes, Peder's long eyes were open, watching him through the faceplate of the exo. He looked away from Peder's stare, sat up shaking, and the little dream washed out of him in a flood: the long black breathless dive, he was nauseous, astonished, afraid, he said, "What!" or "Wait!" and struck the bottom of the blind slide in a burst of noise and percussion. In the dream, as in life, he had known he would die. He had thought, *This is how people feel when they are dying, this surprise.* But none of them were dead. If they had struck the lava field or the mountain, maybe it would have killed them; anyway Luza said it might have, she was the medic among them, and she knew dynos and forces, she'd studied physics as well. But they'd come down in water, the big lake at the edge of the old lava flows, clear of the mountain, clear of the stony field, and had saved the blown hatch door and a broken cupboard of tools, and Peder, who was broken too, and so none of them were dead yet. And they had still the finder-seekers: Bjoro's made a pip every little while, he felt it moving his blood like an ersatz heart.

They had leaned the hatch cover against piled-up rocks to make a roof between them and the sky, and a wind blew, rattling gravel or pellets of ice against the metal. Bjoro sat under the eave of the hatch with the heels of his gloves against his eyes, and only slowly let his hands down and looked out across the lake. The prevailing color of this world was gray, the patchy snow and the gravel soaking up the colors of the sky, the lake fuliginous with silt. While he had briefly slept, there had come a thin streak of violet and cobalt blue across sixty or seventy degrees of the western horizon, obliquely defining the serrate peak of the mountain. It seemed a bruise on the sky, a sign of something dire.

Luza said, without looking toward him, "We'll have night, eh?" and then she did glance toward him, she may have looked to see if he feared the darkness.

This world had a long slow turning, thirty hours forty-seven minutes in a revolution; they were not yet at the spring equinox. At this season of the year, there'd be seventeen hours of night. Bjoro wasn't afraid of night, he knew what a vast blackness looked like. It was the sky that daunted him, its great tenebrous clouds sweeping toward them ceaselessly from behind the peak. The air was incredibly cold, bristly, it smelled of sulphur; he could feel its cold and its enormity in his chest, his mouth, when he took in a breath.

"Where is Isuma?" he asked Luza. He didn't mean *where* but something else. He could see Isuma walking away from them following the icy margins of the lake, keeping to the rocks that bound the shore. She looked small and distant; her white exo against the grayish landscape made him think of Juko on the sail and filled him with sudden, helpless grief.

Luza kept looking out at the long lurid edge of the overcast, the night falling. "Walking down the lakeshore. Seeing is there a flat place to lay an aerostat down."

Before they'd ever left the *Miller* they'd constructed a hundred elaborate emergencies and worked out a hundred elaborate responses: If the *Lark* was lost on landing, they would get a balloon to ride them up one at a time in its gondola. The *Ruby* hadn't any other heavy-lift craft but the *Lark*. There were three on the *Dusty Miller* but they might as well be useless; it would take forty days to get one here on board the *Ruby's* twin, the *Dream*. They had conceived the balloon rescue seriously, the six of them lounging on the floor in Isuma's house, pushing beads around on an abacus and interrupting each other with gestures and details. If they dumped the survey equipment, there'd be room for sixty kilos; none of them weighed more than that in the .8 gravity. They'd wear exos. It would take a while is all, rising a meter a second. Would be best if they had a good landing space, flat and unimperiled, for the montgolfiere, the open balloon below the closed one, to settle its voluminous sheets out in vast array when the cold nights sank it down to them.

There was a spinnaker the *Ruby* could deploy for steering the unmanned balloon to their finder-seekers, and when the mild day-heat lifted the thing off the ground Arda and Hans would steer by remote again, bring the *Ruby's* low orbit to intersect with the apogee of the balloon.

It had been a crazy construct. They had been playing, pretending, none of them had believed it, and here was Isuma walking over the snow after a place to land the damned balloon. Bjoro laughed. But Luza's startled look brought his fear out, and instinctively he stood up to walk away from it. Then he found he was climbing the back of the lava field to look for a landing place himself.

The ridge of stones was vast, a couple of hundred meters high, bounding the northern lakeshore in both directions out of eye's reach, a great bulk of gravel and basalt boulders, obsidian sand. Likely the stones had spilled down molten from the shoulder of the mountain and dammed the lake; from where they were, there was no telling how wide the field was spread, no way to guess the direction of the old flow. He went up slowly on it, laboring.

His legs quickly ached; he had to stand every little while and pull the cold air in his chest. It was opposite to his whole experience: On the *Miller* there was diminished effort with altitude, the hub was "up," free of gravity, effortless. He felt a wave of homesickness, standing alone and broken-winded with the storm-driven clouds and the immense mountain at his back. He had spent much of his life making ready for this venture, for this crash, even; he hadn't expected to be rotten at it, to find his mind occupied childishly with a desperate ache for his wife and his home. He had thought, in the filmcards he had studied of unbounded landscapes, of storms and snows and seas, there remained no surprises. It hadn't occurred to him, the vast depth of the third dimension. He hadn't thought he would fear the sky.

Ronaldo Inomoto had made boots for them all from studying old clothes and old landscapes. Bjoro had to think about his walking, had to set these heavy boots with care among the rocks; they made him feel he was stumping on numb feet, clumsy, no sense of the ground through the thick soles. They had near drowned him. He'd splashed his arms and gotten to the floating tool cupboard with his weighted feet hanging below him, worse than useless, dragging down the buoyant exo, and Luza had got out of her boots, let them go down in the water, but she was sorry for it now, hobbling in the thin-soled feet of the exo. The ground on this world was stony and gnarled, even the snow sharp, crusted—Ronaldo had guessed some things right.

Bjoro stood, finally, hunched and wheezing at the top of the ridge of rocks, and found the view north was an immense sweep of world, beyond imagining, many hundreds or thousands of hectares of broken ground, lava fields blackish and denticulated, dirty snow in the clefts of the teeth. There was no dust in the air; the edges of things were sharp, utterly clear. He could see to the northeast a green thread raveling through the canyons of lava, maybe it was a river, and almost at the sky's edge a line demarking two shades of gray—he had a sudden remembrance of the topo map of this continent and knew that line for the edge of the sea. Staring toward it, he felt a sort of vertigo, a dream image: He was standing on the slope high up under the ceiling of the torus but the trough of land below him slipped downward forever without a turning up. The land was immense, alive as an animal, unutterably powerful. The big mammals had been gone, all of them, decades before the *Dusty Miller* was built, Bjoro had seen them only on filmcards; but he thought this must be what people had felt once, staring in the face of the bear, the cat, the wolf—this terrible humbling before the thing so beautiful, and breathing death. He stood stricken, his breath gusting in white clouds.

He was a long time going over the rocks down to the lake-shore, stumbling slowly in the failing light. There'd been a hand-lamp in the tool cupboard; he saw Luza under the roof-hatch holding the lamp so the cone of light fell over Peder. On the cold wind he heard her voice, wispy, without words, and then Peder. "Enough," he said, or "Rough." When Bjoro crouched on the groundsheet beside them, Luza was holding Peder's hand, saying the end of something, ". . . ought to sleep; are you keep-ing warm?" and Bjoro was struck with a brief, pathetic wish to be the injured one, to lie dependently under the sheltering roof and be tenderly comforted and guarded.

There were flocks of little dark birds or bats working the surface of the lake now, grazing the water and wheeling upward and then dropping to it again in close throngs. Isuma, who had come back ahead of him, was crouched under the metal roof on her haunches, looking out at the big flat sheet of the lake, and the flyers. "What is behind us?" she said in a loud voice, a voice ringing unnecessarily across the water. None of them had spo-ken of anything but concrete matters—what they had saved of tools, what time it was, was it Peder's rib that had put a hole in his lung. But this bluffness in Isuma's voice was something new; maybe she'd become angry at their situation, or blamed one of them for it, or anyway Bjoro imagined that was it and not shakiness she was hiding. She was fearless, Isuma was, and solid. He thought if he heard her voice break, it would break him.

He meant to keep his own words flat, steady, but they jumped out too quick for him, mimicking Isuma a little, edgy and loud. "This field of lava goes on north to the horizon," he said. "Northeast a little river cutting it, and then maybe the ocean. There's no place that way."

"Well, no place round this lake is flat enough, big enough, and anyway all sharp stones," Isuma said. She looked at Bjoro. "How far would you say, to the ocean?"

Bjoro shook his head. "Far. I don't . . . My eye . . ." He shook his head again. "What's between is bad land, old lava," he said angrily. He realized he was grateful for Peder's flattened lung. They would need to carry him, and that would keep them from crossing the vast black canyons to the river delta and the sea.

"South is the mountain," Luza said in a moment, the only one of them with a mild voice. She looked at them both. "So we're left only the east and the west, between the peak and the lava bed, either end of the lake." She gestured vaguely.

Isuma said, growling, "We ought to find a place quick, and get our selves and our finder-seekers onto it, before they bring the damn balloon down in the middle of the lake."

"They'll wait, I bet," Luza said. "They'll wait to see if the seekers move: If the seekers don't move, they'll be thinking we're killed." She grinned slowly, baring her teeth. The plan had been to mark a diamond of landing field by the four finder-seekers. No one had said what the plan would be if the seekers never were made to mark a diamond.

Isuma grinned too, and finally Bjoro did, something to do with not being dead.

They agreed they would do turns with Peder, two would sleep while one sat up, getting a pulse and a breath count every little while and clicking on the handlamp to feed him painkillers. There was a med box that had been kept in the tool cupboard but no respirator in it, no possibilities for reinflating the lung. Luza wasn't a surgeon anyway, and the lung had a hole in it. She said he wasn't bleeding much into his belly, only the rib gave him pain and the empty lung made him wheeze. She said they ought to keep a lookout for ashy color, bubbles in his breath, blood from his mouth or his nose.

They fell silent, and in a while, without speaking again, Luza put out the handlamp and they faced the cold darkness. Their own weather was a Costa Rican analogue, humid subtropical, its two seasons warm-wet and warm-dry. The hub was the only cold place on the *Miller*, it was ten degrees there, or even less; but Bjoro's imagination hadn't made him ready for a true coldness of the air. It was zero in the daylight here, would drop to minus ten or fifteen overnight. The exos were proof against the cold, but a bared scalp, the back of the neck, one's eyes, let the heat out of the torso as if the exo had been breached. There had been skullcaps made by the Fiber Arts Committee, tuques knitted tight from kapok yarns, but lost in the crash. Escaping the *Lark*, they'd thrown off the hardhats and afterward only recovered two, the things cumbrous in the gravity anyway. They put one on Peder because of its respiratory assist, but none of them used the other, they crouched together, shaking, with the black wind blowing to their bones. There were no stars. The wind shook the air noisily. It was, after all, not the blackness of space.

Luza and Isuma lay down together on the groundsheet

behind the windbreak of the tool cupboard and Bjoro hunched himself into the close space between Peder and the women, with his arms clasping his knees to his chest, and his head sunk down between his arms. Gradually he found he couldn't keep from tears, and it was only the touch of the others, an arm, a leg pressing against him, that saved him from crying out loud. His mind felt crowded with an ill-defined horror, wordless, inchoate. He worked his mouth silently. After a while the repetitive action comforted him. He began to think about his wife, an aching, aimless jumble of details and remembrances.

He had a habit, when Juko wasn't with him, of recasting a gossip he'd heard, an argument, an occurrence, for later telling to her. He liked to imagine elaborately where they would be when they were next together, at supper or lying in bed, and his words, and Juko's face listening to him, her voice making a response. The actual telling never was much like his imagining. He knew he went over these resumés and over them, to extend his enjoyment of some events, and to get a sort of control over others. In his mind he had told and retold Juko every consequential thing that had happened to him since the *Ruby* had gone ahead of the *Miller*. But he had done little of it in these hours since the *Lark* crashed. What he had seen from the ridge looking out toward the sea was unspeakable—*I don't . . . My eyes . . .*—and Juko wasn't where he could find her in his mind anyway. He'd lost track of real time, didn't know if it was night there now, or day, if she was on the sail, or eating, or sitting in the bath, or saying his name in her sleep.

He realized suddenly: By now she might think I am dead. He imagined her, imagining him killed, lying on her back in their bed, looking up blindly into the ceiling. She was not prone to tears, but he imagined her weeping for him, and for a childish moment he felt contrite, as if he must apologize for living on. But then it wasn't childish, and he was apologizing for something else, something to do with the vast gray landscape and the frigid wind blowing out of the sky.

He never slept. When he had done his third of the night sitting up, he lay on his hip behind the windbreak, his body clasped together with Luza and later with Isuma, his eyes shut and his teeth locked against the cold, waiting for daylight, which was only a thinning of blackness to gray.

The wind had subsided in the last hours of the night and now the air felt depthless, bated; Bjoro felt its slight tremble when any of them made a motion through it, or spoke a word. He had a sense that their movements would rouse the wind again, that they ought to lie still and silent, becalmed. But in the scant early light, Luza and Isuma took turns walking away along the stony shore to empty their bladders and then he had to do it too, stumbling stiffly in the big, hard boots and standing to relieve himself on the piled-up rocks. He kept his back to the flat, lead-colored field of the lake, the great bleak sky, the mountain. From where he stood watching the steam of his urine, he could hear Luza and Isuma speaking to one another, breaking loose the stillness.

They ate tubes of lemon paste and, while Bjoro fed one to Peder, Isuma and Luza went over their little bit of saved rig. Isuma piled up tools: a big, light hammer and a theodolite; a narrow rock pick; a seismograph; a sack for rock collection. She cut a corner out of the ground sheet and found in the tool cupboard a pen that would write on the plastic. She was a geologist, and knew a little about surveying, so it became clear: She meant to do some of what they'd planned, meant to get samples and take measurements and make maps, while she looked out for a place to bring down the aerostat.

Luza was gathering together Bjoro's tools for measuring climate. His field was mechanics and after that meteorology; the machine they had was dead, drowned, but he had spent years studying weather and Luza was methodically piling up his pressure tester, anemometer, hydrometer, the old-world devices unneeded for 175 years—accoutrements of another people, another place, and utterly alien to him, he realized now. Bjoro wanted to laugh at these women's scrupulous diligence, had to set himself against a rush of anger and despair. What were they thinking? That this was a world they might, in fact, want to live on?

"There's only the one binoculars," Luza said. Her brow was drawn up, worrying over this. She was a fussy person, she liked to arrange things systematically. Bjoro didn't want to take the little instrument onto his stack, hadn't any wish to see this world writ larger. But Isuma was quick; she pushed the old Japanese binoculars at him. "I see farsighted," she said. She squinted her eyes, then widened them childishly.

Luza kept looking at the organization of their choices, adding to one pile and then the other some of Peder's things—specimen kits for soil and water, packets of biological sample sheafs—and her own things—a rad counter, a flat little thermocouple. When she was satisfied, she pulled her mouth out slowly. "Don't get lost," she said, and let her teeth show.

It was Isuma who laughed, expelling whitish clouds of her breath. It sounded like, "Ha! Ha!" and the loud, hard words reporting across the lake startled birds into the sky, not the flyers of the night before but three big water-birds, long-necked, beating their wings in hard, slow effort. Bjoro started too. He hunched his back, anticipating the wind, but the birds wheeled and gradually settled again, the air closing like a skin of water, shivering, and then seamless.

Without a word, Isuma went away along the edge of the lake toward the west, carrying her tools in the rock-collecting sack. She appeared resolute, walking short-strided, not swinging the sack. Bjoro, pushing his own tools in a duffel, looked after her with sudden desperate loneliness. Luza stood to watch her go. Then she looked at Bjoro. A tear had run down beside her nose, though her mouth was still set in a kind of smile, earnest, intent. He couldn't smile, himself. He stood up and walked away quickly east, shaking.

He looked back every little while. The ridge and the lake lay in an oxbow, the curve hiding Isuma from him, but he could see Luza standing before the tipped-up hatch cover watching after both of them, one and then the other. The daylight had come into the sky by then and the air was shadowless, pellucid, under a flat overcast. The light in the *Miller* was yellowy, rich; he didn't know why the shallow gray light here, the colorlessness, seemed blindingly bright. He was able to see Luza's face clearly, the faint line of frown, her pursed mouth, even from a distance. Once, he raised his arm to Luza and in a moment she lifted hers in a broad sweep. He might have been a kilometer from her at that point, but the clarity of the air allowed him to see her bare open palm, the spread of her fingers. The sight of her standing small and distinct and familiar against the unfamiliar, outspread, scabrous landscape, evoked in him something like awe and tenderness.

When he had finally got beyond seeing Luza, when he was alone with the variously gray, utterly empty fields of dirty snow and of rock extending boundlessly before and behind him, the sense of his solitude flooded him with anguish. For a moment he was paralyzed, his breath letting in and out in quick, choking huffs, the clouds of his respiration remaining sharp and white and motionless in the air. At last he heard the finder-seeker, its steady slow pip inside his exo, against his skin, and he put his hand to it, spreading his fingers, pressing until he could feel its beat against his palm, irrationally reassuring.

The lake was incalculably long, stretched out along the depression at the foot of the mountain. It was slow and effortful getting across the old snow and the rocks, but the quality of the cold was changed without the wind—it had a purity that he suffered more easily than the blowing—and he found that walking between the skirts of the lava ridge and the long impoundment of the lake gave him some little sense of narrowness, of margin. He felt himself steadying, settling into a work. He became used to the sound of his own breathing in the stillness. A couple of times he climbed the rocks partway and looked out unwillingly upon the long sweep of the lake, the high, serrated chine of the mountain, and ahead along the edge of the lava field—everywhere rocks—but he didn't use the Japanese binoculars, and he kept his eyes mostly away from the horizons.

The lake was shallow at its eastern end, a margin of water weeds and gravel, and he took a weed as a specimen. Where the shore curved away to the south he thought he would go on following it stubbornly, feeling if he kept to the lake's edge there wasn't any way to lose his own trail. But there was an outlet—an incredibly white chute of water falling away steeply downhill from the lake into the canyons of the lava field—and he was stopped by it, had to stand at the fall line of the swift little river and consider where to go now. After a while, a chill slid down along his spine and he started to shake, so he turned and went on doggedly, following the bank of the stream now, east into the lava.

It was difficult to keep the river in sight. Anxiously he pulled out his compass every little while and took a line on a pile of stones, a hummock of ice, the shoulder of the peak, sighting out to the horizon and noting his place in the pages of a little notebook meant to record the weather.

Finally, from a high vantage, he looked out to the east and saw the land flattening gradually and the field of lava tailing off. Where the river slowed and widened, turning north to find the sea, there were plumes of white, a cluster of them. He sat down, shaking, and got out the binoculars. The focus was wrong: He fiddled with it until the horizon jumped up in front of his eyes and drove his breath out in a burst. There were six or seven sheer white columns against the gray, rising straight until they blurred and tore along the line of their joining to the overcast. He watched through the glasses, stricken for a moment with a wordless fear. For years they'd been making the unmanned fly-arounds. It was known there were no thinking beings living on this world: It was a young place, nascent, populated with birds and invertebrates and small mammals, small reptiles. What he saw was steam, or smoke, climbing up from a volcanic cleft, a solfatara. But for that one speechless moment he imagined the straight shafts of white were spokes holding high the ceiling of the sky.

The plumes stood together and far off for quite a while

without his getting any nearer. Only when he came up on the first one, he could see the rest were spread out over dozens of hectares, the last of the six maybe another two or three kilometers north and east of the first, on the slope that fell off beyond the northern end of the lava field. What they marked was a company of stinking mud pots, the ground between them thawed and sloppy, yellow, spotted with tufts of brownish grass. The air was sulphurous, spoiled; he skirted around the field with his chin sunk down in the neck of his exo.

Where the lava field finally flattened out and was finished, the river sloped off northeastward across broken shelves of rock; he went on following it to the edge of the mud field. The view dropped off to the north suddenly, and there was the river spreading out, edged with low basalt cliffs, scattered with little islands, the water shallow, gray-green, the islands brownish gray, flat, pocked with hardened snow, or ice. Away from the canyons of rocks, the volcanic sweepings, there was a small wind blowing off the water, wet and smelling of salt. He stared out at the sudden vista, appalled, his eyes filling with tears. The edge of the sky was unbearably distant. He had to turn away from it until he had his heart back.

They had not spoken of how far to go, when to come back. He had come near turning back when he had first got clear of Luza—he had stood minutes there with his hand on the finderseeker, intending it. Maybe, after all, the aerostat would lay out gently on the rocks, wouldn't be torn—he had thought of arguing for that. Now he thought of it again. He was afraid of the wind, and of walking away from the comfort of the lava field. It was a kind of relief that the widening ground south of the river mouth kept on stony to the horizon.

By an effort of will, he got the binoculars up and made a slow search north and east, the land sprawled vast before him now without the ridge of rocks, the lake to bound it. Through the eyes of the binoculars, he saw birds were nesting in the hummocks on the little islands. Water fell down in several narrow white lines across the face of the basalt cliffs—what did this mean? He had thought he had come to the delta of the little white river, but now he realized it might be the incision of a fjord.

As a sort of balm against guilt, he put a few blades of grass in bio sheafs, took little specimens of mud from the boiling pots, made perfunctory measures of pressure, altitude, humidity. And then he started back west along the skirts of the river toward Luza, and the shelter. He knew the few landmarks, going back, and ticked them off in his mind as he went past them—it was a reassuring exercise, it shortened the way. But the wind came on a little, blowing out of the east and down through the combes of the lava, and he feared worse weather. He pushed himself to go quicker, the long muscles in his thighs and his calves burning and shaky. He hadn't any sense of time of day, had to keep looking at his timepiece to orient himself to the long solar period, comfort himself that he had hours yet before the sky would blacken.

When he came in sight of the lakeshore, he kept watching for Luza until the watching became an anxious yearning. He got out the Japanese binoculars and searched up the long rock-bound margin for her, and the empty sweep of shoreline raised in him an unreasonable, sudden fear he'd been left alone, the others gone off without him. After that he carried the binoculars in his hand, stumbling swiftly among the stones and over the patchy ice and stopping every little while, frozen with terror, to look where he remembered Luza had been, standing with her open palm raised to him. It was a while before he understood, he had all along been seeing the sheltering roof there among the big stones, the long white smooth hatchcover defined by the black gasket. He stared at it through the lenses, and when Luza came out from under it and walked down to the edge of the water, swinging a plastic bottle, he began to cry.

He put away the binoculars and wiped his eyes and walked deliberately down along the lake toward the camp. When Luza saw him, she came out to meet him, grinning madly in the unreal daylight. "Thought I'd been left forever!" she called to him. He shook his head, smiling dimly.

They sat under the hatch-roof with Peder and stared out at the lake. There weren't any birds. The wind made the water rough, its shine colorless. "It's rocky land, all of it. There wasn't any point going farther," he said to Luza when she asked him. "I thought Isuma would be back." For the most part they were silent, waiting for Isuma, listening to Peder's tired wheeze. Every little while Luza walked out to the edge of the rocks and looked off to the west and then walked back slowly without speaking. Bjoro watched his timepiece, and the edge of the mountain where the sky had shown color the evening before.

The daylight was thickening when Luza, standing out by the lake, shouted and lifted her arm in a broad gesture and Bjoro stood and saw Isuma coming at a fast walk, with the loops of the samples sack hung from her shoulders.

"Hey!" Isuma called to them from a long way off, and lifted both her hands above her head.

They sat under the hatch and ate tubes of corn paste and

papaya and drank water Luza had distilled from melted ice and hand-pumped through the little medical filter. Isuma talked while she ate, describing the route to the western end of the lake—rocks, and rocks—and then the climb up over the saddle of a ridge and below the short scree the land unclenching finally in a lovely big plain, hummocky under a nap of grass. "It's a good field, but it'll take some getting to. Wouldn't choose it if you got a better place, eh?" She peered at Bjoro.

He let out a short, stinging laugh. "Nothing," he said bitterly. "I've found nothing." He kept his head down, telling what he'd seen going east—rocks, and rocks. He told about the mud pots and the river and the basalt cliffs, the water falling over them. It wasn't necessary to say he'd seen no place as good as Isuma's plain.

Isuma had made a map and she spread it out on her knees and showed them, tracing the tip of her finger along the way they would need to go, here the hard part, the saddle, it was rocky and a steep climb; getting Peder up it and down the other side was a worry, she said. She looked at Luza, and at Bjoro, and finally at Peder. Peder's face inside the clear bubble was a frown; he may have been sleeping, or his eyes were squeezed shut against pain.

They fell silent, in the manner of a Meeting when there was a difficult thing needing deciding. Bjoro sat with his gloved hands clasped in his lap and his eyes fixed blindly on his boots. He waited for the silence to enter his mind, so that he could focus upon this question of moving Peder the long distance to Isuma's field. But his thoughts were helplessly chaotic; since the crash of the *Lark* he had felt himself drowned in futile detritus and vague horror.

The wind rose suddenly in a little gust that blew sand against their backs and clattering against the metal of the hatch. "If it's a good flat field?" Bjoro said, low-voiced, hunching his shoulders stiffly. "There's no good place nearer, eh?" He was embarrassed to hear in his words a kind of impatient quality. He looked at the women and then out to the lake shore with sudden nameless anger.

No one spoke. Bjoro imagined himself on Isuma's flat field, watching the balloon's slow descent. He couldn't keep from thinking of himself rescued, embracing Arda and Hans in the close familiarity of the *Ruby,* weeping, speaking over the radio to Juko, waiting the crackly moments for her voice to reach him in return.

"It's a good field," Isuma said. "Just a long damn way." She looked from one of them to the other, grimacing painfully.

Luza was holding Peder's hand, rubbing her gloved thumb measuredly across his gloved palm. She sat hunched with her eyes on her other hand where it was clasped inside the bend of her knee. "We would need to make a kind of litter for carrying Peder," she said finally, murmuring. "Maybe Bjoro can get the hatch door to come apart, we could use a panel from it?"

An exquisite relief sprang from Bjoro's chest and out to the ends of his fingers and his feet in a quick, cleansing wash. He stood and got his tools out of the cupboard.

The sky had filled with grays, blacks; the mountain's peak and the edge of the horizon were lost behind the lowering overcast. Isuma held the handlamp for him while he backed out screws and turned nuts from bolts and cut metal with a little torch. He was comforted by the work. When he had the sheet of metal free of the hatch, he kept on in the utter blackness, with

Luza or Isuma turnabout holding the light while he bent up a rim, strengthened the underneath, rolled a smooth edge on the handholds. He quit finally when the others asked for sleep, but afterward, lying with Isuma in the cold blackness, he imagined new improvements, and invented ways to get them done with the tools he had at hand. *I thought of lessening the weight by cutting out holes in the metal,* he would tell Juko when he was with her again.

The weather worsened overnight and in the morning a needly snow fell on the wind. There was no seeing the mountain now, but no comfort in the closing in of horizons, as the great black clouds came down to the southern margin of the lake. They got Peder into the litter and carried him west without waiting for Bjoro's remodeling of the metal. The wind was frigid, blown at them across the sweep of the lake so they were driven to walk with their shoulders twisted sideward, heads bent, crablike. Two carried the forepart, one the rear, changing about their places every little while. Bjoro thought the weight seemed light in the first minutes but then swiftly it was heavier. Isuma had guessed the distance to the landing field at eleven or twelve kilometers, and he had imagined himself walking the circle around the torus ten times. *All right. Not so far.* But it wasn't the torus they were circling, and Peder's weight was leaden, cumbrous. They had to stop often and let him down and stand over him, all three of them, gasping, with their backs hunched to the wind and the stinging, bitter snow.

Gradually Bjoro's hands began to bleed through the gloves where the edges of the handholds sawed against his palms. His back, his shoulders, his legs ached. He became grateful for Luza's blistered feet slipping in Peder's big boots, a reason for more and more frequent standstills. It occurred to him, none of them had ever carried a heavy thing more than a short way. Heavy work was in the hub, where tools and metal pieces and equipment weighed little or not at all.

He took to sorting back through his life methodically, seeking the times he had carried weight, but it was all trivial, occasional: He had used to carry his son, Eneo, his daughter, Abigajlo, years ago, home from someone else's house when they'd fallen asleep there; he'd pushed wheelbarrows piled up with dirt or oranges when the farming people were at their busy times; he had carried a box of tools or a piece of equipment from one śiro round to another. He was unprepared, inapt, they all were, for this terrible labor. A sudden new despair gripped him: Had anyone thought, before now, how they would get their hard work done on this world, without a freefall place for doing it?

Whenever they stood hunkered around the litter, Peder's eyes watched them through the clear faceplate, a childish look, confused, afraid. Once, his mouth moved, he was telling them something. Luza got the skull off and put her ear close to hear his whispery voice: "Where are we going?" His mouth made a strange twist, a sort of smile.

Luza's face was stricken with guilt. She couldn't find an answer. She looked at Bjoro, and at Isuma. A sudden heat rose in Bjoro's neck and his ears. He crouched stiffly. "Isuma's found us a landing place for the balloon," he said. He twisted his own mouth in a burning grimace. "You'll get the first ride up, eh?" Peder breathed a sound, shut his eyes slowly. Someone else made a sound too: Bjoro heard the low whining clamped behind teeth. It was Isuma, or Luza, or the sound was in his own throat.

When they went on slowly across the stony ground with the wind driving the hard snow against them, Bjoro found the distance between his body and his thoughts began swiftly to widen. He was aware of the voices of the others, and of stopping and going on, lifting and setting down, he knew he was chilled, that his hair was a wet mantle clinging cold along his scalp. He continued to turn things over in his mind—regrets and forebodings, imagined quarrels, reimagined events—but his body's discomfort separated itself from him, became dreamlike, translucent. He imagined he was outside, floating directionless upon a gray space, in the silence and warmth and shelter of an intact exo.

He remembered that he had had a surgical repair when he was seven or eight, a benign cyst, and coming up from the anesthetic afterward had felt as he did now: unable to focus on any visual image, detached from his pain. *If I spoke, I would be clear of it,* he thought, but could not get his mouth to move, words to come out. *This is how people feel when they are dead,* he thought. *This bodiless stillness.*

He heard a shout, it was Isuma, but there was a long slow suspension before he knew what she had said. "Here! The saddle!" And he shouted too, it was his own voice he heard, an incoherent yell of joy, as he broke the surface in a dazzle like sunlight.

They set Peter down on the ground below the ridge and Luza stayed there with him while Bjoro climbed with Isuma to the top. It was a hard steep going, they had to find handholds, footholds, on the icy stones, the frozen mud. Bjoro kept from thinking of how they would get Peder up this way. But from the swale of the saddle, the plain lay white and smooth under new snow, a great startlingly open reach, a landing field.

They had brought all of the finder-seekers, Peder's and Luza's and their own. They climbed and slid down the gravelly scree onto the plain and paced out a big diamond, stuck the little robot devices down in the snow at the four corners. Bjoro stood a hundred meters across from Isuma at the last corner, the snow falling between them, and lifted his arm, then both his arms, grinning madly. He was filled with a keen hope now. Isuma's shout came to him on the wind, a flutter like paper, he didn't hear it all: ". . . saved!" she said.

The scree was fine gravel, they had slid down it abruptly on their haunches; now the climb up was a ceaseless, inefficient struggle against the little sliding stones. The east side, the big icebound boulders, seemed to Bjoro to become abruptly less formidable, and getting Peder up that way began to seem possible. He went over in his mind a plan for rigging the litter—hanging it from a sort of harness at the shoulders so their hands could be free; two of them to carry Peder, one to steady the others, give a hand up, scout the best way. The balloon would be a while yet getting to them, there was time, they would go slowly.

Luza stood below, watching them climb down from the saddle. Her yell came up to them in pieces: ". . . okay?" they heard, and ". . . set?" Isuma straightened and cupped her hands at her mouth, shouted back, "We've done it!" Bjoro thought when he saw Juko he would tell her the way Isuma's voice had sounded then, fierce and joyous.

There were cords in the waists of the exos, tethers for the sail work, and Bjoro made use of them for his rigging, though it was little enough like his imagining. He made the straps short on a first try, to bring the litter high enough to clear the rocks; but it was too high to lift from the hips. When one of them let go to seek a handhold in the rocks, or put a hand out for balance, the sway was wild, Peder's face in the exoskull a white mask, terror. So he had to fiddle with the length of the cord until the weight hung lower, hip-height, and he rigged a waist yoke to check the sway. Better. Isuma and Bjoro carried, Luza scouted the path up, and came back to help them clear the rocks, lift the weight over the worst places.

Bjoro's hands went on bleeding, and his knees now, his elbows, from crawling over the rocks, from stumbling to catch the litter when Isuma fell, from falling himself. The cords of the rigging dug into his shoulders, whipsawed his hips. He sweated within the exo, and the suit gradually lost ground, could not keep up with the diaphoresis. While he worked, he wasn't cold, only wet, but when they sat to catch their wind, the sweat chilled him swiftly and he would shake, was a long time building back the heat when they stood again to drag Peder on up the ridge.

Luza led them an erratic way up, switchbacking across the steep face following the flattest stones or the brief open ways across little deltas of gravel drifted with the new snow. Sometimes she led them to an impasse; they had to go back and find a new way, or muscle the litter up over the boulder that stood in the path. They didn't speak, any of them, except as they had to: There was little enough breath for climbing, and it broke from them in loud, white explosions. They hoisted Peder's terrible weight above their shoulders, shoved it through old crusted drifts, dragged it up through the great stones.

Bjoro began gradually to take a kind of offense at Peder's terrorized look and the rigid clench of his hands on the edge of the hatchcover. He found he couldn't keep from watching the sky for the descent of the balloon, irrationally fearful it might land and rise again without them if Peder's unwieldy burden kept them from getting over the ridge in good time.

Unexpectedly, Luza came back to them, shouting, her boots sliding little rocks down the hill. "We've got there! You're at the top, the catbird seat! Bjoro! Isuma!"

They went up the bitter end of it, shouting weakly, foolishly, and letting Peder's weight down at last on the other side of the saddle, along the south-sloping talus. The wind blowing fierce over the top drove the snow like sand, but they sprawled there in the lee of the ridge, spent and joyous, looking out on the plain, the landing field. They would lower the litter down the gravelly scree on a cord, it would be quick and easily done. They had got over the damned thing.

Luza said, "Oh," suddenly, in an odd voice, and Bjoro looked, blinking, wiping the snow-crusted sleeve of his exo against his eyes. There was a spray of blood on the faceplate of the exo; Peder was hidden behind it.

He watched stupidly while Luza pulled around the pack she had carried, dumped their tools and supplies, pawed through until she had the med kit. She slid the hardhat from Peder's head and, kneeling there on the gravel in the snow, cleaned her hands with the sterile packets of wipes and then swiftly rolled Peder's exo down, cut a hole in his neck and pushed in a little piece of plastic tubing. She cut a hole in the chest of the tough exo and in Peder's tender skin, and threaded in another plastic tube that filled immediately with pink, frothy blood that ran out in a stain on the snow. The sound of Peder's breath above the whistle of the wind stopped Bjoro's heart.

He remembered suddenly it had been Peder's wife who had been afraid. It had been Peder's wife, a woman Bjoro didn't know, a woman named Juanita or Juana, who had worn that smile between set teeth, on the day the families of the *Ruby* had sat down together on the matted cottongrass in the Mandala orchard and held a sort of celebration, a good-bye supper, though no one was calling it that. It had been Peder's wife whose eyes had followed her husband.

Bjoro had watched Juko privately to see if he might catch something like that in her eyes, but she was like his mother, autonomous, solid, not given to dreams of romance, or adventure; when he looked, she was intent on something told to her by Arda Mejina's husband, or she was laughing and pushing Hans Arnesen away from her for the bad joke he told. And obscurely, he had envied Peder Ojama his wife. Had not imagined, then, that any of them might really die. Had felt that Peder's wife's fear was a kind of pleasure, a prize. Now he was suddenly appalled by the childishness of his feelings, the incompleteness of his imagining.

He had not prayed, nor believed in the efficacy of prayer, since he was seventeen, but he began to repeat and repeat in his throat soundlessly, *God, please, please, please, God,* and finally, rocking on his heels in the stinging wind, he gave himself over to it, began helplessly to pray Hans and Arda hadn't gone away without them; that the balloon could be brought down accurately in the wind not once but four times; that the *Ruby* would find and retrieve the damned aerostat four times over when it rose again out of the sky. He prayed for life, and for home. What was prayer but the listing of hopes that were otherwise irrecoverable? *God, please, please, please, God.*

They went on sitting beside Peder, crouched shaking in the blowing snow in the scant shelter of the rocks along the top of the ridge, while Luza kept the tubes clear with a little pump she worked in the palm of her hand. She said she was afraid to move him further until he'd rallied. *Or died*, Bjoro thought desolately. He listened to his own breath and his heartbeat, and Peder's, and helplessly frowned out across the plain where the blown snow rose in immense gauzy curtains.

He was too cold and too worn out to keep on feeling things deeply, and fell into a tired numbness and then into a short, unquiet sleep. When he woke, the wind had died. The stillness of the air confused him; he looked out on the plain in bleary disorientation. The light had begun to fail. The sky and the snow were sooty gray, and in the vast midsky, the silvery sheets of the descending montgolfiere soaked up the dull ochre color of the horizon.

Isuma was asleep beside him, but Luza sat up with Peder's head on her thigh. The skin of her face was chapped, her lips swollen and fissured. She made a stiff, pursed grimace and shrugged her shoulders when she saw Bjoro looking. The skin of Peder's face was grayish, there was a line of old blood below his nose. Luza rested her hand across his brow lightly with the fingers spread as if she hid his eyes from the luminous shine of the balloon.

4

Kristina

Ebb, ocean of life (the flow will return),
Cease not your moaning you fierce old mother,
Endlessly cry for your castaways, but fear not, deny not
  me,
Rustle not up so hoarse and angry against my feet as I
  touch you or gather from you.

BECAUSE HER SHRUNKEN old bladder couldn't be made to wait so well anymore, Kristina sat herself in the doorway of the lavejo, leaning against the jamb so she could get to the toilet if the Meeting ran long. In the last year, Meetings for Business had naturally been drawn out with all these matters to do with the New World, but since the *Ruby* was gone ahead of them even the weekly Meetings for Worship had been lengthening—people were anxious or ebullient by turns, they wanted to speak of the eventful times.

It was up to members of the Ministry and Counsel

Committee to sense the end of a First Day Meeting and bring it to a timely close, and increasingly they had trouble apprehending the moment, erring always on the side of inaction. That was all right—Kristina liked their inefficient spiritualness. This domaro had had counselors in the past who were without sufficient silence, people who would interrupt thoughtful quietism. Luisa Jamaguči, who was clerk when the domaro held a Meeting for Business, and Iteja Peron, who was clerk of the Pacema Monthly Meeting, were both of them better at bringing an overlong Meeting to an end, but neither would sit at a Meeting for Worship—Kristina considered it a weakness in those two, that they never had written a Minute having to do with the Holy Spirit.

There were six apartments in this domaro and twenty-four adults, but only twelve or fourteen who regularly came together on the First Day of the week: Meeting for Worship. What were they thinking, those other people, the ones who stayed away? Kristina wondered. Did they think there was an explanation for the soul, for its feelings of truth and beauty and goodness, for its moral imperatives and its intimations of wider scope—did they think there was an explanation for this that did not involve God?

She pulled her knees up to her chest and rested her forehead there, eyes closed, to allow the silence to take form. There seemed always a little while at the beginning of a Meeting when the silence was trivial—people would cough and squirm, it was clear in their faces that they were thinking about commonplace things. Only after the first restless quiet was there real silence—the silence of God, as distinct from the silence of people, Kristina thought.

She waited with her eyes closed, her forehead pressed against her knees. Her mind wandered, touching on large and small worries to do with her son, Bjoro, with the broken grouting between the floor tiles of the lavejo, and the piece of drafting work she had been doing for some people over in Kantado širo, a plan for the rerouting of an irrigation aqueduct. Eventually—perhaps it was when the silence began to belong to God—she also thought of Linda Florencio, whose son Alberto had killed himself only the evening before. On Last Day, she realized suddenly.

She saw little of Linda now, but they had been friendly once, during the years their children were central to their lives. Linda had been on the Waters Committee, and Kristina had drafted projects that involved her; because their younger children were of like ages, eventually they had confided a few things, difficulties and satisfactions having to do with mothering. Kristina never had known Linda's older son, Alberto Poreda, so her allegiance was with Linda, and it was hard not to blame Alberto for causing grief to his mother. Death was inevitable, universal, and that rendered it meaningless, she felt; people had to look for meaning in the way they lived their lives. She never had given much credit to this thing people called the šimanas, was impatient with suicides generally, believing people just looked for too much happiness in their lives. Her own husband, Aŭgustino, had been that way, imagining that happiness ought to be a kind of reward for managing your life well. *God is love* comprised Kristina's whole system of ethics, and there was not much allowance in it for a husband who gave himself up to despair, or a son who killed himself while his mother still lived.

Perhaps other people were thinking of Alberto, as well.

Kristina felt a damp, heavy mood among them, and an image gradually settled in her mind: the limbs of blooming locust trees slouching under the weight of rain.

"Today something has come in my mind of a very serious nature." It was old Arno Masano, who was often given to inward voices; he stood to speak rather more often than other people, and liked to cite ancient Quaker documents without attribution. He spoke with his eyes fixed on the hunched shoulders all around him on the floor. "I have had a revelation that I believe makes our obedience to God a very simple thing. It is this—that the voice of God comes through our judgment, and not through our impressions." He pronounced the words sincerely, solemnly, waiting for their understanding to come in on the following silence. Kristina waited for it too, in impatient confusion. "When people go by impressions, rather than judgment," Arno said, "they turn from the true voice of God, and follow the false voice of self. When they are led by God—that is, by careful judgment—they make very few mistakes." After a moment, with evident satisfaction, he sat down among the shoulders and knees of his neighbors.

Kristina rested her head back against the door jamb of the lavejo. She closed her eyes again. She had learned to give Arno's words as much regard as someone else's unborrowed leading—it had occurred to her, God might find it necessary to repeat some things more than once. But she thought Arno ought to have given them a little more help, this time, distinguishing between judgment and impression. If it was so easy, we always would make correct choices, she thought irritably. But in the lengthening silence after Arno had spoken, she began to think of Linda's son Alberto, following impression, and not judgment, when he killed his mother's son. *The false voice of self.*

After an interval, Silvia Troelsen stood slowly. She lived with her husband and his family over in Revenana, but until her marriage she had lived with her mother in the apartment next to Filisa Ilmen's. She had a new baby tied against her belly; one of her hands was cupped beneath the solid roundness of the manta, lightly balancing or guarding the child there. "I worry—" she said, with her eyes cast down, her voice thin, timid, "—is it impression only that makes me fear this New World we are coming to? How am I to know if it's my fear leading me from it, or God's voice warning me away from quakes and storms? If it's the weather scares me, is that good judgment, or only cold feet?" Smiles went around the loğio, but Silvia's face was solemn, earnest, she may not have meant the little joke her words played.

For 175 years they had gone on talking and thinking and making ready for leaving this world. They had lived for 175 years in a kind of suspended state, a continual waiting for change, but it was a balanced and deep-grounded condition, an equilibrium. They knew their world, root and branch, knew its history and its economies. The human life of the *Miller* and the life of its soil and its plants and animals revolved together, in a society that was well-considered, a community that was sustaining. Some people thought they had lived for 175 years in a world that was a kind of Eden.

Now they had come to their sea change—it was an enormous revolution that was pending in all their lives—and it had become common for people to raise the issue of being afraid. Before the *Ruby* had gone ahead of them, before they'd known the dimensions of the unpromising weather, the stony landscape, when people spoke of fear, it was of direful dreams, vague apprehensions. Just lately, as a result of all this bad news, these weather reports from the *Ruby*, people were more precise, speaking of the weather, vulcanism, rocky soil, instead of dim dreads. *Well, it's all right to be afraid*, Kristina thought. *Only don't count it as judgment.*

She found, though, that she held a certain sympathy toward Silvia Troelsen, who had this new baby and a young child, and had gone against good advice when she'd married a man without patience in anything, a man everybody knew was lazy and short-tempered like his father. Her husband, over there in Revenana, wasn't likely to come to a First Day Meeting; Silvia may have come to this Meeting in her mother's domaro to say this one thing on her mind.

Kristina thought, *It isn't the weather you're afraid of, dear girl,* but she wasn't moved to speak this thought, knowing it to be opinion, which she was prone to put forward too often. Only afterward, in the long silence after Silvia's witness, she felt a gradual restlessness, an agitation she recognized: She would, after all, eventually be driven to stand and share some leading, though there was no telling what she would say; she never did know that until the words were out.

After a while of increasing unease, Kristina stiffly got up in the little space where she had sat. She looked at the broken grouting between the tiles of the lavejo, just left of her left sandal. "I've been thinking of locust trees," she said finally. Her voice was husky, its sound a surprise, though not the words—now, it was as if she had known all along what words would come out of her mouth. She kept from clearing her throat, she let the speaking clear it. "They have blossoms like sweet peas, they're violet-pink or white. They bear them in big loose bunches, and when it rains, the weight of the water and the blooms makes the limbs hang down, they're very yielding, even the thick ones will droop as if they haven't any strength." She sent a look around to her neighbors, considering whether she had given them a sufficient image. "But the locust wood is very hard—the young limbs, even, are strong wood—and proof against rot. Some of you may know, the prunings are favored for the carving of eave ornaments, and canes." She gestured toward old Arno Masano, who lifted his cane and flourished it in the air.

She kept standing a moment, waiting as the others waited, to see if she might have any more to say. But the silence felt solid, comfortable, so she sat down.

The metaphor satisfied her. With her eyes closed, she turned it over in her mind, examining it, looking for ways it bore on Arno Masano's leading about judgment and impression. She had thought, hearing the words come out, she had spoken a straightforward symbolism of the strengths and weaknesses of their community. Now she saw, as well, a parallel between the locust tree and this unnamed world they had been steering toward for nine generations. It might be they should look for advantages in stormy weather, stony ground—maybe there was a hidden luck in them—canes to be made from broken wood. She wondered, also, if they lacked the information that would better their judgment—there were the two failed balloons. She thought, with something like stubborn insistence, Now the *Lark* is landing, eh? we'll see.

After a while, Hilda Fugate stood. She was a woman forty or forty-five; she and her husband had only lately come to live in the Pacema district, in the household of Virdela Rota, who was an aunt of Hilda's. Kristina knew Virdela Rota, but not this niece, yet. She had a broad nose, an intelligent face, not much like Virdela—maybe their relation was by marriage. "The image of the locust trees," Hilda said in a murmuring, diffident voice, "has made me think of the tree called mule's-kick. I don't know its botanical name."

Someone spoke out, "miconia," and another voice said, "styrax," which Kristina knew as snowbell, and not mule's-kick, though some trees had more than one common name. Hilda's eyes went briefly across all the heads, focusing upon no particular place. She nodded and said, "I know about this tree because my mother was a forester"—two or three old people nodded as if they remembered Hilda's mother's tenure—"and when I was eight or nine years old she had an apprentice who was killed, cutting one of those trees down after it had died on its feet. Some of you probably remember that apprentice who was killed, Rubeno, I think was his name." People nodded. Kristina remembered it herself. The man's name had been Rubeno Mendoza, he had been the young son of her husband's cousin. "That mule's-kick wood is hard, but it splits, and if a dead tree needs cutting down, then it likes to fall before it's cut through, and as it goes over, the trunk splits lengthwise and kicks out, or upward."

Hilda let a silence fall. She stood at the edge of the logio, and Kristina was drawn to the outlook behind her. There was a draft slightly stirring in the strands of a weeping willow tree that stood beside the alteja aqueduct. When her children had been young, they had liked to play in such places, under a willow's trailing long tresses, in the secret dimness. She wasn't able to remember what a mule's-kick tree looked like. In her mind's eye, though, she saw the split trunk recoiling, and Rubeno Mendoza's startled face.

After a long while of standing looking across all the heads, Hilda said, shifting her weight self-consciously, "I don't know what this means—my remembering that man's death, and the mule's-kick tree—but his name I think means *ruby*, so perhaps God knows." She said this in a voice of hesitation and tenderness and then sat down slowly beside Virdela Rota.

The silence vibrated slightly with Hilda's words. Kristina felt it enter her own body and ring inside her skull. The mood of the meeting was abruptly changed, but who knew in what direction? Afterward, Virdela, and old Arno, and then Leo Furuso spoke wildly various leadings, to do with cautious decision-making, with precipitate death, with souls hiding a malign bent, or a durable. Kristina nodded when Karlo Eŭbioso stood and simply said, "The voice of the Holy Spirit, in these times of anxiety and decision, must be listened for, both in strength of spirit and the breaking of it."

In the very long silence after Karlo's witness, finally Arno Masano and Kristina's neighbor Filisa Ilmen—both of them were of the Ministry and Counsel Committee—clasped hands and stood up, and the shaking of hands went around the room. Coming onto the logio, people had been quiet, had come by ones and twos, or by family groups, silently, establishing the hush of the Meeting, but now bunches of people at once stood and began to talk. No one tried to keep silence. The Meeting was finished.

Kristina used the toilet and then came out to stand and talk with Arno Masano. "It was a gathered meeting, eh?" Arno said happily.

It had been a while since a First Day Meeting had been Gathered Into the Light—not since the *Ruby* was gone ahead of them, Kristina realized suddenly. She and Arno believed with the old Quakers, when words were truly spoken In the Light, they didn't break the silence but continued it, the silence and the words all of one texture, one piece, so when the words ceased you had a sense of the silence continuing uninterrupted, seamless; and it was in such silences that God's voice could be heard. She nodded. "I guess it was." She had felt it herself, when Hilda Fugate had spoken, though afterward no one had seemed to know what her words meant.

Arno's look was serious, confiding. "It was after Hilda Fugate spoke her witness. She surprised me, when she stood up. I thought right away, it might be God's witness we'd be hearing out of her mouth because I don't think she used to speak at Meeting much, over there in Bonveno where she lived. That's what I heard."

He leaned his head nearer Kristina. "Somebody said she moved because her husband and his brother had a falling out. Her husband's brother is Ĉito Mejia, you know Ĉito, eh? You drafted for him, I bet, because he was an engineer, or something like it. Now they've moved here from Bonveno because Hilda's husband and this brother lived in the same household and they have hard feelings or something, and he doesn't want to keep living with him in the same house. That's what somebody said." Arno knew everybody's business. There was an unfocused look of happiness that would come in his eyes when he was standing in position to overhear someone else's conversation.

Kristina wanted to ignore this talk of Hilda Fugate's family life—she was in a religious mood just now. She said, "You gave us the first words to think on, Arno," which was true.

"Well, it may be I spoke In the Light, myself," Arno said. He nodded and smiled modestly. "God does speak in me, from time to time."

She looked away. She never could make up her mind if his spirituality was honest—maybe it was just too forward for her liking. "In all of us, Arno," she said flatly, and moved away from him. She found other people to talk to, Filisa Ilmen and her husband, Leo, and then Karlo Eŭbioso made a beckoning gesture and she went to stand with him and young Silvia Troelsen.

"We were just speaking of locust trees," Karlo said, beginning to smile.

Kristina made a disrespectful sound with her lips; she thought Karlo might have been teasing her a little. "Don't chide God's words, Karlo, whoever speaks them."

Karlo laughed. "No, no chiding. We liked those words ourselves." His look became more tender, more serious. "Silvia liked them."

Silvia gave Kristina a timid look. She said, "A man I know, his father was killed yesterday, killed out on the sail—the šimanas, I guess, that's what people say. I thought of him—that man I know, and his father—when you told about the locust tree. Who knows why? But there was a little comfort in it. It was like poetry."

Kristina wouldn't have said anything so sentimental as that, even when she was Silvia's age. And she was suddenly angry with Alberto again. She hadn't thought of him leaving his own children. *What were you thinking of, damn your selfish eyes.* "Then it must be God who is the poet," she said irritably. "I never have had a facility that way."

Karlo nodded happily. "God's words, whoever speaks them," he said.

Kristina reached out to stroke the palm of her hand across the silky crown of the baby's head where it lay bundled against Silvia's breast. "Who is your husband—is it Ole?" she said to Silvia, and the woman said, "Ole Hiroŝi," nodding.

She'd had a slight notion to offer advice, or take Silvia to task for accepting a bad husband against the advice of her neighbors, her family, the Pacema Clearness Committee. *You can always divorce, take a new husband, but your children will have only the one father,* she thought of saying. But she kept still, and petted the child again. Sometimes a person would come right, when the job was rearing children. You could learn patience: It wasn't like left-handedness or poetry, something you were born with or not. Ole Hiroŝi might still master it.

When people began to leave the loĝio and go on with other things in their lives, she put on a clean shirt and collected her flat clay bowl and a little sack of ground breadnut, a lime, sapotes, a knife—there were always too many people at a mortafesto, and there was never enough food—and she hunted up her clarinet, because sometimes people would play music and dance at a funeral. She didn't know if Alberto Poreda's body would be laid out at his mother's house, or at his wife's, but she went over to Linda Florencio's house in the Esperplena ŝiro.

She kept a deliberate pace, swinging in one hand the battered old clarinet case and in the other the string sack with her groceries in it, and the shallow bowl. Her eye told an uphill way, the curve of the torus always rising ahead, and behind, following the architecture of the wheel, but it was flat to her feet, easy walking—it was only the distance that made her sweat a little, made her calves ache, now she was gotten old.

Esperplena was half around the circle from Pacema; it wouldn't have mattered if she'd gone east with the turn of the world or west against it. You could walk clear around the torus anyway in a few minutes, if you were young and in a hurry, though there were the fields and neighborhoods and the spokes to be got around, aqueducts and ditches to be crossed; and if you kept down along the maltejo, there was the bridging of the Ring River and the rebridging, as the watercourse was deliberately roundabout. There had once been woodland between Mandala and Alaŭdo, a belt of trees that stood across all the incurvature, and in that place the through path rose high up on the altejo. It had been, in old days, a narrow, shadowed, duffy track winding along the shoulders of the uncut forest at the edge of the ceiling. In Kristina's childhood, those trees still were living, but she remembered the quick plague that had killed them, and now the path along the altejo made a winding way among orchards of pear, sapote, persimmon, fig.

She saw people she knew, especially in Mandala where she had lived twenty-eight years, before marrying Aŭgustino Mendoza and moving to his mother's house in Pacema. But she kept walking steadily, just calling a word or lifting a hand to people who spoke to her, in a way that made it clear there was a place she needed to get to.

It had been years since she had been in Linda Florencio's house, she remembered poorly where it stood. At Esperplena she meant to ask the way, but there was a stiff yellow kite stuck on the roof of a house down in the maltejo, an old practice, and she knew it was Linda's house flying it, announcing a death.

People crowded the loĝio and all the apartments in that

domaro, standing about in bunches or sitting on the floor, not
many of them making themselves useful. Some young people
were decorating a bier with flowers and the fronds of ferns,
streamers of yarn and rag—they would put Al's body on the
decorated bier and his family would carry it once around the
circle of the torus before he was burnt. Among the children
tying ribbons to the cart was Juko's son, Ĉejo Indergard, and
a girl, a cousin by marriage of Kristina's granddaughter's husband. What was the girl's name? Kristina couldn't remember.
She let both of them kiss her cheek, but she had come to visit
the body, not to visit with her own relatives, she told them, and
went off looking for the dead man. Alberto's body had been
laid out on a rug in one of the rooms of his mother's apartment. The skin was blackish and taut—he had breached his exo,
Kristina remembered. She looked at him critically, but the look
he returned was pitiful, despairing, and she found after all she
must forgive him. *Bad judgment.*

She went among the people until she found Linda Florencio.
Their friendship was remote, disused, she didn't pretend otherwise. She looked in the woman's face—it was a surprise to
find she had gotten old—and said simply, "I'm sorry for what's
happened to your son," and embraced her until they had both
quit crying, and then left her among her relatives, her neighbors. She pulled up a short table in a corner of the loĝio, sat
on the floor and began to make tortillas. She could do it without thinking about Linda's son, or her own. The fast, rhythmic slip-slap, slip-slap, of the patties against the palms of her
hands was a comfort, and it masked other sounds—she never
had had much tolerance for the silly words that were spoken in
sympathy at a mortafesto.

"I hadn't thought you were a friend with Alberto." Juko squatted beside her at the low table. Her face was sallow; she liked to wear that yellow shirt that had been resewn from her mother's old clothes after that woman was dead.

"I was a friend with Linda Florencio, eh? and Al killed her son," she said flatly. Then she said, "Did you go to Ina's house?"

Juko made a gesture with her head, not an answer. "People over there were coming over here."

"Did you see the body?"

"Yes."

"Somebody should have let the blood out of him. He looks bad that way, not himself."

Juko looked in the sack with sapote in it. She spilled the fruits out on the table and made a start at paring them, halving them, without speaking about Alberto's body. In a minute she got up and went to hunt for a plate. When she came back, Kristina said, "I had forgot you and Alberto Poreda were friends."

Juko shrugged, though her eyes became bright with tears that did not fall. Kristina kept patting the tortilla quietly, slip-slap, slip-slap. Juko laid the sapotes on the plate in a careful manner, spiraling the yellow fruit from the rim to the center.

"Did you know? my nephew spent his green years with Alberto and Ina?" Juko said this without looking up.

"Vićente? Oh, I did know it. I'd forgot." She had forgotten Ina, the wife, too, when she'd been stoking her anger toward Alberto. *What were you thinking of? Selfish, selfish.* "Which is Ina? I never did know her."

Juko looked about. "I don't see her now." She set the plate of sapotes away from her and shook some of Kristina's ground breadnut into the shallow clay bowl, squeezed a lime into it, began to knead the dough and flatten it. "Alberto and Ina have a son born with only one hand," she said in a low voice.

Kristina looked at her. Juko seldom would speak about such children. *The fey ones,* people called those kids, and were chary of them—babies born without hands, or with toeless feet, twins joined at the ribs. It was blamed on insufficient shielding, cosmic radiation in the interstellar space. Juko's own fey child had lived four years? five? and Kristina had been harsh in her judgment of her own behavior, then. She had felt stiff and tactless and false-hearted, had believed that she was not a sufficient friend to Juko. This was something she and Juko never had spoken of—Juko was shrouded in her own guilt, in those days, brandishing a shield of anger. In the years since Vilef's death, looking back through a lengthening lens, Kristina gradually had become more forgiving of herself; but Juko deliberately refused to speak to her of those years. She spoke as if she had no other child but Ĉejo.

"I heard a man say, once, those children are touched by God's finger, and that way of seeing it has stuck with me afterward," Kristina said.

Juko's face became sour. "Is that a complaint against God? that God's touch always brings these calamities?"

Juko was someone who would not sit at a Meeting for Worship; if she once had followed a religious leading, she had turned away from it after the death of her son. She and Kristina often had argued about God, but they kept away from certain tender places, and this was one. Anyway, Kristina could see in Juko's face that her daughter-in-law's irritability had nothing much to do with her. Both of them went on working the tortillas, slip-slap, slip-slap.

"Well, there is Ina," Juko said.

Kristina looked. The woman was forty or fifty, with fair hair, a tall body but her posture poor, her shoulders rounded over. Her face was anxious, tired, without grief. She hadn't yet felt this death, Kristina thought. Kristina's own husband had died young—she remembered standing among her friends and neighbors at that mortafesto, conscious of wearing sorrow like a garment, but feeling only confusion, and anger and fright. It was months before she had understood in her breast that Aŭgustino was dead.

It may have been one of Ina's children with her, a young man standing with his arm clasped about Ina's waist, inclining his head to listen to something Ina spoke. There was a likeness about their wide mouths, and the younger one was built like the older, muscular and long-waisted. The young man's face was blowsy from weeping, the tender skin around his eyes dark and swollen.

"Is that her son, then? That boy standing with her—is he the son without a hand?"

"Yes. Beto, his name is." And at that moment the boy flourished one arm, gesturing to his mother, and Kristina saw the smooth rosy knob at the end of his wrist. "There's a daughter, I don't see her," Juko said. "You wouldn't know either of them for Al's children, they're fair, like their mother, neither of them took Al's color." She looked at Kristina. "Do you want to speak to Ina?"

"No." She shook her head. "Yes," she said, and got up stiffly from the floor.

The widow Ina pulled her mouth out in a joyless smile when she saw Juko. "Romeo was here, did you see him? And Orval

Wyho. They said you were with Al, eh, when he was killed?"

Juko made an uncharacteristic gesture, thrusting one of her hands back through the cap of her hair in a jerky movement as if she were fending off with an elbow the thing Ina was asking her. "Well, he was dead when I reached him, Ina." Ina stood with her son's arm around her waist again, the two of them leaning into one another, waiting, expectant. "He may have meant to cut a tangle in the halyard," Juko said after a silence. "None of us was there to see. Who can know?" Ina went on looking at her unhappily. Finally Juko said, "Maybe if the sheet had held flat, eh? then he might not have been killed."

Kristina was embarrassed for Juko's lie, but Ina leaned toward Juko with yearning and nostalgia, as if this lost opportunity were a gift she might still receive. The son looked at his mother sorrowfully. "Well," he said, and pushed the rounded heel of his wrist across his cheek, though there were no tears there.

Juko said to Ina, touching Kristina's sleeve, "Do you know my husband's mother, Kristina Veberes?"

Kristina had stood back, but she came up now, and stood alongside Juko. She had lately had to struggle with an old-woman's compulsion: She often wanted to share her painfully gained wisdom with people who weren't able to make use of it. *You'll get over being afraid, get used to being alone,* she wanted to say. *When my husband was forty-seven, he killed himself, so I know your feelings.* Stupid. She looked in Ina's stiff face. "I'm sorry for what's happened to Alberto," she said flatly. Ina's eyes strayed away from her, dry, skittish. That was all right. She hadn't cried much either, those first days.

After a moment, Juko came forward and put her arms briefly

around Ina—the widow looked like a long bent pole Juko had got her arms around. Kristina didn't know this woman, but she knew what sort of loss she was living, so she also gave her an embrace. With her cheek against Ina's she found she was compelled to murmur, "When my husband was forty-seven, he went mad and killed himself."

The woman made a slow sound, a lament, let her head fall on Kristina's shoulder as a child will do, beginning to weep. Well hell, not so stupid then. She patted Ina's back and kissed her hair and murmured, "Yes. Yes. Yes," in a steady rhythm, the word empty, a mantra.

She and Juko made pots of tea and put them out for people to find, and they sat with tea themselves, on the boards in the open center of Linda's house, watching people, and talking with ones they knew, Sonja Landsrud and Virdela Rota, about the *Ruby,* and the little boat *Lark* that surely by now was set down on the world, and Kristina's son, Juko's husband, maybe by now walking under a sky, a sun's light, in unmade weather.

Later, Armando Poreda—who was dying, Juko said, and was Alberto's father—came and spoke with Juko nostalgically of childhood things to do with Al. This man Armando would have been Linda's husband during the years of their friendship, but his face was unfamiliar. She thought they had never met in those days, she had known him only through his wife's words. Now none of that was in her memory; he was an old man with smooth dark skin pulled close over a fine skull, and she could see in his eyes that he'd found some secret about death, and hadn't any need to grieve for the loss of his son.

He had been a handsome man, still was handsome if you took into account he'd gotten old, and was dying, and she liked his equanimity, a quality she still waited for in herself. She wished, not quite seriously, that his marriage to Linda and his dying were not in the way of her enjoying sex with him. She was ashamed of herself for the irreverence in this thought—it was First Day! they were meeting at the wake of this man's son!—but it had been a year since she'd copulated with anyone, and she wasn't ready to be finished with that aspect of her life, just yet. In fact, she had been surprised to find that, in her old age, she was relieved to be unmarried. She liked having the scope to enjoy sex with different partners. Anyway, marriages had to be remade, once your children were no longer children, and she had seen in other people that it was difficult work, something she was glad to do without.

The mortafesto went on being silly in the usual ways. People laughed and gossiped, children ran through, but every little while a self-conscious silence would fall in one of the rooms or a corner of the logio and then someone in the middle of it would be moved to stand and share some thought about Al, or about God, or death. Sometimes a person would fill one of these silences with foolish or pointless advice for Al's relatives—"God's will be done," people liked to say, but drawing it out to some dreadful length. Kristina, squirming irritably, would comfort herself with a conceit: She had kept her own words to them short and private, and had offered no advice.

She was impatient with melancholy music as with barren advice, and when a flute began to play a sad melody from the room where Al's body lay, and two women's voices joined it, a lyric about loss and truth, she took her clarinet from its case and spitefully toodled something amusing, a bit of a song. Let the sad people go and sit in that room with the body and the flute, she thought. Over here, we'll have a festo. Eventually Roaldo Forman brought his horn to play with her, and then someone with a guitar, a woman she didn't know; they settled into playing in earnest, variations on an old tune they all knew. A few people began to dance, and more instruments were brought out, and people who were sitting drummed the floor or their knees, or made timpani of the shoulders of the person sitting in front of them, and Kristina let go of her irritation.

After a while she had to give up playing and unbend her legs—she had an old woman's body, something she regarded as a betrayal. She stood up, flexing her knees ungracefully, putting her hands to kneading the small of her back, and when she was standing there she saw Linda Florencio and her dying husband dancing together, leaning into one another with the tenderness of children. When you move something, you discover new meanings in it, Kristina thought, watching them.

Juko found her again and said quietly, "I have some wine I got from Leo Furuso. I've been hiding it from you. People are getting ready to carry Al around the world; are you going? or maybe do you want to go home and help me drink up that little wine now?"

Kristina lifted her eyebrows. "You are damn selfish, eh? Didn't bring it for sharing at this funeral."

"No. Oh hell no," Juko said, and both of them looked sly, and smiling. They sat on the stoop of the domaro putting their sandals on, and then went up through the close-built houses. There was a wetland at the east edge of Revenana, the leaching field for that district's wastes, and the footway went high up on the wall to skirt it. Kristina's bones felt lighter up there close to the ceiling, and climbing up was a diminishing effort. It was the downhill that was hard, a thickening of weight on her old bones, her aged heart.

On the path between fields of jackfruit and bananas, walking swiftly uphill to them, was someone they knew, Leo Furuso's wife, Filisa Ilmen. Her face was pink—Kristina saw in it some bad news she was coming somewhere to give. She was a homely woman and not very bright but Kristina liked her; she was a good mother, and rightly had kept up a friendship with her husband's family even though Leo had some old grudge against them. She expected Filisa's bad news was for someone else, but then her round face, lifting, seeing them, darkened to red, and Kristina's heart began to drum in her ears.

"The *Lark's* crashed," Filisa told them, and her eyes filled swiftly with tears.

Kristina hated the way her body felt when it was surprised by fear—light, breakable, shaken, like the rattles people made from gourds. She had not expected to find the attachment to one's child so strong after fifty years. *My son isn't dead,* she thought, but she couldn't make her body believe it. Her body waited for Filisa to say that Bjoro was dead.

Juko said, "Where does this come from? Who is saying it? Are people dead?" with her voice rising in a kind of anger. She didn't speak Bjoro's name, neither had Filisa.

She looked at Juko with her brows raised in appeal. "Someone from the Radio Committee came and said it. You know how they never tell clear things, eh? the radio always will break up." She shook her head, opened her hands out from fists. "They said there was a mechanical failure—something—and a short falling; there was water, they've come down in water, I guess."

Juko made a choking sound and Kristina was startled and

frightened by that, more than by Filisa's chill words. She took Juko's arm, held it fiercely. "Now don't, don't," she commanded. Then she let go her hold and they all three stood without looking at one another, without speaking or touching. After a while Juko said, "I've got that wine," with her anger back again, and went on down through the fields toward the houses of Revenana, walking stiffly erect, swinging her arms. Kristina arranged her mouth. She said to Filisa, "The radio people believe they are killed, eh?"

Filisa lifted her brow again, childlike, sorrowing. "I don't know, Kristina." She put one of her arms across Kristina's shoulders. Kristina wanted not to be touched; she felt breakable, cracked, but didn't want to hurt the poor woman's feelings. She reached up and patted Filisa's hand on her shoulder. "Well," she said meaninglessly. "Well."

5

Humberto

A song of the rolling earth, and of words according,
Were you thinking that those were the words, those
*   upright lines? those curves, angles, dots?*
No, those are not the words, the substantial words are in
*   the ground and sea,*
They are in the air, they are in you.

BECAUSE IT WAS May, farming was a work that wouldn't wait for grief or fear to be spent. In May there was rain every night, and long days of bright light, and the rain-washed air was charged with fertility. The rice was delicate, not as swift or as coarse as maize; if it wasn't to be overgrown it had to be kept weeded, and weeded again. It stood knee-high in straight rows of vivid green, and Humberto went between the rows, scraping the ground with a broad mačeta curved like a scimitar.

Asian people had grown a rice that thrived in flooded

fields, but it was the upland Costa Rican rice that had been brought onto the *Miller,* a kind of rice that sprang from well-drained ground, and yielded well on poor soil where heavy-feeding crops would sulk. For the latter virtue, Sven Fujino and Humberto had planted it to this field, the Shepherd's Crook, which was always impoverished by the old trees standing at the east edge of the śiro, the remnant of a woodland that once had separated them from Esperplena. Humberto had gone along, jabbing holes in the earth with a pointed stick, while Sven followed him with the rice seed in the hollow shell of a calabash gourd. Humberto's lines were straight as if he'd followed a cord strung across the field. It was something you had an eye for, or not; Sven always laid crooked rows.

Now Humberto went alone between the ranks of green, skinning the ground with the blade of the maćeta in short, even strokes. His son had gone to work with Ĝeronimo Zea, digging up and chopping the spent stalks of okra now that that crop was finished, and Humberto had gone into the rice without asking anyone else's company in his work. He thought he wanted to be alone, and not to talk to anyone about the crashed boat. Weeding was not a job he liked overmuch, but he liked the small, repetitive sound, the scuffing the blade made against the earth, and when he straightened his back and glanced behind him, he liked the way the row looked, the soil clean and dark, and the cut weeds lying in little wilting windrows. It was work you could do without thinking about anything, your mind absorbed in the short, methodical swinging of the tool.

Houses stood nearby the field of rice, and the path between Alaŭdo and Esperplena went along the south edge of the Shepherd's Crook; people frequently walked by on the path or went up the ladder of a house or down from one. He kept at his work with his head down, meaning to give a message about his wish for solitude, but not many people respected it. Because he was related to actors in the event, they steadily brought him their well-meant sympathy and their speculations about the *Lark*.

Years before, Luza Kordoba had stopped his bleeding to death when he had stepped into the edge of Henriko Lij's cane-cutter. And though he and Luza had never had a sexual union—Luza was sapphic, her lovers all had been women—people knew that Humberto had loved her for a while, and tried to interest her in loving him, and that their friendship was charged with an old sexual energy. They wanted to bring him consoling words—he must be suffering grief for Juko's sake, eh? and for the loss of Luza Cordoba—but he was already tired of the weight of his sorrow. He wanted to find peace in his weeding and be allowed to let go of the people lost on the New World.

After a while Pia Putala walked out into the rice with another long blade and went to work beside him. She was silent for quite a while, as if she must have guessed his wish for privacy. But then she said, looking around, "There is a word just gone around from the Radio Committee, a rescue is being done. Did you hear?"

He hadn't heard that. He stood up straight. "No. They're not killed, then?"

"Well, maybe not, somebody among them has given a kind of signal. I guess it was a plan they all made in case this might happen. They've got a balloon going to bring them up one by one, people are saying."

Humberto stood looking across the several rows of rice

at Pia. Since word had come of the crash of the *Lark*, he had secretly thought they were dead, all four of them, or would be shortly, as there wasn't any way to get them back up to the *Ruby*, was there? He hadn't imagined they could use the balloons. The idea startled him, made him feel stupid.

"When?" he asked her.

She straightened from her work and looked thoughtfully at the ground. "I don't think there was a time said. A balloon isn't something you can move precisely, I guess. But anyway they've started on it." She eyed him cautiously. "There's no sure telling this rescue will work, I don't suppose."

He was surprised again, feeling there must have been something in his face or his voice that made this woman, twenty years younger, think him so naive. "No," he said, in a tone of astonishment, and bent to his weeding again. He wondered if people had gone to tell this news to Juko and to Kristina Veberes, but was afraid of asking it, embarrassed.

He had thought there was only one possibility and now suddenly there were several. He kept on with the maćeta, but his peace was now completely lost, he was preoccupied with imagining the manifold details and difficulties of this balloon rescuing. Deliberately, he kept from reimagining Luza and Bjoro alive. He was cautious of pouring much hope into a fragile vessel.

Once she had told her news, Pia became silent again, focused upon the repetitive weeding, and after a while Humberto surprised himself by restarting their conversation. He asked her, "Are people wanting to go on with Meeting for Business, have you heard?" He didn't want to go to the Farms Committee Meeting if people only meant to stand around and guess at how things would come out with the crashed boat.

"I don't know," Pia said. "I heard a clerk over in Bonveno saying, how could people come together on ordinary business matters until the *Lark* was a settled trouble? But he doesn't farm. I don't know what other people, farming people, are thinking. Maybe they wouldn't want to put it off. Nothing is ordinary these days, eh? There's a lot of studying and weighing of things that still needs to be done."

They had been studying and weighing for years, but now there was accurate information, useful detail. *The more known, the more is known to ask,* was an old maxim lately become timely. "The answer to every question is ten new questions," Humberto said unhappily, and Pia nodded without speaking.

He straightened, pushing a little stiffness out of his back, and looked across the field of rice into the woodland. For a while he had been hearing a ringing high whistle—a nunbird, he thought it was, objecting to their voices. He looked on the long slope at the edge of the woods, in the patchy, concealing shade under the trees, the ferns, for the bird's low nest. He had once been privileged to see the mouth of a white-fronted nunbird's nest, an inconspicuous hole a few centimeters wide with a long anteroom of twigs and dead leaves hiding it. It was Ridaro Rogelio who had shown it to him a lifetime ago, when he was still green and had thought he might want to take up Ridaro's work, be an ornithologist. For a while he had followed Ridaro at his slow, painstaking practice of netting and banding and counting and releasing certain birds, and then netting and killing others. When the cats had taken a plague and died, people had found they must act as keystone predators of some species, and this killing was part of Ridaro's work. Humberto never had been able to get a distance between himself and the killing and he'd lost his eagerness for ornithology. But he never had stopped watching birds.

"Are you doing a committee job?" Pia asked him.

He nodded without taking his gaze from the edge of the woodland. There had not yet been agreement on the question of whether new species, Earth species, ought to be introduced to the New World. People researching this question had brought up plagues of alien rabbits in Australia, of alien cheatgrass in North America; but evidently there had once been a landmass connecting America with Asia, and animals had crossed in both directions, some killing off others—how was this natural event different from human ones? While they waited for agreement, quite a few people were going ahead, looking at the *Miller's* library of frozen cells for plants that would take cold weather, poor soils. Humberto's little committee studied the wild things—cold-tolerant natives that might, if cultivated, be edible, or pharmacological, or useful as a textile.

"I'm put to studying subarctic natives, the xerophyla," he said to Pia. "It isn't known yet, but if the water in the soil is frozen, a tundra, then when it thaws there will be too much water, the roots will stand in it."

She grimaced. "All these bad accounts."

Humberto lowered his eyes to the earth, his dirty feet, the toe strap of his worn sandals. "Some things will grow in those circumstances. I'm reading, looking." He began slowly to weed again. By the time he thought of saying something about esculant willows, the moment for it seemed to have slid by.

Pia let her maceta rest on the ground but she didn't straighten. She looked toward Humberto diffidently from her hunched-over pose above the handle of the long knife. "You have relatives on that boat, eh? Someone said you had a lover, or a brother, on the *Lark*."

Humberto shook his head, his face flushing. "I know Luza Kordoba, but not in that way. My son's mother is now Bjoro Andersen's wife." Pia's wrong information humbled him. He realized with embarrassment, maybe his links to the crashed boat had made him feel speciously self-important.

Pia said, circling backward a bit, "I guess I'd find it hard to keep a clear mind for a Business Meeting, myself, with the *Lark* still unsettled."

He seldom spoke in Meetings. He thought the clarity of his mind maybe wasn't the issue. "Whatever other people want to do," he said, straightening again so he could shrug.

Pia had two young children at home, one was a baby still sometimes nursing at her breast. Around the midday her nephew carried the crying baby out to the rice field to see if Pia's breast was what the baby wanted, and after that Pia quit the field. Humberto worked on alone until the weeding of Shepherd's Crook got done, then he went down to the tools house and washed and honed the maćeta he had used, and rubbed a little oil onto the metal, and hung it up by the handle on a hook. He was tired, his back ached, his skin itched with sweat, but he had not altogether lost his wish for solitude, and this was a time of day when there would be several people in the baths. So he went up the ladder of the domaro to his own apartment.

There was only Alfhilda there, heating a soup. Humberto brought out the old books and the tapes he had from the bor-rowing library and sat on the wide sill of the casement with his back braced against the frame in the pasado wall and his knees pulled up to rest a librajo there. Humberto had lately begun a hunt for relatives of the tough, adaptive willows and birches whose stunted forms had once made a rug across the northern plains of the Earth. The possibilities he listed went to Kilian Bejrd, who studied each of them for their dietetic values, digestibility, or to Andreo Rodiba who was an herbalist, or to Edmo Smith, a spinster and weaver. And then to Anejlisa Revfiem who was tinkering with hybridizing different ones to see if they could be recast in a more useful or a more productive form. It was slow work—after a year of this studying and tinkering, they had two dozen possibilities that might furnish a marginal crop, might nourish or clothe or heal a person in need. But Humberto liked the difficult progress. He thought there was a certain satisfaction in untangling a small tight knot in a piece of thread—maybe more than in straightening out a big kinked rope.

He read the botanical works on the screen of the librajo with his eyes pinched to force the intricate old languages, the unwieldy namings, through a narrow strait. When his eyes or his mind tired, then he set the botanicals down and read old, general geographies about tundra soils, subarctic climes, their language of landscape by now comfortingly familiar. Much in those books was reiterative, but he wasn't tired of them. He had caught from some of the essays a kind of reverence for the strategies animals and plants had used, surviving in an arduous climate.

Alfhilda brought him soup and sat on the floor with her own bowl in her lap. She was his brother Pero's only child, a girl with a broad brown face, unreticent, impulsive, a songbird. She had a potter's wheel in the Alaŭdo work shed, and frequently went about with clayed hands, had to be reminded to wash. Her ceramics were plain and artless—her gift was for biology, and lately she had apprenticed herself to Anejlisa Revfiem. She liked to read from Humberto's botanical books, and talk seriously with him about the genetics of draba mustards and tundra grass and stunted mountain heather. He had had a quiet life for several years in a small household, himself and two old people. Now his brother's daughter and his own son had moved into this apartment, along with his mother's friend Heza Barfor. His privacy, his time for solitude, had become brief and erratic, but he wasn't sorry for it. He regarded, with astonishment and fondness, Alfhilda's swift mind, Ĉejo's earnest ideality.

"Do you know, there's this rescue to be tried?" Alfhilda said to him.

He nodded over the soup.

"They'll bring them up one by one in a survey balloon, dump the equipment and come up in the gondola," she said, without looking at him to know whether he had made an answer. "Avino went over to Luza Kordoba's house to tell them—in case they didn't know it yet."

Humberto's mother hardly knew Luza or her family. People would wonder why she was taking this upon herself, or they would guess: it was a slight, cunning gesture of malice toward Juko Ohaŝi. Maybe by choosing to bring the rescue news to Luza's family, she was deliberately, conspicuously choosing not to bring the news to Bjoro's wife. She and Juko had an old enmity, grounded in guilt and blame, dating from the death of Humberto's son, and he had long ago lost the energy for trying to heal it.

"What is it you're doing with Anejlisa just now?" he asked Alfhilda, by way of turning the talk away from the *Lark*.

"We're growing a hybrid from willow stock, a sort of mutation of the—" Humberto saw her tongue come forward, licking the soup, or the intractable word "—setsuka sachalinensis. Trying to get it to grow a root mass like the pussy willows, edible," she told him.

"On the setsuka? I never hoped much for that one." He lapped the soup thoughtfully. There was mushroom in it, and bright paprika; it was sharp, sweet. "I thought Anejlisa would go at it the other way, fiddle with the pussies."

"She's doing that too." Alfhilda lifted the bowl, maybe hiding her mouth, her beam of satisfaction, behind the rim. "But I helped with the setsuka. Fixed the plates, and the droppers, and scraped the cells." She looked at Humberto. "Are you reading the Kovalak book? I like that one."

"I'm reading it. What? Are you picking it up when I set it down?"

She grimaced. "Only sometimes. I read wherever your marker is, a page or two."

Kovalak's was one of the old books he had from the library, its pages rebound between stiff boards and the paper sprayed with something slick and inflexible, a fixative or a mold-inhibitor. People handled such books with care—they were talismans, holy objects, and Kovalak's work was lyrical, a kind of spiritual geography. Humberto read it not for instruction but for its gift of imagination, its passion and compassion for Earth's lost species, its informed evocations of storms and migrations, aurora borealis, icescapes. Kovalak had been dead for two hundred years, but in the photo image on the frontispage he was in his forties, hunkered down on his heels on a gravelly scree and peering off narrow-eyed toward something behind the camera. He was long-jawed, bearded, had a look of dignity and reproach. Humberto said, "When I'm finished with it you can read it yourself, not just pieces."

She made a childish face, rolling her bottom lip down. "Anejlisa has given me a lot to read: eight books, one is French."

When they had finished the soup, the two of them took up reading companionably, though Humberto gave up trying to get at the complicated botanicals with Alfhilda asking him frequently the meanings of words, and reading things aloud when they struck her interest. Shortly Heza came in the house with a bundle of dyed yarn, and when she let her load down in the front room and started in about the balloon rescuing, Humberto had to finally give up trying to be alone. He put his reading away and got clean clothes and a towel in his arms and went along the pasado from his apartment to the men's bathhouse.

Two men were washing, and one man and a child were in the tub. He nodded to people, got his clothes off, crouched naked under the spigot of a shower beside Karlos Onoda and Edvard Penagos. Karlos and Edvard kept on with what they were saying to each other, something to do with thermostats and parabolic mirrors; both of them worked in the smeltering of metals. They were married, raising young children, their lives marked off different circles from his. The dribble of the water-spout was tepid and soothing; he sluiced it over the back of his head, his neck.

"Probably you heard about this rescue that'll be tried," Karlos said to him.

He pushed the water out of his eyes. Both men were looking at him. "Yes. A balloon," he said. Karlos's chest was extravagantly hairy. In the stream of the shower, the hair lay against his skin in a smooth pelt which Humberto admired from the edge of his eye.

"It seems a risky thing, eh?" Karlos said, raising his eyebrows. Probably Karlos wasn't asking a question, but Humberto felt he should nod, agreeing with a sort of wordless distress.

"Well anyway, there isn't much mechanical can go wrong with a balloon," Edvard said. "I'd trust it more than another go-down boat, was it me." He said it in a grimacing way, as if he held mechanical things in high scorn. No one knew why the boat had tumbled, so people were placing blame on a vague failure of technology.

"How long will it be, before there's some word of them?" the man in the tub called out above the water of the showers. His name was Umeno Flagstad, he was short and thick-bodied, his skimpy hair stuck up in a wet cockscomb. Umeno ground lenses for eyeglasses and for laboratory microscopes. Humberto thought he had spoken generally, but the others seemed to wait for Humberto to answer the question, as if his relation to Bjoro or Luza gave him a kind of authority.

"I don't know," he said. Then he also said, "A balloon isn't something that can be moved precisely, I guess." He spoke up, so his words borrowed from Pia Putala would reach Umeno sitting in the tub.

"Those radio people are sending down stingy notices," Edvard said with bitterness. "There's only a few words of news comes out from the hub every little while, but people say there's a steady talking going on between the *Ruby* and the hub, should be ten people carrying the words down here if they were sharing it, but they're keeping the most of it to themselves. I don't know what they think they're doing, those people."

Humberto knew one of the people who worked at the radio, a man who had married a cousin of his. Before the *Ruby* had gone ahead, Noria's radio work had been a sometime talking with the miners who went out on the slow tugs to capture little asteroids. Noria was a furniture maker, the radio had been something he did seldom and unhurried. But when the *Ruby* was launched, all the people who worked radio had had to drop their other work, just to keep ahead of the listening, and transcribing—putting committees' belated questions to the *Ruby*, and running to get answers to questions that came back from the boat. What must it be like now the *Lark* was crashed?

"There's more work than they can keep up, maybe," he said, but Karlos was speaking at the same time, asking if there maybe had been a trouble with the radio. When Edvard complained again about mechanical failings, it became clear they had all heard Karlos's words over Humberto's. In discomfort, he waited for an opening to repeat himself, but they went on talking, and in a little while the talk got away from that matter, and there wasn't any reason for him to keep on waiting to say it.

He left the waterspout silently and sat in the deep water in the soaking tub, on the wooden bench beside Umeno Flagstad. The child was Edvard Penago's son, a boy about three or four whose name Humberto didn't remember. In a moment, Edvard and Karlos came into the tub. Edvard blew bubbles on his son's wet belly before he sat on the bench. When he was bent over the boy, his clean pink anus displayed itself for Humberto and Umeno.

After everyone was settled, Humberto closed his eyes. People were finally done talking, and for a few minutes he heard only the water lapping against the underneath of his chin. The bath was hot, it smelled of mint and the camphor wood of the tub. Shortly, behind his eyes, he began to construct wild, empty landscapes of rock and sky, his mind's work, dreamscapes that could not have been put into words. The person he placed in the world of the dream wasn't Bjoro or Luza but himself, poking holes in the pebbly dirt with the end of a pointed stick.

The little boy said loudly, as a sort of declaration all at once, "I have a penis." Men knew, three or four years old was an age for making these announcements, and they laughed or smiled. Humberto felt a brief pang of nostalgia. He was glad, usually, to be past his own child-rearing days; his friendship with his grown son felt easy as loose clothes. But sometimes, as now, he felt something like a loss. Where was that little boy, eh? vanished into the person Ĉejo had become.

"Bridge Troll has a penis that floats," Umeno Flagstad said to the boy quietly, and that got the adults to smile again.

The boy looked down at his own penis in the water. After a while he said to Umeno, "Mine floats."

Umeno studied himself in mild surprise. "I see mine does too." There was a silence, then he said, "Bridge Troll has a penis as long as his arm. It must be the size of his penis that got Bridge Troll into trouble, eh?" Some laughter went around among them.

The boy examined his penis again, and his long thin arms bobbing in the water. "What trouble?"

Humberto had told this same tale more than once to Ĉejo,

and now he thought with sudden happiness, *I'll go on telling this to my grandchildren.* Umeno said, "Oh, it had to do with Koi, and the Plum Rains. Do you know that story? That time in the Plum Rains, it was hot and clammy and Bridge Troll lay down in the Ring River to cool himself. He was under the Tailed Frog Bridge where the water is very shallow, but he didn't remember: In the mornings of the rainy season people always open a gate on the Mandala dam. The little flood came along while Bridge Troll was lying there sleeping, and his big penis floated up and carried him along the water like a boat."

The boy's eyes were fixed wide on him through the wet scrim of his bangs.

"Old Bridge Troll," Umeno said, "thinking he might have to swim around the river forever, called out for somebody to rescue him. Koi swam up to see who was crying, and when he heard what Bridge Troll was worried about he laughed and said, well, he had lived all of his life swimming around the Ring River and it was a fine life. Bridge Troll, you know, has a short temper, and he had lived all of his life under bridges and wanted to go on doing it—he said he wasn't interested in living the foolish life of a fish. Well, this made Koi spiteful and sly and he said, if Bridge Troll wanted to stop floating around the Ring River he'd have to cut off his penis."

One of the other men, Karlos, made a scissoring gesture with his fingers in the steam rising from the water. "Ouch," he said, and there was laughing again. The boy fidgeted, looking at their faces, waiting for the end to be told.

"Bridge Troll by now had floated half around the Ring River," Umeno said. "And was just then under the Wake Robin Bridge. That bridge has a booming echo living under it, from the pump and the falls over there at the edge of Pacema."

"The Falls From Grace," Edvard said to his son, and the boy knew that place. He nodded solemnly.

"Fum-Grace, where Mario lives."

Edvard nodded too.

"Well, there's the pump brings water up to the head of the falls, and the water falling, the sound they make under the bridge is pretty big, eh? And when Bridge Troll heard it he got more afraid, and he told Koi to cut his penis off quick and save him from going up in the pump and down over the falls. So Koi cut off the Bridge Troll's penis with his teeth and carried it away for his children to eat—and Bridge Troll sank to the bottom of the Ring River."

Umeno waited for the boy's mouth to open in understanding surprise. Then he said, beginning to make a crawling motion through the water with his hand, "Bridge Troll had to crawl along the bottom like a crayfish going round and round the Ring River forever. Or anyway until drier weather, when the river got low enough for him to crawl out under the Tailed Frog Bridge." He began to grin slowly. "But later on old Bridge Troll stole one of Koi's children and stitched the little fish on to his body in place of his penis. So maybe Koi was sorry for that joke he played. Do you think?"

Edvard Penagos made a sound of fright and nipped his little son's penis under the water, between two fingers. The boy squealed and laughed, and began a game of holding his breath and crawling on the bottom of the wooden tub like a crayfish, pinching toes and penises.

When the boy and his father and Umeno Flagstad had gone home, Humberto went on sitting in the bath with Karlos.

"Here's something new I've got to wonder about," Karlos said to him. He grinned. "Is there a bridge troll on that New World, eh, if there's no bridges?"

"Trolls are canny," Humberto said, smiling himself. "They might think of living under rocks."

"Oh hell, there's plenty of those, that much is true. What do you farm people think about it?"

"What? The rocks, you mean?"

"All of it. The ground, the weather. That world's got a short year, eh? How can a crop be raised in a month?"

People who weren't farming often didn't pay attention to the reports, or didn't remember them. Humberto looked away. "Fifty days. We can get crops to ripen in that time, if we have the long days. At the midlatitudes, summer daylight is either side of twenty-two hours."

Karlos raised his brows. "How would our bodies get used to that, eh? They say we've all got a clock in our bodies tells us when to sleep and wake and eat. I guess I wouldn't like to stay awake twenty-two hours, maybe plants wouldn't like it either."

Humberto began to feel tired and blunted. These were arguments he had heard many times. He said, "It would spur a plant to grow, I guess," but that was only what his instinct told him. There had been three or four mathematical studies without clear result, statistical remodelings to do with atmospheric pressure, surface gravity, irradiation, axial tilt; the research was built upon known agricultural responses. Not many people believed in the studies, anyway. Reports about what had been grown in the summers at Reykjavik, Iceland, or Yakutsk, Russia, seemed too remote from them to be any longer truthful.

Karlos touched his groin, smiling boyishly. "Maybe those

long days would grow me a penis long as my arm, eh?"

Humberto answered without joy. "Well I guess we could get used to it, then."

When other men came into the bathhouse, Humberto dried himself and put on his clean clothes and went out, before the talk could get back around to the *Lark*. He carried his dirty clothes down to the laundry, and while he waited for the washing machine to finish its job he took a piece of needlework from his pocket, a square of linen he was hemming in a fine stitch. He sat on the flagstones at the edge of the path in front of the laundry, with his legs folded under him and the needlework on his knee. He had meant to give the finished piece to his cousin's daughter on the occasion of her marriage, but then had imagined it might be needed as a funeral gift for Juko on the death of her husband. Which, now?

The sewing was not an occupation for his thoughts, and because the path in front of the laundry house was not much on the way to somewhere else, he was frequently left alone to turn things over unsystematically in his mind. It was impossible to keep from thinking about the *Lark*, and gradually he began to worry along a new line. All the spacegoing boats were old, original equipment; the *Lark's* failure maybe was age, or maintenance. He didn't know if it was possible for the people on the Mechanics Committee to warrant a reliable go-down boat.

Parts of houses were old as the torus, and many trees, wooden chests, tables, many of them were Earth-built. The clothes washers were old stock, a clever Japanese invention; they made an ultrasonic noise that shook the dirt off into very little water. In the kitchenhouse of the domaro Humberto lived in, the stove was Earth-built, it had a short phrase in Norwegian, raised in relief on the ceramic base. Ĉejo, who was fascinated by it, had worked out the meaning. *Root and Leaf,* it said, and Ĉejo, every little while, would offer some new sense he had made of that old, quizzical message. But original machinery had gradually become rare. The mechanisms that survived tended to be of two kinds: simple things with few moving parts, like the clothes washers; and things too problematic for their small manufactory to re-create—spacegoing boats, sewing-machine motors, the heavy equipment of manufacture itself. Humberto imagined an absurdity: After so long a course getting to this world, they might only lack the fundamental machinery to deliver themselves and their belongings down to it.

When he carried his clean laundry home his mother was there, delivering to Heza all the guesses and certainties and dreads she had gotten from the crowd of people at Luza Kordoba's house, all the people who were helping the family to wait, or bringing news about the rescue. Earlier, he had thought he might not want to go to the Farms Committee Meeting, in case the talk was all of the crashed boat. But now he went out to it—it would have been pointless to stay away, since even the people in his own house were keeping up their talk about the *Lark* and there was no escaping it.

The Alaŭdo Farms Committee for many years had made a habit of meeting in the field above the aeroponics shed, the one named The Whisper Behind the Tree. There were five carob trees standing in a rough circle in a field of cottongrass, and the committee fitted their own circle of people inside the circle of trees, people balancing tablets on their knees if they had to write something down, and bringing mats to kneel on at certain times of the year when the grass was stubbly or littered with St. John's fruit. There were twenty people who farmed in Alaŭdo, but not often twenty at a Farms Committee Meeting—today only nine. With the fate of the go-down boat at the front of people's minds, maybe quite a few were following the maxim that a person ought to stay away from a Meeting if not able to bring an earnest sense of listening and sharing.

Humberto seated himself between old Nores Panko and Ĝeronimo Zea in the circle, and let his eyes close for the beginning of silence.

"Ĉejo says, tell you he has gone to his mother's house," Ĝeronimo said, touching Humberto's sleeve, whispering hoarsely. "Waiting for word of the *Lark*, eh?"

Humberto nodded. "The balloon," he murmured, before Ĝeronimo could say it.

The committee clerk was a woman named Elisabeta Bojs, a good clerk with a facility for finding the open way. She liked to let the silence at the beginning and end of a Business Meeting go on a little longer than other clerks were inclined to, and in the long quiet Humberto felt a slow centering down, a sloughing off of his fretfulness about the crew of the *Lark*, until finally he was able to fill his mind with an expectant, living silence.

"Do people have concerns?" Elisabeta said at last.

After all, nobody brought up the boat. There were things to do with weeding, with getting the pejiba palm fruits down from the taller trees, and planting late mustard. People reported about the repair of the mezlando aqueduct, and raised pessimistic questions from the data sent by the *Ruby*. A query had been sent down from Quarterly Meeting about the possibility of burying heating cables underground to warm the soil for farming, and about the drilling of wells—whether people had considered the eventual problem of depleting the fossil water. Humberto reported on his own work with Killian Berd and Anejlisa Revfiem, and his second-hand information about the genetic tinkering Anejlisa was doing with the setsuka willows. Intermittently, Elisabeta stated her sense of the meeting, and if there was no disagreement with it, Gil Roko, who was the recording clerk, wrote it down as a Minute of the Meeting.

When there were nine recorded Minutes, and new issues weren't being raised anymore, she brought up the problem of the leaf-cutter ants, who had built two enormous labyrinths in the midst of a hedge of cinnamomum. This problem had been brought up before, without anything being decided. The ants were in a cycle of abundance this year—new colonies had been springing up suddenly in fields and in the woodland everywhere—and Aleda Laitowler thought, when the ants had exhausted the foliage of the hedge they would begin to attack the citrus trees. He thought people ought to act before this happened, to take the role that the extinct army ants once had taken, invading the leaf-cutter ants' subterranean galleries and chambers in the cinnamomum. Some people agreed with Aleda, but other people thought, in a few months or years the leaf-cutters would become suddenly rare again without farmers disturbing them. The population of insects was unpredictable, prone to puzzling fluctuations, this was something everybody knew.

Elisabeta had steered the arguments gently and let silence inform the spaces, but people had only put forward information to support one belief or the other, and no advance had been made. When they had last met, she had asked three particular people to study this issue, to gather information and reformulate it, set it forth in a clearer light. Out of the three, only old Nores Panko was there to make a report. He stood up slowly when Elisabeta at last raised the subject of the leaf-cutter ants. Nores never had been what people called a "weighty Friend"—someone whose voice was always worth listening to—but his old age had given him a kind of stature. He was seventy-nine years old, probably had seen other invasions of leaf-cutter ants, must have been living when the army ants inexplicably disappeared.

These leaf-cutter ants were a kind of farmer ant, he said, cutting pieces of leaves into tiny fragments like sawdust and heaping them up to make a compost in their underground chambers, which they fertilized with their own feces, and on which they sowed a fungus that produced nodules like tiny, fuzzy kohlrabi, that the ants then ate, just as human beings inoculated compost with the spore of mushrooms, and ate the mushrooms. A female ant going off to establish a new colony carried in a pocket of her cheek pieces of fungus for sowing in the new place, just as human beings transported and preserved seeds, bulbs, cuttings, for propagating their own crops.

There was a silence while Nores kept on standing. He was white-haired, but his bushy eyebrows still were dark; they made a fierce line across his face. He had a wide tender mouth that belied his brows, and a kind demeanor. He stood without a cane, leaning a bit forward with his hands folded together behind his back. Humberto sitting below him could see the slight tremor in his hands—maybe that was why he clasped them. And looking at old Nores's hands, he began to imagine himself a member of a guild to which the peaceful fungus-growing ants also belonged—both of them vegetarian agriculturists. In the midst of the quiet, he thought of saying this, but he kept silent, waiting for someone else to bring it up. Too often he found he wasn't able to give his values, his judgment, any coherent expression. He had formed a gingerly habit of not speaking when there was serious disagreement.

Another clerk might have counseled a longer silence, for people to consider the problem before probably tabling it again. But Elisabeta Bojs said to Nores gently, "I feel maybe you have something more you want to say, Nores," and he took a slightly different grip of his hands and sighed.

"Well I guess I do," he said finally. "Here is something else I will tell you. I was a boy when I saw this, and I'd forgot it until I took up this reading about ants." And he told about once seeing a colony of leaf-cutters invaded by raiding army ants. He hadn't seen the battles, he said, only afterward the many hundreds of corpses of leaf-cutters' soldiers strewn dead around the entrances to their galleries, and scattered for yards along the paths to and from the city. Some of the dead and dying soldiers had lost limbs or were cut in two, but there were scores without an evident injury—perhaps they'd been stung to death, he said, or they might have simply fallen dead of exhaustion; who knew how long they had kept up this defense against invaders? The army was passing in a steady stream along the paths to and from the leaf-cutters' chambers, in and out of its portals, carrying off to their bivouac the white bodies of larvae and pupae.

Though they had killed the leaf-cutter soldiers, Nores said, they only stripped the poor nursemaid ants of their charges and left them wandering about sorrowfully, uninjured. Who knew why? After a moment, Nores added, "I guess it wasn't anything like clemency made them do it. I suppose, in the natural way, they were leaving survivors so the ants' city would recover, and be there when they came round to pillage it again."

He loosed his long-boned old hands. "That's all I wanted to say," he said, making a shaky gesture. He sat down slowly beside Humberto, pulling his knees up slightly and resting his thin forearms across them.

There was a profound silence after old Nores sat down. Humberto thought he ought to refuse the shameless ascribing of human nature to these ants, but what he felt was a sudden deep ignorance of the quality of an ant's psychic life. He looked down at the ground in front of his crossed knees. There was a beetle with an iridescent carapace making a slow way through the cottongrass and the dry leaves.

Elisabeta let the silence go on quite a while. Perhaps she knew the direction of Nores's leading would make itself evident if they all waited long enough. Eventually someone stood and simply told about watching the ants on their narrow, beaten highways, endless columns of them homeward-bound, toting tiny pieces of green leaf that rose gigantically above their backs like great banners or rainhats. And someone else told of seeing a piece of leaf borne along by a big ant, with two or three small ants clinging aloft—the little ones had tried to help carry, maybe, but the big one had simply lifted the cargo, helpers and all, and marched away with it. And finally Gift Ŝu stood up and said, "I wonder. If we put leafy cuttings near their city, would they snub them, or be glad of the extra? When any of us have got fresh prunings, if we brought those over and laid them on their paths, maybe they would cut them up and carry them home and maybe that would lighten the pressure on the cinnamomum."

Elisabeta raised her brows in surprise. She looked at Nores. "Will they take leaves cut fresh for them, Nores?"

The old man considered this before nodding solemnly. "They have a little preference for certain leaves, don't like every kind. But what they like, they'd take cut as much as not, I think. In that book it said they would take from downed branches."

And so a way was opened. Talk turned to the kinds of leaves the ants would accept, particular plants and shrubs, trees, herbs; and people made rough guesses about the kind and volume of pruning they'd be doing in the next weeks. Shortly, they got to speculating why some leaves weren't suited for the ants' use, and whether the ants' little species of fungus was related to mushroom, or to lichen. When the discussion seemed to get around to repeating itself, Elisabeta interrupted and stated her sense of this last part of the meeting: An effort would be made to minimize the defoliation of the cinnamomum by furnishing leafy cuttings to the colony of farmer ants who had taken up living there. No one disagreed, and Gil Roko wrote it down as the tenth Minute of the Meeting.

That was all the business anyone raised. In the silence at the close, gradually Humberto found he was adrift in the space behind his closed eyes, a sort of dream, himself in a cavernous black chamber on his hands and knees weeding a white field of woolly kohlrabi.

He meant to get away from the Meeting quickly afterward but people stopped him, wanting to talk now about the *Lark* and the rescue, and he was slow getting home again, the light by then already lowered for dusk. Heza was out of the house, she'd had a meeting herself, of the Fiber Arts Committee, and frequently was late from those meetings, was one of the people prone to sit around afterward and do handwork while catching up gossip. Humberto's father was playing cards with his cronies in the sadaŭ of a house over in Mandala. His mother and Alfhilda sat alone in the apartment, quietly playing Go. Alfhilda's soup was eaten up, so Humberto went round to the kitchen house and steamed some bulgur in orange and ginger, made a ragout of beets, leeks, squash, cold lentils. He left some of this in the refrigerator for other people to find and brought his bowl back into the apartment, but then his mother and Alfhilda complained and he had to go into the kitchen again and bring the rest of the bulgur and the ragout for them to eat while they played Go.

"Ĉejo is waiting at his mother's house," Leona said. She was focused on the game. "Until there's word of the *Lark*."

He nodded. "The balloon." He ate slowly while he watched them play and then he took his turn at it, finding a kind of relief in the concentration on strategy. He won with Alfhilda and then lost to his mother, and while he was waiting out their next game he got up, carrying their empty bowls, and came back with a banana and a bowl of figs. He and Alfhilda ate figs and kept on playing after Leona had gone to bed, but when Alfhilda had lost twice in a row she gave up in frustration, and Humberto went to bed himself rather than sit alone with botanical reading. He was afraid Heza, when she came in, would want to talk with him about the *Lark*.

As soon as he lay down he was half-asleep, thinking suddenly, *I am too tired to worry tonight.* But he woke when the boards of the floor groaned quietly in the darkness beside him. Ĉejo was coming to bed. How late was it? His limbs felt rigid, expecting a blow.

"What has happened?" he asked in a low voice.

"Bjoro is rescued," Ĉejo said softly. "And Luza Kordoba. But Peder Ojama and Isuma Bun are killed."

Humberto rolled onto his back. He stared blindly up into darkness. He didn't know the two who were dead—he had been thoroughly spared grief. Immediately a kind of guilt settled on him, as if God had made this selection by considering Humberto Indergard's interests ahead of other people's.

"Isuma Bun is a second cousin to Katrin Amundsen," Ĉejo murmured after a silence.

Katrin Amundsen was a name Humberto knew without a face, the most recent of the girls Ĉejo had loved in the last year. She lived in her grandmother's household in Revenana, in the domaro where Ĉejo had spent his green years.

"I went to see if Katrin's family had heard about the death," Ĉejo said. "Maybe Katrin is a close friend with this cousin, or her grandmother could be also Isuma's grandmother, and maybe they would want to know. But no lights were on in their rooms. I didn't know if I should wake anybody."

"It's all right if they don't learn about it until morning," Humberto said quietly. "What can be done anyway, but crying?"

In the darkness, Humberto heard his son's voice break. "I wanted to be there with her if she cried," he said, crying himself. Ĉejo hadn't yet grown out of an overemotional romanticism.

He was fiercely monogamous and loyal but his couplings tended to be brief. Almost as soon as a girl returned his attention he would put her in a desperate, smothering clasp, and when the girl tired of the weight, she'd quickly wriggle free. Humberto himself had been a casual lover at Ĉejo's age, had accepted copulation as a kind of gift from girls without imagining romantic love was being offered too. Now that he was forty-six years old and for the last six years unmarried, he found he was more analytical. He seldom had coitus with a woman without wondering if he loved her; and he wondered about the quality of the love, and if it might become relaxed enough to support a marriage.

He remembered suddenly that time he had walked into the swung blade of Henriko Lij's cane cutter, the long moment while Henriko gaped at him in astonishment and fear, and then the woman he didn't know, Luza Kordoba, pushing by old Henriko and past Humberto's own clutching hands to put her fingers deftly to his neck, pushing down in the hole through the spurt of his bright red blood, the swift, sure gesture that stopped him from bleeding out. While Henriko ran to get other people to help, people with surgical tools to close the hole, helplessly he had gripped Luza's wrist and fixed his eyes on her, and she had squatted over him with her hand at his throat, in his throat, talking to him quietly about farming and weather, and when she was short of those subjects, instructing him irrelevantly about things she knew in her own fields, kinematics and linear momentum, acupuncture pressure points and homeostasis, until the warmth and even pressure of her hand on his pulse had become as compelling and sexual as an erection. It was the single time he had loved someone as Ĉejo loved, brief and burning, urgently holding on.

PART TWO

UNNAMED LANDS

6

Humberto

After the dazzle of day is gone,
Only the dark, dark night shows to my eyes the stars;
After the clangor of organ majestic, or chorus, or perfect
*   band,*
Silent, athwart my soul, moves the symphony true.

HUMBERTO HAD A habit of sitting together with Anejlisa
Revfiem, Edmo Smith, and Andreo Rodiba at Meetings of
the Alaŭdo ŝiro—this was something that had started when
they formed a little committee to study arctic plants and they
had thought they might be asked to give a report at Monthly
Meetings for Business. Now their work seemed irrelevant and
ignored at these big Meetings where the issues shaped themselves around larger matters than plant genetics, but they had
gone on sitting together for the pleasure they all had in arguing
together afterward.

There were something near two hundred adults, ten houses

in Alaŭdo. By the natural order of things only fifteen or twenty or twenty-five people were likely to gather on the loğio of one of the houses for Monthly Meeting if there was nothing needing deciding, nothing consequential. Not many things really affected everyone; most decisions were made in Meetings of a domaro, or in committees. But for more than a year the Meetings of Alaŭdo ŝiro had been preoccupied with the New World and this was a matter that no one considered trivial. Habitually now as many as sixty or seventy or eighty people, whole committees and households, would come to answer the Queries, argue the Advices put to them by Yearly Meeting, or to raise issues they thought should be sent on to the clerk of Quarterly Meeting.

Isaba Aguto, who was clerk of the Alaŭdo meeting, had taken to dragging a table out onto the loğio and sitting up on it so she could see faces and be heard in the crowd. Some people had complained about this, saying Isaba was putting herself above other people. But who knew the best way to guide a Meeting of such size? Poor Isaba was doing the best she could, some other people said.

Humberto wondered if all this arguing about Isaba's methods came from people being closed-minded, or afraid of the real issues. He thought Isaba Aguto had a tendency to let an argument go on too long before putting the matter in the hands of a committee, and she had some habits that annoyed him, nervous mannerisms, but he never had thought she was self-important. When Isaba sat on a table, they all could see her and hear what she had to say, even from the edge of the loğio where they were able to lean their backs against the outer wall of the kitchen. Humberto thought if Isaba sat down on the boards of the loğio with other people, he and his friends might have to move in closer to hear what was being said, and Edmo Smith was stubborn, wouldn't bring a repozo for sitting against, though he had a curved spine and couldn't sit for long without support.

"Well, I don't hear a unity of judgment," Isaba said in frustration, and looked around at all their faces for someone who might disagree—someone who might want to put forward a leading that she hadn't recognized. She had a long torso, looked tall while she was sitting, but when she stood she became short, and her long waist thick and straight, hipless as a man's. She never had borne children, but Humberto didn't know if this was related to her narrow pelvis, or to her marrying a man who already had been married once and had three living children.

People had been arguing about geothermal heat. There were innumerable hot springs on the New World, thousands of surface vents emitting hot gases or vapors, and the Energy Committee of Yearly Meeting had delivered a report saying the steam from those hot springs could be used for running machinery, making heat and light, for warming agricultural greenhouses, and that this might be a simpler thing than the complicated and slow process of cold fusion they relied on in the *Miller*. The geothermal sites stood mostly on the flanks of volcanoes, were prone to quakes, and there was considerable disagreement about the jeopardy; they had sent a query to all the śiros asking whether people wanted to build houses on firmer, flatter ground, and then find a means to pipe the heat and the power to those houses, from springs, solfataras, fumaroles, which might be dozens of kilometers away.

Humberto felt himself caught in an anxious, muddled thinking, while he strained to hear something that would open a way, free him from doubt. But Isaba hadn't been able to keep people on the question. Inevitably the argument had deteriorated, sliding down to smaller and smaller issues. Who could say what was a reliably safe distance from a volcano? If houses were apart from the power plant, how would people who ran and repaired the machinery get from their houses to their work? Would they be expected to live, themselves, on the volcanoes, the fault lines? What if power-plant workers wanted to live at the power plant on the shaky slopes, but their families wanted to live in the houses on safe ground?

Isaba interrupted frequently, trying to broaden the question, to turn things upward, but people went on arguing logistics, making claims and counterclaims, and the important question was lost in ever-narrowing lanes and culs-de-sac. It was a compulsion they all had, a need to divide a question into its smallest components. Most people had given up the old wrangling over whether the New World would support human lives—they understood that it would, that the question was something else, something indecipherable, and that the scientific reports never would be able to explain the things that really mattered. But they went on suffering from a vague, irrational hope that if everything, every mystery of the New World, could be examined and known, then they would reach an understanding of how they felt about it.

Isaba Aguto prodded her chin with her fingertips. "The committee that's been studying energy—are you on that committee, Lucina?" She gestured toward a woman and then returned her hand to her chin. "Will you take this Query back to them, ask them to restate it a little? Maybe if you bring it next month in different words, or another shape, we can all find some way to an agreement." She went on exploring her chin thoughtfully a moment, pulling on it, looking out at people's faces, before she tipped her head toward Samčjo Penaflor, who was the recording clerk. "This geothermal matter is held over, then," she said irritably, "until the question can be restated." A long sigh went around while Samčjo wrote down this Minute—people were frustrated by the inconclusive, discursive nature of the Meetings lately—but no one objected to Isaba's conclusion, it was obvious no agreement had been reached.

A silence settled on everyone after Isaba had stated her sense of the Meeting. Humberto began to wonder if he ought to speak, now that the main business was set aside. Since he had been going on with his arctic studies he had lately had a dream: his bookish imagining of something he took to be a glacial tongue at the margin of a sea. In his dream, a bleak immense island broke from the edge of the glacier, fracturing slowly under the weight and pressure of the ice. In a bluish tableau, people stood on the ice floe and others at the edge of the broken shore ice in separate, wretched confusion, while the distance between them inexorably widened.

He hadn't yet told the dream to anyone, but he thought it was rooted in his worry about the New World, or was something vaguely to do with their increasing disagreement and paralysis. People sometimes brought up impressions and inklings at the end of a Meeting, and he had been wondering, in the last few minutes, if his dream might be that kind of vague leading. But he seldom had spoken to a gathering larger than the Alaŭdo Farms Committee, hadn't spoken at a meeting of the whole širo since the numbers of listeners had become so many, the questions of such weight. He had little confidence in his judgment, felt himself easily swayed.

After a considered silence two or three people stood up abruptly and began to talk to one another, signalling that they considered the Meeting at an end. Humberto stood, and Edmo grunted and grimaced as he got himself up, pulling on the hand Humberto held down to him. Edmo wasn't old—his youngest child wasn't grown yet—but as he had aged his crooked spine had given him increasing pain. He had to stand up to spin thread, with his spinning jenny raised on a sort of platform. People made obscene jokes about Edmo and his wife, that they had intercourse standing up, and this was why his wife walked bowlegged. If Edmo had heard these jokes, he never had said. He reached around to knead the small of his back and straighten gingerly from hunching. "Well, hell," he said, complaining. "That was a useless Meeting, eh? When there's too many people, things get off the track. Here's what I think: Every house ought to send only its clerk and maybe one other person to Monthly Meeting. Twenty people. That's always a good size for coming to agreement."

"Everybody's entitled to a voice," Anejlisa Revfiem said irritably. "You can't tell people to keep home from a Monthly Meeting. They want to know what's being said, even when they don't speak out."

"Well, nothing will get decided, then," Edmo said grimly. "How can we get to any agreement, with so many people having a say in it?" He made a rude hand gesture that took in the bunches of people standing around them on the loǵio. "Must be eighty people, eh? ninety? a hundred people! A meeting will break down when we get these crowds, you know, that's something we can count on."

A rule by majority or by representation always had been

anathema to the old Quakers, but it was mostly the size of the gathering that had kept Humberto from speaking, and he thought other people were daunted too—lately it was the same dozen or so who would stand and offer their voices, people not known for the weight of their judgment but for not being timid. Still, he had been coming to the širo Meetings himself because he didn't want to hear second-hand what was being decided or talked about now that the issues had always to do with the New World. He looked from one of them to the other but kept out of this argument between Edmo and Anejlisa, not knowing which side of it he stood on.

Andreo Rodiba had been looking down at his feet, considering. Humberto had a good opinion of Andreo. Often in the talking that went on after the Meeting it would be something Andreo said that would bring a thing into focus for him, make it comprehensible. Andreo wasn't known for his gifts as a speaker but for a penetrating wisdom, a seeing-through to the simple truths.

Now he said cautiously, "I don't know if it's crowds that break down a Meeting—or not *only* crowds. It's always been a spiritual method, eh? And it stops working when people give up being spiritual."

Humberto said, "Be quick to hear and slow to speak, and let grace season the words," which was an old Quaker maxim his grandmother had used to recite to him.

Andreo nodded. He had a long, fissured face, ears that sprang from his skull. When he gathered his mouth, the tips of his ears pulled nearer his head. "We've all been bringing quarrels to these Meetings and leaving grace at home," he said.

Andreo seemed to mean the four of them as much as

anybody, though none of them had spoken for the last several Meetings. Maybe Andreo thought they had all given something intangible to the temper, the atmosphere of dissension—none of them had stood up and spoken of love, of fusing differences, of a desire for unity. Humberto was pierced by a belated wish to tell his dream.

Edmo was still fixed on what he'd been thinking about the size of Meetings. "Maybe a big siro Meeting could be held in two or three parts; minutes could be read one to the other, so people would know what the other parts were saying."

Anejlisa grinned sourly. "Maybe you should tell that to Isaba, get her to put it on the agenda, next Meeting. But there's a double-bind, eh? We'll never have smaller Meetings because there's too many of us to come to any unity about how to have smaller Meetings."

They stood on the logio arguing and talking in this way without getting anywhere. Other people were standing around in little schools doing the same thing—assigning blame for the failure of the Meeting, and arguing about Isaba Aguto sitting herself above them. In the past, the time following a Meeting had been good for thinking and discussing and persuading—for people to move slowly toward agreement on a hard question. Increasingly, now, no one could agree on the question. Where was the foundation for agreeing upward?

Knuto Mursawa had been standing near them, seeming to listen to what they were saying. Knuto was an aeroponics engineer, a man somewhere in long middle age, with a flattened nose, moles on his face. He was as likely to say something scatterbrained as something that would open a way, but he hadn't spoken while people were arguing about geothermal power, or while Edmo and Anejlisa quarreled over the size of Meetings.

Now he cleared his throat and said, addressing himself to Andreo, "We always have lived in this world, in its body as in the body of God. It's a sufficient world and a blessed one, I would say, and I wonder why we ain't been thinking how we can go on living inside—build something like the *Miller* down there and live inside it." He may have wanted to say this momentous thing to the Monthly Meeting, and not been able to bring it out—it had a formal sound, rehearsed. Now he seemed relieved. He shifted, standing mostly on one foot, looking around vaguely without pinning his look on anyone.

None of them spoke. Then Andreo said, spreading his mouth down mournfully, "Well, Knuto, that's a pretty big question to bring up when we thought this Meeting was over, eh?" No one else spoke. Humberto looked in the other faces for a sign of what he felt, himself—a kind of stunned realization. He had thought he had learned to admire the elegant complexity of the subarctic ecosystem not less than the lush intricacy of the one he lived in, but now he felt his heart clench with a sudden, inexpressible yearning to go on living under a roof, without vagaries of weather, eating cerimoj and mangoes.

Andreo went off and brought back Isaba Aguto who listened to Knuto repeat his little speech, the same words brought forward in the same order, *as in the body of God.* A small bunch of people had gathered around Knuto by now, and argument began about whether the chronic mechanical failures and deterioration of machinery, the śimanas and plagues of illness, the steady irrecoverable loss of plant and animal species, would be prohibitive problems for a planet-bound biosphere.

Isaba said, interrupting, "We can't be talking this out today, do people agree? We had a long Meeting already, and some of us got to get on to other work. Maybe three or four people will meet with Knuto, and make a start at seeing if this idea is possible." A few voices called out. Isaba nodded, gripping her chin. "All right then." Knuto's lugubrious face was flushed.

After Isaba walked away, people finally began drifting off, going on with the other things in their lives. Then Humberto, who had been hanging back, talked to Anejlisa about the possibility of her brother-in-law's sister's second cousin maybe someday making a marriage match for Alfhilda. It was something that was still years away, but arranging a marriage was an important responsibility, and people who loved Alfhilda were already thinking about it and looking around unhurriedly for someone compatible. His brother Pero had asked him to talk to Anejlisa about her relative. Did she think this boy might be suited to Alfhilda? Would she keep an eye on this boy as he grew older, watch him to see if he might make a successful partner for Pero's daughter?

Humberto spoke his brother's request quickly and then struggled to get away from Anejlisa's interested, insistent scrutiny of the idea. He never had been comfortable with questions like these since his own marriage had come undone; he had a vague conviction that his divorce made him unfit to involve himself in other people's marriages. When his mother had talked to him about matching his son Ĉejo, he had felt a nameless fright, and had resisted having a hand in it. When she went on pressing him, bringing up names of girls, gossiping about this one or that one who might make Ĉejo a wife, he had finally, irritably, told her to bring her reports to Juko. Her face had flattened, as if he'd accused her of something—she hadn't spoken to Juko in years—maybe she thought he was blaming her for arranging his own failed marriage. But afterward he had gained a little peace: Now she and his aunt Lavka and Heza Barfor were looking at possible matches for Ĉejo without telling him about it.

He got away finally from Anejlisa and the śiro meeting, but he didn't go back to his own house. His mind was jumping helplessly from one thing to another, picking at odds and ends of worries; he wanted to go up into the altejo corn and be alone a while and turn things over systematically. He took the narrow path between the houses into the small terraced fields of pumpkins and beans, plantains, pepinos. A dead chicken lay on the dirt at the edge of the mezlando rice, and he squatted and turned the hen's stiff body over, examining it. There was a puncture wound in the breast, the feathers surrounding it black and clotted with blood. Chickens frequently disappeared—at daybreak they came for corn, in the evening they simply failed to go to roost; tayras carried them off, or opossums. It was rare to find more than feathers, but this one had made a brief escape, maybe, and then died alone. He sighed unhappily and carried the dead hen back down to his domaro, went into the kitchenhouse and plucked it, eviscerated and washed the body carefully, wrapped it in a piece of linen and left it to cool in the refrigerator.

People came in the kitchen and went out again while he was working, and he was required to talk to each of them—to give a report of the śiro Meeting to people who hadn't been there; to listen to opinions about geothermal power plants from people who had been shy of saying what they thought in front of sixty or a hundred people; to repeat what he had heard Knuto say about the body of God, to people who had already heard about it second- or third-hand. When he had finally, scrupulously, sorted the clean feathers from the bloody and left the clean ones in a basket in the sadaŭ for anyone who needed them and brought the offal out to the compost pile, then he went on with what he'd planned to do, going up into the altejo corn to be alone.

In the corn field he was hidden in the verdure, the maize rearing its powdery tassels an arm's reach above his head. Weeds had given up trying to grow in the shade under the spreading, strappy leaves, and he went through the field easily, pinching earwigs between his thumbnails, smearing aphids with his fingertips.

He had thought he would spend this time looking for a clear way—grappling with images of grace and unity, or turning over ideas to do with the body of God, or geothermal machinery, or Meetings that were too crowded for consensus; but the smell of the dry heated ground and the must of the corn at this time of year began to be linked in his mind with the scent of sexual intercourse, and helplessly he began to drift into the interstices of that connection.

People who wanted to keep their sexual relations private had to look for secret places or times, and when he was sixteen, seventeen, he had been embarrassed to bring a girl into his own bed with his family members and his neighbors listening on the other side of the wall. The corn field was a place of concealment, of seclusion—he used to lie down with girls on the stubbly dry earth among the stalks of the maize. That was so many years past, the memory of it so abraded, it might have happened to someone else. Now his mother teased Ĉejo about his failure to bring a girl home, and there were places in the altejo field where the stubble of weeds was pressed down flat under the corn in a shapely nest, and twice Humberto had glimpsed a flutter of movement, not an armadillo, not a sloth, someone scuttling away from him through the brake. He had begun to keep out of the maize when he saw a girl of a certain age walking up the path toward his son in the altejo corn.

He remembered without nostalgia the heated urgency of those years in his life, and wasn't much interested in recapturing it. But he was sometimes surprised and obscurely worried when he realized he'd gone weeks without a real need for sexual contact. He missed the settledness of marriage, the casualness of its sexual relations. He knew people—his brother Pero and his wife—who had fallen into a methodical pattern of intercourse that didn't much allow for appetite. Pero once had said to him, looking sly, "When Natčja takes my penis into her hands, that's when I'm hungry to have a little sex with her."

This made him think of a woman he had coupled with once, while he was still married to Juko. This woman, Naoma, had had a husband dying slowly from a cancer, and Humberto's younger son had only just died. Naoma had been a loud talker in those days, had a blotchy, coarse face, and she smelled of her husband's slow death; he hadn't thought of laying with her. But when she deliberately pushed her breast against his arm, put the tips of her fingers inside his trousers, he discovered after all a hunger for her, and they had copulated wordlessly on the floor of the tools shed. Afterward he had wondered if it was intercourse she had needed from him, and not something more generous. She had moved into her sister's household, after her husband's death, and become an ascetic—was this something he ought to be blamed for? he wondered. And his divorce from Juko must be blamed on other things, not on this adultery, but he had maybe stopped trying hard to find a clear way with his wife after he had had intercourse with Naoma Samuels.

When he cast around in his memory for the last time he had had sexual relations, he was only able to remember bringing the carpenter, Berta Ule, into his empty house while the members of his family danced at the christening of a neighbor's new-born son. That had been months ago, the baby creeping now, or walking, so he realized with a start that he had become celibate without planning it.

He didn't know why he had lain with Berta only the one time, and now that he was thinking of her he began to turn over the idea of seeing her again. He didn't know many people over in Revenana where she lived, didn't walk over there very often. Their meeting in the first place had been accidental; he'd gone to talk to someone who was on the Revenana Farms Committee, a man who was helping Berta Ule rebuild a shed. He thought suddenly of asking that farmer to ask Berta if she would welcome his company again; he didn't know if she might by this time have someone else in mind to become married to.

If you were out of the seed years, had been divorced or been widowed and still were wishing to marry again, you could make a reliable match for yourself, most people thought. By that time you ought to be free of the well-known tendency to choose a lover as a mate—perhaps even through being ruled by your sexual organs. But Humberto missed the assurance, the abso-luteness, of having other people organize his partnering—it wasn't Leona's fault his marriage to Juko had failed. It might be a healing gesture, after all, if he asked his mother to find him a second wife—if he asked his mother, rather than that Revenana farmer, to talk to Berta Ule about renewing their friendship.

For a moment he stood in the close swelter under the corn, deliberately recollecting Berta's pendant breasts, the wide dark areoles, the nipples rising against the palms of his hands. He remembered her long freckled arms and a belly that rounded neatly above her pubic hair. Immediately his penis stiffened, suffusing with heat, reassuring him. The sound of a gamelan and of drums and people dancing at the christening had come rhythmically through the walls, and Berta had stood up playfully after copulating with him and had danced beside the bed, beating her feet against the floor, slapping her knees, her big teeth flashing.

Humberto swayed dizzily as if he were dancing himself, and the heat in his groin swept out to his limbs suddenly. His eyes watered, peering against a yellow blaze. He shut them, but the shimmer went on blinding and dizzying him. He felt himself absorbed in a kaleidoscope of fleeting movement, of impressions and shifting featureless patterns and colors, impermanence. For a moment, he wondered stupidly if he had become an infant again: He felt he hadn't yet mastered the intricate skill of seeing fixed three-dimensional objects in the great rushes of movement and light. Wonderingly, slowly, as a person born blind and suddenly sighted, he realized what hung before his eyes: the delicate arched bones of the distant ceiling, the array of the daylight xenon lamps.

His arms outflung, he was lying in a tangle of broken canes of corn. One of his eyes was shut, he realized, and when he opened it, the brilliance made his mind stop. The earth burned against the skin of his shoulder blades, his buttocks, his heels; the bowl of his skull held a searing fire. In a flutter of confusion, he wondered if it was the whole torus that had flashed to apocalypse in a dazzling moment of heat and light. But then he understood what his ears were hearing: the hum of bumblebees, blackflies, mosquitoes, going on with their lives. He became aware of children laughing. A woman shouted something and she or someone else banged on a pot. The world was going on living, and he with it, lying on the ground. He thought he should be afraid but felt only a kind of surprise, and a flattened, distant interest in what had made him fall.

He sat, and in a moment realized that he had only imagined sitting up, that he was still lying there, looking through the blades of leaves and overarching tassels of corn to the ceiling. He put his whole attention scrupulously on the task of sitting, but his mind seemingly had separated itself from his body, and the body ignored the mind's decision, went on lying quietly on the ground, peering up at the glare of daylight. He shut his eyes; shut his one eye, because the other, disobeying him, went on looking into the sky. A mote swam into his field of vision, became a cowbird or a young starling flying against the distant girders. People once had examined the flights of birds for auguries of the future. He wondered what he should understand from this single cowbird flying across his single eye.

A wordless anxious shakiness moved into his chest. *Do you know what this means?* he thought desperately, but without knowing where this question came from or who it was meant for; it was nonsensical, unanswerable.

An involuntary tear scribed a slow arc down to the hinge of his jaw and into the nape of his hair. "Uh," he said, not a word but a vague protest, and the sound vibrated dryly on his tongue. He was surprised by the small hoarse moaning and tried to say something more definite, a coherent complaint or an appeal, but couldn't get anything more to come out of his mouth. And his mind, too, disobeyed him, becoming independent of his desires. He began helplessly, silently, to turn over and over the irrelevant repetitions of jumping-rope rhymes, of lullabies and work chants, ritual blessings for tools and crops, *bless this, bless this, bless this seed.* The center slowly gave way and he drifted into a jumble of unconnected words, a silent stream that flooded his brain with impression, with indecipherable meaning—*when show don't ever where next come call me come call heaven call to me don't don't,* and from that unknown place he slid seamlessly down to fragments, syllables, and finally into a silence that poured into him and washed his brain clear, and he lay mindlessly, not thinking at all, simply feeling in his bones, his blood, the swift wheeling of the earth, the weight of his body against the ground, the clammy June heat against his skin.

The dirt sifted dryly, and a snake came up on the rise of his ribs. A measureless time had passed. He was startled, muddled, as when he would sleep in the daytime and wake without knowing if it was early morning or twilight. The snake was black, very long. Humberto wasn't afraid of it—musaranaj ate other reptiles, even venomous snakes—but his skin shuddered involuntarily, a belated intent to move away, to let the snake get by him without touching. From the lower edge of his tearing eyes he watched the snake's head and forepart resting delicately on air, centimeters above the buttons of his shirt. It tasted his smell silently with a thin, scissored tongue.

In the snake's lidless eyes it was impossible to see its soul, and after a moment Humberto shifted his own eye away uneasily. What was this distance between human beings and snakes? He felt a closer kinship with ants and fish than with the utterly alien intelligence of snakes. There wasn't anything in a snake's life he was able to recognize: no family ties, sociability, playfulness, joy in living, no devotion to their young. It seemed to him, a snake was all predation, toothless jaws that took animals in whole. They were lengths of thick vine that had become unexpectedly muscular, fluent, blood-filled—who knew why?

If it ever had looked at him, the snake looked away now, the broad shovel-tip of the head turning indifferently as it gathered its thick limb to get over his obstruction. He was obscurely ashamed to be inanimate, to be taken for a warmed stone or a toppled tree lying between the rows of corn. The musarana insinuated itself languorously across his body but then settled into the triangular space between his outflung elbow and his ribs. The snake was heavy and sinewy, two meters long, but it coiled neatly into the small enclosure there, in the tented heat and darkness beneath a fold of his shirt.

He had touched wild birds, several of them, during the little time he'd been apprenticed to Ridaro Rogelio, the ornithologist. And a few times, in the sutago beneath a house, gathering up drifts of leaves or taking a look at the kitchen plumbing, he had found sick opossums or porcupines recuperating or dying, had touched a few of them accidentally or because he had thought them dead. He had touched snakes and lizards in the rescue of chicks or chicken eggs. But he realized: This was the first time he had *been* touched by a living, unrestrained, undomesticated animal. He was inexplicably gratified by the snake's settling against his body, as if its trust in his innocence was something he could take credit for.

He was conscious of holding still, of holding in a breath, stilling a heartbeat; but gradually the unmoving weight of the snake began to seem an extension of himself, a massy benign tumor obtruded from his armpit, and his stillness became devotion, a kind of exaltation. When he shut his one movable eye he imagined himself imbued as the trees are, with silence and equanimity in the midst of irrational things. He began simply to wait, growing passive, receptive. Waiting for what? he wondered. For night? sleep? death? the stars?

His mind wandered, and he dreamed that he slept. When the weeds stirred softly and a draft opened against his shirt, he said, "Vilef," to keep his son from wriggling away from his side. Vilef was four, had been mobile for more than a year, could move himself small distances by an undulating flapping of his elbows and hips. Or he was dead, had been dead for more than eight years.

"There's beetles in the grass," the boy said, not wanting to be held.

There was a particular perfume he gave off when he'd been lying asleep and flushed with heat. Humberto breathed it in, the piercingly nostalgic smell of his son's skin. He opened his eyes. "Vilef," he said.

The boy's shortened arms were single-digited, atrophied, his body a kind of writhing divided limb without hips or buttocks, the thin legs flaccid and unjointed, but he rolled his skinny, pliant body on the canes of fallen corn, looking back at Humberto. His small head was slung sideward on the long thin stalk of his neck, his mouth open in that heartbreakingly familiar way, a sagging grin, the small rows of teeth straight and neat, perfectly formed.

"I want to look for beetles," the boy said, stubbornly pleading.

He was naked, his pale skin rosy where it clung to bone at elbows, heels, chin, the tips of his pointy single fingers; deep mauve where there was heat, darkness, dampness—his genitals, the cave of his mouth, the smooth hollows at the axilla of shoulder and arm. Humberto fixed his eyes on the small dark muscle of his son's tongue moving in the dark mouth. Vilef never had spoken in his five years of life. Whose voice was issuing from his mouth? "Come here," Humberto said. "Come and lay down here with me."

The boy wobbled as if boneless, as if he were a curved blade of grass trembling and swaying, weighted by a bead of rain. The leaves shook slightly with his nervous fidgeting. Humberto was helpless, must wait for his son to come or to wriggle away.

"You fell down," the boy said, explaining something.

"I'm just sleeping. Come here and sleep with me."

Vilef grinned foolishly, rocking up on his flexuous waist, and then he settled himself against Humberto's ribs again. He lay with his small head flung back, his face turned up to the daylight, his mouth open to catch the falling rays of the xenon lamps. His heated fragrance filled Humberto with an excruciatingly indefinable impulse.

Vilef breathed noisily. "Tell the names of birds," he demanded.

Humberto stared skyward where the spars of the ceiling were wound with thready clouds—a gathering of afternoon humidity, the incipience of the evening rain. A cowbird still flew there, beating back and forth within the frame of Humberto's view, the coarse fringe of leaves and tassels of corn.

"There is a brown cowbird," he said. He felt around for the nib of a memory, something he once had known. "They slip into other birds' nests, Vilef, and leave their eggs to be brooded and hatched by that other family."

The boy made a dry *cht*, birdlike, a sound of puzzlement. "Why?" he said.

"I don't know."

"Do those other birds care?"

He considered. "I don't know that either. They raise the young cowbirds with their own children. I don't know if they mind doing it."

He and his son watched the cowbird in silence. The bird drew a barely perceptible network of lines on the sky, its wing-beats snagging and trailing the mist.

"More," Vilef said solemnly.

"Gray's thrushes, and ruddy ground-doves," he said, "build their nests on the bananas, right on the ripening bunch, where the fingers of the fruit reach up and hold it cupped like this." He formed the intent to gesture delicately, stiff-fingered with one hand, but nothing came of it. His hands remained outspread, lying on the ground, inattentive. Vilef held one of his own formless hands up, the single finger pointing from his bird-like, truncated arm. "Like this," he said, and Humberto, smiling, feeling that he was smiling, answered, "Yes." Then he said, "Tanagers hide their nest in the center of the bunch, between the hands of the fruit. Sometimes, in the days between building the nest and feeding the babies, the fruit thickens, and the gap where they pass through becomes so narrow they finally can't slip in and out; then sometimes their children must starve."

"I would widen the doorway," Vilef said staunchly, and Humberto said, "Yes, I have done that."

"What else," Vilef said after a small silence.

He cast around in his memory. "Some woodpeckers live in families, aunts and uncles and parents and children all together sleeping in a single house. And the ani birds live in great shared domaroj, laying all their eggs together and rearing their children in a bunch without setting one apart from another."

"More."

"They perch in long rows, anis do, all facing the same way, ten or fifteen or twenty of them crowded together; when a bird at an end of the long row wants to move to the opposite end, it walks over the backs of the others." Vilef made a wet loose sound in his throat, his habitual choking laugh, and Humberto's heart, from habit, clenched and released in a spasm of love. How easily the old responses reinhabited his body!

"I have looked for you," he declared tearfully, meaning something that was unfathomable even to himself. Vilef rocked his small round skull, and the heat of his breath blew intermittently against Humberto's ribs.

"Where did you look?" the boy asked dreamily.

Humberto felt himself caught in a mindless turbulence, a flood of echo, chord, vibration. Something latent and formless, long preparing, had arrived. "Where should I have looked?" he answered.

Vilef made a cunning sound, *huh huh huh,* the same dry, calculated chuckle he used to make in his sleep all those years ago, before the sheer weight of his own outsize heart had progressively strangled and killed him. Humberto strained to see his son's face; from the lower edge of an eye he watched the tip of a tongue searching the corner of a mouth, not able to distinguish whether it was his own tongue, his own mouth, or Vilef's. "You know where," Vilef said slyly.

He did know. Something turned inside him. He gave up straining to see his son's face; he looked up through the halo of light into the faraway framework of the ceiling, but then shut his eye, and through the transparent membrane saw the paths of blood in a carp's eye, in a dragonfly's wing, in the body of a tick.

"Pac̆jo," his son said, and touched his outflung wrist. The heat in the touch startled him, jerked his eye open, and his grown son Ĉejo stood leaning down to him, his round face creased, worried—"Pac̆jo, why are you lying here?"—and behind him, another face, an unknown girl with eyebrows thin as fingernail parings, her mouth an open bow. His other son, Vilef, had already slipped away from his side as swift and silent as if he'd been delivered whole into heaven.

On the old terms, he said, clutching his son's hand, or meaning to clutch it, meaning to say, *It must be on the old terms.*

A small hoarse croaking came out of his mouth, and the sound drained him of anguish—he felt suddenly empty and free, as if his soul could leave his body in the next moment. He hovered there, at that charged balance point of his existence, holding out to his son on the delicate upturned cup of his hand as if it were a construct of moss and twigs and brown maize, an unnamed land. Ĉejo shook his head or shuddered, uncomprehending, and the moment went forward with a small stir of Humberto's heart. He fell back inside the days of his life as into a hollow vessel, full of familiar voices and people, of seasons repeating themselves, of sorrow and joy going out, returning, waiting, undreamed of.

7

Bjoro

I sing the body electric,
The armies of those I love engirth me and I engirth them.
They will not let me off till I go with them, respond to them,
And discorrupt them, and charge them full with the
*   charge of the soul.*
Was it doubted that those who corrupt their own bodies
*   conceal themselves?*
And if those who defile the living are as bad as they who
*   defile the dead?*
And if the body does not do fully as much as the soul?
And if the body were not the soul, what is the soul?

WHEN THE AIRLOCK was opened, the quick rush of the draft was like a wind, piercing cold, bitter against Bjoro's skin, and at once he began to shake. He had had thirty-one days in the closeness and warmth of the *Ruby* to get over his chill, but now his body swiftly gave up its heat and he felt as he had when

Luza had strapped him in the gondola of the balloon, the bones of his ribcage enclosing a central, numbing cold. Eighty or a hundred people were gathered there in the south pole of the *Miller* in the big open docking arena, a great daunting welcome, and it struck him bitterly that this was a mortafesto as much as a celebration of homecoming.

When he looked for his wife in the faces suddenly crowding him—a jumble of grins and moving mouths, unrecognizable—he had a sudden, unexpected glimpse of Luza. On the *Ruby* they had made an unspoken agreement not to say too much; they had kept to things that were devoid of pain, had kept clear of talk about the crash, Peder's dying, the pale, fluttery tangle of Isuma's balloon pitching down the night sky. In the silences between them there had been a kind of tender closeness. Now all at once he wasn't able to bear Luza's look, bear looking at her. When their eyes touched, he shifted his own away jerkily. A clot of anguish and impenetrable rage swelled in his throat. He knew if he let his mouth open, a thick dumb wordless shout would fly from it.

Juko appeared suddenly among the faces. She was keeping a fierce smile, her lips in a wide line which she pressed against his ear. "Where've-you-been?" she said, whispering their old homecoming usage. He wasn't able to answer: *out-of-the-way*. He had imagined this reuniting, imagined that she might be moved enough to weep, and he would taste her tears on his tongue. But her face was familiar, unsentimental, and his body was stiff and numb with cold, he wasn't able to bend it to his will. He lowered his head effortfully and let his mouth down against the crown of her head; on his tongue was the dry, acerbic taste of her hair.

Some of the faces around him became members of his family, his sister, niece, cousins, brother-in-law, an intricate web of relations he felt helpless to negotiate. "Paćjo," his daughter murmured to him, and put herself under his armpit in her familiar way. He put his arm around her shakily. Juko had been on his other side gripping his hand, but now she let him go, and it was his son Eneo holding that hand suddenly and saying something to him, and he was grateful for the cacophony of people's voices relieving him of the necessity of hearing the words, or of speaking. He felt distanced from his wife, his relatives, his children, as if years had passed and meanwhile they had become other people.

Someone, maybe it was his sister Olinda's husband, said irritably, "Make them a way through. Let them go home, eh?" and other people gradually took up this proprietary mustering. The crowd opened a little, swimming slowly against the free-fall, and let the crew of the *Ruby* and their families go out of the docking arena and up the winding corridors to the gallery of lifts. When people spoke to him he tried to smile, but went on unable to speak, his brain filled with a jittery misery. The heat of his son's hand became his point of concentration. He felt mercurial, transient, was dimly grateful for Eneo's clasp anchoring him to a fixed base.

For years he had been piloting tugs, had made three or four space junkets as long as this one—longer. He always had dreaded the heaviness, coming down to the torus after those long periods of free-fall, had been days getting back his land legs. But now crowded in the lift with the nine or ten members of his family, he found an obscure comfort in the way his body felt taking on quick weight, substance, falling heavily down from the center. He thought, *All right. All right, now,* giving himself a kind of rebuke.

He looked for Juko. She stood holding the hand of his young granddaughter, but she was watching him with a look that was anxious and wary—a surprise. He reached for her suddenly, put his arms around her in a fierce clench. Her back shook briefly under his hands—she was letting go of a few tears—and when he understood this, he experienced a moment of exhilaration and loosening. "Ended," he said in a hoarse voice, and sobbed out loud. Other people in the lift began to weep too, their hands reaching to touch him, to stroke his cheek, pet his arm. "Yes. Yes," his family said, "the old *Ruby* has got home. Gift of God."

It was a vast surprise to come out into the *Miller's* yellowish, humid daylight and find the jacaranda trees still in bloom, their lavender blossoms seeming impossibly glorious after long days and nights at the edge of the gray lake, weeks of incandescent lamps and tiny metal rooms in the *Ruby.* He was a technologist, not a botanist; a mechanic, not a farmer. It struck him that he had lived his life until now without ever looking on the landscape of his world. Now the brilliant green of the rice, the scarlet passionflowers against the rank verdure, the high-up ceiling, hazy with cloud and refracted light, filled him with helpless longing and love.

He hadn't thought of his mother being absent from the homecoming until he saw her standing in front of the house, squared on her feet, peering with her bad eyes down the path into the bunch of them coming up toward her. Maybe it was the hub she had stayed away from, she had a hatred of the free-fall now she was old. Neighbors, his mother's friends, his wife's relatives, were with her, standing about in the narrow path and the little garden before the house, waiting for him.

When he saw how many there were, a kind of exhausted panic made his legs suddenly unsteady: He wanted to be let alone, not be made the center of their celebrating. Kristina's eyes picked him out finally, gave him a long narrow look, and then he heard her dry voice suddenly over the others, she was turning to her friends, pulling at their arms. "My son is way-worn, used up," she was saying. "We'll let him sleep, eh?" It was a terrible moment, realizing his mother had seen this in his face as if he must still be a child. But when people started going off meekly, he was weak with gratitude.

He hadn't believed her advice to people was meant to be absolute, but when he came up the ladder onto the loǵio of the house she pushed him into the little apartment, the little room he and Juko slept in, and the two women rolled the bed out and put him onto it. His skin was rough with cold, and they covered him with a sheet, put a pot of tea on the floor beside the bed, closed the shutters over the window casement to shut out the daylight and people's voices. They behaved as if he were sick, and he let them behave that way. He submitted to everything helplessly, not having the strength for explaining, the will for protesting.

They left him alone in the room. As soon as the wall was closed, a burning anguish sprang up in his chest. He worked his brain, grappling to give a name to his feeling. He had yearned to be alone, but now, alone, he realized he wanted his wife to get into bed with him. He wanted her to lie with him on the bed without speaking, with the heat of her torso pressing against him in wordless, undemanding sympathy. He wanted her to hold him like a sick child until he slept, and he blamed her for not realizing this.

He drew his knees up and huddled on the mat, under the heavy weight of the air, shaking with cold and self-pity and irrational resentment. He could hear his relatives and neighbors talking softly on the other side of the thin wall, their voices an indistinguishable murmur. When he heard a word, it was meaningless, irrelevant. "Point," he heard someone say, and later, "Carry down." He realized he was straining to hear his own name, he wanted to overhear them talking about his health, his grief of heart, how much they had missed him, how much he had suffered.

He wasn't able to keep his eyes shut. His look jumped anxiously, distractedly around the room, not settling anywhere, not focusing on anything. The house had a quality not just of unfamiliarity but of transcendent strangeness, as if his whole experience had been a life in the branches of trees. He thrashed about, restless, until he was crouched on his knees with his forehead pressed against the mattress. He rocked on his head, his knees, the pressure behind his eyes making a wavery kaleidoscope of yellows and reds. Gradually the rocking soothed him. He slept a little in a milieu of feverish dreams and woke exhausted, sweating under the sheet. It was dusk, and the room's shadowiness, the dim light cast through the papery panes of the wall, disoriented and oppressed him. He saw that Juko, or someone, had gotten the room unaccustomedly clean, the individual motes of dust on the floor boards a testament to recent washing.

He sat on the mat, his body heavy and dull, and held his head in the cups of his hands until he was fully awake. Voices were still speaking softly somewhere in the house, a sound that made him feel excluded and vaguely sorrowful. He stood up and slid back the door. Juko sat in the dimming light beside the casement in the common room, braiding rattan. His mother sat near her, shelling beans in a battered clay bowl. When he opened the door, they both looked at him critically.

"When did you eat, eh? Are you hungry?" his mother said, and made a movement as if she might be drawing her feet under her. Juko murmured something and stood up, put on the lamp in the galley, and Kristina settled again with her fists sprouting long fingers of beans. Bjoro stood in the doorway of their sleeping room, watching his wife heating soup, shredding cabbage, putting a thin knife to mushrooms and leeks. When she looked at him, he kept his eyes on the blade of the knife.

"People are worrying about you," Juko said. From the edge of his stare he could see his mother's face in a gathered-up frown, and between Juko's straight eyebrows a shirring of pleats. But the other members of his family had gone. What should he understand from that? That some people had become impatient, waiting for him to be over his suffering? He shook his head. Then he said, "It was all right," without knowing what he meant. The crowd of people at the dock? Peder's dying? Isuma's?

Juko, with the edge of one hand, swept the greens to his bowl, poured the soup over, brought the bowl steaming to the low table. "Bjoro," she said, reaching for him. "Come and eat." She had a gentle tone of voice, and her eyes touched him lightly as if he had become fragile. He sat on the floor with his knees under the table and ate Juko's soup. It was an unspeakable luxury after weeks of pastes and reconstituted freeze-dry. The two women watched him eat, their faces smoothing out, evidently taking pleasure in it. When he had emptied the bowl, Juko stood and filled it up again.

Bjoro said, trying to smile, "It was almost the worst thing, the bad edibles."

Kristina nodded firmly. "You can bear anything if you have good food," she said. This wasn't true but it had truth in it, and his mother doubtless believed it; she was someone who always would bring bread to a mortafesto, soup to the sick, though she never had liked to prepare daily meals. Her preference as cook was a breadnut tortilla rolled around scraps and leavings of food.

"And sleep, a good bed," Juko said, murmuring. The two women exchanged a closed look. They had a habit of leaving him out of certain things, never would tell him their meaning unless he asked, and maybe not the truth then. He always had resented such moments, and gradually had got away from asking for explanations. But he thought he understood this one. Juko, when she was divorcing Humberto Indergard, had moved in with Kristina and mostly stayed in her bed for weeks. His mother had had the Clearness Committee in to see her, but mostly let her sleep, and sleep, so long as she came out to eat healthy meals.

He said, his voice hoarse, "There was not much sleeping on the *Ruby*."

Their faces looked at him in constrained surprise. "No. No, I guess not, Bjoro," they said to him, without either of them asking what it was that had kept him from sleeping. *It was dreams of the dead*, he had planned to say bitterly, and the unspoken words settled in his chest, constricting his breath.

They talked around him. Maybe they were resuming a

conversation they'd been having while he slept. "Old Kelling is getting off the Advices and Queries Committee," Kristina was saying. "He's been telling everybody his health is broken."

"Oh, he always worries too much about his health, Kelling does." Juko's attention again was on the wickerwork. She worked the strands deftly, examining them under the lamp. "How old is he? Seventy? He'll get to be a hundred, but he'll complain every day until then, about his bad health."

Kristina nodded. "There's a man in my family who has a loose valve in his heart," she said. "He never has spent a minute of his life complaining about his health, eh?" She was back at her work too, shelling the beans. She took them out of a gunny bag two or three at a time. The pods were mottled, purplish, papery; she had made a little loose mountain of the empty ones beside one of her knees. The beans in the bowl were creamy beneath faint purple whorls.

"Is that Orid Finĉ?" Juko asked her, glancing up from the braiding.

His mother nodded. "Orid never complains about his heart. Only he has a pale look, and if you put your head on his chest you can hear a kind of whistling sound when the blood moves."

Bjoro knew Orid Finĉ. Orid was seventy, his hair white and silken framing a long face, without any resemblance to Peder Ojama except in the sound blood made, leaking behind a breast bone.

Juko teased Kristina solemnly. "You had your head on Orid's chest."

His mother showed her yellowing teeth. "That was a long time ago." Then she said, closing her mouth to a sly smile, "He is only a relation by marriage."

Juko laughed. In a moment she said, "When I was little there was a blind woman in our neighborhood. Did you know her? I don't remember her name. Maybe it was Pena? Or Lena?" Kristina shook her head. "Well anyway. This woman had a cane and walked about without any trouble, it seemed to me. I liked to play as if I was blind, eh? Shut my eyes and go out on the footway or the fields and find my way around. But I never could keep my eyes shut all the way tight." She smiled ironically.

They went on telling these stories of health and infirmity, first Kristina and then Juko, while Bjoro silently emptied the bowl of soup by spoonfuls. When he lifted the bowl to his mouth for the last of it Kristina said, eyeing him, "We sent everybody away. We swept them out of here with a broom, eh? They can come back tomorrow when you've got rested up. You know Leon Thorssen is clerk of the Yearly Meeting now that Guner Ĝohanesen has died? He maybe hasn't got old Guner's patience: He came with five people from that Planning Committee and wanted you to tell what you saw. What was he thinking! Some of them went over to Luza Kordoba's house, too, but I bet Luza's spouse—what's her name? Tereza?—pushed them out the same as we did. To come today, the very day you are home! the very hour! We told them to come back tomorrow. All that business can wait, eh? You won't forget how to tell what you saw. Anyway, they won't be publishing the Advices and Queries anytime soon. We said you needed a sleep. And to eat. Are you full now? Do you want to get into bed again?" She touched Juko's arm. "Put him to bed, Juko. He has something he wants to give you, I bet, something he's been saving." She flashed a narrow smile. She considered intercourse, along with food and sleep, essential to life.

Juko laughed and put her hand softly on his back. He didn't

know what this touch meant—whether she was telling him she was anxious to copulate with him, or consoling him for being too tired, too filled with grief, to consummate his homecoming in that usual way.

He didn't feel interested in intercourse with Juko—moving his body was a ponderous effort in the unaccustomed gravity, and he had had only brief, edgy rest for weeks. But he had lost his craving to wrap his cold legs around his wife and lie in her arms like a sick child. Her hand on his back patronized and irritated him.

"I haven't needed fucking, only sleep," he said harshly.

This startled them, and they looked at him in a guarded way. It wasn't their usual practice, this tiptoeing around his feelings. The two of them always had shared a directness, a willingness to chide him, and their silence seemed a kind of humiliation. He felt a sudden impulse to say something else, to accuse them of something, but his brain wasn't able to bring it forward.

Juko stood with the empty soup bowl and washed it at the galley's little cold-water tap, put away the scraps of food, wiped down the chopping board. While she was doing this, Bjoro's mother watched him across the heap of shelled beans. Gradually his choking anger loosened, and he said tiredly, "I've not had much sleep for more than three weeks."

This was a condition they felt able to understand. They looked at him with affectionate tolerance. "I'll come to bed with you," Juko said, and reached her hand down to him. He stood slowly and let her lead him back into their room.

It was close and hot and dark, and smelled of his sweat. She went to the shutters to let the night air come in, but he said, low-voiced, "No. Will you leave them shut, Juko?" Her face searched him out blindly in the darkness.

"Are you not over being cold, then?" she said to him in a murmur. He wasn't able to answer, but she came away from the window again, left the room closed up.

He sat on the mat heavily. She knelt behind him and began to knead his shoulders. She was tender, thorough, she knew the places that held on to tiredness. He shut his eyes.

"Do you know?" Juko said softly. "Peder's wife dreamed her husband's death, before the *Ruby* was gone, but kept from saying so." Bjoro's eyes became hot with unshed tears. She waited, and when he didn't answer, she went on. "I'm sorry for what happened to Isuma and Peder." Her voice became almost a whisper. "I'm sorry."

He didn't know why her insistent sympathy, the urgency of her thin voice, angered him. He realized, he didn't feel grief for Peder's wife, but for himself.

"Dreaming of death is something we will do every day, on that world," he said bitterly.

She kept kneading his back and shoulders in silence. Her fingers were strong. Sometimes she flattened her palms and pushed the heels of her hands up and down the valley between his shoulder blades, either side of his spine. Gradually the rhythmic stroking aroused him a little. He was still wearing the caparajos they all had favored in the *Ruby,* and he thought his erection was hidden in the freedom of the loose trousers, but Juko whispered, "Do you want to lay with me now?"

"Yes," he said hoarsely.

He stood and pushed his trousers down from his hips. Juko laughed. "I guess you do," she said.

He lay heavily on the mattress, inert, and she knelt over him kissing his chest lightly and his soft belly and the urgent rigidity of his penis, stroking his cold skin with her hands and her mouth. She was patient, willing, and that built his inexplicable anger. He didn't know what he wanted from her, but when she took one of his hands and put it under her shirt, cupping a breast, prompting him, he convulsed suddenly with rageful passion. He seized her with both hands, rocking up wildly and then turning onto his knees to put her body under him. She braced her arms against his weight but she was pulling at her own shirt, working ahead of his pent-up rush. In an urgent fire, he grappled her trousers down, shoved her legs open with his knees. She was moving under him, murmuring, words he wasn't able to hear. He climbed on her, his elbows across the bones of her arms, and she twisted and her breath let out a high gasping sound of pain that made his skull hum. He pushed himself against her, groping, his penis beating against her pubic bone. Behind his teeth a whining sound arose, as he thrust against her uselessly, wild with defeat. He became aware that her mouth was open, that she was letting out a continuous whimpering complaint. She struggled under him, pushing against his weight.

In a frenzy he jerked her by the arm, the leg, onto her belly and hooked his arms under her thighs, lifting her buttocks to him. Another, higher sound came from her, or a word, *what* or *wait*, but eclipsed by the heavy booming inside his skull. It was another wife, it was Hlavka, with whom he used to have anal sex. But recklessly, uncontrollably, he forced himself into Juko's anus, and the sound she was making became a toneless, gasping crying, a thin wail that raised a singing under his scalp. He pumped against her with a terrible fury, his arms braced rigidly beneath her thighs, until his muscles loosened and shook with fatigue, until finally he was too heavy, too tired to keep on with it, and he rolled away whimpering, without release, and held his penis in both his hands, pulling on it in an exhausted rage until a short hot spurt of semen wet his thigh.

He released a few hot tears as well, and a clenched moan of misery. Then in the slowly cooling sweat of heat and fire, lying on the bed in the darkness with his hands still clasping his flaccid penis, he felt relieved of something, as if he had emptied himself of waste. When he realized he was searching for something in the blackness of the ceiling, he deliberately shut his eyes.

He became aware of his mother moving in the small alcove where she lay at night; and then he began to hear Juko's short huffing breath containing some louder sound of tears or fury. When she moved against his back, shifting away on the bed, he rolled his head toward her. She crouched on the mat of their bed, her hands pressed over her mouth, her knees flattening her breasts. Behind her hands was the sound of grievous breathing. Bjoro's limbs filled with a ponderous dull guilt and pain. Reflexively he began to go over and over what had happened, conceiving other endings, other beginnings, words said or unsaid, until he was no longer certain what the truth was, though he imagined the detail of gestures, silences, tears. *I forgot which wife I was with*, he thought of saying. In his mind, in the peacemaking that had not yet begun, Juko was mournful and forgiving; she took some of the fault onto herself.

"Juko," he said sorrowfully. She made a sound, a catching of air, and stood up, pushing away the tangled shirt and trousers stiffly and going from the room naked. He lay in a heavy lethargy in the darkness while water ran in the sink, and his mother's voice asked something. Kristina knew the sounds people made, wrestling on a bed, she maybe had heard Juko's held-in wailing and imagined—what? He wasn't able to hear what she asked, but his wife's harsh answer, illuminating nothing: "No, go to sleep, Kristina, go to sleep."

When the water was shut off, he thought he heard a door sliding, and imagined Juko taking the old manta they kept hanging above the shoe bench, a cape against the rain for people who walked anywhere after dark, and settling angrily on the narrow boards of the pasado with the cape pulled up like a blanket over her breasts. Then he imagined her putting on the cape and walking around to Senlima or Alaŭdo, to her brother's house or her son's, and a cold anxiety rose in his body. But she came into the room again. Her shape moving against the darkness was erect, stiff-limbed, her small breasts lay against her ribs. She went around him lying on the mat, went to the casement and pushed open the shutters. Then, in the night light falling into the room, she got into a clean shirt and trousers, her arms swinging in short, jerky arcs. He sat up on the bed and watched her with a kind of thrilling dread.

"I haven't—" he whispered. "It wasn't—"

Without stopping what she was doing she said to him in a furious whisper, "I won't have a husband who thinks I am a hole to stick his penis into."

He put his head into his hands. "I have killed our marriage," he said piteously. Juko blew a wordless sound through her lips, something made up equally of anger and amusement, as if she considered this bathetic. He looked at her. She had taken her dirty shirt and begun to push things unsystematically into the middle of it, unrelated objects from shelves and trunks: a hat, a hank of thread, old sandals, a scarf embroidered by Humberto Indergard. He stood shakily. "I was crazy," he said, opening his hands, murmuring. "There isn't any reason why you should forgive me. It was a bad thing to do. I was crazy."

She pulled the sleeves of the shirt into a bundle and held it against her chest. In the darkness her face was a shining mask of pain and bitterness. She said, thick and low, "I'll live in my brother's house until you are sane again."

He made a lost sound, and when she shifted her weight to move he put his arms around her desperately, the bulk of the bundle between them. She became rigid, standing with her face turned from him, waiting to be let go. Through the open casement of the window he heard voices speaking, the clack of a loom, someone's child crying, an enigmatic, quick patting of hands. He realized irrelevantly that the daylight was barely gone. In the incomplete darkness, not many people were sleeping yet. In Kristina's little grotto under the stairs of the sadaŭ, there was silence. She had a practice of intruding herself in their arguments, of taking Juko's part in any quarrel, and he felt her reticence now was a fearful sign. He stood holding his wife hard in his arms, unable to speak or act effectively. Her breath going in and out of her mouth made a bristly sound that he felt along his bones, like a scraping of metal.

In a while she said, "Let loose, Bjoro," her voice shaking under the weight of anger.

He said hoarsely, "Please, Juko, make peace with me. Please. I behaved in a bad way. I was crazy." He put his mouth against the crown of her head, whispering desolately, "I didn't know I was hurting you."

She reared against him, jerking her head, and his teeth

rammed the inside of his mouth. He tightened his arms con-
vulsively and went on holding her, rigid with fear. She twisted,
turning her face toward him, her mouth misshapen. The bottom lids of her eyes brimmed with tears. *"Don't say you didn't
know you were doing it!"* she said in a wild whisper.

He didn't have an answer. He looked away helplessly. "I was
crazy," he said in a rising wail.

Juko sobbed suddenly, and this unexpected sound from
her drove the air out of Bjoro's lungs in a hiccup of surprised
terror. He hooked his chin over the pitch of her shoulder and
turned his face into her neck. The heated, pungent, woman-
ish odor of her skin overwhelmed him with grief. "I'm sorry,
Juko. I'm sorry," he murmured repeatedly, and tears ran in his
mouth and stung him where his teeth had cut the inside of his
cheek. But when she had loosed three or four long roupy sobs,
shuddering against him, he understood that her tears signaled a
kind of yielding, an adjustment. His own crying became relief,
and when she made a weak, insinuating effort to get out of his
clasp, he loosened his arms. The bundled-up shirt slid down to
the floor.

Juko brought the heels of her hands to her face and let them
rest there, standing breathing hard over the little hillock of
her goods. Bjoro stood, not touching her, with his arms still
raised slightly, unfinished with letting her go. After a while
she dropped her hands and made a slight, tired movement of
indecision or despair and then lay down heavily on the mat, on
her hip, crossing one arm over her eyes. Bjoro in a moment sat
carefully below her feet. He waited, and when she didn't speak
he put a hand on his wife's foot. It was bare, clammy.

The world moved under them in a ceaseless regulated

sweeping. In the darkness, her smell was familiar, the sound of her breathing familiar to him. His fingers, closing on the small bones of her foot, warmed it slowly. Finally he came around the bed slowly and lay down beside her. He felt heavy and exhausted, tired of anxiety. Lying on his back looking into the ceiling, he realized he was waiting for the damp weight of the darkness and the silence to deaden their crisis. After a while she sighed, her little breath descending in him, rising out of him, sweeping up a windrow of weeds and old leaves.

He slept and woke, slept and woke. Juko lay unmoving, her eyes hidden behind her arm, her breath heavy and slow. It was impossible to tell if she was awake or asleep. The third or fourth time he woke and looked at her, her arm had slipped down and she lay with her mouth slack against the mattress, her eyes jumping behind the lids. He felt a brief spurt of shame, as if what he saw was intimate and revealing, but he wasn't able to stop watching her dreaming, the tips of her fingers spasming helplessly. A tenderness and love for his wife engulfed him suddenly, and when the dream slipped out of her, when her face became minutely tighter, less defenseless, he wasn't able to go on watching her, or loving her. In the darkness he put on his trousers and went softly out of the room, the house.

It was preparing to rain, the night air humid and heavy. The weak light cast out of houses threw black shadows along the walls. Chickens slept along the eaves of roofs, on the tops of walls, and among the yellow trumpets of the ajamanda vines that climbed over arbors at the edges of fields. Bjoro stood on the bottom step of his house, looking without holding anything in his mind, and then started downhill following the footway between the crowded houses, under the star-shaped shadows of the trees. The murmuring restlessness of people inside the houses was an inescapable field of sound. As he stood beside the clamor of the Falls From Grace waiting for the lift, a rain began, and his breath came hard in the clammy night. The ambient light was dimly yellow; the rain falling through it looked fine and white as snow. It was an unexpected summoning of another landscape, and brought with it a sudden, vast conviction: The division between himself and Juko was as impenetrable as death, this wife as lost to him as the first. He was choked with self-pity. At Hlavka's death he had felt a fear and knowledge that had overpowered his reason—it had been impossible not to blame her for dying, for succumbing inexplicably to an asthma she'd withstood for thirty years. Now he realized that he blamed Juko, too, in a vague but certain way, for not understanding what he had been unable to articulate.

He took the lift up to the center of the world. He had no expectations, no intentions, but he understood darkly: The metalline, strident, fluorescent chambers of the manufactory were a sacred space for him. Other people oversaw the machinery, kept up the ordinary maintenance and repair, but when there was a breakdown Bjoro was someone they asked to help them with it; he considered the glass kiln and the complicated apparatus of the paper mill and the foundry to be his province. This was a familiar landscape, manageable, ordered, and his yearning for it now seemed a kind of prayer.

In the hub, where certain machinery needed tending, there was work done around the hours: People fiddled at panels and boards, clambered over the machines, in rooms Bjoro looked into. He felt charged with loneliness, with separation, and kept away from the people he saw, kept to the Byzantine passageways in a kind of furtive agitation. No one stood by the keys in the glassworks. Without thinking of doing it, he scaled the batch hopper there, pulling up with his arms in the light air and retreating urgently into the narrow space between the ceiling and the furnace.

The air was hot, thick. When he had climbed the glass kiln, working, he always had protected himself, worn a stoker rig, but now he was barefoot, barechested, and the heat against the skin of his belly gave him an unexpected feeling of liberation, of abandon and risk. He put his hands down delicately, deliberately, against the feverish surface of the furnace and walked on his palms across the metal, his legs and feet following, drifting and buoyant. Beneath him the furnace made a continuous, hot susurration that entered his bones through the burning tips of his fingers.

At the center of the furnace where the batch was fed to the cauldron down a gullet and windpipe, he cooled his hands on the standpipe. There was a place among the conduits, an awkward cranny there, and he settled onto it, giving himself over to the effort of getting a breath into his lungs and out again in the dim heat. He felt pleasantly giddy, empty-headed. His body gave up a little of its lightness, and when his breastbone came down slowly against a gas pipe he reached through the webwork of flues and lines and siphons and scrupulously rested his palms, then his forearms, against the surface of the furnace.

He had once crouched in the narrow chamber of the kremaciejo, holding a wrench on a nut while Opal Nansen had slowly turned the bolt out from the other side. But the furnace had been shut down for days by then, and the crematory cell had been cool and dim. It was inlaid with heat-bearing tiles and

there had been a minute dust of ash on the tiles. He had felt
something integral and clarifying when he had run water in the
sink afterward and carefully rinsed his hands, imagining the
little trickle of gritty, grayish water in the catch basin delivered ultimately to the feet of cabbages, cassavas, mango trees.
Inside the kremaciejo he had been able to slide down onto his
back, stretch his legs out, without imagining his own death. It
was now, in the heat and the narrow, dirty darkness among the
pipes of the glassworks, that he had a sudden apprehension of
his body consumed in fire.

He shut his eyes, with his arms laid trembling against the furnace, and looked inward, following the slight rush of air across
the back of his throat, the intake and outtake of his breath. But
he couldn't keep his attention there, his closed eyes following
the breath out across his teeth and then flying loose in a gasp,
and his arms betraying him involuntarily, recoiling. His eyelids
started open, and he lay in the narrow interstice, huffing his
breath. Clumsily he turned his palms up, examining them in
the dimness; the fleshy pads of his fingers, the heels of his hands
began to whiten and blister as he looked. He extended his arms,
peering at them through a screen of tears. The tender skin on
the inside of his forearms was striped ruby red. He squeezed his
eyelids closed in an exaltation of agony. He had to push himself,
clambering once, twice with his elbows, his heels, to get clear
of the pipes, to free himself from the cleft space between the
conduits before he had the room to pull his arms up, to clasp
the pain like a pillow against his chest.

They had left Peder Ojama's body on the stony ridge, lying
on one hip under a thin sheet of snow. Isuma had told them a
body might lie more or less intact for months, or a year: The

prevailing weather made a slow process of decay. Not many scavengers lived on this world. Bjoro had wondered if she was saying something else, something revealing—that there would be time enough for Peder's family to come back for his body, to collect it for burning. Was she saying, then, that this bitter place was to be their world? He had wanted to argue with Isuma—he had wanted to set fire to the body there on the ridge, in the snow. But she had begun tenderly to arrange the limbs, drawing the knees to the chest, crossing the arms, fitting the hands under the armpits until Peder lay in the posture of a child protecting his center; and Bjoro's mouth had only filled with sourness and heat.

Afterward Luza and Bjoro had stood on the ridge in the blowing wind, watching the spectacular burning of Isuma's wrecked montgolfiere, the lifting flurries of sparks in the black night. And later, in the daylight, in the long waiting while the *Ruby* brought a second balloon round to try again, they had walked over the hummocky grass a kilometer or more to look for Isuma's body among the cooling ashes. The brief hot burning had left a blackish mass on a skeleton, and standing over it, Bjoro had felt something incomprehensible, something brutal and requited.

8

Kristina

*I go from bedside to bedside, I sleep close with the other
    sleepers each in turn,
I dream in my dream all the dreams of the other
    dreamers,
And I become the other dreamers.*

BECAUSE NO ONE in her own household had taken sick, people were quick to ask of Kristina her time, her hands, in families where several people were down. She took on the fetching and the laundry for her neighbor Lavka Valen's household, and then the household of Jakobo Saldado—Jakobo was her dead sister's son—but when she was coming or going from those houses other people would catch her up, to ask if she would do a particular thing: carry the baby a minute; stir the pot; go and see if so-and-so needed a drink or had taken sick overnight. She found the urgent work of getting round to committees had to be done in the odd respite.

She had lately let herself be named to the New World Advisory—they were gathering a consensus on this matter of whether the New World would physically support them. It was this question that would shape the larger one, the question of staying or going, so it wasn't a light matter. Two or three more generations of people must finish their lives out and die on board the old, deteriorating *Miller,* if they gave up the idea of making a niche for themselves on this cold-weather planet and went on looking for another place more amenable.

It was her charge to listen to what people had to say in the committees of Pacema, Bonveno, Revenana. Farms and Waterworks and Science Committees she was seeing ahead of others, but in the end she must see all of them, even Fiber Arts Committees and potters, who would be thinking the point at issue was whether this New World had good seed hairs and stems for weaving, malleable clay for pots.

Eight people had been asked to be on the New World Advisory, their names settled on by agreement of the district clerks. Kristina, when she saw that five of the eight were old people, wondered if the clerks were thinking age was the same thing as wisdom. She didn't quite believe this herself, having known some foolish old people and some sensible children, but she thought people could turn a long life to good account if they worked at it a little. She wasn't unwilling to have this weighty work given to her. But there was a vanishing four-month window for making up their minds about it—it was a work that shouldn't be put off for plagues of illness, she felt.

In Pacema, there were forty people stricken; in Kristina's domaro, five. The sick people had a pungent, stinking urine; their kidneys ached; they took fever and lay weakly in bed, craving water and complaining of burning behind the eyes and on the tongue; and when they'd been sick for seven or eight or nine days, some few died and others began to be well again. No one in Kristina's domaro had yet died. Or only old Edita Salvera who probably would have died soon anyway, she had gotten to be more than ninety years old and in the last few months had slipped into a kind of dream, calling her children and grand-children and great-grandchildren by the names of friends who had been dead for twenty years. Edita, when she took the fever into her body, simply fell into sleep and peacefully let go of life.

Grace of God, people said of Edita's death, which made Kristina twist her mouth in irritation. She wanted to be mind-ful and attentive when she went out of her body. She had an abiding curiosity about the moment of death and considered it a loss to die in one's sleep, ignorant, oblivious. But her irrita-tion had more to do with platitudes than with God. She never had blamed or credited God for things that happened in the world, though it was hard not to hold Someone accountable for all this bad timing.

The accident of chronology had brought a persistent, wide-spread feeling that these particular microbes had come inside the *Miller* by way of Luza and Bjoro, though none of the six in the *Ruby* had come down sick, and the *Miller* always had been prone to epidemics. The population of micro-organisms always had been lively, capricious, unpredictable—in times past, this was blamed on the humid environment and irradiation and the two-thousand-some people living as close to one another as the pages in a book. But now, with a kind of plaintive urgency, people were blaming the New World. Ruby Fever, people were calling this new illness, and no one wanted Luza Kordoba treating the sick members of their family, though Luza always had been a well-respected kura.

It would have been hard enough work to make up their minds quickly without a plague delivered into the breach. *Better the brakes than the spurs,* was a well known axiom, and some problematic questions had gone undecided on the *Dusty Miller* for a hundred years, awaiting unity. Consensus was a method that was understood to be inefficient, cumbrous. It slowed down the introduction of new ideas, made sure that change was well-considered. No one had any experience with decisions that couldn't be put off.

In the press of God's bad timing, Kristina had become impatient with sleep. She had got in the habit of napping once in the daylight, once or twice in the night, and sitting under a lamp while other people were sleeping, holding a magnifying glass over pages of cryptic balloon data, Minutes of Planning Committees, replies to old Advices and Queries. Her own apartment at night was still, empty, no one objected to the light or railed about an old woman ill-using her body. Her son had made a frenzied mission of overhauling the steel mill robotics; he seldom slept in the house. Juko kept away too, was sleeping in her brother's house where someone—Naja, the sister-in-law?—was sick and the old man, Juko's father, had a dementia and needed habitual looking after.

This had given Kristina's neighbors something to gossip about: Maybe Bjoro was working too hard out of a guilty conscience, something to do with his bringing home the plague in his body; and maybe Juko stayed away from her husband because she was afraid to catch a sickness from him. Or maybe she had a guilt of her own—her brother might have scolded her for always, in the past, leaving the old man, old Ŝilko, for him to watch. Of course, there was other gossip as well—neighbors had heard the whispered arguing and crying the night Bjoro came home in the *Ruby*—but Kristina kept herself from listening to it. She didn't know fully what was between her son and her daughter-in-law anyway, only that it had become thick, a shroud, and when both of them were in the apartment it had filled the rooms, silenced them all, kept them from looking in one another's faces. The plague had been a kind of bitter deliverance from that, perhaps one of God's small graces, the timing not off after all.

She turned the pages of the bound Minute book slowly, her watery eyes peering among the endless tedious arguments and petty deliberations of the Bonveno Planning Committee. A man Kristina knew, Gilberto Osborn, was the recording clerk, and he had a neat small hand but a compulsion to write everything down. There were long, irreducible harangues from people whose words would finally carry little weight, and people who would stand aside or be discounted when the sense of the Meeting was gathered up. She had to read pages to find the scarce words of clearness, of judgment, the communal leadings, the congruences. She always had had a short patience for drivel, and from too much reading of Minutes lately she had maybe become intolerant. It wasn't Gil Osborn's fault there were stupid people living in Bonveno district, she thought, but he shouldn't have written down their words. And the clerk over there in Bonveno, Toma something-or-other, shouldn't have let them go on talking after it was clear they weren't saying anything with depth or insight.

She pushed her knuckles against her eyes, a pleasant burning pain. *Oh hell.* She stood effortfully and went out of her apartment and down to the lavejo, as much for relief of tedium and stiff joints as relief of the little pressure on her bladder. The toilet box gave up a thin smell of rot and sweetness, a composting perfume she secretly savored, and once there she made herself comfortable on the seat and waited for a slow, small bowel movement. *What's the matter with them, over there in Bonveno?* she thought irritably. When at last she stood up from the toilet seat, a tiredness settled suddenly into her chest and her pelvis. When she came out from the lavejo and saw the small yellow circle of the lamp in her apartment illuminating the loose stacks of papers, her flattened cushion, her magnifying glass, she thought *Oh hell*, and put out the light and got into bed.

For a while against her closed eyelids there were dim traces on the darkness, the neat handwriting of Gil Osborn. But she wasn't able to apply her mind to those serious matters; she went helplessly over and over the trifling things in her day—the sorting of the Saldados' unfamiliar laundry, an unfinished piece of drafting, the words she had traded back and forth with her nephew about the sexing of chicken eggs. *Why are there so many stupid people over there in Bonveno?* she kept thinking uselessly. In the apartment occupied by Filisa Ilmen's family, some couple began to copulate—the little huffing of the man's breath broke the first delicate skin of Kristina's sleep. In the undefended moment she was struck with grief, and thought suddenly, heavily, *Who can know what he was thinking?*

She went round irresistibly in the early morning to see Luza Kordoba, where she lived over in Senlima. There was a heavy mist along the incurvature so the houses down in those neighborhoods were in fog. Because the gray mornings made her glum, she went above the warm drizzle, keeping to the narrow footway at the edge of the ceiling. Walking up there along the high curve, she was sometimes prone to see the world in a bad way—to catch sight of it suddenly as tubular, meager, ersatz. But she was too tired, today, for farsightedness: The view across the long roofs, the heads of the light poles standing above the fog, was utterly familiar, without the capacity for surprise.

She didn't know which house was Luza's and had to ask a person pruning a tree and then two people cooking on a brazier on the high narrow pasado of the domaro where people had sent her. Senlima houses were down along the maltejo in a tight cluster, with the terraces of their fields climbing up either side. The domaro that Luza Kordoba lived in was built at the edge of the maltejo aqueduct, and Luza and her brother's family and her spouse had a house with a view through the legs of trees that stood higher up on the slope.

Kristina climbed slowly up the stairs to them in their tree-trunk house, standing on every second or third step to press a fist behind one hip where she was aching. Then she had to go from apartment to apartment looking for Luza until she'd found her, she and the woman who must have been her spouse, sitting puzzling over the parts of a little motor, maybe it was a refrigerator motor, that was neatly arrayed on the floor between them. Luza's foot rocked slightly, working the treadle of a cradle where a sick little child slept ruddy-faced, wheezing. The room was a storm of disorder. A strung hammock had become a landing stage for disheveled bedding and towels, unwashed clothing. The table was adrift with unrelated things—a dirty shirt, greasy cutlery, a tangled wad of yarn stuck through with needles.

From the threshold of the apartment Kristina said quietly, "I've brought a cold soup for that sick child."

People had told her there was a baby sick with the plague in Luza's household, and she had made this a reason to come, though she never had known Luza Kordoba more than off-handedly, didn't know her family at all. The sick child was a pretext. Among the Planning Committees and the business clerks of the Monthly Meetings, there was a mistrust of the bal-loon reports and a need to hear the weather and the landscape as human eyes had seen it. Her own son Bjoro had told a few things flatly once, and after that sent people away, but Luza had been patiently telling and retelling everything she'd seen. Twice, Kristina had listened to her long, thorough account and was ashamed that she had a compulsion to hear it again. She didn't know what she expected to get from the repetition except once more a glimpse of her own old bones standing in obdurate cold, her own watery eyes peering toward an unap-proachable horizon.

The woman who might have been Luza's spouse murmured, "Dankon," smiling slightly, and Luza said to Kristina, looking up, "You are Bjoro's mother, eh? Kristina? Do you know my wife, Asa? Come in and talk to us, will you." She gestured over the scattered parts of the motor and grinned. "You can tell us how to get this put back together again, eh?"

Kristina considered her son's mechanical knack had come from her, but she made a polite mocking sound and said, "You're thinking I've got somebody else's know-how." She stepped out of her shoes on the doorsill and came into the house. The narrow galley table was pulled out, littered with rinds of oranges, slime and seeds of pomegranate. She had to pile up bowls in a dirty cooking pot to get a clean space at the edge of it, a place to set down the jar of soup. And then, because she was lately in the habit of making herself helpful in other people's households, she went on for a minute, gathering up the unwashed dishes. Luza's wife laughed quietly when she saw her doing this.

"Our mess hasn't got to do with any of us being sick, eh? Luza's the only one leans toward neatness in this household, and she was gone a hundred days—this is how we lived. Now she's got home and she's not rational, she thinks she's punishing us, not to pick it up." Asa wasn't sheepish. She looked at Luza in amusement.

Luza blew an obscene sound through her lips. "Come and sit down, Kristina. When they have mice making houses in their filthy towels, they'll pick things up maybe."

Kristina's own leaning was toward tidiness—it was all right with her if dust was on a shelf, but she wanted people to put things away in their places. She admired Luza's unflinching stubbornness. "Well hell, then," she said, and began deliberately to undo the work she'd done, to put the dirty dishes back where they'd been, and that got the two women both to laugh.

She came and sat down stiffly beside Asa, on the bare floor. The tatami mat in the room was folded up so they could lay out their work on a sheet of plastic, and the floor was hard against her buttocks. She shifted her weight, easing her bony ankles cross-footed.

Luza was getting at the greasy dust in the motor's little intake, inefficiently poking a twisty rag down each narrow cell of the grid. There were two metal boxes sitting between them with the lids open: One was a tools box and one held a cache of nuts and washers, screws, wire. Asa rummaged in the tools box and got a wrong-sized wrench and tried it against the head of a bolt on a piece of motor that was in her lap. She held the nut on the other end with pliers while she tried another wrench and then the right one and methodically loosened the bolt. Kristina watched this impatiently, without comment. Luza's doorstep declaration might have meant, *Don't* tell us how to get this put back together.

The three of them talked politely about fractious refrigerators, and the view into the legs of the trees, and people's habits of neatness or of sloppiness. Every little while Asa's eyes went over to the sick child, and gradually this moved Kristina to forgive her jumbled house. She watched the baby herself. It had been more than half her life since she had sat watching a sick child of her own, but the sweetish smell of fever on the baby's skin and the whistle of air going in and out of the child's mouth brought a rush of vivid memory. Olinda had been prone to get infections in her ears, her sinuses, and Bjoro three times had grown cysts in his belly. She hadn't thought of those baby days in years.

"What is that child's name?" she asked them.

Luza looked at the baby. "Paŭlo," she said, and looked down again, watching her own hands working. "My brother's son," she said, and after a silence she added, "They have another one. My brother's wife has taken him—the other boy, Jeno—to live with her mother in Mandala until this plague is finished. She thinks maybe she can keep him from getting sick, eh?—no one's caught plague in her mother's house yet."

Asa lifted her eyebrows without raising her eyes to Kristina, and said, "She should have stayed in her own house, here, with her husband and her sister-in-law. People will be thinking all this shit-talk is reasonable, that the plague is rightly named. Ruby Fever—ha! *Luza's own family believes it,* people will be saying now."

Luza released a thin sound, a hissing, without looking up from her twisting of the rag. "People will say what they want. Some people will say, Luza and Bjoro were in the *Ruby* with Arda and Hans for twenty days and nobody got sick, eh?" She shook her head. "Shit-talk sinks to the bottom."

Kristina said glumly, "Sometimes it ought to have a weight tied on to it." She was ruled, these days, by the feeling of time urgently slipping away from them all.

When the sick baby whimpered suddenly and kicked his legs, Asa pushed the motor away from her lap and took the baby boy into it. His little fingers went straight into his mouth. Asa petted him, her spread hand lifting the fine damp strands of the child's hair. "So, so, so," she murmured, rocking on her hips. He lay listlessly with his eyes shut, his mouth loose around the fingers. He went on whimpering dully. Kristina stood up with a soft groan and crossed the room to the sink. Asa said, rocking the child, "Is it fruit, in that soup?"

"I put papaya in it. That's an easy thing to go down." She washed a spoon and brought the soup and spoon back to the woman sitting on the floor with the boy clasped to her chest. Asa coaxed the child to take a little, not on the spoon but on the tip of her finger, whispering in his ear.

Luza said, finishing a long thought, "If people want to blame this New World for the plague, they don't have to be saying it's a bacillus." She looked at Kristina. "It's all the worry and nervous strain puts souls out of balance, and then sickness is let in, eh?" It was an old belief—any kura knew it to be true—and in calmer times most people had faith in it. Kristina believed it herself, and it may have been Luza's words that made her see suddenly from the edge of her eye the aura of her world, a fluttering of colorless anxiety distilling until it became physical: red streamers. But when she startled and turned her head to look, there were the trees standing windless beyond the open casements, and rising above them a light-pole holding skyward its delicate cluster of globes, illuminating the vault of heaven. She had spent a lifetime striving to glimpse what was in the crack between her world and God's, but these small epiphanies always came at inattentive moments; they were shadows that vanished when she focused her eyes. She sat down again with painful stiffness and pressed a fist behind her hip.

"It wasn't sickness my son brought home with him," she said heavily. "I thought it was grief, eh? horror of those deaths, but people just die badly sometimes, I've seen one or two die badly, myself, it wasn't only that. I don't know what he brought home inside him—but something, I don't know, something." She shook her head helplessly.

Luza said in surprise, "I guess I know what it is, it was in both of us." Kristina was able to see the tender pale scalp between the individual hairs of the woman's head—a babyish look. She must have kept her hair cropped short as stubble while on the *Ruby,* and by now it had begun to grow out in a bristly dark corona. But her broad face was dour, intent, considering what she would say. "The weather was bad, and the . . . hugeness. We were afraid."

She looked at Asa first and then Kristina, frowning. "We killed Peder, carrying him, do you know? Ought to have sat where we were, brought the balloon down along the lakeshore. We didn't—We should have sat where we were." She went on looking earnestly from one of them to the other, as if she'd asked a question.

Her face had reddened a little. These were things she hadn't spoken of in other tellings. "I don't know what killed Peder, if it was the cold, or the carrying. We should have let the balloon come down there, right there in that damn field of rocks where we were, not carried Peder over the ice to Isuma's field, he'd maybe not be dead, eh? if we'd done that. But we thought . . ." She gestured blindly, lifting her hand and closing it in a fist, taking hold of something difficult in the air there in front of her—holding her fist out as if it represented the words she couldn't articulate. "I thought we would die, all of us, if the balloon tore." Then her voice broke a little and she said hoarsely, "I thought it would be better if Peder was the only one who died."

There was a silence. But after a while, smiling ruefully, Luza said, "Do you know? the sky on that world begins at your feet? People say you can see the face of God in the way one thing is connected to another, and I think I saw the face of God in that sky, the way it was connected to the ground, the way my body stood inside it!"

Kristina said furiously, the only matter she felt able to speak to, "God is in every place." The other matter, the culpability for Peder's death, frightened her in a vague way. She thought, *That's between Bjoro and Luza and their souls.*

"In the *Miller*, God's face is on the ceiling, eh?" Asa said with a narrow smile, glancing at the other two women across the restless limbs of the baby. Luza laughed, and Kristina after a moment made an appreciative sound with her mouth, *Huh*, feeling they were loosening something, all of them, coming out of a tangle. "Yes. On the ceiling."

Her eyes were burning painfully. She sighed and put the heels of her hands against them, rotating her wrists methodically, kneading. A universe of stars wavered briefly in the blackness. *Oh hell. Hell. Here it is now, and I don't have time for lying about sick in my bed.*

She stood up with difficulty, pushing on Luza's shoulder. "This is a hard floor, and I'm old," she said, and petted the woman's lustrous cropped hair. "My hair was black, black as that, you know." She touched her own wild white hair with her fingers, an uncharacteristically fussy gesture. "I never have learned to comb," she said, grimacing unhappily.

"Oh, I like your hair. It's thick, and I like the ribbons you tie in it, the colors against the white."

Kristina accepted this flattery without a reply—Luza was a kind woman. "My house is in Pacema," she said. "Come and visit me when this damn plague is finished with us all." She touched Asa's head too, and the sick baby's, conscious of a kind of blessing in this gesture, and then put her feet in her shoes and went down the steps of their house stiffly, clutching one of her aching kidneys with her free hand. She went slowly, beginning to shake already like an invalid, round to her own domaro and then to the door of Filisa Ilmen's apartment.

"Send somebody to tell my son, he ought to take care of his own mother before any damn machinery," she said tremulously, giving in to misery and self-pity.

Filisa, who had a sister-in-law sick in her own house, said, sighing, looking up from the little galley sink where she ran a bowl of water, "Well, hell now Kristina, I was thinking you'd got by without it."

It was Filisa's husband Leo who helped Kristina out of her shoes, her trousers and shirt, waited while she peed, helped her from the toilet, put her into bed. He was a man she always had liked, quiet and sweet-tempered, his cheeks round and florid in a lean face. She was ashamed to be seen by him in this weak state, her thin shanks trembling when she stood up from the toilet, and her embarrassment made itself over into bitter impatience, complaints, petty demands. *That's a good shirt, Leo, don't be letting it lay there on the damn floor. No, no don't fold it now, it's got too dirty, the way you let it lay.*

He was matter-of-fact, tolerant. When he stood her up from the toilet and pulled her shorts around her bony buttocks he said mildly, "Worst thing, eh? The way the pee stinks." She clutched him gratefully, though she was helpless to stop being petulant. "Oh hell, pinch your nose closed if you can't stand it, Leo, it's a damn little thing to complain about."

When he unfolded her bed and let her down onto it she groaned quietly and turned her back to him, clasping the thin bedsheet. She heard him clattering, dragging over the little table, arranging things within her reach. "Can you sleep?" he asked her, and when she muttered resentfully he pretended not to hear it, his hands fussing, letting her hair free of its red ribbon tie. His fingers raised a thrill across her back, something to do with fever or with anile foolishness. "I'll come back in a while. Or somebody will. They've sent off for Bjoro, eh?" He patted her shoulder and went away.

She struggled over onto her other hip, out of a childish need to see what he'd brought next to her bed. There was a bottle of water standing on the table, cloudy, drifting shreds of lemon, and a shallow bowl with a wet bit of sponge, maybe meant for cooling her face. At the edge of the bed he had put an empty pot for peeing into, and papers for wiping. She had a sudden longing for an orange, and resented Leo for not thinking of it. With difficulty, she lifted on an elbow and drank two swallows from the water bottle, her mouth burning, the tepid water a brief ease. She closed her eyes, let her body settle heavily on the mat. I don't have time for lying in bed, she thought fretfully, but fell at once into the vague dissociation at the borders of sleep.

"Panja," her son said. She wrenched up suddenly and clung to him, helpless even to control her tears. "Oh. Oh. This damn plague," she cried irritably. For only a moment, she had thought he was a little boy whimpering feverish and she his mother, sitting up drowsing beside his bed. But then she knew who was sick, who sitting by the bed, and his calling to her out of childhood with that old babyish name, *panja*, seemed a vaguely dreadful sign. What did he think—that she was dying? "Will you get me an orange?" she asked him impatiently, and she stopped her tears with her fingertips jabbed against her burning eyelids.

He went away and came back. "Here. Kristina," he said, crouching beside her bed. He began to peel the orange in his hand, piling up the little saucers of rind on the edge of the table. The piece he fed her was a mass of tasteless pulp; she pushed it around with her tongue and swallowed stubbornly. Her mouth was coated and sore, she'd lost interest in food. When he held out another finger of fruit she grimaced and looked away.

He put his hand against her cheek and then her forehead. She was parched, fever-ridden. Beneath her skin, behind her eyes, a dry fire was burning, and his cool hand sliding across her face was intensely comforting. "Do you want me to bathe you?" He was patient and kind but detached, a manner he took on when he tended to the sick—his first wife Hlavka's chronic asthma had inured him to invalidism.

"Let me have some water to drink," she told him.

He held the water bottle while she swallowed. Her own fingers curled shakily around her son's hands. When she let her head back onto the bed again, she said, complaining weakly, "Oh hell. I don't have any time for being sick just now."

"No," Bjoro said indifferently. He began to bathe her limbs with the wet piece of sponge, drawing an arm and then a foot out from under the bedsheet. Her skin was tender, crawling with feeling, the cool wash delicately painful. She watched her son's face. He was forty-seven, had a long sloping bony brow, wide and thin mouth, not her husband Aŭgustino's look nor her's, but a family homeliness that had been in her own mother's face and an uncle's. There was no little boy in that look anywhere, and since he had come home in the *Ruby* there had been a defeat, an unknowability, a core of anger, a miserable unhappiness. Her eyes began to tear slowly, watching him, and in the blur she received a gift, saw him a lanky child again, with pale hair sticking up straight along the crown of his head.

"I want to see that world," she said, breathing out harshly. This had been at the edge of her consciousness for days, a numinous whispering that unexpectedly, suddenly, became coherent. A shudder went along her skin like a loosening of clothes: Her body's understanding of something still inarticulate, something that transcended language. *I want to lie down on that earth and embrace it.*

Her son went on sponging her skin. "I have seen it," he said contemptuously. Her own feeling was nonrational, beyond arguing, but she said, clasping his wrist, "God's face!"

He looked at her in incomprehension. He was angry, anguished. "There's no God in that world, Kristina, I have seen it! I felt when I was standing between the ground and the sky in that world, I was nothing, unremembered. There was so much space, air, emptiness, distance, and no meaning in it, eh? Where was God? When I was in that world, what I saw was—" He threw her an urgent look, flourishing his hands, grappling with something. "I don't know! What did the mountains mean? What were their names?" His eyes filled with sudden tears. "There was a wind!" he said wildly, as if that explained everything.

Kristina became inexplicably tearful herself. She was surprised and ashamed when the words that were in her mouth turned and came out banal. "We can't know all the meanings of things," her mouth said, and the sound of her voice shamed her too, seeming only flat and stubborn.

Her son blinked impatiently. His tears fled onto his lashes and vanished. He looked away, beginning again slowly to push the sponge across her fevered skin. "There isn't any meaning at all, Kristina. There's chaos." His voice was low, murmuring, as happens when you know an argument has gone past the point of usefulness. Kristina's shame deepened. She hadn't felt they'd been arguing.

"We must just try to make our lives coherent," she said sorrowfully. "To go on gathering ourselves into the Light."

"What does that mean?" he said harshly. "What are you looking for, in this Light? God's face? What does that mean? That it's implacable? Beyond knowing? Yes! God's face, then!"

At times in her life she had felt she had an understanding of God—for a few inexplicably clear moments she had recognized the essential value, the equal wonder, of everything in the universe. She had understood, there was utterly no distinction, no separation, between the parasitic beetle, the anibird, Wolfgang Mozart, the evacuation of a bowel. But it was easier to let this understanding go than to confront the terrible weight that lay inside it. And it was something like that that made her loosen her grasp now, made her let go her desperate embrace of the New World and withdraw into the frailty and effortlessness of her illness. "Help me onto the toilet," she said pitiably. "I don't want to use this damn pot Leo put by the bed."

She wasn't able to remember when she had last stood naked before her son, and she clutched the bedsheet ineffectually while Bjoro supported her by the elbows. "How cheaply we take good health," she said through her teeth. Bjoro brought his arm around her, murmuring impatiently, "I've seen naked old women, panja."

She tightened her hands tremulously on the sheet—a medicine bundle against her breastbone. "Do you think old women don't have any dignity to keep?" she said wretchedly.

But swiftly afterward she lost the strength for modesty, became indifferent to such things, undignified. She lay naked with the sheet bunched under her when the fever broke a sweat; she gave up the effort of getting into the lavejo and took to using the pee pot beside her bed. She no longer cared if it was her daughter-in-law Juko, or her grandson Eneo, who sponged her naked limbs; if it was her daughter Olinda who helped her to squat and pee, or Olinda's husband Axel.

She dreamed and woke, dreamed and woke, in a brief

shallow circling. Objects in the room slid away from the walls and down into her dreams, allusory, intangible, transient. Or she entered the walls and became permeable, imbued with light. She was a person who always had tried to interpret her dreams, but was too sick to redefine these—or they meant nothing, they simply were. In a sudden feverish insight, she accepted them for what they seemed—another domain of life, having equal weight with her waking life. *The face of God.* She thought she might die, and it was a relief to let go her old dread of dying in her sleep—it had been an arbitrary habit, she realized, assigning more reality to the waking world than to dreams.

When she began slowly to be convalescent, it was Bjoro's daughter Abigajlo who kept her company in the daylight hours. They played Go, or chess, and in the long afternoons Abigajlo read to her, with the librajo propped on her knees: poems and moral philosophy, religious mysticism and the metaphors of physics. Abigajlo was twenty. All of her life, she had seemed to absorb from the air the shape of things unseen—intimations, flashes, whispers, bodings—and from that seed ground had sprung a lively interest in spiritual matters that her parents never would share in. Hlavka's beliefs had been narrow, she had been grounded in a concrete reality, was strictly humanist: A soul was the fundamental force for good in human beings, only that. Bjoro, if he ever had been open to hidden things, had shut those doors one by one until now he stood behind a stolid disinterest. He regarded his daughter's beliefs with remoteness. For years, Abigajlo had been bringing her spiritual interests to Kristina, as she never could do with her parents: She had a passion for the unknowable shadowy edges of things, and Kristina was a religious woman.

They argued mildly about the principle of *abimsa,* which wasn't a tenet of Quakerism but of Hinduism, and practiced by certain Jains and Taoists. Abigajlo was fierce in her belief that all living things sought their own happiness, and people ought to do what they could to keep from interfering with that.

"What is your practice when the happiness of mosquitos or little black flies involves your blood?" Kristina asked her in amusement. "What will you eat if you give up cutting lettuces, whose happiness is to flower and go to seed?"

Abigajlo had thought these problems through, and only grinned back: If people went on struggling toward an ideal that was unattainable, then in the striving itself they might find something unexpected, an insight.

Abigajlo also flatly believed natural objects, rocks and ponds, sky, had souls, and Kristina put forward a problem: On the *Miller,* what was natural? The river and the lakes were engineered. Was there soul in a cloud called to life by machinery? But then both of them began to trade apocryphal stories about self-conscious vehicles and malevolent generating plants. "There is anima in any damn machine, eh? If you ask a mechanic."

Kristina made an effort to tell her grand-daughter some of her dreaming, but the brief, evanescent images became ordinary or absurd when she impounded them in language. "There was something I understood . . ." she said, muddling to a stop. She waved a hand vaguely, irritably. "It's gone again. . . ."

Abigajlo sat beside her bed chewing on a loaf of bread and swallowing it down with tea. "When you're in my dreams, we're always arguing," the girl said, as if she thought this might help Kristina to find what she'd lost. Kristina croaked a helpless laugh. She liked their amiable, discursive quarrelling.

In the evenings it was Juko or Bjoro, one or the other, who came and slept in the house. Kristina was thin and weak but driven by urgency: She coerced each of them in their turn to read to her from the pile of Minutes, and Advices and Queries, and sheets from the modem and the exploratory balloons, while she lay in bed with her burning eyes shut. They were always tired, themselves. They stumbled over words, lost lines, fell into confusion. Bjoro, when he was fed up with boggling the words, would say, "Enough," and shove the papers from his lap, go off to bed. But Juko sometimes would sit with a finger on the page, frowning wearily through long baffled silences, until Kristina finally would open her eyes and see her sitting there, and murmur, "Go on to sleep, leave that, it's all right."

Juko was private, withdrawn, and Kristina let her be so, afraid of something that remained vague, a shadow that was in some way an umbra of the new world. While they ate together, or while Juko combed Kristina's hair or shook out her bedsheet, they went on as they ever had, in conversation and argument about food and work, sewing, people they both knew. They went on telling confidences, Juko complaining about her brother, and telling the little oppressive details, the resentments and sorrows of seeing her old father, Silko, circling back to childishness; it had now come round to peeing his pants and mashing foods with his fingers. But she and Kristina avoided speaking Bjoro's name, both of them did, and Kristina understood this slight scission was a gulf—they were isolated from one another suddenly, their friendship of twenty years brought down as easily as that, as if it had been a bridge made of paper and string, negligible, irrelevant.

"Do you remember Dačjo Otersen?" Kristina asked her

suddenly while they were standing at the sink in the women's bathhouse. Kristina gripped the edge of the splash board shakily, steadying herself while Juko stood in front of her soaping and washing her face, working the washrag deliberately into the hollows at the hinges of her jaw, into the crevices of her ears, the creases of her eyelids and cheeks.

"He was Helena Hajnzel's son, he was one of them on the *May Snow*," Juko said after a moment. This man Dačjo Otersen and two more had been lost on the tugship *May Snow* when it went out ranging for rocks and never sailed home. "I didn't know him, much. I knew Liliana Olavo, better," Juko said, naming one of the others who were lost. "Liliana's sister married a cousin of my father's, that was how I knew her." Scrupulously, she began to rinse Kristina's face of soap.

"He was in a dream of mine, I think," Kristina said. She didn't know why this dream had reappeared to her just at this moment. Or why she had dreamed of Dačjo Otersen, a man she knew only slightly.

"Dačjo?"

"He was . . ." Kristina felt for the thread of the dream. "There was a red sky and he was a bird, I saw his feathers, and the beak, his eye was ringed in black—I don't know how I knew it was Dačjo." In the dream, he had sat on the lofty cap of a light pole with wings folded, one black eye fixed upon her, and then flown into the sun, which had become visible in the ceiling behind him, beating his wings in a hard, slow rhythm the way a heron flies, or a swan, though she had known he was neither, was only himself, Dačjo Otersen, flying, feathered.

Juko said without interest, "What was he doing?"

She was suddenly irritable. "Oh I don't know, it was a

dream." And then, irrationally, tears sprang in her eyes. She put a trembling hand to her mouth, and Juko let one of her own hands down and looked at her, alarmed. "What? The dream?" Kristina wasn't able to answer, wasn't able to understand what the dreaming or the crying meant. When finally her throat opened and spilled out words, they weren't any she'd expected. "I always have wondered, do you have poor Vilef in your dreams?" she said sorrowfully. She was surprised, both of them were, by her breach of an old, unspoken agreement not to speak of this dead child.

"I don't dream!" Juko said fiercely, and began to wring out the washrag. Kristina was startled by the scrim of fear in her daughter-in-law's eyes, and felt herself flooded suddenly with self-reproach. What was in her mind, to bring up that poor dead baby after all these years?

Juko folded the washrag neatly, hung it from the faucet. She took Kristina's arm and walked her wobbly back to their apartment. A burning silence charged the air between them, and this quickly was a pain Kristina couldn't bear. When she was settled in the bed and had her breath back, she said unhappily, "Are we finished being daughter and mother to one another, then?" and Juko looked at her in astonishment.

"No! Where does that come from? Because I won't speak to you about my dead son?" Her face became very bright. "Because Bjoro and I aren't sleeping in the same bed?"

An inarticulate dread rose in Kristina. "That isn't anything to do with me," she said crossly, and turned her face away. In that moment, she understood: It wasn't the keeping of these secrets but the baring of them that she feared.

Juko made a small frustrated noise and put out the light,

went to her own bed. After a while, into the darkness and silence she said flatly, "Once, I dreamed the air was water and he swam in it, smooth as a fish."

A gift of fever and sickness, a lost memory, rose up slowly in Kristina. "Some of the world is visible to us," she said, sighing, "but some of it can only be seen in our dreams."

9

Ĉejo

And these things I see suddenly, what mean they?
As if some miracle, some hand divine unseal'd my eyes.
Shadowy vast shapes smile through the air and sky,
And on the distant waves sail countless ships,
And anthems in new tongues I hear saluting me.

OLAVA MORGAN'S HANDS were thick, blunt-fingered, the nails etched with indigo blue as if she might have been dying yarn before she came to lay her hands on Humberto. "This is holding me," she said, sighing. It wasn't clear if she was speaking to Humberto or to Ĉejo. Ĉejo was watching her, sitting cross-footed beside his father, who was lying on his mat on the floor with Olava's large hands spread across his eyes. "Right here, the eyes, my hands are stuck here, the pull of the energy is so strong, maybe it would pull some skin off if I moved my hands. It feels like that."

Ĉejo said earnestly, "One of his eyes won't close."

He knew that Olava knew this. She had been in their house daily since Humberto had suffered his stroke. He didn't know why he felt compelled to tell her, *One of his eyes won't close.*

Olava said, nodding, "I can feel that. This eye, the right one, eh? I can feel the heat." She shifted her hands, drawing the thumbs under, bowing the knuckles. There were twenty hand positions in the rijki healing art; Ĉejo knew this from his grandmother, who had learned a little rijki therapy from Olava in the hope that it would ease Humberto's sleep. He had been sleeping badly since this stroke had paralyzed him, and often, late into the night, he lay muttering and beating his motive left hand against the floor. All of them had had to learn to sleep with the commotion—Leona's inexpert practice of rijki therapy never had brought him peace.

"I can feel the heat," Olava murmured again, her hands making a shape like two long narrow mounds of earth hoed up for planting pumpkins. She narrowed her eyes and shifted her weight on her knees. She was a big woman with a cap of gray curly hair, pointy front teeth. She had a sloppy way of dressing, sometimes wore crumbs of food at the corners of her mouth— her untidiness put Ĉejo off, and he and his grandmother had argued over this in the past. But Olava had been kura to his father's family for more than thirty years, and in the first days after the stroke she had tenderly cupped Humberto's pulse in her palms for hours at a time while they all waited to see if his brain would swell enough to kill him. She had been daily explaining things, relieving anxieties, serving as a sort of clerk at their family Meetings. What was a doctor's chief work, any- way, after inoculations and setting broken bones? It was help- ing people through difficult times, even through dying. Ĉejo had lately given up thinking that sloppiness was an obstacle in those matters.

"Well Humberto," Olava said quietly, "I missed your face, eh? At my sister's grand-daughter's wedding." She sat behind his head, her fingertips resting on his cheekbones, his mouth spread out just below the tips of her fingers. Ĉejo had become accustomed to his father's crooked grimace, the one corner pinched and the other loose, but now with Olava's big hands over his father's eyes the mouth drifted alone, isolate and unfamiliar.

"That singer, Signe Pilsen, do you know her? She came and sang for my niece, a gift, a wedding song. Some people say she has a voice but it's a loud screech, that's what it sounds like to me. All the time she was singing at my niece's wedding, I was thinking, that would be a good song if somebody else was singing it."

Ĉejo had expected Olava to meditate while she was laying hands on his father. His grandmother always would shut her eyes and fall silent when she tried rijki on her son; Ĉejo thought if you were conducting the body's $ĉi$ from one person to another, you wouldn't want to be talking about weddings and singing. He said cautiously, "Are your hands feeling anything now? Is any healing going on?"

Olava opened her eyes, beginning to smile slowly. "There's always healing going on, eh? Healing and dying both." She shifted her hands, flattening and spreading the fingers. "Here, put your hands on now, lay them on mine," she said, wriggling her thumbs slightly. Ĉejo placed his own hands scrupulously over hers. "There's heat," she said, "and a pulling. Do you feel it? Right here over the bridge of the nose."

The backs of her hands were cool against Ĉejo's palms. He closed his eyes and waited to feel something. Olava began a wedding tune behind her lips. Her hands carried Ĉejo's hands slowly outward; their four hands began to hold Humberto's long face, his skull, tenderly between their palms. Olava went on humming quietly, not seeming to need to be focused on the touching, though Ĉejo went on trying to meditate, his eyes shut. As his hands became slowly heated, filled with a kind of charged weight, then finally he had to look, had to say, "Do you feel this, paĉjo?"

Olava's hands, moving outward, had let his father's eyes come out from under. His left eye was following Olava, his right eye looking up to the rafters, the floor of the sadaŭ. He stirred restlessly and said something inarticulate, a quick glib collection of meaningless syllables. He looked at Ĉejo and Olava urgently, jumping his left eye from one of them to the other. Ĉejo shook his head, scowling, turning the sounds over in his mind. His father's tongue was thick, intractable, but some few words were clear, and sometimes a garbled word could be understood. *Pe! Jos duble!* he may have said. Ĉejo didn't know what these particular sounds meant.

Olava moved her hands and Ĉejo's with methodical care, lifting them from Humberto's face, setting them down on his right shoulder. She said quietly, "Well I don't know that language you're speaking, eh Humberto? You'll teach it to me, I bet, if I keep paying attention. Through the skin, though, I know what you're saying: *Sure Olava, I feel that healing touch there, that heat, and I'm sorry I missed that wedding, that Signe Pilsen singing those songs in her screechy soprano voice,* but I don't know if you might be saying that, something like that, with your mouth.

Or something else, eh? I don't speak that fey language yet." She smiled sorrowfully.

Ĉejo's father, watching Olava's face, stirred again and sighed. He was drooling from the loose edge of his bottom lip, seeming not to know when saliva had accumulated in his mouth. Ĉejo had a habit of wiping it away with the pad of his thumb, but his hands were occupied resting on Olava's hands, on his father's useless right arm, conducting the heat and power of his own body into his father's, so he let the little dribble run down into the crease of Humberto's chin. "Right here," he said to Olava, "I feel this pulling right here."

Olava nodded solemnly. "Yes. It's pretty warm, I feel it drawing pretty strong." She gave him a look. "You got a good touch. Your grandmother, she couldn't feel it, couldn't get her hands sensible to the energy. Humberto, we can show your son how you like to be touched, eh? He can lay hands on you, himself, after this." She brought her hands down over his father's abdomen, lifting her elbows out slowly, linking her fingers in a thick mat. "The spleen," she said, murmuring. "You know the spleen? This is how to touch it, how to find a balance by touching. You make a path between your body and Humberto's and let the ĉi flow along it."

The warmth of the soul's energy moving from his own body into his father's was palpable, compelling. He watched Olava's hands and followed them. She went on showing him how to touch his father in a healing way, the pancreas, the stomach, the liver, and then his father's hips and legs, his feet. Eventually Humberto's right eye rolled up and he shut his left eye and breathed noisily, sleeping, but Olava seemed not to notice this—she still sometimes talked to him in a low, soothing drawl, telling inconsequential gossip and news, or asking him something and then delivering the answer she said she could hear through his skin. Ĉejo listened intently without understanding anything through his palms, only the inaudible whisper of heat and life.

"Well, you got to listen awhile," Olava said when he told her this. She nodded. "You'll get to hearing it. But your hands are good. You got a healer's hands, I think. Anybody can learn it, get some of it right, but certain people are just born to it, they got a certain spirit, a certain touch that's right for rijki." She held her own hands up and examined them with unselfconscious pleasure.

Ĉejo made a pot of tea when the laying on of hands was finished, and he and Olava drank it, sitting beside Humberto as he slept, the two of them talking quietly about the rijki therapy, what had been accomplished—harmony for disharmony, quietude for worry, ease for strain; and the harvest, what was being brought in—corn and breadfruits, pumpkins, pejibayes.

They traded certain gossip about Heza Barfor. Olava knew Heza from the Fiber Arts Committee, and Heza's sister-in-law—the one she always was quarreling with—had been in Olava's care for a while. It hadn't been possible for people to keep the sister-in-law from dying, Olava said, but that woman had used the energy from her illness to heal her relationships with her relatives. This was something Ĉejo had wondered about. During the dry season, Heza had moved back into her brother's household—helping her sister-in-law with the hard work of dying, people said.

Afterward, Ĉejo had expected the old woman to go on living with her widowed brother. It was a surprise when she came promptly back to their apartment again. "My brother's grand-children are rude and loud," she had said, as if this explained it sufficiently. Cejo, repeating these things to Olava, added thoughtfully, "Living in our house, maybe she had got out of the habit of being patient with children." He felt very distanced from his own childhood.

Olava said mildly, "I thought Heza came back to live with your family because of her friendship with Leona, eh? now that Leona's son has decided to have a stroke, and this family needs comforting."

Cejo hadn't thought of his grandmother in this way—a friend, having a claim to someone's loyalty. And he hadn't con-sidered that Heza might be a comfort to them.

Their household had become chaotic, prone to storms. Humberto, who always had been a mild and tolerant person, was an impatient, irascible paralytic. He cried out unfathom-able demands, and fell into a fury when no one understood his needs. His clear words were all obscenities: "Fuck!" he would shout in the spasms of his defeat, his left arm hurling out in a wild frenzy, his left leg beating the floor in rage. "Shit! Hell! Piss-you!" In these storms, Cejo's cousin Alfhilda was prone to burst into tears, and Cejo, who could not bear the crying and the rageful cursing, would pace helplessly up and down the pasado while his grandmother and grandfather lashed out at one another or shouted back at their son in frustration and misery. Now Cejo searched around in his memory: Was it Heza, after all—going on unperturbed, making reply as if Humberto's meaningless sounds were speech—who always would restore the peace?

His father went on sleeping in the middle of the floor after

Olava Morgan had finished her tea and gone home. Ĉejo slid back the wall of the apartment to listen for him if he woke, and sat on the loĝio in front of his loom. He laid down the narrow lines of brown tapa, and wider ones, quince yellow, the border of a woven rug, while he followed people's arguing and haranguing with each other, their whispering of scandal, without taking part in it himself. He had lately made up his mind that he was a person with a brooding disposition: He liked to practice sitting out on the loĝio, not joining in people's idle talk. He liked to work silently, watching other people in an abstracted way as if he didn't know who they were. When no one was saying anything that interested him, he turned over solemn thoughts in his mind—not the old, weighted questions to do with death and grief, but a thicket of slighter terrors, things to do with helplessness and whining.

Shortly, his father began hawking up sputum, and this became a kind of gagging. He was inclined to cough on his slobber—needed someone to lift his head and help him swallow his saliva. For a moment Ĉejo couldn't keep his hands from going on pushing down the beater of the loom, pressing the thread tight and even. Some neighbors' faces were registering alarm before he was able to make himself stand and go in. Bleakly, he helped his father's shoulders off the floor, waited for this spasm to be finished, wiped the spit with the edge of his hand, dried it on his trouser leg. His father's eye followed the movement, his right hand stirring vaguely. In a moment he murmured to Ĉejo, an unfathomable, insistent plea. Ĉejo looked away, sighing. He didn't know which eye he should be looking into, the fixed or the roving.

His father had to be helped to sit on the toilet—his body

wouldn't support itself. He had to be propped against a repozo or turned from one side to the other every little while if he were lying on the floor; someone in his family had to spoon his food, sponge his sweating limbs, shave his cheeks, pull his shirt on over his head. And one or the other of their household had always to be showing in, overseeing, and turning out the stream of people who came to sit with him, bringing their extravagant reassurances and overly fervid prayers, their gossip and pointless jokes, believing this was help he needed as much as medicaments and therapy. Cejo thought bitterly that more of them could be helping to wipe his anus and his leaking mouth, to hold his head up when he choked.

"I'll get you up," he said in a bare whisper. "You need to pee. Here, sit, I'll get you up." Humberto helped him ineffectually, clubbing about with his left leg and arm. He could stiffen his left leg to hold his weight when he was upright, and he stood leaning into his son's body, breathing harshly. His penis had stiffened too—he was prone to useless erections since the stroke had brought him down in the corn field. Women had been teasing him for it. Even Cejo's grandmother was likely to laugh and say something lewd when she was helping him to urinate, or to bathe, but Cejo was ashamed of their shamelessness, and he pushed his father's thick penis down in the neck of the bottle silently. After a little pause Humberto got his stream of urine going and the two of them stood together thoughtfully watching the piss rising steaming in the glass. A little dribble spilled over the edge of the bottle onto Cejo's hand. "Pacjo," he said on a long note, uselessly angry, and Humberto mimicked him, "Ahg," on a long note, guttural, meaningless.

"Do you want to come out to the loĝio?" he asked his father sorrowfully. "Watch people? I'm at the loom." Humberto made an inarticulate noise and twisted the left side of his face in a grimace—who knew what he understood? But he let Ĉejo bring him out of the apartment, clubbing along on one leg, and when he was seated, propped against a wicker repozo, his left eye watched people at their work, as they sorted seeds or straightened bits of old wiring, wrote notes for committee business, sharpened maĉetaj. People talked to him from time to time, but some of them spoke as they might have to a child or someone they barely knew.

An old woman, Pata Vilasenor, used his feet for winding her yarn while she told him a long, complicated story about an argument she had had with someone on the Metals Committee, a disagreement over the design of a thermocouple. Ĉejo sat at the loom and went on silently with his rug-making while Pata went on talking. Humberto's eye wandered away from the woman; he began to watch Ĉejo throwing the shuttle, bringing down the beater in a hypnotic rhythm.

Ĉejo's grandmother and his cousin Alfhilda came up onto the loĝio. Alfhilda squatted beside Humberto and studied her feet while Leona stood over her disabled son and her grandchildren and briefly unburdened herself to Pata Vilasenor. She had taken Alfhilda over to Kantado ŝiro because some people thought there was a boy living over there who might make a match for Alfhilda, but that boy would grow up stupid, Leona was saying. He had a mother who was loud and arrogant, bragging of things her son knew—what could be more stupid than that? Ĉejo looked at Alfhilda and she shrugged her thin shoulders, disinterested. They would be at this business for another ten or fifteen years; Ĉejo's own marriage hadn't yet been settled on, and he was years older than Alfhilda.

The old woman, Pata, at once began to tell tedious stories of marriages she had arranged in her own family, and Ĉejo's grandmother fell silent, nodding politely as she lifted her feet one after the other and fingered crumbs of dirt from her sandals.

Some people were in the kitchenhouse boiling tikisko, and maybe it was the smell of their cooking that began to make Humberto's mouth run with water; while Pata went on talking tiresomely to Leona, Alfhilda wiped his drool with the edge of her hand, wiped it again, and cleaned her hand on the hem of her shirt. Finally she stood and leaned into Leona, speaking to her in a whisper Ĉejo wasn't able to hear, then she squatted beside her uncle again, stroking his hand soothingly as Humberto began to shift his weight more and more restlessly and mutter secret words. When finally old Pata took her yarn from his feet, patted his ankle kindly and wandered away, Leona sighed. "That woman talks too much," she said quietly. "And her daughter is the same way. I wonder how they can keep from starving—they don't want to stop talking long enough to chew their food."

Alfhilda said, wiping Humberto's lip again, "Doesn't she know it's time for people to eat their supper?"

Ĉejo helped her to lift his father by the arms and bring him to sit inside the house. It was sweltry in the evenings at this season of the year, and other households ate their evening meal on the loĝio, or they slid open the pasado walls of their apartments to let the slight, cooling draft blow through, but the loose right corner of Humberto's mouth made his eating a strenuous, sloppy ordeal, and Ĉejo thought it was a humiliation for his father if they spooned his food into his open mouth while people who were not his family members watched them do it. He had pushed his family into a habit of shutting the walls of their apartment, eating in isolation, in the hot, dusky rooms. Now they fed Humberto slowly from their own plates, sweet mangoes and boiled cassava root, and wiped the dribble from his chin, while Ĉejo's grandmother and his cousin argued about Pata Vilasenor—whether it would have been rude to tell her she was talking too long, and that Humberto was needing to be fed.

Heza Barfor came into the house with cotton-silk seeds tied up in a manta, and she sat down without speaking and began methodically to pull the floss out of the seed pods. She seemed not to notice that the other members of her household were eating. It was Ĉejo's grandmother who had boiled the root of the cassava and beaten it to a pulp the day before, and she said in a hurt tone, "Don't you want to eat? Can't you wait to do that another time?" as if Heza's failure to eat the cassava were a personal affront to her.

Heza looked up in surprise. "There's that big old ceiba tree that stands over there between Alaŭdo and Esperplena. People have been gathering in the seeds as they fall." She had no eyebrows, only a few wiry sprigs of hair above the inside points of each eye to suggest where her brows should be, and she lifted these in a questioning way, as if she were asking something: *Is this a sufficient answer?* She never would answer a question herself in a straightforward way. Ĉejo's grandmother looked away plaintively. In a moment, though, she brought up with Heza this matter of Pata Vilasenor talking too much, and Heza took Leona's part in it, coming down on the side of politeness. After that, the two of them began to trade stories about Pata's family, old anecdotes and hearsay going back to women who had been old when Heza and Leona were children. Cejo stopped listening. He wandered off into a daydream about Katrin Amundsen, following her into the musky shadows of the corn field, lifting her shirt, putting his mouth upon one of her nipples.

"Did Olava Morgan come and show your grandson how to lay hands on your son?"

Cejo's penis was searching inside his trousers, and he looked between his grandmother and her friend in a flurry of self-conscious confusion, but it was his grandfather, standing there, who had asked this question of his wife. Old Petro had been sick with the plague and stalled in a long convalescence, imagining himself not yet well, but well enough to complain: This restless night-time thumping of his son's was keeping him from sleep. He'd been living in his brother's apartment to escape it, or to escape his wife's pitiless good health, but every little while he shuffled home to proclaim his lingering illness.

Cejo's grandmother was helping Heza with the cotton silk and both of them were fixed on this work, their hands stripping the floss from the seeds. She said, looking toward Cejo, "I forgot to ask. Did she come? Did she say you've got the hands for it, Cejo? You know, mine are worthless, I told her that, I told her she'd have to give this work to my grandson, he always has had a thin skin, I told her, for letting invisible things come in."

Heza turned her head, peering at Humberto anxiously as if it might be possible to see Olava's work in his face. "Did she get this eye to close, yet?" she said. She put her work down and touched the tip of one finger to Humberto's eyelid. When she pushed it down gently, it rose open again slowly, and his crooked mouth released a clicking sort of sound—anger, or a sour laugh. He flopped his left arm vaguely. "Ga!" he said with bitterness. "Ga!" Maybe he was offended by Heza Barfor's finger pushing down his eyelid, or he might have been frustrated with Olava's rijki therapy. It was impossible to know. Maybe he just wanted to go on being fed. Heza murmured, "Oh, that's to be expected," as if the two of them were carrying on a lucid conversation.

It was Heza's belief that he understood all of them as well as he ever had, and she had half-persuaded Alfhilda of it: Sometimes Alfhilda tried to go on sharing with her uncle the parts of her life she had always shared with him. Now she leaned toward him, whispering beside his neck. "There is this pea sort-of vine we've found on the northern continent, it fixes nitrogen in the soil so this other plant, something like a draba mustard, will grow with it, and the draba gives off a smell and keeps this certain fungus away from the peas. Anejlisa said it was a perfect little arrangement. *Elegant,* she said." She bared her teeth for him in a shining grin.

The left side of Humberto's mouth shuddered with the effort to speak. His eye strained in its socket, demanding something of her. Alfhilda was always in fear of her uncle's angry eruptions, and she cast a quick pleading look toward Ĉejo. Why was she looking to him for a remedy? He felt overburdened, oppressed, and shrugged his shoulders impatiently.

His father's mouth went on working, while Alfhilda stroked his hand and whispered urgently about edible seaweeds, and bacteria that might protect plants from dying back in a mild frost. Ĉejo, against his will, began to feel Alfhilda's anxiety.

Perhaps Heza felt it too. She suddenly quit her hand work, cleaning the cotton silk, and held out to Humberto a long sliver of mango pinched between her thumb and forefinger. "Here, it's sweet, a mango, do you want it?" Humberto's lips twisted, retreating from the offer, but the wildness abruptly went out of his face. He sighed and gazed off into the middle distance. Alfhilda, sighing too, lapsed into silence.

Ĉejo's grandmother opened the pasado walls of their apartment as soon as they were finished with eating, and then it was possible to hear families noisily washing their dishes, children getting into trouble, old people arguing with their older parents, chickens fighting and posturing. On the loĝio of the house there was to be a Weekly Meeting for Business, and some people began to go out there and sit down. Ĉejo fled quickly onto the loĝio himself, escaping his family, escaping care of his father, and distancing himself from his family's usual place at Meeting by sitting with Udo Blades and his family along the wall of the kitchen. Udo moved over to make room for him, but they were both silent. He and Udo had grown up together, yet the easy alliance of their childhood never had become friendship—Udo always had been inclined toward superstitious fears and aversions, and Vilef always had been at Ĉejo's right hand, a totem of horror.

As small children were sent off to play in neighbors' houses, gradually the quiet that people practice before a Meeting began to rise up and wash over other noise. The seventeen adults of the house were beginning to prepare themselves for thinking about business. They were studying the boards of the floor, or searching for peace behind their closed eyelids. Ĉejo mournfully watched his grandmother and his grandfather let their son's clumsy weight down to the floor at the family's usual place in front of the bathhouse wall.

"Any announcements?" Luizo Medina said, and people who had been meditating lifted their heads and looked around. Luizo was clerk of the Weekly Business Meeting, a short old man with a poorly repaired hare-lip and a lispy voice, proficient at keeping to an agenda and getting through a Meeting in a timely fashion. There were a few things announced: a woman giving a public reading of her poems; a change of venue for Waters Committee Meeting; odd jobs needing doing; things available for trade. Then Luizo opened the Meeting by formally listing all the pending business matters, and he reminded people not to wander too far off from the agenda. No one had to follow the order of his list; an agenda only defined limits. It was common, in fact, for a single question to rise up, and speaking begin to focus on it. Then other matters would go undecided, held over for another Meeting or put in the hands of a small committee. Not many things, after all, concerned everyone.

On Luizo's agenda was a long report to do with the New World's zonal soils, and Celia Fuǧinaka read this aloud, not every word of it but the gist. Some of it people already knew: There were great tracts of lifeless sands and gravels, moraines and glacial outwash and the abandoned diluvium of transient lakes—a dead and stony lithosol—and vast ice-scoured and stream-eroded slopes with immature soil profiles. There was mature soil under the grasslands and in the shallow valleys, but typically the A horizon was thin and gray, leached of iron and aluminum, with the minerals deposited in a dense hardpan in the illuviated B horizon. Short summers and low temperatures and the soil's sharp acidity discouraged the biological process:

The layer of humus was a discrete and undecayed litter of stems and twigs, leaves, petals of flowers, the mummified remains of insects and small rodents. The Geological Arts and Sciences Committee had been saying that if people tilled the grasslands soil it would quickly lose its scant organic content and the loose silt would blow off on the wind. It was this committee which had been sending down to Farms Committees a steady procession of Queries to do with cultivation. The Alaŭdo Farms Committee, Ĉejo knew, had been sending back a steady string of Advices, ranging from digging-sticks and peat-drills to very ancient, cautiously provident strategies of slash-and-burn.

But now the people studying soils had got through looking at all the new information from the balloon surveys and they wanted people to know: There were intrazonal soils in the depressions of glaciated plains, in bogs and marshes underlain by thermal basins. The heat and dampness in those places encouraged decay, and so the soil in the wetlands was enriched with the remains of grasses, sedges, rotting marsh plants. Where the C horizon was clay or loam, the soil scientists thought the valleys could be drained and made tillable. They had sent a Query to both the Designs Committee and the Waters Committee, asking those people to look at feasible plans for drainage fields.

A few times people interrupted Celia to ask questions or make comments. Had the Ceramics Committee been brought into this planning? someone wanted to know. After all, what was a drain tile but a big piece of pottery? Someone else said, well, there were other ways of draining a field, metal pipes and tubes—wouldn't it make sense to just adapt and relocate the systems that were already in place on the *Dusty Miller*? Had

the engineers thought of that? And inevitably, two or three
confused people wanted to talk about the difficulties of living
above a marshland—would houses be prone to sinking? would
people be able to walk across the ground without fear of falling
down a mud hole? But this was a report, not a Query, so Luizo
tried to keep everyone from too much turning aside.

When Ulfo Amsfred began his habitual stump speech—
"We'll have a much harder time down there, no matter if this
drainage works. There'll be more deaths, we'll have to work
harder, life will be more dangerous—" Luizo made use of it to
shift the talk away from soil, bringing up a question sent over to
them from Monthly Meeting, this matter of whether they ought
to give up trying to make the New World amenable—whether
they ought to build a biosphere flat on the ground there.

"They want to know what we think, in general. And then
the questions that would have to be addressed if we began to
plan seriously to do this." He said *"theriouthly,"* pushing the tip
of his tongue against the cleft in his upper lip.

Knuto Mursawa's words—*We live in this world as in the body
of God*—had long since gone clear around the śiro—all the śiroj.
People were ready to speak to the question. If this had been
a Meeting for Worship they might have waited, might have
expected a reasonable silence to give weight to their words, but
old Karla Asida stood quickly and said with fierce heat, "This
work we've already done, all this research and planning on how
to live on the New World, I suppose that's all wasted, then, if
we build a roof and live under it, eh?" She looked around at
them resentfully, as if the research and the planning were all
work she had personally accomplished, and the idea of a biosphere was a personal affront to her efforts.

Ĉejo didn't know what he felt about the biosphere plan, but he saw other people giving back Karla's look without speaking. No one thought she was raising an important issue. At the edge of his mind, Ĉejo began to repeat, *theriouthly addrethed theriouthly addrethed,* his tongue following his brain, pushing against the front of his teeth in a reflex of silence that mimicked Luizo's delicate lisp.

Hugo Lagrimas stood and said, "It's one thing to keep a closed system like the *Miller* running along without too much trouble, but building one is another thing, eh? We've got a smithy that makes steel for needles and knives, and they turn out a new light pole now and then, little machine parts, tools and whatnot. We haven't got the know-how, haven't got the raw goods or the machinery—have we?—to build a thing like this"— he gestured broadly with his two hands, a motion that took in the whole of the *Miller's* metalline sky—"this big and difficult."

Ruben Bera, old Pata Vilasenor's son, had arthritis in his hips—people didn't expect him to trouble his body to stand up. From where he sat on the floor of the logio, he said, "They're thinking that we could dismantle the *Miller* and move it piecemeal down to the ground, that's what I heard."

Luizo said, "Is that right?" and looked at Laŭdia Ortega. Laŭdia's brother was a design scientist, an engineer. None of the people living in this domaro were scientists; for that kind of wisdom and apprising, they had to ask people in other houses, other family members and neighbors.

Laŭdia said, nodding, "Not a part-for-part rebuilding, but reusing the materials, anyway, the joists and sheathing, in a new architecture."

Someone murmured irritably, "Well, they ought to have

said so in the first place. What kind of a Query is it that doesn't lay out the circumstances of things?" Someone else answered this, but the only part of it that Ĉejo heard was the naming of Isaba Aguto, clerk of the Alaŭdo Monthly Meeting.

Their own experience was with small projects of farming and transport, small constructions of plumbing and electronics—they didn't have the knowledge for arguing—but they started blindly down the path, raising questions of engineering and technology, general difficulties they imagined might come from dismantling the *Miller* and reassembling it on the New World. Would people go on living inside the *Miller* in the early part of this project? What would be the living conditions for people working down there on the New World, building the new place? There would be excess heat, surely, from the taking apart of the toroid—how were the engineers thinking this heat would be discharged? Maybe a land-bound biosphere wouldn't need an absolutely closed system; maybe it would benefit from an exchange of air, of water, with the New World's own envelope? There must be particular tools and machinery needed for taking this big structure apart; would they first need to devise, build, test, perfect, the very means themselves?

Luizo spoke every little while, keeping people from too much arguing, keeping them from following a question too far. "All we're about, is to flag the stones in this field," he kept saying.

Eventually, Pata Vilasenor stood alongside her son and said, "What is the point of taking the *Miller* apart and rebuilding it down there? If we're going to go on living under a roof, shouldn't we just go on living right here? I think it's crazy, this scheme. And going down to live on the New World, that's crazy too. If the Maintenance Committee thinks this torus will last another fifty years or one hundred, then maybe we should let our grandchildren be the ones to worry about finding a new place to live. If we're going to go on living under a roof, we ought to just stay right where we are, is what I think, where old people with tired hearts can move up on the altejo, eh? and go on living easily. And people with arthritis can go on without the weight getting into their bones."

Maybe Ruben was sorry to have his mother bringing up his unlucky health in this sideways manner. His face became bright; he looked intently into the palms of his hands. His mother went on without seeing this, saying, "If we go down there—under a roof or not—many of us will die, it'll be a hard life, like Ulfo always is harping on. On that New World, I think Ulfo is not far off, I think we'll have a hard time of it." She looked around at her neighbors doggedly. "I don't see why we need to come out in the sunlight. We're doing pretty well, after all. It's like Knuto Mursawa said: This place is an Eden, it's the body of God. Only he didn't take it far enough. We ought to just stay right here, inside God's body, that's what I think."

Pata's leading turned them in a new direction. Instead of going on arguing about steel manufacture and know-how, Irma Lindberg slowly stood and gave them her own reasons for wanting to abide in the old *Dusty Miller,* a complicated argument to do with people on this world having to be mindful of every detail of their living environment, their souls and minds put to work always in keeping the whole world from collapsing, every act an act of conscious worship—for what else was it but worship, eh? loving and protecting this soil, these trees, these animals, against the void of space. Irma thought their ceaseless life-giving work made them completely and fruitfully human. On the *Miller,* she said, there were certain human potentialities that hadn't been in reach of people on the Earth.

This seemed both mad and rational to Ĉejo—irresistibly appealing. A quietness settled into all of them. Maybe other people, like Ĉejo, were waiting for sense or understanding to come out of the two women's speaking.

When Humberto made a small noise, a meaningless sound, Ĉejo's family ignored this distraction as if it had nothing to do with them. His grandmother's eyes were shut, her mouth in a pucker of concentration. She had a longstanding fear of leaving the *Miller,* and a longstanding resolve to live long enough to accomplish it. Ĉejo wondered: Did she think this planet-bound biosphere stood at the intersection? Ĉejo's grandfather, old Petro, sat beside his wife, his hands clasped behind his neck and his elbows pointing downward; he stared along them as if he sighted down an azimuth to the floor. A morbid torpor was in his face. Probably he wasn't thinking about people's leadings but yielding to his recent habit: sighting down the short end of his life. Alfhilda's face was creased and intent. When she saw Ĉejo looking toward her, she rolled her lower lip down thoughtfully, displaying a pink gum.

Sesilo Hurtado got slowly to his feet. Sesilo was married to Alfhilda's mother's sister. He was known for a certain stew he liked to make, of sweet potatoes and eggplant, tomatoes, summer squash, ground peanuts, and seasoned with ginger, garlic, coriander. In Ĉejo's family, this stew was moderately famous. "Where there's a hardship," he said, "generally there's a grace to be found in it," and people nodded, as if Sesilo had said something they all understood to be true. "On that world, eh? it's all hardship, and I wonder: What is the saving grace?" He looked around at his neighbors before offering them his own considered answer: Maybe that marginal landscape would force them all to economy, frugality, where a rich world might make them prodigal. There were old, historical understandings, available to anybody who would read the old books: Humans tended to be destructive exactly in proportion to their belief in abundance. It was people of meager lands who had gone on longest, on the Earth, holding to an economy of sharing and of thrift. "Maybe it's in a bare-bones existence that we'd be enriched," Sesilo said. "Maybe the hardships would be a good thing."

After Sesilo had spoken, Pia Putala stood and said that hardship was the sort of thing people liked to romanticize and think about endlessly, but there were plenty of hardships everywhere. "We don't need to go down to the New World to find hardship," she told them, indicating their own world with her hand.

Someone else said, Sesilo's argument about the destructiveness of humans might be a reason for them to keep to themselves, up here in the *Miller*. If people carried the possibility of apocalypse inside them, shouldn't they seclude themselves behind barriers?

People had finally come around to what the question was, and they went on speaking to it without the clerk needing to keep them to a center path. "The New World, it's forbidding of people—all that cold and the long days, the stony soil. This place, the *Miller*, at least it's made for people, eh? as the New World was not." "This world we've made in the *Miller*, it's simpler by orders of magnitude than any natural world—we can keep it going ourselves, it's not confusing to us." "We've got a life and death reliance on each other, right here, eh? It's our hardships binds us together."

Until recently, Cêjo had had a habit of not listening to much that was discussed at a Meeting for Business—it was always tiresomely repetitious. People always were bringing up questions of sanitation and repair, arguing whether a diseased tree ought to be cut down, and what should be planted in the vacated space. He would often drowse dully, or wander in daydream. When there was a matter that concerned him, he fidgeted restlessly, waiting for it through tedious negligible discussions. But these days, everything circled endlessly around the New World. There were always Advices and Queries from Monthly Meeting, and matters people felt had been overlooked by Quarterly or Yearly Planning Committees. Lately, Cêjo kept his attention scrupulously focused, and cast around in his mind for an opinion on every question. When the issues had to do with farming, sometimes his mouth opened and words came out—this, he had lately realized, was what people meant by The Inner Voice.

He didn't have an impulse to speak on this matter of how to live well and where to do it, but he wanted to hear every word spoken, and Humberto went on restless and noisy, shifting and banging his left leg, his left hand, and muttering meaningless phrases. Cêjo became restless himself. He and Alfhilda exchanged glances. If he gave up sitting with Udo Blades and went over there where his father was, nothing would be accomplished by it—he didn't have a gift for quieting his father's noisy outbreaks—but he suffered from dim guilt, as if it was in his power to put an end to the distraction. He wanted someone who was already sitting over there, his grandmother or Heza or

Alfhilda, even old Petro, to bring his father inside the house, so people could go on with the Meeting without this noisy commotion. In the same long braid with guilt was something like embarrassment, and aggravation.

For a while his family went on ignoring Humberto, but finally Heza began to whisper to him and then to Leona, and finally, when no one was speaking and Humberto's steady muttering was filling up everybody's silence, Ĉejo's grandmother stood up to pull at her son's arms. Heza helped her, and they got him standing. But then Leona looked out at people and said, pushing her lower teeth forward, "My son, Humberto, wants to speak to this Meeting."

People turned their heads in surprise. Ĉejo's father was braced on his left leg, his right leg trailing heavily useless, the fingers of his right hand curled like a flower against his thigh, and the two old women were standing there steadying him in their arms. His mouth was loose at the right corner, the shine of spit on his chin. His long eyes were unpaired, the one moving restlessly and the other staring, a vitreous bubble in a sagging fold of eyelid—maybe that eye was sightless. His mother kept his hair untangled and clean, but he never would sit quietly for it to be cut; it hung in a ragged curtain over his brows, caught in his eyelashes. His look was ferocious, pitiful.

His mouth shaped two words with agonizing care, two meaningless sounds, something like, *Forbar! Ardo!* Some people looked at him gravely and some other people looked away. Ĉejo studied his own hands, the line of black under a thumbnail—a horizon of soil. There was a long, following silence. Silence was a language people understood, and an expectancy and patience began to find its center in the stillness. Ĉejo went on looking at his hands, but then, irresistibly, he looked at his father. Humberto's working eye was moving among the faces of his neighbors, focused on someone, and then someone else, and someone else. When the eye came around finally to him, Ĉejo was surprised by it. His father's look behind the scrim of his uncut bangs was tender and reasonable, entering into the silence.

He felt suddenly at the edge of something—an abyss, or a continent.

Humberto grappled again with his tongue, and his urgent whisper when it came out was meaningless and unknowable, but the feeling in it overleaped consciousness, passed into Ĉejo's brain as a vivid, feverish intuition. He thought, *What is a human being for?* imagining this, or something equally solemn, something that reverberated through all the nights and days of their lives, must be what his father was asking them all. In the silence afterward, while people were considering Humberto's impenetrable question, Leona took a better hold of her son and closed her eyes. Heza, on his other side, fixed her look somewhere indefinite, somewhere in the center of the stillness.

Ĉejo understood that something had come onto the loĝio with Humberto's painfully achieved words, his unknown syllables, and that people were waiting to see what it was. And when his father began again, pressing on them his mysterious, necessary truths in hidden phrases, fluent silences, then the thing all of them were waiting for seemed to enter into his voice, where it became familiar, became allusive, and Ĉejo wondered how he had ever thought there was but a single pronunciation in the sound of a word. He thought Humberto was speaking to them in his own language or theirs, in the bones of their ears or in their blood, his words a sigh.

Are we thinking we've created something? he was saying. *Are we thinking, because we've put ourselves and some other creatures inside a container, that this container we've made is Eden? There's only one Creation, eh? and we're among its members. What is this torus except a smaller circle within a larger one? Are we thinking we can go on living forever inside the little circle of each other's arms, without returning? without joining ourselves to the cosmos? without letting our arms open to touch the arms of the rest of Creation? What is this torus except a solitude? There isn't any meaning in anything except in its relations with other things—what is the anther of a flower except in its relations with the bee, eh? And what is the meaning of people who have uprooted themselves from ancient soil and are trying to go on living in a container of air and water, separate from the rest of the Creation? What is that meaning except a skeleton of bones from which the soul has escaped?*

There was a charged silence, a resonating peace, in which all of them were enclosed: the completeness and consciousness and life of the Meeting. At last someone murmured, or the air stirred in a coherent way, and Humberto's afflicted body moved slightly finding a new balance against his mother's breast. His tongue touched his lips silently as if it might be feeling around inside his mouth for more to say. Finally he sighed, and Heza and Leona stirred in the wake of that breath, letting his clumsy weight down on the floor and then sitting themselves, sighing too.

People waited in a long silence. Eventually, Udo Blades's mother stood. Her lips were moving in a whisper before she had quite got all the way to her feet, as if she spoke out from the middle of something: ". . . we're in the care of Wisdom beyond our knowing. Are we thinking we are God, then? What is God doing, freed of the obligation to order the waters and the skies?" She looked around at people thoughtfully. "I wonder, what is our ambition, in building this roof? Is this an issue of our trying to manage things? Do we think we've got control of everything here, because this place is small and simple and we're in charge of it? It's so obvious we're in control, I guess we may have forgotten we're not in control. And I wonder if those people on the Earth, because it was so clear they weren't in control, forgot that they were."

Ĉejo had lost her leading, by the end, wasn't certain if she had finally argued for or against their going on living in the *Dusty Miller*. Was she saying the *Miller* was a living organism? or a dead mechanical object they were laboriously keeping alive themselves? When he looked out through the open logio of his house, across the crowns of the breadfruit trees to the incongruously huge architecture of the Alaŭdo spoke holding up the roof of the sky, his confusion was charged with agitation, excitement: In the uncertainty itself, there seemed an indefinable meaning.

He was surprised when his own body stood up—surprised by the words coming out of his mouth: "If we make a container and put things inside it—what is left out? Are we thinking those things aren't valuable?" He quickly sat again, his shuddering knees unwilling to hold him.

Verner Bjornson, whose mother was a cousin of Ĉejo's mother, later stood and said, "People weren't built in God's image, eh?" He sat again and then looked around for agreement, but Luizo, also looking around, said that people didn't understand what Verner meant, and prompted him to get up a second time and explain himself. "Well, it's this business of the śimanas," Verner said, standing again. "We're living in a mechanical thing, eh? and we got to work hard to keep it from coming to ruin. People can't be expected to carry such a burden, can they?—knowing it's our human intervention prevents the whole world from collapsing. We weren't meant to be godlike in this particular sense, were we? I wonder if maybe that's the cause of so many people going insane—the śimanas, eh?" He filled his cheeks with air and rolled the little balloons around thoughtfully. He was small, with bulging eyes, and this grimace turned him to a toad. If he hadn't been saying something weighty, somebody would have teased him for making himself so ugly. When he let the air out of his face, Verner said, "People suffer from this knowledge," looking around as if this was intended to clear up any last little confusion about his meaning. Then he sat down beside his wife.

Immediately Sven Fujino stood and said, "It's true, there's no escaping the possibility of apocalypse—people just carry that possibility inside them. But nothing in life is certain, eh? Nothing but the circling round of things." And he brought up an old Quaker tenet, a belief in the progressive revelation of God's will through the ages. In order to discover new truths, they must look, each time around, for ways to widen the circle. "New paths around old habits," someone else said, and Sven nodded.

Between long silences, other people spoke: "This New World is how God created it. What are we thinking? that God's work needs remaking?" "We ought to be listening to this New World instead of asking it so many questions." "We ought to be asking whether there's a place for us there, and what it is." "If we want to live there, it ought to be on the old terms, eh? as the old Quakers lived, joining our hands to the world God made."

Gradually, people began to return to Sesilo Hurtado's leading—that the marginality of the world might be a saving grace—and they followed that leading toward adaptive strategies, ways to live lightly on a fragile land. This time around, no one brought up drainage fields or tillage.

Cêjo went on listening to people talk, but without looking at their faces. Once, he looked at his father. His eye was shut, his head bearing off loosely sideward as if he had been released, finally, from the burden of its weight. Cêjo had a sudden, excruciatingly vivid recollection of his brother Vilef's heavy round skull balanced and swaying, a hibiscus blossom on a spindly stem.

It seemed to him that on the day of Vilef's birth his family had been set afloat above an abyss and had been straining ever since to make out what lay in the darkness below. Now in a flash of apprehension he realized he had never had Udo Blades's friendship and so never had lost it. And he understood, all at once, that his brother hadn't changed his life, only shaped it.

On this little eddy, drifting, he lost the stream of people's talk. Was it Heza's old voice that he heard finally? a few words, floating, transcendent in their meaning. *God's world*, she said. *Here we are, re-entering God's world.*

10

Juko

Dazzling and tremendous how quick the sun-rise would
  kill me,
If I could not now and always send sun-rise out of me.
We also ascend dazzling and tremendous as the sun,
We found our own O my soul in the calm and cool of the
  daybreak.

JUKO AND HER neighbor, Filisa Ilmen, helped Kristina from
the tub when the old woman complained that the water was
too hot, that her thin old skin was letting the heat through to
her bones, but then both of the younger women got back in the
water—Kristina hadn't yet become so old that she wasn't able
to put on her own clothes, she told them.

While they went on talking about the man over in Mandala
who was a hoarder, Juko watched her mother-in-law stooping
over her pants, putting her clean knobby feet in the leg open-
ings, shakily pulling up the trousers around her hips. Kristina's

solidity, her sturdiness, was still in the bones of her broad face
and hands, the wiry patch of her pubic hair, the splay of her
feet, but she had seemed to shrink in the last years until now
her skin was a loose fit, slumping in little shirrs at her breasts
and elbows, buttocks and knees. And after the plague had finished with them all, the old woman never had recovered her
whole strength. She had always been thin but after the plague
her collarbones stood out from her neck in long delicate arches
as if they might be the scaffolding of wings, and there was
fragility in the sprung bones of her shoulders and hips, in the
tender dark cups of her inner thighs as she stood bowlegged
getting her pants on. Now her hands rattled the paper as she
lofted lines on a drafting board. Other people had to thread the
needle when she took up a piece of sewing. She was prone to
fall asleep at unexpected times—talking, sitting over a bowl of
unshelled beans or a lapful of reading—her chin dropping irresistibly down to her breastbone and her eyes sliding in a secret
search behind the closed lids.

At such times, watching the spittle gathering at the edges
of the old woman's mouth and her uncombed hair trembling
with her breath, Juko would fall into an impatient, resentful
melancholy. Her own mother had died at forty-seven, a bacte-
rial infection of her lungs; her father's mother had died in her
sleep at fifty-three; her mother's mother, bleeding out from a
torn uterus, hadn't survived her own youngest child's christening. Humberto's mother, Leona, was as absolutely lost to her
as if she had died with her grandson, Vilef. Juko had thought,
in marrying Bjoro she had acquired a mother who was proof
against that lineage of early death. She had imagined Kristina
still standing flat-footed and erect at ninety, brandishing a

cane, going on stubbornly well. Her failing health was an unexpected defeat, an offense, but who should be blamed for it?

"When she sweeps up the dust from the floor of her house, her husband gathers it into bowls and keeps it," Filisa said insultingly, and this made Kristina curl back her long upper lip.

"Maybe he thinks he'll get enough dirt to grow carrots in."

With little enough to share, it was their practice to share everything, and this man Rajdaro Furbo was widely known, defined by his selfishness. He stored corn in baskets in his apartment. He was contemptuously tolerated, his family pitied—gossip and scorn were the chief line of enforcement in their lives.

"Does he think he's living alone?" Filisa gestured with her thumb. "Does he think, if his children are fat, his family is living well?"

Kristina was sliding her feet shakily into her sandals, looking down to find the toe loop, frowning. "I don't blame him for it; he's crazy," she said. "Only I blame his wife, what's her name, you say? Helena?"

Juko let out a small scoffing breath through her lips, *Puh.* "For what? For sweeping her house?"

Kristina was shuffling off, sounding the tile floor with her sandals, and she waved a hand irritably without looking back.

Filisa knew this miser's wife, Helena, from having served with her on the Pacema Sewage Committee, but she seemed to take Kristina's point of view without a qualm. She said, nodding, casting her answer toward Kristina, "Maybe she ought to bring those hoarded things out and give them to other people, eh? And if that old shithole gets mad, she can divorce him."

In a flurry of dim exasperation and bewilderment, Juko

thought of saying, *A wife can't be held accountable for her husband's corn, any more than his sins.* But she was following Kristina with her eyes, the old woman already through the doorway and her bent shadow moving across the openwork of the pasado wall, and in a moment she only said bleakly, "Maybe she doesn't want a divorce."

Filisa turned her head toward Juko, a canny look. "Well, maybe not," she said, as if these were weighty words, a pronouncement. Juko's own marriage was the object of neighborhood gossip and speculation, she knew, and people doubtless were asking Filisa, who was an old neighbor, a friend, for news and judgment. Probably now Filisa would tell people, *Juko Ohaśi doesn't want a divorce. Oh, she said it was to do with Rajdaro Furbo's wife, but I could see, it's her own marriage she was talking about.* Juko shifted her weight in the water, looking away from Filisa rudely, stung by the truth in this presumption. Her life had become melancholy and insupportable; her marriage felt broken, unfixable; but she didn't want to be divorced again.

"Who knows why Helena del Rio stays married?" she said unhappily. *It might be my mother-in-law and not my husband that I go on living with, will not separate myself from.*

"Well, some families think divorce is a scandal," Filisa murmured. "Or maybe she thinks, because he's crazy, it wouldn't be right to leave him." She gathered up her mouth. "Or maybe she likes the way he touches her in bed, eh? doesn't want to give that up?"

Juko had kept silent with her friends and her family about the thing that had happened between her and Bjoro—obscurely, she imagined that if she didn't speak of it, it might become faraway, equivocal—but she had become impatient in these last weeks, expecting illogically that people would stop making their jokes about sexual matters, out of kindness to her. Yet Filisa Ilmen, heedless, lifted her hands out of the water in order to make a lewd gesture in the steamy air: "Or maybe she likes to be let alone, and Rajdaro keeps her happy by sleeping with his corncobs." Filisa's face was round, her nose wide and flat; when she grinned, a crease folded across the bridge of her nose in a childish way. "Or maybe it's Helena who sleeps with the corn," she said, laughing, making that childish face, and then Juko was irresistibly drawn into it, delivering an insult common in women's bathhouses: "Any corncob will do—what's the use of men, eh?" In the gibe was a small, satisfying loosening, a release from inexpressible bitterness and anguish.

Filisa laughed again, rocking back in the tub so that her breasts broke the water. She floated, eyes closing sleepily, the cups of her ears flooding. Her breasts stood up like the soft brown crowns of earth in a field beset by gophers.

They got away from talking about Rajdaro Furbo, began to trade reports of their children, to gossip about other people's children, and complain about their parents. That got them started on other things, matters of aging. Women liked to say, when they were old enough to be done with the business of being women they could finally be persons. In their old age women were expected to make a lot of noise, be disapproved, be fearless. Filisa, grimacing, said she always had been loud and disagreeable, and who could stand her if she worsened? As if it were all part of the same thing, she said, "I'm getting to a rough place, myself—me and Leo—between the woods and the fields." She meant an old axiom, *The forest is always waiting at the edge of the fields.*

Juko was pierced by a sudden wish to confide in Filisa: to say, *I'm at that place myself—in the rough weeds;* to say that she had not let Bjoro into her body since the night of the *Ruby's* homecoming. But Filisa went on with a flat reporting of the habits of Leo's that bored and offended her, and gradually Juko's urge to speak went out of her. Someone on the outside of the pasado wall was shaking a long mat, the person's shadow moving, bending, swinging arms, in the interstices between the upright bamboo. Juko watched this without seeing it, listening indifferently to Filisa Ilmen's complaints. Leo shirked small decisions, she said. He habitually asked for answers she had already given. And what was this proneness he had, for making himself scarce when there was argument between his mother and his wife?

They had been married a long time, she and Leo, their youngest child by now twelve or thirteen. Filisa was at an age celebrated for women's sexuality and men's erratic emotionalism. Couples who didn't divorce at the end of their child-rearing years often ceremonially reaffirmed their marriages then, when fidelity was a more difficult sacrament. It was a recognition of a hard truth: There could be no possibility of allegiance, of faith, without the possibility of choice. Juko understood what Filisa was asking. *Should I go on being married to my husband?* She understood that Filisa was listening for the answers inside her own mouth.

"Humberto Indergard—he's marrying, I heard," Filisa said suddenly. "Has he got so much better, then? I thought he was crippled, his mother had to wipe his mouth for him when he ate. Who's this woman? Someone his mother chose for him? A caretaker wife?"

"I don't know," Juko said in surprise. She had heard from her

son that Olava Morgan, the kura, had begun to keep company
with Humberto, and she had thought Olava was walking out
with him to bear up his weak right side. If they were sleeping
in the same bed, Cejo hadn't said. Were they marrying now?
She didn't know. Olava Morgan was a big, beautiful woman,
had gotten to be fifty-five or sixty without ever deciding to
marry. Maybe Olava wasn't the woman people were talking
about. Or maybe Humberto's coming marriage was a matter
of gossip and rumor. People said it was Humberto's words that
had cleared the way on this question of the New World, and
now some religious people might be searching his life for signs
and portents; maybe this was a guess that had jumped wide of
the mark, something trailing illogically in the wake of wonder.

Filisa's thinking may have been going down this same way.
She said to Juko, "It was God's voice coming out of his mouth,
eh? How else to explain it?" Her body had settled in the tub so
that the front of her face was the only part above the waterline,
a small, crested island fine-grained as a dune. From between
her damp lashes, she peered thoughtfully into the crosspoles
of the bathhouse ceiling. "It's a mystery. The world's a strange
place. We go along imagining it's ordinary, and then something
happens and we're reminded: It's all inconceivable, every bit of
it. Cockroaches. Bananas. People speaking in tongues. Why the
hell ever did we get to thinking it was commonplace?"

Juko's own faith and practice always had been mundane.
She valued the Quaker way of silence for leading people into
scrupulous listening, slow judgment. A few times she had seen
a certain power rise up out of the silence of a Meeting and
bring speakers to places they never could reach alone, raise
them to a kind of eloquence they never had shown before

and perhaps never would reveal again, but if she didn't know what this power of the Meeting was, she always had accepted its presence in the world without presupposing some kind of junction with God. She and Kristina had spent years arguing such questions, all the proofs and rebuttals wrung out of both of them by now. When they had heard of Humberto's speaking, how all at once he had made himself understood, Kristina had pulled up her mouth, had nodded without surprise. "Music is in you; it awakes and comes out when you're reminded by the instruments," she had said firmly, as if this were part of their longstanding argument, a persuasive finding.

"I guess none of us can stand to know it every day," Filisa said, answering something else. "We'd be crazy, eh? if we always stood balanced at the edge of the mystery, looking out at the world with wide-open eyes. We got to take it in little glimpses through our fingers."

Juko said, murmuring, "Or send someone else out to look."

Filisa rocked her head, pushing a wake across the water. "Well, yes. We sent Humberto, eh?"

Juko had been keeping away from Humberto's sickbed, and telling people it was because of old Leona's rancor toward her. She didn't know if this was true. Humberto was someone who'd always been apt to complain about little maladies, her years with him a litany of queasiness, twinges, lesions and loose bowels, and for months after Vilef's death he had been chronically sick. Now he'd fallen down with a stroke. A few times she had sent along to him, by way of her son, some stupidly trite words of pity and support, but she had not gone to sit with him herself. There was a core in him, of helplessness and pathos, and she was impatient with it—or afraid of it, as a kind of proof of what might be at her own core: an unfeelingness, an indurate heart. But this gossip about his remarriage made her feel anxious and nostalgic. She yearned suddenly to say to Humberto every small thing that had not been said between them. She wanted to say: *I once loved you for your perfect acceptance of our imperfect child.*

She was fifty now, her menses had been erratic and skimpy for more than a year. Maybe she would be finished with that part of her life entirely, before long. How was it possible that she still remembered exactly the way her body felt, the hugeness, the intimacy, of harboring a child inside? And the absence afterward, the unexpected pang of becoming solitary again— she never had forgotten that. She was struck all at once by a flurry of precise physical remembrance, bare of nostalgia, the body's memory: the salt-burn of her milk letting down, the briny-sweet taste of her son Ĉejo's toes, the smell of his feces, Vilef's narrow, membranous breastbone—the palm of her hand cupped to the heated pulse there.

She stood up suddenly from the tub, sighing. In the close, humid heat of the bathhouse she combed her damp hair, smoothed her chapped hands, heels, knees with coconut oil, put on her shirt and sandals, tied up the strings of her trousers, while Filisa sat on in the water. "I think sometimes, when you set your mind to work at understanding your life, that's when you lose sight of it," Filisa said thoughtfully. She was looking into the ceiling, her tongue exploring her teeth. Maybe it wasn't meant to be advice for Juko.

Juko gathered up her towel and unclean clothes and went out, padding in flat bare feet along the narrow poles of the pasado to the door of her own apartment. People were waiting inside—Ĝan Sorensen, Svalo Smit, Dagmar Lopez, the three of them sitting with Kristina, talking quietly together while they waited. Bjoro was waiting with them, sitting in a half-lotus as if he might be meditating, his palms resting across his knees. When he saw her, he flushed slowly. She stood at the threshold, her bones taking on weight. "Oh hell," she said, from a kind of tired helplessness.

The three Clearness Committee people looked up at her, laughing, understanding. Dagmar said, teasing her, "Don't cry, Juko. Hey, we started without you, but it's a long work to find a clear way out of troubles. There's enough to do—you won't be left without." Ĝan, grinning, said, "She looks happy to see us, eh? She's got a good attitude. She wants to try to find a way through, doesn't want to do any dodging."

Juko didn't think any of this was funny. She gave Kristina a look. The old woman was sewing, her eyes fixed on her hands, but she knew Juko's eyes were on her. She made a small, flatulent sound with her lips and tongue. "Should I have let your marriage go on being sick to death, then?" she murmured.

The Clearness Committee people looked from one of them to the other. Dagmar said, not yet becoming entirely serious, "Are you blaming Kristina for bringing us into this? Did you think your troubles were a secret?" She gestured loosely, the swinging of her hand taking in Bjoro where he went on sitting as if none of this concerned him, his face turned from people, a mask of disinterest. "A husband and a wife can't stop sleeping in the same bed—hell, the same house!—without neighbors seeing it, you know. Anyway, people heard your shouting. Some people think they know what's the matter between you and Bjoro, and they asked us to help you find a clear way through.

Maybe you should thank them, eh? for bearing witness. Maybe you shouldn't be looking around for someone to blame." Her voice was low, good-humored.

Juko always had liked Dagmar Lopez, a woman her own age whose sense of humor was on the sour side, whose laugh was a pleasure to listen to, low and chuckling. But now she said bitterly to Dagmar, the words spilling out from a jumble of shame and anger, "Maybe you should look around for someone else to counsel. I don't need help finding a place to put the blame in my marriage." From the edge of her eye she saw Bjoro drop his head and then lift it, seeming to search the ceiling. *Don't look up there for it,* she thought angrily, irrationally.

People on Clearness Committees were respected for their patience, and for a certain kind of graceful common sense, a considered or instinctive wisdom. All three of them looked at her quietly, Dagmar's face becoming serious but not taking on any offense. Svalo Smit said in a flat, reasonable way, "Where do you put it? This blame?"

She meant to look deliberately at Bjoro, to deliberately name him, but in a moment she let her armload of dirty laundry heavily down to the floor and sat down with it, her eyes fixed upon Kristina's hands, the bird-like clench, fingers stiff as pin feathers as they pulled a needle through the cloth, in and through, in and through relentlessly. Juko's mouth when she finally opened it said sorrowfully, "If there's a way not to blame my husband, you'll have to help me look for it."

Ĝan Sorensen nodded. He turned his head toward Bjoro before turning it toward Juko again. "I don't know if there's a way not to blame Bjoro. But there's always a way out of troubles, eh? and we'll all of us look for it." He didn't say, *Sometimes the*

way out of disease is death. Sometimes the way out of a troubled
marriage is divorce.

They let a fairly long silence clear the path a little. Then
Dagmar said quietly that people had begun to know there was
trouble in Bjoro and Juko's marriage on the night of the *Ruby's*
homecoming. She said that people knew there was trouble in
their marriage when Bjoro butt-fucked his wife as if this were
an entitlement rather than a matter for mutual consent. She
said, looking from one of them to the other, this was something
everybody knew, or supposed to be true, and if it wasn't, then
Bjoro or Juko ought to say so now.

Juko's body filled with heat; there was a dim ringing in the
bones of her skull. She had fixed her eyes on a point in the wall
behind Svalo Smit's shoulder but was blind to it, her seeing
turned inward following a shifting confusion of memory, the
fine pale hairs along the curve of Bjoro's knee lifting to straddle
her, the hollow below the hinge of his jaw clenching and then
loosening, the involute plaiting of the rug pressed beneath her
eye—an incomprehensible landscape, dim and vast.

"Some people think Bjoro is ashamed of his behavior and
hates his wife for this shame," Dagmar said in a little while.
"Some people think Juko hates her husband for his behavior
and is ashamed of herself for this hatred. Anyway, everybody
knows that Juko and Bjoro have given up having sexual relations with one another since the night of the *Ruby's* homecoming. And that the person who came home inside Bjoro's body
is not the same person who went away in it but somebody else,
somebody who can't see a clear way through. And that the person inside Juko's body has lately become solitary—she thinks
she's living alone, eh? anyone can see this." Dagmar looked at

Juko and at Bjoro without seeming to expect either of them to reply. "So people have asked us to help Bjoro find a clear way, and take Juko by the hand so she can stand up with the rest of us and stop this crouching down."

There was a longer silence while people waited for an inner stillness. Juko's head kept up a clatter of noise, meaningless and distracting. She did not look at Bjoro but began to be conscious of the precise placement of his body in the close air of the room, the weight and balance of his head carried at the top of his spine. She didn't know what she was feeling except a buzzing, unfocused anxiety. The Clearness Committee allowed the silence to stand and stand until it began to seem solid, a support, and finally it became possible for her to bring a few words out: "I don't want to be known as the woman who was twice divorced."

She was surprised by the pitch of her voice, low, a murmur of piety and self-disgust.

"I wonder," Svalo Smit said, "who *would* you want to be known as?"

She went on being surprised, separate from her mouth, from the words that finally came out, dismally sentimental: "The woman who was married so long that she and her husband would finish each other's sentences." Fragments of dialogue, pointless and unidentifiable, unwound themselves in her brain, the voices of old people overlapping one another in an amiable, winding braid of storytelling.

Without seeing it, she felt Bjoro's head turning. The turning of her own head brought the frame of reference around, a disconcerting sideward slip, a coriolis effect, and then he said, looking at her, "Do you want me to be that husband? the one who finishes your sentences?" with something in it that was anguish, and something else, a wildness, a charge. He may not have been asking her anything. Maybe he was angry with her for disclosing a maudlin side; their history together had been agreeably bristly, unimpassioned.

"Yes! You!" She was angry too, and wild, and the surprising thing was that she began suddenly to cry, a choking cough of grief or denial. Maybe Bjoro cried too; he put his face down in his hands. She didn't know what she wanted from him, but not weeping, and she hated him for it suddenly, remembering that she had thought this was something left behind in her other marriage, with that other husband. Swiftly she was finished with tears herself. She stared bitterly across the casement of the pasado wall, up the narrow slope of the tube to the houses and fields of the Bonveno ŝiro.

Svalo Smit said mildly, "As far as that goes, I wonder if you want to be that husband—eh, Bjoro?"

Bjoro reared his head, exactly as opossum sometimes will do, a kind of blind searching, and when he found Juko he twisted the heels of his fists against his eyes harshly. "I want to go on being married," he said. His voice was rough, hopeless. In his long homely face there was something unfamiliar to her, a desperation that transcended loneliness. In that look, it was impossible to separate the gentle from the terrible, the suffering from the harm—what should Juko understand from that look? She turned from it in a confusion of anguish, as if he had deliberately peeled back a bandage to show her an ugly wound.

"My wife never did finish my sentences, but she retold everything I said," Svalo said after a while, uncomplainingly. "She said I never could get it right, eh?" He was an old man

eighty or more, and had been divorced from his wife after their
children were grown.

The Clearness Committee might have gone on talking in
this vein, a mild bantering—they may have thought this was
a bridge to something—but Kristina said suddenly, bitterly, "I
don't know what all this talking about unfinished sentences has
to do with my son covering his wife's back." Then unexpectedly
she gave Bjoro a furious look, her lips twisting, "What were
you thinking? What were you thinking?" she said to him, and
went on glaring at him a moment—his burning face. Then she
pulled her head down again, going on with sewing. Her lips
were drawn up in a tight gather as if she had just now sewn her
own mouth shut. They all could hear the slight hush of thread
drawing through the cloth, and the stick of the needle.

"What do you want me to say, panja?" Bjoro said to her,
spreading his hands. "I was crazy. I told Juko that. I went crazy!
I don't know what I was doing, why I was doing it. Shall I go on
apologizing for that until you make up your mind how much
penance is enough?" He looked around at all of them. "I don't
know what I should do, after I apologize to my wife," he said
angrily. "After I tell her I want to go on being married. What's
the next thing I should do? I want to have sex with my wife
again, but she never comes into my bed. What is the next thing
I should do?"

Ĝan said, in the habitual way of Clearness Committees
everywhere, "Oh, well, I don't think any of us know the answer
to that; it's not our business to tell you what you should do,
after all."

Bjoro made a sound, a low hissing of unhappiness, of frustration, and looked off from everyone.

"You say your wife never comes into your bed," Svalo told him after a while, "but as far as that goes, you never come into your wife's bed either."

Bjoro said fiercely, "My wife doesn't want me coming to bed with her." Juko believed this, herself. *I won't let him in my bed!* she was thinking, but in the silence, when those words didn't speak themselves out of her mouth, she knew that she had been lonely for his weight lying by her in the night, his back against her hips, his whispering in the darkness. The loss of her husband's company distilled itself into a pang of longing. It was her body, not her bed, that she didn't want Bjoro coming into.

When she spoke, finally, the words that came out were a bitter chiding. "I don't have any interest in having sex. You've made that a hateful thing. What do you think? That if we lie in the same bed, we must have sex?"

Then Dagmar said, nodding, "There's nothing wrong with Juko keeping celibate, eh?" She thought and then she said, "Everybody knows how it is with women who miscarry, how their bodies go on feeling the effects of grief and they have to wait for that to be finished before they get pregnant again, or they're liable to lose the new fetus, too. It seems to me, this is what Juko is doing, waiting a while, letting her body get over this grief, before she lets her husband into her again. There's a healing that has to take place."

"In Bjoro, too, as far as that goes," Svalo said, and Ĝan, nodding, told everyone that celibacy had a well-known value, especially in treating sexual matters.

The silence after that had a different quality, the vague weight of satisfaction; probably the members of the Clearness Committee were thinking a little progress had been made. Juko couldn't have said what the progress was. Something pent-up had been released; maybe that was all.

They went on talking a little while more but it was no longer a counseling. Dagmar asked Juko if it was true, this gossip about Humberto marrying. "I heard it was Olava Morgan he was walking out with," she told Juko. Kristina, without looking up from her sewing, said pointedly that Olava was a woman who had no interest in marrying. "People have too much empty space in their minds, that's where this kind of stupid gossip comes from," she said, mumbling in irritation.

They drifted off to discussing the New World, and Humberto's magical leading, and the *Dream,* gone out ahead of them to put a new landing party down in the southern archipelago. Bjoro listened to this talk dourly, not joining in. When Ĝan Sorensen asked him if it was true—from the face of the land there was no seeing the curve of it?—Bjoro gave back a harsh look. Juko thought he wouldn't answer. But then he said, staring away from them all, "I think of the sky." She saw that he was flushing slowly. He said bleakly, enigmatically, "It's the lack of incurvature on the sky."

After the Clearness Committee people had gone home, Juko and her husband and her mother-in-law went on sitting silently inside the apartment. Juko drew her unclean laundry into her lap and began searching along all the seams with her thumb and forefinger as if she believed she might find a place where some stitching had come apart. She didn't look at Bjoro, but felt him watching her hands.

"I miss the settledness of things, Juko."

What did this mean? She wasn't able to answer. Then he stood, grunting, and went down the ladder, out of the house.

She began to fold the shirt and trousers, the towel and shorts, went on folding and refolding them in her lap while Kristina went on with her sewing.

"What is it, anyway, this business about Olava Morgan marrying Humberto Indergard?" Kristina asked her finally.

Juko looked at her. "I don't know. Do you want me to ask Ĉejo?"

"We ought to go over there and ask Humberto ourselves."

"That woman, his mother, doesn't want me in her house."

"Oh, she can go to hell. What does she think—that the mother of Humberto's sons shouldn't come and see Humberto when he's sick? She can go to hell. I always have liked Humberto Indergard but his mother must be a fool." She looked at Juko. Her eyes were rheumy, the lids trembling, but the look she gave was hard and intent. "Where is that house he lives in, over in Alaŭdo, eh? We ought to walk over there now. We ought to sit down with Humberto and talk with him."

There was something Juko had wanted to say to her once-husband: She remembered the impulse but not the substance. What she felt now was her old determination to stay away. "I don't want to go into Leona's house, Kristina."

Her mother-in-law looked at her. Then she looked away. "Well, that's an old matter, eh? Settled."

A heat rose up the back of Juko's neck. "Yes. It's settled. That marriage, that child's life."

Kristina turned her head again, her mouth loosening sorrowfully. "Well, I don't know what that old woman is thinking—" she said after a while. "—what she's blaming you for."

Juko understood that this had nothing much to do with Leona Arntsen. After a long silence something yielded in her and she said without looking at Kristina, "Do you remember how a child will sleep tangled? How you want to straighten their bodies on the bed? My son Vilef slept so light—so light, Kristina. If I pulled his legs out straight, he always would wake and cry."

She didn't know why this memory had come up in her; or why, in a few moments, an ancient, latent culpability came out of her mouth: "Some people think sailmenders and other space-going people should keep themselves childless; the rads are higher for people outside. Maybe Leona thinks I'm to blame for making that fey baby." She grimaced—a concealing, joyless smile. "Or it may be she just blames me for not loving him more."

Kristina pulled her chin down. She said nothing, and then she said, "It's bad luck, is all it is. You know my son has gone out in the boats for twenty years, eh? and both his children were born whole. Who does that woman blame for her grandson Cejo, born whole?" After a long silence she sighed. "Ah, Juko," she said, as if this naming were a benediction.

They walked around to the Alaŭdo ŝiro, Kristina tired and slow, leaning into Juko. "Old age is not all it's cracked up to be," she muttered once, and flashed a sour grin.

One person, a woman they didn't know, was in Humberto's apartment, separating seeds from cottonsilk. This required them to sit down politely and help her get the work done, before it became possible to ask where Humberto was. "People are digging up the malanga taro, eh? this time of year," she said. She went on pulling out the seeds with her quick old fingers while she gave them an earnest look, drawing her skimpy brows forward. Juko didn't know if this was an answer.

They left the apartment and asked a man who was gathering eggs: Where was the field of taro planted? Looking for it, walking up the narrow beaten footway between the Ring River and the tiers of Alaŭdo fields, they saw a woman digging a test hole at the river's slack edge and when she stood up it was Leona—Humberto's mother—her trousers rolled at her thighs and her bare old legs glazed with mud. She made a sound when she saw Juko, a breathing out. In a moment, the old woman's chin convulsed and she deliberately stooped to her hole. Juko's impulse was to say something serene, something commonplace, as if there was no history between them, but her brain was suddenly filled up with too much that was consequential.

Kristina said, when they had walked past Leona, "Was that woman your mother-in-law?" and Juko said irritably, "You're my mother-in-law."

The big heart-shaped leaves of the malanga taro were brown and dead, and Juko's son was standing out in the spent field digging up the tubers with a wide-tined fork while Humberto sat at the edge of the field watching the work, his weight on one haunch with his other leg outstretched. Kristina put her hand on his scalp, petting. The shaky, weighted turning of his head was obscurely evocative: Juko's heart turned with it. Someone had cut his hair very short, baring around his ears a curving bow of skin that was pale and tender; his face had become bony, unfamiliar, asymmetrical. He looked at Kristina and then Juko one-eyed without surprise, or he had lost the knack for displaying it. "Ha," he said, twisting his mouth.

Ĉejo came out of the field and the four of them sat together and talked about the taro harvest, and a repair someone was making to the plumbing under a nearby domaro, and rumors and gossip to do with the people crewing the *Dream*. Humberto sat clasping one hand with the other, his outstretched leg trembling slightly, his bidden eye following people as they spoke. It was an effort for him to speak himself, the words thick and slow, but Ĉejo had developed an ear for making out his father's meanings, and sometimes Juko understood the gist of Humberto's words from Ĉejo's responses. It occurred to her, watching the two of them talking slowly back and forth, that if Humberto had once stood at the center of the Light, he was standing somewhere else now. But gradually she understood some of his words herself. When they were arguing about an opossum that had become a pet, Humberto said laboriously, "Gives up. Rightful. For safe," and his eye moved from one of them to the other. When he looked at Juko it was an old look, natural and dear, his brows rising in that self-effacing way, and she was pierced suddenly with a sad, indefinable longing. *None of us are standing in the old places*, she thought.

She and Kristina made a slow way home in the afternoon light. When they were stepping over the narrow channel of the mezlando aqueduct, she said, "Oh hell," and stopped suddenly, straddling the little ditch. "We forgot to ask about Humberto's marriage." Kristina shook her head, going on up the footway without slowing, beginning the easeful climb to the high houses of Pacema.

Their rooms were empty, mournful with the yellowing light of dusk. Juko and Kristina did not speak, sitting over separate handwork. When Kristina's chin fell to her breast, when she began to snore softly, Juko studied her sleeping. She thought of going out quietly, going onto the sail. After a while she did.

In these last weeks, the little orange sun had gradually

become a source of light. Now in the blackness, objects were bright. Inside the exo, in sunlight, Juko's skin was warm, and on the shadow side of something, cold. The purity of the unreflected light was a comfort, clarifying. She went out to the field called the Wayward Gate and climbed to the head of the flymast. The sails were a vast wheel of light, luminous in the perfect blackness. From the head of the mast, it was possible to see the edge of light bound to the blackness in an intricate, inextricable coherence. Over the broad, bright field of the sheet she became exact, contained, a foot or an elbow like an oar dipped in still water moving her precisely. In the soundlessness, the depthlessness of space, there was the sense of a slight shudder, a susurrus on the black brightness. She floated on it, drawing her body through the light.

Vintro

(Of many debts incalculable,
Haply our New World's chiefest debt is to old poems.)

THAT TIME WHEN the *Migremo* fell into the sea, I was standing with my sister Kikuma in a small open boat in the Ŝiblingo Fjord below the houses of Holds Loneliness, getting in the kelp with rakes. Little squalls of rain came and went, but in the still air between them the sea was green, the color people call marblua, and the skin of the water was lacquered, glossy, beneath a colorless sky. A puso weather was moving in from the northwest but we weren't worried yet, only watchful. We were working between the beach and the stacks, a kilometer or a kilometer and a half from the shore, riding a heavy sea anchor, and the boat had a high waist, tipped up horns, it was built for handling a surf. Both of us had heavy-weather gear. And the puso weather would be a while getting here: The cloud wrack was faintly bluish white, lit by the Sea Is Groaning ice fields that stand off the coast there. We wouldn't begin to worry much about the weather until the belly of the clouds, moving toward the coast over the open water, became the griseous color people call Water Sky.

There was another, bigger boat within shouting range, five people in it. One of the five, Adria Berelo, had a progressive disease of her muscles, a dystrophy. All of them kept this in their minds—it was a serious matter—but they were not governed by it, and no one in that boat was solemn: There was a good deal of talking going on and laughter, and Kikuma and I in our own boat sometimes yelled over there to ask what was making those people laugh; I guess we suffered a little from feeling excluded, deprived.

Kikuma and one of the men in that other boat, Davido Cêkli, began to trade insults back and forth over the water. They were longtime kite fighting opponents, and you know how it is with kite people—when they aren't crossing their strings they're crossing words. They think when people are gathered in one place, digging roots or laying out kelp in wracks, and then stopping to eat their lunch, if you raise a kite it's an open challenge, and they want to be the last one to hold the sky—they coat their strings with ground glass. When the *Migremo* came apart, the two of them were shouting their gibes and I was laughing, and you know how it is when thunder is so far off you can only hear it in your bones? That was how I heard the breaking up of the *Migremo*, just in that way, its shudder going through the air as a dull booming, and when I lifted my head, looking, there was a daylight star scribing a long arc across the overclouded sky, trailing embers and ash, going down to the western sea. "Hey. What," Kikuma said, turning to look. "Hey, Ana, what did we see?" and I wasn't able to think of how to answer.

People say, all truths wait in all things. Here is something waiting inside something else: When I was a child we would go up, summers, to that place people call Embracing, and live in my great-aunt's latajo on the steep west side. You know how a latajo's walls are open? How they let in the air and the daylight and people's voices—the whole world? From the inside of that latajo you could look the long way out onto the maltejo, or up the long slope of land to where the mountains broke above the alta, and at night when Kikuma and I were lying in our bed we could see the old stars, and the little new star sliding like a bead of ice over the roof, and it seemed as if you could look a great long way up into the sky.

Once in the winter, after my family had moved back under the berm at Having Wind, I went up on the alta looking for some particular stones—some of us were laying out the pattern of a vocero on the flat of the plain—and I came up to Embracing and looked into my aunt's latajo and the light that lay inside it was a certain color, had a certain quality. That was in the years people call the malsataj. Do you remember those years? The famine and the hard living? People were making their winter tea from pouring hot water over gravel, in those years.

Later in my life, when I flew in a balloon over Holds Loneliness and saw for the first time the color of the deep ice along the edge of the glacier, I thought of that latajo, the light inside it, lying empty in the winter. And later when I was standing in that boat in the Ŝiblingo Fjord watching the long curve of fire, the *Migremo* falling over the edge of the sky and into the sea, I remembered the way the land looked when I was hanging from that balloon above Holds Loneliness, everything seeming to move in sweeping arches, the stones off the shore standing in long curving palisades, and the breaking sea rolling slow and broad, grayed with sand, and the long grasses streaming under the wind, and the falls along the edge of the fjord flying on the breath of air, upward like smoke, and the beads of rain falling so fine that it was still possible to see the sun and the violet sky, but spreading the light in a great, brilliant, doubled cielarko, its shining feet seeming to rest on the oxbows of the mountains with the tongue of the glacier framed within it. That's why the people of the coast have that certain look behind their eyes, I was thinking then. That's why they don't want to live anywhere else.

So afterward, after I had moved into my sister's household at Holds Loneliness and was standing in that boat on the Ŝiblingo Fjord getting in the kelp, and the *Migremo* fell out of the sky in a flaming arch, I didn't think of people's deaths—that I was standing watching people dying. I was thinking of the winter light inside an empty latajo, and the way the beads of ice in a fine rain bend the light in a vivid rainbow.

Afterward, a little while afterward, there was a moment while I wondered if it was the old *Miller* giving up its orbit at last, but somebody in the other boat yelled, "Was that the *Migremo* falling?" and then I remembered the *Migremo* had been up there getting salvage from the empty houses, the feral woodlands, inside the torus, and coming down today onto the long landing field southeast of Divided. I wondered if the people over at Divided, listening on the uplink, had heard the dull clap, had felt it shuddering along their bones.

We watched the tendril of smoke thicken, become a brume of steam rising out of the sky line. Kikuma said quietly, "Are they lying in the Owl Strait, Ana? Off the Mizerido estuary?" and then someone in the other boat yelled out, "In the Owl Strait, looks like!" After a bit, those people in the other boat put their oars in the water and rowed over to us so they wouldn't have to keep on shouting. We looked at one another. Then people began saying how much sea they thought was between us and the wreckage of the *Migremo* and how quick they thought we could get across it, and whether our little boat, the *Pulls Together*, being quicker than their big boat, the *Keeps Steady*, ought to wait up or go on ahead without waiting, and whether it would be better to run on across the strait to the Goes To Grass Islands and lie snug, after we'd got the *Migremo* people aboard, or try to beat back along the lee of the cape, back here to Holds Loneliness.

We didn't want to get out in the Owl Strait and not be able to make land when the puso weather came in from the sea—we didn't want to go down into the water with the *Migremo*. But no one said this. No one said, The winds are northwesterly. No one said, Look, that puso weather is over there, over the ice. Only Magdalena Ulsen's young son, earnest and distracted, said, "There won't be anyone alive, do you think?" and Magdalena looked around sorrowfully and said "Oh, I suppose not," and began to coil up the lines in readiness for getting under way.

There were five of them to get their anchor up, their mast on the wind, and they were off ahead of us, beating west-northwest around the little skerries, the Fisted Rocks, but when we stepped our windpipe the *Pulls Together* made a little twitch, taking a breath, and skated off nimbly on the light air.

I had to look behind once, to the heavy white foot of the glacier and the berms of Holds Loneliness cockling the steep last downhill at the head of the fjord, and seaward from the berms the fretwork of low stone walls sheltering people from the sea winds, and below on the outwash plain that once was a glacier, the cobble of the beach, mossy bogs and hummocks of grass where terns hunted down the fingers of the streams, and people laid out kelp in long wracks, drying in the wind.

I don't know what I was looking for.

We passed the *Steady* in the open water west of the Fisted Rocks and when they fell behind us we dumped wind and kept them to our starboard side. Kikuma steered off the ragged brume, south-southwest into the Owl Strait. The Comes-Between Cape reared its head along the port beam, a great prow of basalt pocked with indentations and ledges, a summer nesting place for thousands of ribb'd gulls but now a many-roomed empty house. In this season of the year, the *vintro,* people like to visit those rooms—when we sailed into the Owl Strait looking for the *Migremo* there was a tiny figure, maybe it was a woman, standing high up on the whitened bluff of the cape, watching our boats, or looking out toward the smoke of the wreck, or offering something into the sky. I've climbed up there myself. On a clear day you can see the Goes To Grass Islands riding in the strait like boats, the tidal currents running so fast through the channels there, they drag long wakes astern. But there was no seeing the islands in that weather, the day the *Migremo* fell, and anyway people don't climb the Comes-Between Cape only for that view across the Owl Strait. When people are feeling the weight of their own lives, they want to see the life other animals are given, and there is something mysterious and revealing about the discarded machinery of birds' lives. In abandoned flakes of eggshell, emptied seed cases, the hollow stems of cottongrass, in the delicate attenuated backbones of fish and the teeth of desiccated crustaceans, you can sometimes glimpse the bare and intricate structures of God.

The mountains of Abides were shrouded in cloud, so when we had come clear of the cape it was the long thin line of the escarpment that fixed the eastern edge of the sea. Westward, there was no line dividing the sky from the sea, and in the distant bourns of the strait we could not see the islands. Southward lay the long spine of Resting-Waiting; in other weather it might have defined the whole southern range of the horizon, the narrow peaks impounding the cirques of old glaciers, the steep headwalls streaked with snow and stone, but it was hunkered, like Abides, beneath a lowering sky. Sailing up the Owl Strait in this kind of weather, you're at the edge of the world, engirt by emptiness.

The little estuary of the Mizerido was bound in shorefast fog, so we kept an ear out for the voices of seeking-browns, those brief and reluctant flyers wintering over in the brushy aits of the Mizerido. We took our bearing from the faint ululations of their barks, and veered west by northwest, crossing and re-crossing the *Steady's* tack, our two boats scribing a braid on the water. Gradually the column of smoke from the *Migremo*, blowing off eastward, became flat and gray, indistinguishable from the overcast, and then I went up on the bowstalk to look out for the wreckage. The wind was cold and dank. For a while I called down to Kikuma, stupid questions or remarks about the boat, and I kept looking over to the northwest where the puso weather was stalled above the ice fields. But after a while I got finished with that.

You know how it is when your mind enters into a silence

with the land? when you give up speaking, and you give up listening for gulls or watching for a shift in the weather, and just begin to place yourself in the world? That was how it was when I was up on the bow stalk looking for the wreckage of the *Migremo*. Long patches of ruffled water, families of the great silver-backed balenoj going up to their wintering place in the By Far fjord; squalls of rain shadowing the sea; rafts of flag-dippers, gray-green against the gray-green water, the yellow bills of those seabirds seeming to slide like a scurf of petals on the water: I recognized and understood these patterns of light in a dreamy unvoiced way while I waited for my eye to take in what was not of the land—floating plastic, aluminum, the suf-flated exo of a dead person—and say it to me on a breath, like a word spoken aloud—*There*.

We came off the wind, steering for a big piece of a shat-tered bulkhead, ribbed white, streaked with soot, and we grappled with the kelp rakes, getting it up into the boat. None of the people on the *Migremo* were known to me, not even their names, but in the illegible letters on the smooth facade of that bulkhead, beneath great flakes of sodden ash, broken blisters of paint, I could see their faces. That piece of wreck-age was a ghostly thing. Kikuma and I passed a sorrowful look between us.

We beat a zigzag path over the water, going after a sud-den swarm of flotsam—more plastic and forced aluminum, a spongy piece of batting, a tangle of flash tubing. We shouted our finds to the people in the *Steady*, and they called theirs back—*a ravel of wiring! here's some webbing! got a piece of a bolster, looks like, or a seat!* We went off to gather up a flotilla of broken crates, and when the *Steady* was a distant white figure on the water someone over there shouted, the voice feeble, indeterminate across the wind. We raised up from what we were doing and looked. A person gestured with upraised arms. I understood something all at once, with my body, with my blood; and I took hold of the tiller, brought the boat around wallowy on the waves. "They've found one of those people," I said to my sister.

There had been four, crewing the *Migremo*; one of them was tangled in nylon line in a wrack of bladderweed that Adria Berelo on the *Steady* had pulled up to the side of that boat with a rake. This was a small woman, young as my daughter, her white exo breached at the chest—pale rags of fat and muscle flapped from the hole. Her face was open and calm, her mouth slopping in the gray lees of water inside the exoskull. Her eyes examined the sky.

My daughter, when she married, might as well have stuck her finger up my nose. That man she married, Armando Fujino, had been married twice before—he had proven to everybody but my daughter that he couldn't be a decent husband—but he was shameless, and my daughter was stupid, and we hadn't spoken a word to one another since that day, though the Clearness Committee came around every little while and tried to counsel our quarrel When I saw the face of that dead woman, the woman who died in the *Migremo*, her face broad and brown as my daughter's, I didn't think about our quarrel. I thought of how, in the afternoon when you sleep the dormeto, and wake before other people, you can try to be as still as everyone else, or if you haven't been married very long or are lying with a lover you can have quiet intercourse. Or if you're a child you can whisper until you wake someone up. I thought of how, in the weeks before my daughter was born, I slept restlessly, and took up a habit of going out of my own house and standing in cold bare feet at the narrow fenestroj of other houses, bending to peer through the wavery panes of glass at the shut eyes of sleepers. In the low winter daylight, people sleeping have a solemn expression, they breathe quietly, lying loose and still, children tangled on a mattress, married couples sleeping face to face with their knees pressed together, sisters lying down without touching, a grandfather wrapped up with his little grandchild.

A few times people woke up startled to find me peering through their windows while they slept—I may have had a brief, mild renown that winter, as a crazy person. But in those last weeks while you're waiting for a child to be born, you're expected to be restless, beside yourself. I wonder what I was looking for in the faces of those dreamers? The face of that dead woman made me think of an old poem, something about the newborn emerging from gates, and the dying emerging from gates; how, when the wildest and bloodiest is over, all is peace.

Three people on the *Steady* pulled this dead woman up into their boat and laid her body on the deck, and Adria Berelo sat with her under cover of the aft tarpaulin. The swells were slapping against the boats by this time—in the bottom of the *Pulls Together*, in a slurry of blackish water and kelp, our tangle of salvaged plastic and aluminum slid around and knocked against the ribs of the hull—but we went on hunting. We were a fit match for seas running a couple of meters, and then we'd begin to think about getting off the water, out of the weather. We gave up bringing in every little piece of wreckage, though—we remembered why we had come out into the strait. Finding that woman's body had rekindled in us a longing to find the bodies of the others.

For a while we veered here and there after indistinguishable shapes on the water, and when one became a company of wandering-tatters, or a cracked piece of plastic or metal, or a baleno breaking the surface to breathe, we veered away after the next. Hunting for a body on the sea was something some of us had done before—Kikuma had lived along that coast for thirty years, and once had gone out into the channels of the Goes To Grass Islands looking for the bodies of her brother-in-law and his daughter; I had been on the *Eye of the Moon*, when a murso breached under the stern of the boat and a woman, a cousin of my sister's friend Eŭnisa Pare, was swept over the side. There is a certain image you learn, the discrete shading, form, drift, that distinguishes a dead body from other things, and gradually we recollected it. Then we became more deliberate, more intent, carried along by the tide, peering for that particular shape lost on the water, and now and then steering around the edges of tangled alĝo, leaning out from the heaving boat to scratch through the jams with our long-handled kelp rakes.

A silence came into the hunt and inhabited it. The near water was blackish now, glossy, but my eye was drawn far out, to the edgeless gray billowing of the sky, the sea. On the smoky distance it was only the birds who measured the world, gave it dimension. Some plum gulls sprang suddenly up—a shifting figure of birds rising into the sky and vanishing on a soundless blackish flash of wings—and then Kikuma said to me, "Look." I saw a chip of white sliding down the pitch of a wave, and when it came up again and down the next slope, it became an exo spraddled on a broken piece of a hatch cover.

We quartered the waves, crying out strategy to one another for making intersection with the drift of the raft; we were signalling the *Steady,* too, with lifted arms, useless shouting, until they made us out and brought their windpipe around to follow us.

We were wary of having that heavy piece of steel pitching alongside our little boat, our hull of paper and aluminum, reeds and string, so I made a line fast to the girdle of my overalls and waited, crouching along the gunnel, while Kikuma brought us near. When the raft slipped laterally, lifting gently up to meet us on the swell, I leaped out and scuttled onto it, clutching a bent end of rebar, scrabbling my boots in the hook of a steel step. I shouted, holding on in the cold wash of the sea, and paid out my line as the *Pulls Together* veered neatly off again without a bump.

My heart had come up into my throat—I had to wait to get a breath before I could make my hand let go its grip on the rebar and touch the gloved wrist of the exo. The body was lying front-down, the suit breached up the back. In the ragged purplish rift were the crenelations of vertebrae. The hands were outspread and clenched on the coaming of the hatch—a death clutch I thought, but when I touched the arm, the fingers of that hand opened and closed, taking a new hold. The faceplate was down in the spillover on the surface of the hatch—it was maybe with my mindseye that I caught sight of a man's mouth in a rigor of terror. I shouted to Kikuma. She made a glowering face and shouted back, a wordless gusting noise, and I knew she hadn't heard what I'd said. But she brought the tiller around and let the boat come into the wind, veering to close with us again.

I put my line through a D-ring at the man's hip, cinching

him loosely to me, and then I peeled his fingers from the hatch and grappled his loose weight into my lap. His skin was pallid, translucent, and his eyes fixed on me with dreadful yearning. I put my head close to the faceplate but when he didn't speak, I wasn't able to think of anything to say myself.

Sometimes we are reminded. I suppose I had in my mind those few years while I was clerk of the Waters Committee, while I lived at Prolonged Singing with my in-laws. We never were done with repairing the fluejo, over there—those people at Prolonged Singing are still repairing them, aren't they? That domaro is situated along the edge of the fault scarp and the culverts and aqueducts are prone to break every time the earth shakes; in a hard quake walls slip, roofs let down their loads, people die. Do you know that little river over there? the Crouches by a Grave River? the one that long ago agreed to share itself with those people? the small water wheel that powers their machine shop and their mill? One time there was a strong seism and the housing for the pilot rod broke away from the tube in the wheel. Next day two of us were fitting a new draft tube below the little dam, and while we were doing that repair there was another harder tertremo. It sat me down in the tailwater. Birĝita Ŝiomi was crouching between the draft tube and the dam head, and in the moment before the struts broke and let down the dam on her, she looked over at me. Sometimes we are reminded: All of us live steadfastly in that moment, the one between hope and the exercise of God's will.

I pulled the man's loose weight up over my shoulders and when the *Pulls Together* came alongside, I let out my shout again. "This man is still living!" Kikuma's face opened in surprise. Coastal people say, piloting a boat is one of those things like playing the flute or writing poems—you are given it or not, and no amount of apprenticeship or striving will bring it to you. Kikuma never had been one of those people, but she delicately maneuvered, bringing the *Pulls Together* alongside and then pulling away again time after time without much banging against the hatch. And she went on being patient, not yelling much advice, while I crouched there with that man slung over my shoulders, getting up my nerve, imagining I was waiting for a perfect alignment.

The lacuna between the boat and the raft always was shifting, capricious, and I think it was finally on just an instinct of motion that I went plunging outward. His weight made me awkward, top-heavy, or I was clumsy; I struck the gunnel hard with my shins, there was a breathless pitching moment—I saw Kikuma lunging for me—and then the cold breaking of the sea. I lost hold of him or let go, stupid with surprise, grappling along the sliding hull in an urgent confusion. His breached exo must have taken on a quick weight of water, because when he sank to the end of my line he pulled me like a millstone and I lost hold of the boat and sank with him, straight down.

I had been afraid, waiting to jump, but now I wasn't afraid. How quickly our ties and ballasts are cast off! I was of the Owl Strait suddenly, my elbows resting in fjords, my palms outspread on the cobbled beaches. Inside my body there were forests of lichens, galaxies of starfishes and lamp jellies, and in my bones the shields of turtles, the teeth of balenoj. I felt in my blood the long slow tide, straining after the sun—I was water, and its unknowable alchemies, dreading nothing, simply streaming and alive. This was one of those times when your mind and body cohere and you understand suddenly what the poets say: To die is different from what you had supposed, and luckier.

Then inexplicably I began to rise up through the muffled darkness toward the dazzle of the daylight—Kikuma was hauling me up—I remembered I was tied fast to the *Pulls Together*. That was a curious moment: I had a sense that I must now make an accommodation to the world, as if I had lived a long time under the sea. Then my sister's hands took a grip in my hair. I reached up blindly and caught the rail and the boat heeled over steeply—she pulled me across the gunnel, washing in on the sea, and I knew as soon as I was in the boat that the knot binding me to the *Migremo* man had come undone. Kikuma pulled the end of the line into her lap and then she clambered back to the tiller to get the boat turned into the wind while I sat cold and shaky among the salvaged wreckage. The *Steady* had come up behind us on the starboard side, and people over there were shouting back and forth with Kikuma but I didn't try to hear what they were saying. I was too cold and wet through to take pleasure in my survival. I looked out over the water for birds.

The domaro where I lived after I married is the one people call Becoming Death, though its older, truer name is Prolonged Singing. At that domaro, before I was born, a man killed his young daughter by drowning her in the water where they were bathing. Or she died without his help, going down in the water silently while he was looking away. In the hot springs there, black-legged pipes raft on the water, and the little side-by-sides live in it, they don't seem to care, those birds, that the water is scalding hot. Their outcry, the slight splashing of the water, the rustle of their wings among the clouds of steam is unending, and after a while you just begin to not hear it.

One day some of us were bathing in that hot springs. You know how it is sometimes, when you see something? when there is a moment? when your eye is drawn to something vanishing? and in that moment something sacred is made known? While I was soaking with other people in the stone basin of the bath—I remember we were shouting harassment to Nona Asaki who was repairing the tiles of the conduit by the outtake of the spring; I remember there was a weather moving over the sky but it was a facila wind, a squall bound for somewhere else—I felt a sudden glimpse of those birds—pipes, side-by-sides—their voices like exclamations, and the fleeting dip and rise of their bodies in the steam. And in that moment I thought, They are calling the name of that man, the one who looked away, whose eye was caught by birds, just as his daughter sank. And that time when I was in the *Pulls Together* with Kikuma, after a man had come loose from my line and gone down into the sea, I looked out over the water to see if any birds were calling my name. But then Kikuma said to me, "Ana, here, get warm," and she peeled away my soaked clothes and put my arms in dry sleeves, my legs in dry trousers; she folded me under a tarpaulin.

I was grateful, exhausted. We were laboring through heavy seas with the edge of the puso weather whining in the windpipe, but I didn't try to hold this or anything in my mind. I lolled in the bottom of the boat, my skull rocking dumbly among the sliding scraps of salvage. While Kikuma was steering for a lee shore, I suppose I stood up from my life and let it stream around me in a clear cataract. I was freed from time, not lying inside a dream but standing in the compass of heaven where everything goes onward and outward, nothing collapses—and when I lay down in my life again we were beating northeast along the Comes-Between Cape. When I looked over the gunnel of the boat, across the strait toward the Fisted Rocks, there was a break in the sky and the sun broke fleetingly across the water in a long bright reef—the puso weather had gone over our heads toward Abides.

A bird's wing brushing your shoulder—or a fortunate weather while you're traveling—how can these small blessings of the land be set apart from God's will, any more than the bloody death that is inescapable, inherent in the world? When you open a hole in the earth by setting aside the turf with a spade, when you lay in the frame for a house and place the fenestroj to accept sunlight, and then mindfully replace the turf—when you do this work with skill and love and you stand at the edge of the field looking at it and see only the smooth grassy rise of the berm, isn't that a moment as vital and defining as a sudden death, bloodshed, cataclysm?

I think of the Woman's Frozen Toes, between Having Wind and Divided. In winter, the climb up from Having Wind is icy and relentless, people have died, even in good weather—it's a fine place to bring your body and soul together. But from the crack between the Woman's Toes, you can stand on your skis and slide down to Divided: It's all gradual downhill and wide turns, intermittent glimpses north and northwest across the shoulder of the mountain or south to the distant summits of Sisters Getting Homesick. A lot of people use that way over to Divided in the winter, and on particular days in a certain kind of weather, once you've got over the Woman's Frozen Toes you only need to set your skis in the tracks other people have laid in the snow and push downhill, a long lazy run.

For a while when I was still green, I was in love with

someone who lived at Divided and one winter I made that climb over Woman's Frozen Toes three or four times—my brain was in my sexual organs that winter! Skiing down, it's most all in the cold shadow of the north side of the mountain until the last bend of the track where the ŝildo stones crouch in an open field close-shouldered under the snow, and on fair days the sunlight, crouching among the stones, leaps out brilliant, blinding. That time when I was in the *Pulls Together,* sitting up to look out toward the Fisted Rocks and the mouth of the Ŝiblingo Fjord, when the sunlight made a brief long glare on the water, I remembered suddenly the winter I had climbed over Woman's Frozen Toes—I remembered how it was, skiing out from the shadow of the mountain into the unbroken glare of the ŝildo field, how I was blinded by the light—how I flew down the red darkness by the brief fierce burning of my heart.

No one stood on the beach waiting for us. Daylight was seeping out of the sky by then, the overcast taking up blackness slowly; they thought we had long since gone to shelter among the Goes To Grass Islands, or been caught by the puso weather and overturned in the Owl Strait. So we were left alone to haul out the boats along the lee shore, and our tiredness came out in a muttering of complaint and disagreement. We argued over who would carry the dead woman's body, and which of us would keep her in their house until her family came after her. When that was settled, there was quarrelling over whether we ought to carry everything, all of the *Migremo* salvage, up the steep path to Holds Loneliness, or only drag it a little way and pile it up like a cairn of stones among the drift at the foot of the scarp, and let other people carry it up in the morning of the next day. Finally people just did as they liked, and it was the

big, unwieldy pieces that were left behind on the beach, while
glass and wire, small plastics and aluminum, damaged crates,
the metal globes of xenon fixtures, those bits and pieces went
up the path with us, shouldered or dragged or carried, behind
the body of the unknown dead woman slung in a hammock of
canvas between Kikuma and her friend Davido Ĉekli. What I
carried up in a cracked plastic box were dozens of bound books,
sodden and heavy, and masses of stained wet paper. Nothing is
ever wasted, or can be; if the Library Committee gave up trying
to salvage the books, people of the Paper and Ink Committee
would slurry the wet pages, re-form and dry them.

That climb from the beach up to Holds Loneliness is long
and steep. My shins ached from striking the gunnel of the boat,
so I trudged painfully, scuffing my boots. I had to stop every
little while and shift the big crate to the other shoulder, and
then Adria Berelo, Paŭlo Medina, Magdalena Ulsen and her
son, one after the other went by me, some of them not even
excusing themselves for this rudeness, and leaving me finally
to be the last.

The air was sharp, hoary; in the rucks of the fjord where the
light was already gone, the cold fog people call *griza* was cleav-
ing to the stones. I don't know why a fog, by diminishing the
world, declares its vastness. But in a while I stopped climbing
up through the narrow rift in the land's edge and stood there
leaning into the uphill rock, holding the box of books. I think
I may have cried a little. A person, ambiguous and small, came
downhill out of the fog—became Kikuma. "What," she said in
surprise, and she took the box out of my hands and peered at
me across the edge of it.

You know how it is between sisters in their middle age?

that old old friendship, how loose-fitting it is? the comfort and safety in it? how you can let silence lie between you without it taking on any weight? how you can let words out of your mouth without wariness or precision because you know your sister will listen to what's worthwhile and let the rest fall out of her ears into the air? how you can be surly, unreasonable, stupid, in the certainty of her grace? We had hardly spoken through this long day, but I said, gesturing impatiently as if this was something we had already argued about, "Oh, this leg hurting, and this damn crate too heavy, I was left behind with the ghosts, eh? Something. My stupid daughter. A dread. I don't know." I was by then crying bitterly.

Kikuma looked at me, shifting the weight of the box. Then she turned sidelong to me and rubbed her cheek along mine. I clung to her until I was finished. Then she said tenderly, "Let's go up, Ana," and I followed her along the narrow notch, the dark lead rising to Holds Loneliness.

When we came out at the head of the fjord it was not yet night—the sky was dark but holding the light beneath it as a hand cups a flame—and the wind had fallen utterly away. The other people had already gone to ground ahead of us, and from the edge of that fell there's no seeing the fenestroj of the houses, or the light cast out from those windows into the shadowed swales—it was a world without humankind in it, the land falling and rising and falling like swells of the sea. Across the shoulders of the berms the long wiry stems of the pinion poppies stood erect, holding their seedheads above the myriad shorter grasses, the brindled pelt of false skipper and flywing, hightail and boozy. Against the darkening sky, over the black water of the fjord a flock of bush owls hunted mites and moths, their dip and rise profoundly synchronous, silent. On the flanks of the glacier there were patches of shadow, thousands of pew larks with their twig-legs folded under, lying together in sleep. Out there were sand hares, flicker lemmings, hermit mice, in galleries and corridors under the ice. And in the waters of the Owl Strait, bowfish were choosing a home for eggs in the crevices of a man's relinquished vertebrae.

There is something about that particular time of day, the failing of the light; at twilight, when the air is cold and still and un-colored, when something moves in it the whole world sees it. As I was standing there at the top of the beach path— standing inside my memory of that day as if it were a stream of light—I came to a magic place in my life. I saw that man from the *Migremo,* the one who had fallen into the sea with me and drowned. Something moved apart from the birds, and I saw that man where he walked among the śildoj of Holds Loneliness, looking for a stone to give his name to.

Kikuma stopped with me, looking up the long slope. If she saw the man herself, she didn't say, but stood with me in silence while I watched him wade the swift white stripe of the Bears Grief River, and while I watched him walk across the hip of the hill, his shape gradually becoming indistinguishable, a part of the darkness. Then I said, "Well, he's gone now," and we trudged tiredly across the rocky mezlando, going home with that box of wet pages. People call this world *Reiradi,* an old word that has a tangled meaning, but something like circling back, or maybe returning. I wonder if those pioneer people, the ones who gave the world that name, I wonder if they were thinking of times like this one, coming home late and cold, carrying a weight.

This time I'm remembering, when the *Migremo* fell, we were

living in a house with Kikuma's husband and my niece and our old parents, and a cousin who had quarreled with her husband. Our family's relief made itself known in a little stream of jokes at our expense, while they brought forward bowls and spoons and placed them in our hands and watched us eat our soup. My mother began to sort through the box we had brought up from the *Migremo,* and before long she was standing the wet books open, ruffling their pages with her thumb. When she had a field of books spread in front of her on the floor she stood up and turned around facing the other way and began again, setting out the rest. Then when she was done, she was in the center and couldn't step out and we had to help her move the books and make a path for herself.

My mother has an old, religious reverence for books. I value them myself, though my mother's experience of books is not mine. In her childhood people looked to books as a repository of wisdom about the land; in mine, people looked to the land itself. The child knows the world more sensuously than the adult, and I think my mother's understanding of this world, even after seventy years, is intimately linked to the fusty smell inside the covers of books, the thickened, buttery texture of the old paper, the sibilant sound of the pages slipping across one another. Mine is in waxy panes of riverine ice, in the smell of a mouse's old bones and the spiny rustle of a ring-eye's nest. The landscape we inhabit as children, inhabits us.

When I had eaten my soup, I had an odd compulsion to go out again in the darkness and look among the śildoj for the stone I had seen that ghost giving his name to. I said something else to my family—that I had a compulsion to go to Davido Ĉekli's house and sit with the dead woman. They sighed and reasoned briefly with me—this was something that they understood, but it could wait for the morning of the next day. Still, no one argued very strongly to keep me inside. I suppose they knew what I was doing, though I hardly knew it myself. I put my arms in my coat sleeves again and went out through the darkness between the houses.

The twilight calm had drifted off on the light, and the wind was cold again, a glaciejo wind, dry and lashing. I put my head down to climb the steep alta to the śildo field, walking among the stones in a misery of cold, hunching my shoulders, waiting for something to be revealed. If that man's ghost was there, he didn't speak. At the high edge of the field I stood looking seaward across the long black downsweep of the grass. There was a fine violet line marking the boundary of the sky—a vanishingly delicate memory of the sun. And then something was revealed after all. That dark filament of light illumined an early, childish memory:

Something more than a hundred years ago, people had buried an old woman in the ground east of my parents' domaro, and at Having Wind they were always telling this woman's story—why she wasn't burnt, how she had wanted to lie down in the earth after all those years apart from it. No one knew where this grave was—in my childhood, the people who used to know that were already corpses, their names given to śildo stones, their souls living in the spaces that connect one blade of grass, one crumb of sand, to the next. What I remembered, standing at the edge of the śildo field above the houses of Holds Loneliness, looking out at the violet line of the sky, was a time, as a child, when I stood on the berm of my parents' house watching the weather coming. It was angviso weather, that time, a weather without any experience of abruptness; it moved slowly at an angle toward me out of the east. Between me and the weather the brown grass was sunlit and I thought, When the shadow of the weather crosses the grass I'll see the sunken place where that pioneer woman's bones are buried.

When I first stood there on the roof of the house looking, there was nothing but the land itself, it seemed all one piece and unalterable. But then I became what I was seeing, and my eyes gave life to even the smallest things—blue stems of moss, the veiny ruts where meltwater sometimes ran, a turnstone, a dead-drop of shed feathers, the wind pushing the grass over in an image resembling a human head or a flight of birds. The weather rode very slowly across the grass, and in the shadow there was a deep old silence, and whispering into it was the land. I suppose that was the first time I heard the earth speaking, as inexplicably coherent as an old book in a forgotten language, transcendent in its meaning.

Now I walked across the ŝildo field, across the crackling grass to the bank of the Bears Grief River and stood there a moment, peering into the blackness, hoping I might yet see the ghost of that dead man, the one I had lost to the sea. But the urgency had gone out of the air, out of me, like a breath, and when I started down again toward the lighted fenestroj of the houses, I thought, That pioneer woman is still there under the grass, alive in the body of the world.

GLOSSARY

altejo: highlands, nearest the ceiling; narrow terraces along the upper edges of the torus's inhabited interior

avino: grandmother

caparajo: loose, lightweight drawstring trousers

dankon: thanks; thank you

domaro: a large multifamily house containing several apartments

exo: pressure suit

kremaciejo: crematory

kura: doctor; nurse; healer

lavejo: lavatory

librajo: small laptop device for reading electronic books

loĝio: a covered, interior porch; the public space, the open middle, of a U-shaped domaro

maĉeta: farm implement for weeding and for cutting canes

maltejo: lowlands, in the trough of the torus's inhabited interior

mezlando: midlands; broad terraces along the middle reaches of the interior of the torus

mortafesto: funeral; wake; a celebration of a life that has ended

paĉjo: diminutive, affectionate name for a father

panja: diminutive, affectionate name for a mother

pasado: the exterior corridor of a domaro; a narrow porch that circles the house beneath its overhanging eave

plantodomo: greenhouse

repozo: wicker chair-back for floor use

sadaŭ: attic of a house, used for storage

sutaĝo: the open underneath of a domaro built on poles

ŝimanas: a spiritual malaise; exaggerated feeling of isolation and loneliness, leading toward depression, alienation, suicide

ŝiro: neighborhood; village; consisting usually of ten or twelve apartment houses. There are eight siroj: Esperplena [Hopeful], Senlima [Boundless], Pacema [Peaceable], Alaŭdo [Lark], Kantado [Prolonged Singing], Bonveno [Open Arms], Mandala [Circling], Revenana [Daydreaming]

ACKNOWLEDGMENTS

For the descriptions of leaf-cutter ants, and for details of tropical birds and tropical farming, I am indebted to the published writings of Alexander F. Skutch, a naturalist of profound compassion and thought.

In the mid-1970's, argument over the feasibility and desirability of funding the O'Neill space colonies was an ongoing matter for discussion in *The CoEvolution Quarterly*, and eventually that material, including the invited responses of several notable people, was gathered together and published under the title *Space Colonies* (Penguin Books: New York, 1977). Some of the arguments and insights spoken by characters in this novel (addressing a rather different question) have been abstracted from the discussion in that book.

All epigraphs in this book are from the writings of the sometime-Quaker Walt Whitman, his lifework, *Leaves of Grass*.

Turn the page to read a selection
from Molly Gloss's collection
Unforeseen: "Lambing Season,"
a finalist for the Hugo and Nebula Awards.

FROM MAY TO September, Delia took the Churro sheep and two dogs and went up on Joe-Johns Mountain to live. She had that country pretty much to herself all summer. Ken Owen sent one of his Mexican hands up every other week with a load of groceries, but otherwise, she was alone; alone with the sheep and the dogs. She liked the solitude. Liked the silence. Some sheepherders she knew talked a blue streak to the dogs, the rocks, the porcupines; they sang songs and played the radio, read their magazines out loud, but Delia let the silence settle into her, and by early summer she had begun to hear the ticking of the dry grasses as a language she could almost translate. The dogs were named Jesus and Alice. "Away to me, Hey-sus," she said when they were moving the sheep. "Go bye, Alice." From May to September these words spoken in command of the dogs were almost the only times she heard her own voice; that, and when the Mexican brought the groceries—a polite exchange in Spanish about the weather, the health of the dogs, the fecundity of the ewes.

The Churros were a very old breed. The O-Bar Ranch had a federal allotment up on the mountain, which was all rim-rock and sparse grasses—well suited to the Churros that were fiercely protective of their lambs and had a long-stapled top-coat that could take the weather. They did well on the thin grass of the mountain, where other sheep would lose flesh and give up their lambs to the coyotes. The Mexican was an old man. He said he remembered Churros from his childhood in the Oaxaca highlands, the rams with their four horns—two curving up, two down. "Buen' carne," he told Delia. Uncommonly fine meat.

The wind blew out of the southwest in the early part of the season, a wind that smelled of juniper and sage and pollen; in the later months it blew straight from the east, a dry wind smelling of dust and smoke, bringing down showers of parched leaves and seed heads of yarrow and bitter cress. Thunder-storms came frequently out of the east, enormous cloudscapes with hearts of livid magenta and glaucous green. At those times, if she was camped on a ridge, she'd get out of her bed and walk downhill to find a draw where she could feel safer, but if she was camped in a low place, she would stay with the sheep while a war passed over their heads, spectacular, jagged flares of lightning; skull-rumbling cannonades of thunder. It was maybe bred into the bones of Churros, a knowledge and a tolerance of mountain weather, for they shifted together and waited out the thunder with surprising composure; they stood forbearingly while rain beat down in hard, blinding bursts.

Sheepherding was simple work, although Delia knew some herders who made it hard, dogging the sheep every minute, keeping them in a tight group, moving all the time. She let the sheep herd themselves, do what they wanted, make their own decisions. If the band began to separate, she would whistle or yell, and often the strays would turn around and rejoin the main group. Only if they were badly scattered did she send out the dogs. Mostly, she just kept an eye on the sheep, made sure they got good feed, that the band didn't split, that they stayed in the boundaries of the O-Bar allotment. She studied the sheep for the language of their bodies and tried to handle them just as close to their nature as possible. When she put out salt for them, she scattered it on rocks and stumps as if she were hiding Easter eggs, because she saw how they enjoyed the search.

The spring grass made their manure wet, so she kept the wool cut away from the ewes' tail areas with a pair of sharp, short-bladed shears. She dosed the sheep with wormer, trimmed their feet, inspected their teeth, treated ewes for mastitis. She combed the burrs from the dogs' coats and inspected them for ticks. *You're such good dogs,* she told them with her hands. *I'm very, very proud of you.*

She had some old binoculars, 7x32 mms, and in the long, quiet days, she watched bands of wild horses, miles off in the distance; ragged-looking mares with dorsal stripes and black legs. She read the back issues of the local newspapers, looking in the obits for names she recognized. She read spine-broken paperback novels and played solitaire and scoured the ground for arrowheads and rocks she would later sell to rock hounds. She studied the parched brown grass, which was full of grasshoppers and beetles and crickets and ants. But most of her day was spent just walking. The sheep sometimes bedded quite a ways from her trailer, and she had to get out to them before sunrise, when the coyotes would make their kills. She was usually up by three or four and walking out to the sheep in darkness. Sometimes she returned to the camp for lunch, but she was always out with the sheep again until sundown, when the coyotes were likely to return, and then she walked home after dark to water and feed the dogs, eat supper, climb into bed.

In her first years on Joe-Johns, she had often walked three or four miles away from the band, just to see what was over a hill, or to study the intricate architecture of a sheepherder's monument. Stacking up flat stones in the form of an obelisk was a common herders' pastime, their monuments all over that sheep country, and though Delia had never felt an impulse to start one herself, she admired the ones other people had built. She sometimes walked miles out of her way just to look at a rock pile up close.

She had a mental map of the allotment, divided into ten pastures. Every few days, when the sheep had moved on to a new pasture, she moved her camp. She towed the trailer with an old Dodge pickup, over the rocks and creek beds, the sloughs and dry meadows, to the new place. For a while afterward, after the engine was shut off and while the heavy old body of the truck was settling onto its tires, she would be deaf, her head filled with a dull, roaring white noise.

She had about eight hundred ewes, as well as their lambs, many of them twins or triplets. The ferocity of the Churro ewes in defending their offspring was sometimes a problem for the dogs, but in the balance of things, she knew it kept her losses small. Many coyotes lived on Joe-Johns, and sometimes a cougar or bear would come up from the salt pan desert on the north side of the mountain, looking for better country to own. These animals considered the sheep to be fair game, which

Delia understood to be their right, and also her right—hers and the dogs—to take the side of the sheep. Sheep were smarter than people commonly believed, and the Churros smarter than other sheep she had tended, but by midsummer the coyotes had passed the word among themselves—buen' carne—and Delia and the dogs then had a job of work, keeping the sheep out of harm's way.

She carried a .32-caliber Colt pistol in an old-fashioned holster worn on her belt. *If you're a coyot', you'd better be careful of this woman,* she said with her body, with the way she stood and the way she walked when she was wearing the pistol. That gun and holster had once belonged to her mother's mother, a woman who had come west on her own and homesteaded for a while, down in the Sprague River Canyon. Delia's grandmother had liked to tell the story: how a concerned neighbor, a bachelor with an interest in marriageable females, had pressed the gun upon her, back when the Klamaths were at war with the army of General Joel Palmer; and how she never had used it for anything but shooting rabbits.

In July a coyote killed a lamb while Delia was camped no more than two hundred feet away from the bedded sheep. It was dusk, and she was sitting on the steps of the trailer reading a two-gun Western, leaning close over the pages in the failing light, and the dogs were dozing at her feet. She heard the small sound, a strange, high, faint squeal she did not recognize and then did recognize, and she jumped up and fumbled for the gun, yelling at the coyote, at the dogs, her yell startling the entire band to its feet but the ewes making their charge too late, Delia firing too late, and none of it doing any good beyond a release of fear and anger.

A lion might well have taken the lamb entire; she had known of lion kills where the only evidence was blood on the grass and a dribble of entrails in the beam of a flashlight. But a coyote is small and will kill with a bite to the throat and then perhaps eat just the liver and heart, though a mother coyote will take all she can carry in her stomach, bolt it down and carry it home to her pups. Delia's grandmother's pistol had scared this one off before it could even take a bite, and the lamb was twitching and whole on the grass, bleeding only from its neck. The mother ewe stood over it, crying in a distraught and pitiful way, but there was nothing to be done, and in a few minutes the lamb was dead.

There wasn't much point in chasing after the coyote, and anyway, the whole band was now a skittish jumble of anxiety and confusion; it was hours before the mother ewe gave up her grieving, before Delia and the dogs had the band calm and bedded down again; almost midnight. By then the dead lamb had stiffened on the ground, and Delia dragged it over by the truck and skinned it and let the dogs have the meat, which went against her nature but was about the only way to keep the coyote from coming back for the carcass.

While the dogs worked on the lamb, she stood with both hands pressed to her tired back, looking out at the sheep, the mottled pattern of their whiteness almost opalescent across the black landscape, and the stars thick and bright above the faint outline of the rock ridges. Stood there a moment before turning toward the trailer, toward bed, and afterward, she would think how the coyote and the sorrowing ewe and the dark of the July moon and the kink in her back, how all that came together and was the reason she was standing there watching the sky, was the reason she saw the brief, brilliantly green flash in the southwest and then the sulfur yellow streak breaking across the night, southwest to due west on a descending arc onto Lame Man Bench. It was a broad, bright ribbon, rainbow-wide, a cyanotic contrail. It was not a meteor; she had seen hundreds of meteors. She stood and looked at it.

Things to do with the sky, with distance—you could lose perspective. It was hard to judge even a lightning strike, whether it had touched down on a particular hill or the next hill or the valley between. So she knew this thing falling out of the sky might have come down miles to the west of Lame Man, not onto Lame Man at all, which was two miles away—at least two miles—and getting there would be all ridges and rocks; no way to cover the ground in the truck. She thought about it. She had moved camp earlier in the day, which was always troublesome work, and it had been a blistering hot day, and now the excitement with the coyote. She was very tired, the tiredness like a weight against her breastbone. She didn't know what this thing was, falling out of the sky. Maybe if she walked over there, she would find just a dead satellite or a broken weather balloon and not dead or broken people. The contrail thinned slowly while she stood there looking at it, became a wide streak of yellowy cloud against the blackness, with the field of stars glimmering dimly behind it.

After a while she went into the truck and got a water bottle and filled it, and she also took the first aid kit out of the trailer and a couple of spare batteries for the flashlight and a handful of extra cartridges for the pistol. Delia stuffed these things into a backpack and looped her arms into the straps and started up the rise away from the dark camp, the bedded sheep. The dogs left off their gnawing of the dead lamb and trailed her anxiously, wanting to follow, or not wanting her to leave the sheep. "Stay by," she said to them sharply, and they went back and stood with the band and watched her go. *That coyot', it's done with us tonight.* This is what she told the dogs with her body, walking away, and she believed it was probably true.

Now that she'd decided to go, she walked fast. This was her sixth year on the mountain, and by this time, she knew the country pretty well. She didn't use the flashlight. Without it, she became accustomed to the starlit darkness, able to see the stones and pick out a path. The air was cool but full of the smell of heat rising off the rocks and the parched earth. She heard nothing but her own breathing and the gritting of her boots on the pebbly dirt. A little owl circled once in silence and then went off toward a line of cottonwood trees standing in black silhouette to the northeast.

Lame Man Bench was a great upthrust block of basalt grown over with scraggly juniper forest. As she climbed among the trees the smell of something like ozone or sulfur grew very strong, and the air became thick, burdened with dust. Threads of the yellow contrail hung in the limbs of the trees. She went on across the top of the bench and onto slabs of shelving rock that gave a view to the west. Down in the steep-sided draw below her, there was a big wing-shaped piece of metal resting on the ground, which she at first thought had been torn from an airplane, but then realized was a whole thing, not broken, and she quit looking for the rest of the wreckage. She squatted down and looked at it. Yellow dust settled slowly out of the sky, pollinating her hair, her shoulders, the toes of her boots, faintly dulling the oily black shine of the wing, the thing shaped like a wing.

While she was squatting there looking down at it, something came out from the sloped underside of it—a coyote, she thought at first, and then it wasn't a coyote but a dog built like a greyhound or a whippet; deep-chested, long legged, very light-boned and frail-looking. She waited for somebody else, a man, to crawl out after his dog, but nobody did. The dog squatted to pee and then moved off a short distance and sat on its haunches and considered things. Delia considered too. She considered that the dog might have been sent up alone. The Russians had sent up a dog in their little Sputnik, she remembered. She considered that a skinny almost hairless dog with frail bones would be dead in short order if left alone in this country. And she considered that there might be a man inside the wing, dead or too hurt to climb out. She thought how much trouble it would be, getting down this steep rock bluff in the darkness to rescue a useless dog and a dead man.

After a while she stood and started picking her way into the draw. The dog by this time was smelling the ground, making a slow and careful circuit around the black wing. Delia kept expecting the dog to look up and bark, but it went on with its intent inspection of the ground, as if it were stone-deaf, as if Delia's boots making a racket on the loose gravel was not an announcement that someone was coming down. She thought of the old Dodge truck, how it always left her ears ringing, and wondered if maybe it was the same with this dog and its wing-shaped Sputnik, although the wing had fallen soundlessly across the sky.

When she had come about halfway down the hill, she lost

her footing and slid down six or eight feet before she got her heels dug in and found a handful of willow scrub to hang on to. A glimpse of this movement—rocks sliding to the bottom, or the dust she raised—must have startled the dog, for it leaped backward suddenly and then reared up. They looked at each other in silence, Delia and the dog, Delia standing, leaning into the steep slope a dozen yards above the bottom of the draw, and the dog standing next to the Sputnik, standing all the way up on its hind legs like a bear or a man and no longer seeming to be a dog but a person with a long narrow muzzle and a narrow chest, turned-out knees, delicate doglike feet. Its genitals were more catlike than dog's, a male set but very small and neat and contained. Dog's eyes, though, dark and small and shining below an anxious brow, so that she was reminded of Jesus and Alice, the way they had looked at her when she had left them alone with the sheep. She had years of acquaintance with dogs, and she knew enough to look away, break off her stare. Also, after a moment, she remembered the old pistol and holster at her belt. In cowboy pictures, a man would unbuckle his gun belt and let it down on the ground as a gesture of peaceful intent, but it seemed to her this might only bring attention to the gun, to the true intent of a gun, which is always killing. *This woman is nobody at all to be scared of,* she told the dog with her body, standing very still along the steep hillside, holding on to the scrub willow with her hands, looking vaguely to the left of him, where the smooth curve of the wing rose up and gathered a veneer of yellow dust.

The dog—the dog-person—opened his jaws and yawned the way a dog will do to relieve nervousness, and then they were both silent and still for a minute. When he finally turned and stepped toward the wing, it was an unexpected, delicate movement, exactly the way a ballet dancer steps along on his toes, knees turned out, lifting his long, thin legs; and then he dropped down on all fours and seemed to become almost a dog again. He went back to his business of smelling the ground intently, though every little while he looked up to see if Delia was still standing along the rock slope. It was a steep place to stand. When her knees finally gave out, she sat down very carefully where she was, which didn't spook him. He had become used to her by then, and his brief, sliding glance just said, *That woman up there is nobody at all to be scared of.*

What he was after, or wanting to know, was a mystery to her. She kept expecting him to gather up rocks, like all those men who'd gone to the moon, but he only smelled the ground, making a wide, slow circuit around the wing the way Alice and Jesus always circled round the trailer every morning, noses down, reading the dirt like a book. And when he seemed satisfied with what he'd learned, he stood up again and looked back at Delia, a last look delivered across his shoulder before he dropped down and disappeared under the edge of the wing; a grave and inquiring look, the kind of look a dog or a man will give you before going off on his own business, a look that says, *You be okay if I go?* If he had been a dog, and if Delia had been close enough to do it, she'd have scratched the smooth head, felt the hard bone beneath, moved her hands around the soft ears. *Sure, okay, you go on now, Mr. Dog.* This is what she would have said with her hands. Then he crawled into the darkness under the slope of the wing, where she figured there must be a door, a hatch leading into the body of the machine, and after a while, he flew off into the dark of the July moon.

In the weeks afterward, on nights when the moon had set or hadn't yet risen, she looked for the flash and streak of something breaking across the darkness out of the southwest. She saw him come and go to that draw on the west side of Lame Man Bench twice more in the first month. Both times she left her grandmother's gun in the trailer and walked over there and sat in the dark on the rock slab above the draw and watched him for a couple of hours. He may have been waiting for her, or he knew her smell, because both times he reared up and looked at her just about as soon as she sat down. But then he went on with his business. *That woman is nobody to be scared of,* he said with his body, with the way he went on smelling the ground, widening his circle and widening it, sometimes taking a clod or a sprig into his mouth and tasting it, the way a mild-mannered dog will do when he's investigating something and not paying any attention to the person he's with.

Delia had about decided that the draw behind Lame Man Bench was one of his regular stops, like the ten campsites she used over and over again when she was herding on Joe-Johns Mountain, but after those three times in the first month she didn't see him again.

At the end of September she brought the sheep down to the O-Bar. After the lambs had been shipped out, she took her band of dry ewes over onto the Nelson prairie for the fall, and in mid-November, when the snow had settled in, she brought them to the feed lots. That was all the work the ranch had for her until lambing season. Jesus and Alice belonged to the O-Bar. They stood in the yard and watched her go.

In town she rented the same room as the year before, and as before, spent most of a year's wages on getting drunk and standing other herders to rounds of drink. She gave up looking into the sky.

In March she went back out to the ranch. In bitter weather they built jugs and mothering-up pens, and trucked the pregnant ewes from Green, where they'd been feeding on wheat stubble. Some ewes lambed in the trailer on the way in, and after every haul, there was a surge of lambs born. Delia had the night shift, where she was paired with Roy Joyce, a fellow who raised sugar beets over in the valley and came out for the lambing season every year. In the black, freezing cold middle of the night, eight and ten ewes would be lambing at a time. Triplets, twins, big singles, a few quads, ewes with lambs born dead, ewes too sick or confused to mother. She and Roy would skin a dead lamb and feed the carcass to the ranch dogs and wrap the fleece around a bummer lamb, which was intended to fool the bereaved ewe into taking the orphan as her own, and sometimes it worked that way. All the mothering-up pens swiftly filled, and the jugs filled, and still some ewes with new lambs stood out in the cold field waiting for a room to open up.

You couldn't pull the stuck lambs with gloves on; you had to reach into the womb with your fingers to turn the lamb, or tie cord around the feet, or grasp the feet barehanded, so Delia's hands were always cold and wet, then cracked and bleeding. The ranch had brought in some old converted school buses to house the lambing crew, and she would fall into a bunk at daybreak and then not be able to sleep, shivering in the unheated bus with the gray daylight pouring in the windows, and the endless daytime clamor out at the lambing sheds. All the lambers had sore throats, colds, nagging coughs. Roy Joyce looked like hell, deep bags as blue as bruises under his eyes, and Delia figured she looked about the same, though she hadn't seen a mirror, not even to draw a brush through her hair, since the start of the season.

By the end of the second week, only a handful of ewes hadn't lambed. The nights became quieter. The weather cleared, and the thin skiff of snow melted off the grass. On the dark of the moon, Delia was standing outside the mothering-up pens drinking coffee from a thermos. She put her head back and held the warmth of the coffee in her mouth a moment, and as she was swallowing it down, lowering her chin, she caught the tail end of a green flash and a thin yellow line breaking across the sky, so far off anybody else would have thought it was a meteor, but it was bright, and dropping from southwest to due west, maybe right onto Lame Man Bench. She stood and looked at it. She was so very goddamned tired and had a sore throat that wouldn't clear, and she could barely get her fingers to fold around the thermos, they were so split and tender.

She told Roy she felt as sick as a horse and did he think he could handle things if she drove herself into town to the urgent care clinic, and she took one of the ranch trucks and drove up the road a short way and then turned onto the rutted track that went up to Joe-Johns.

The night was utterly clear, and you could see things a long way off. She was still an hour's drive from the Churros' summer range when she began to see a yellow-orange glimmer behind the black ridgeline, a faint nimbus like the ones that marked distant range fires on summer nights.

She had to leave the truck at the bottom of the bench to climb up the last mile or so on foot, had to get a flashlight out of the glove box and try to find an uphill path with it because the fluttery, reddish light show was finished by then, and a thick pall of smoke overcast the sky and blotted out the stars. Her eyes itched and burned, and tears ran from them, but the smoke calmed her sore throat. She went up slowly, breathing through her mouth.

The wing had burned a skid path through the scraggly junipers along the top of the bench and had come apart into a hundred pieces. She wandered through the burned trees and the scattered wreckage, shining her flashlight into the smoky darkness, not expecting to find what she was looking for, but there he was, lying apart from the scattered shards of metal, out on the smooth slab rock at the edge of the draw. He was panting shallowly, and his close coat of short brown hair was matted with blood. He lay in such a way that she immediately knew his back was broken. When he saw Delia coming up, his brow furrowed with worry. A sick or a wounded dog will bite, she knew that, but she squatted next to him. *It's just me*, she told him by shining the light not in his face but in hers. Then she spoke to him. "Okay," she said. "I'm here now," without thinking too much about what the words meant, or whether they meant anything at all, and she didn't remember until afterward that he was very likely deaf anyway. He sighed and shifted his look from her to the middle distance, where she supposed he was focused on approaching death.

Near at hand, he didn't resemble a dog all that much, only in the long shape of his head, the folded-over ears, the round darkness of his eyes. He lay on the ground, flat on his side like a dog that's been run over and is dying by the side of the road, but a man will lay like that too when he's dying. He had small-fingered nail-less hands where a dog would have had toes and front feet. Delia offered him a sip from her water bottle, but he didn't seem to want it, so she just sat with him quietly, holding one of his hands, which was as smooth as lambskin against the cracked and roughened flesh of her palm. The batteries in the flashlight gave out, and sitting there in the cold darkness, she found his head and stroked it, moving her sore fingers lightly over the bone of his skull, and around the soft ears, the loose jowls. Maybe it wasn't any particular comfort to him, but she was comforted by doing it. *Sure, okay, you can go on.*

She heard him sigh, and then sigh again, and each time wondered if it would turn out to be his death. She had used to wonder what a coyote, or especially a dog, would make of this doggish man, and now, while she was listening, waiting to hear if he would breathe again, she began to wish she'd brought Alice or Jesus with her, though not out of that old curiosity. When her husband had died years before, at the very moment he took his last breath, the dog she'd had then had barked wildly and raced back and forth from the front to the rear door of the house, as if he'd heard or seen something invisible to her. People said it was her husband's soul going out the door or his angel coming in. She didn't know what it was the dog had seen or heard or smelled, but she wished she knew. And now she wished she had a dog with her to bear witness.

She went on petting him even after he had died, after she was sure he was dead, and went on petting him until his body was cool, and then she got up stiffly from the bloody ground and gathered rocks and piled them onto him, a couple of feet high so he wouldn't be found or dug up. She didn't know what to do about the wreckage, so she didn't do anything with it at all.

In May, when she brought the Churro sheep back to

Joe-Johns Mountain, the pieces of the wrecked wing had already eroded, were small and smooth-edged like the bits of sea glass you find on a beach, and she figured this must be what it was meant to do: to break apart into pieces too small for anybody to notice, and then to quickly wear away. But the stones she'd piled over his body seemed like the start of something, so she began the slow work of raising them higher into a sheepherder's monument. She gathered up all the smooth eroded bits of wing, too, and laid them in a series of widening circles around the base of the monument. She went on piling up stones through the summer and into September until it reached fifteen feet. Mornings, standing with the sheep miles away, she would look for it through the binoculars and think about ways to make it higher, and she would wonder what was buried under all the other monuments sheepherders had raised in that country. At night she studied the sky, but nobody came for him.

In November, when she finished with the sheep and went into town, she asked around and found a guy who knew about stargazing and telescopes. He loaned her some books and sent her to a certain pawnshop, and she gave most of a year's wages for a 14x75 telescope with a reflective lens. On clear, moonless nights she met the astronomy guy out at the Little League baseball field, and she sat on a fold-up canvas stool with her eye against the telescope's finder while he told her what she was seeing: Jupiter's moons, the Pelican Nebula, the Androm-eda galaxy. The telescope had a tripod mount, and he showed her how to make a little jerry-built device so she could mount her old 7x32 mm binoculars on the tripod too. She used the binoculars for their wider view of star clusters and small con-stellations. She was indifferent to most discomforts, could sit quietly in one position for hours at a time, teeth rattling with the cold, staring into the immense vault of the sky until she became numb and stiff, barely able to stand and walk back home. Astronomy, she discovered, was a work of patience, but the sheep had taught her patience, or it was already in her nature before she ever took up with them.

Praise for *Hearing from God*

"David Stine's work and pastoral sensitivities flavor this entire book and his grounding in God's Word provides its strong foundation and practical viability. Read it—and move forward toward a goal of learning the joys and blessing that transcends the trials and lessons life inevitably brings us all. You will be profited, your heart instructed, your mind sharpened, and your feet secured on your way as you listen to God's voice."

—**Jack W. Hayford,** chancellor of The King's University in Southlake, Texas; pastor emeritus of The Church On The Way in Van Nuys, California; and author of *Prayer Is Invading the Impossible*

"In a culture where there can be many competing 'voices' in our lives, the voice that carries the greatest weight can only come from God. God desires relational intimacy with all of us and this can only be cultivated by learning to listen and recognize His voice. David Stine has written a powerful and highly practical book that de-mystifies this process. This is a must-read for everyone!"

—**Stovall Weems,** Lead Pastor of Celebration Church in Jacksonville, Florida, and author of *Living the God-First Life*

"Having had the privilege of knowing David and his wife personally for over twenty years, I can say that David Stine knows what it means to walk with God. His life is an example of someone who seeks the Lord with all of his heart. This book will help resurrect your walk with God as David uses his testimony and experiences to help you hear God's voice in your life. David is able to make complicated ideas understandable so that we can apply them to our lives. This book will help you to commit to seeking God first and everything else will be added to you.

—**Joe Champion,** Lead Pastor of Celebration Church in Austin, Texas, and author of *Rocked: How to Respond When Life's Circumstances Rock You to Your Core*

"There is nothing more elemental to Christian pursuit or more essential to Christian living than hearing the voice of God. With equal parts good theology and good sense, David Stine's crack at this age-old question demystifies a cluttered subject and offers refreshing, practical help. With the intellectual honesty of a scientist, the care of a pastor, and the zeal of a man who lives this stuff, he helps us relate to a God who is both mystical and rational."

—**Rob Brendle,** Lead Pastor of Denver United Church in Denver, Colorado, and author of *In the Meantime: The Practice of Proactive Waiting*

"This book is not theory; it is the reality of a man who has tested it personally and vocationally, finding it both true and trustworthy. Reading Dr. David's personal milestone stories will give you hope and help to upgrade your own story of God's blueprint for your life and ministry. The good news is that the author makes the complicated simple without dumbing down the power and life change of 'a Word in season' in your own life.

Because I have watched this book work itself through the life of the author as my student, ministry staff, and now as an overseer for this esteemed and sought after church planter, I can attest to its truthfulness and fruitfulness. On the other side of this exciting read you will have a hunger and thirst for hearing and obeying our Abba Father, who calls you by name and leads you out into this courageous adventure of trusting His daily voice to you."

—**Dr. Joseph Umidi,** Interim Dean of Divinity and Executive Vice President of Regent University in Virginia Beach, Virginia, and author of *Transformational Coaching*

HEARING FROM
GOD

5 Steps to Knowing His Will for Your Life

DAVID STINE

HOWARD BOOKS

New York   London   Toronto   Sydney   New Delhi

HOWARD BOOKS

HOWARD BOOKS
An Imprint of Simon & Schuster, Inc.
1230 Avenue of the Americas
New York, NY 10020

First Howard Books trade paperback edition October 2018

HOWARD and colophon are trademarks of Simon & Schuster, Inc.

For information about special discounts for bulk purchases, please contact Simon & Schuster Special Sales at 1-866-506-1949 or business@simonandschuster.com.

The Simon & Schuster Speakers Bureau can bring authors to your live event. For more information or to book an event, contact the Simon & Schuster Speakers Bureau at 1-866-248-3049 or visit our website at www.simonspeakers.com.

Interior design by Davina Mock-Maniscalco

Manufactured in the United States of America

10 9 8 7 6 5 4 3 2 1

Library of Congress Cataloging-in-Publication Data

Names: Stine, David Isaac, author.
Title: Hearing from God: 5 steps to knowing His will for your life / David Stine.
Description: First [edition]. | Nashville : Howard Books, 2017. |
Includes bibliographical references.
Identifiers: LCCN 2016010292| ISBN 9781501147326 (hardcover) |
ISBN 9781501147791 (tradepaper) | ISBN 9781501147333 (ebook)
Subjects: LCSH: Prayer—Christianity. | Spirituality—Christianity. |
Spiritual life—Christianity. | God (Christianity)—Will. |
Listening—Religious aspects—Christianity. | Devotional literature.
Classification: LCC BV215 .S8175 2017 | DDC 248.4—dc23
LC record available at https://lccn.loc.gov/2016010292

ISBN 978-1-5011-4732-6
ISBN 978-1-5011-4779-1 (pbk)
ISBN 978-1-5011-4733-3 (ebook)

To My Grandfather

I watched you study your Bible, while I studied your life, and you made me want to know the God that you knew. You taught me about hearing the voice of God and, in many ways, inspired the journey that led to this book.
I can't wait to see you again.

Contents

Foreword

In my time as a pastor, I've had countless individuals ask me how to make their spiritual lives more exciting. They want to know how they can have a more dynamic prayer life. They long for a two-way conversation with God rather than their one-sided presentation of a list of requests. These are good concerns, but this truth I share in response may be hard to swallow: if you are bored as a Christian, perhaps you are not actively following in the footsteps of Jesus.

You see, when we have an interactive prayer life and we follow Jesus' lead, irregular and spectacular things happen on a regular basis. *Hearing from God* contains incredible stories of what has happened in the life of my good friend and fellow pastor David Stine when God showed up on the scene. What I most appreciate about this book, though, is that David helps you learn how to hear God's voice for yourself so you can experience your own adventure with Him.

I have known David for over a decade, and he is a gifted leader, a humble servant, and someone who regularly hears from God. When I first met David, we immediately connected over our love for the Washington, D.C., area, as we have the incredible honor of pastoring in the same city. I know that, whenever we get together for dinner, I will hear about his latest experience following the voice of God. What he shares always awakens in me the desire for more "God encounters" in my own life and reminds me of the wisdom of following Him wherever He leads.

Learning to recognize God's voice has been an absolute game changer in my life. In fact, I can't think of a more important skill for a believer to develop than learning to hear God. If you have ever read any of my books, you may have noticed the common theme of reclaiming the adventure of pursuing God and going where His voice leads. Once you've tasted this, you are ruined for anything less.

As I have shared on my blog, the Holy Spirit speaks in lots of different

dialects. He knows every language, including your own unique language. He knows what to say and how to say it. And He is always speaking—but do you recognize His voice? If you aren't listening, you won't hear it. If you aren't looking for God encounters, you won't see them. But if you open your ears and open your eyes, you will hear God's voice and see Him everywhere!

I recommend *Hearing from God* for God-followers who want to learn how to open their eyes and ears so that they, too, can see and hear God everywhere. I appreciate how simple David makes the practice of hearing from God. He gives you a step-by-step guide to position yourself to hear from Him and outlines a forty-day "experiment" in the back of the book so that you can practice everything he teaches. If you read this book and put its ideas into practice, not only will your relationship with God deepen, but I am confident that your ability to hear from Him more clearly and more consistently will grow exponentially!

Mark Batterson
Lead Pastor of National Community Church
and bestselling author of *The Circle Maker*

HEARING FROM
GOD

PART ONE

CONTACT

There is a great sci-fi movie that came out in 1997 called *Contact*. Based on a Carl Sagan novel by the same name, the movie follows the main character, Ellie Arroway, from childhood to her career as a research scientist with the SETI program (Search for Extraterrestrial Intelligence). The preteen Ellie—later Dr. Arroway—has an insatiable desire to make contact with the outside world. What starts as reaching outside of her childhood home through a CB radio develops into a life devoted to searching for life outside our solar system.

In the opening scenes of the movie, Ellie excitedly makes contact on her CB radio with someone in Florida, which leads to questions about the possibility of making contact with the different stars she views through her telescope. Eventually, as an adult, her search for contact from worlds beyond pays off, as she receives a series of communications from the distant star Vega.

One of the most gripping scenes takes place early in the movie after Ellie's father dies. In the midst of the tragedy, while family and friends are downstairs socializing after the funeral, Ellie is up in her bedroom, seated in front of the CB radio, attempting to make contact: "Dad, are you there? This is Ellie. Dad, are you there?"

I called this book *Hearing from God: 5 Steps to Knowing His Will for Your Life* because I believe, as humans, we all want to make contact with our Heavenly Father and hear and recognize His voice. We want to know what He has to say to us personally and know what His will is for us. Many of the world's religions are like Ellie's CB radio, where we call out to God as she called out to her father, "Are you there?" We all

hope that perhaps we will get some kind of reply—an assurance that He exists and is somehow interested in our lives—even if it's only a scratchy, faint hum.

As believers I am convinced that God wants to make contact with us even more than we want to hear from Him. Instead of a faint, indistinguishable hum, He wants to speak clearly to His people. As Jeremiah 33:3 says, "Call to me and I will answer you and tell you great and unsearchable things you do not know."

God speaking to us is meant to be a normal part of our daily lives. Unfortunately, it can seem too time-consuming, inaccessible, inconceivable, or downright frustrating for many. According to a recent study by George Barna, more than 80 percent of Americans pray during a typical week, but only 38 percent are certain that Jesus talks back to them in a personal and relevant way, while an additional 21 percent are only somewhat certain that God speaks to them personally.[1]

The most common question I am asked as a pastor is, "How do I hear from God?" There is so much confusion, uncertainty, and ambiguity related to this subject, but I believe God wants to bring clarity so that conversational intimacy can be developed between Him and any believer. John 10:27 expresses that thought clearly: "My sheep listen to my voice; I know them, and they follow me." This is an invitation for all believers to listen to and hear God's voice.

The longer I have walked in a relationship with God, the more confident I have become that He wants to make contact, speaking specifically and frequently to each of us. So if He wants to speak and we want to hear, the million-dollar question is how do we position our lives to make that contact and hear clearly from God? As a pastor, I fully understand how difficult this can be, and there have been times in my life (which I will share in this book) where I missed God's voice in important ways. However, I have learned invaluable truths and practical applications that have absolutely revolutionized my walk with God and my ability to hear from Him. I have also found that the biggest hindrance to hearing from God is me—not God.

So many believers either do not believe they have enough significance, let alone a significant role to play, in hearing from God, or they don't understand what they can do to recognize His voice. Instead, they buy into the lie that God is not personal—He doesn't speak to them directly—or that there's something wrong with them that keeps them from making contact.

The reality for most believers is that they just need some coaching on how they can position themselves to hear from Him and on how to recognize His voice. There is a concept I call the ministry of Eli. Eli was High Priest in the Jewish temple and was instrumental in helping the young boy Samuel (who later became a prophet) recognize the voice of God speaking to him (1 Samuel 3:1–10). I want this book to become like the ministry of Eli to you. I have benefited greatly from being coached in this area by other pastors, mentors, and friends, and I am excited to share with you what I have learned along the way.

I am confident that as you put into practice what I teach in this book, you, too, will make contact and hear Him. If you already hear from God, I believe this book will help you grow in your ability to hear His voice even more clearly and become even more grounded in your relationship with Him. As new challenges arise where God is calling you to step out in faith, you will be more prepared because your ear is attuned to what He is saying and you can recall His faithfulness through previous challenges to give you confidence to step out again. You'll find that the more God speaks to you and guides you, the more you'll be faced with. The enemy will do his best to distract you as well. Because of this, you can never be too grounded in this process.

The Practical Science

Science has been described as God allowing man to discover the secret workings of His incredible creation. For Dr. Arroway, although the search was not based on a faith in God, it was based on discovering whatever was out there in the unknown universe. I believe God wants to help man

discover not only the secret workings of His natural creation, but also the secret workings of His supernatural realm, including hearing His voice. The term practical science is defined as "the discipline of applying specific knowledge to practical problems." It is the synthesis of these two concepts that coveys the heart of this book.

Hearing from God is written to help believers discover and apply specific knowledge to the practical dilemma of wanting to hear clearly from God so that we can experience more depth in our relationship with Him. Although hearing from God cannot be reduced to an exact science in the typical connotation of the word, I believe there are specific action steps to take and important components we need to include in the formula of our lives to increase our propensity and frequency of hearing from Him. We live in the natural realm, but as believers we are also called to seek out the supernatural realm through a vibrant relationship with the living God. So how do we put this into practice?

The Scientific Method

Do you remember the scientific method from high school or college days? Since I am causing many of you to dig deep into the recesses of your mind, let me give you a little refresher. For those of you who are not science minded, please hang in there with me. I promise this will be simple and even intriguing.

The scientific method is a body of techniques for investigating phenomena, acquiring knowledge, or correcting and integrating previous knowledge. It includes the following six steps:

- ✦ **Step One:** Ask a Question
- ✦ **Step Two:** Do Background Research
- ✦ **Step Three:** Construct a Hypothesis
- ✦ **Step Four:** Test Your Hypothesis by Doing an Experiment

- ✦ **Step Five:** Analyze Your Data and Draw a Conclusion

- ✦ **Step Six:** Communicate Your Results

Although it is not a perfect correlation, when we apply the scientific method to hearing the voice of God, we come up with the following:

We ask God a question or questions, creating space and time in our lives to hear from Him (Step One).

We do background research, taking our question(s) and researching what the Word of God, the Bible, says about the topic (Step Two).

Listening for His voice and researching the Word of God should lead us to a hypothesis of what we believe God is speaking to us (Step Three).

We share what we believe God is speaking to us with trusted friends or counselors—testing to see if they confirm what we are hearing (Step Four).

We analyze what we have heard through His voice, His Word, His counsel through others, and see if our conclusion is confirmed by His peace (Step Five).

Finally, we tell others of what we have learned through this process and of what God has done in our lives (Step Six).

The Experiment

God invites each one of us to know His thoughts. Amos 3:7 says, "Surely the Lord God does nothing, unless He reveals His secret to His servants."[2] God wants to reveal His secrets to us, but we must seek Him. So, as you read through the chapters of this book, I invite you to participate in an experiment. A scientific supernatural experiment of sorts, which I am confident will help you grow exponentially in being able to hear and discern God's voice.

My challenge to you is to spend thirty minutes a day with God for forty days, intentionally positioning yourself to hear from Him. Thirty minutes is a good starting point, and I believe that as you begin to en-

counter God in prayer and His Word, your thirty minutes will soon turn into forty minutes or more. Thirty minutes a day of prayer, study, and allowing God's Word to bring transformation can lead to a radically changed life.

There is detailed guidance on how to position yourself to hear from God in part 3 of this book ("The Experiment—a 40-Day Guide to Hearing God's Voice"). To help you effectively spend your thirty minutes with God and increase your receptivity to hear from—and make contact with—Him, I unpack the five-step process I recommend for your devotional time:

- ✦ **Step One:** Pick a Time and a Place to Meet with God

- ✦ **Step Two:** Be Still and Worship

- ✦ **Step Three:** Read and Pray

- ✦ **Step Four:** Listen and Write

- ✦ **Step Five:** Share and Obey

The "40-Day Challenge" includes forty daily Bible passages to study, a format to follow to help you in your time with Him, and space to journal and record what you are learning and hearing.

The theologian Frank Laubach stated, "Before a scientist tries an experiment, he must have faith in the work of those who already have reported success."[3] This book is a combination of what I have learned from walking with God, listening to Him, and gleaning from the wisdom and experience of others who have gone before me.

I believe that this book could change your life, but it won't happen without an intentional investment on your part. Will you say yes and commit to the experiment of spending thirty minutes a day, for forty days, seeking Him? As you take this step toward God and position yourself to hear from Him, He will come. Just as He said to the Israelites in Exodus 29:42, "I will meet with you and speak with you."[4] Get ready!

The Science-Loving, Want-To-Be Inventor

As a child, I was one of those quintessential science-loving, want-to-be inventors that wanted to compete in every science fair and had a certain obsession with creating something I could patent. My dream vacation was a trip to the Smithsonian Air and Space and Natural Science Museum in Washington, D.C. It was there that I felt like I found my people and realized I was not alone in my passion to discover.

That trip was a catalyst that fueled my desire to explore and discover. If I was going to be the next Einstein or Edison, I figured I'd better start learning to split atoms and create something that would revolutionize society. Okay, maybe not splitting atoms, but I felt inspired to dive headfirst into the world of science.

During those elementary years, it probably did not help my social status that I spent my free time reading science books and dreaming up what my next invention would be. I don't like to brag, but I will tell you that I entered six different science fairs and came home with more than my fair share of prizes. In fact, one year I won first prize in the school and an honorable mention in the regionals.

As a junior "mad scientist," I had one experiment go wrong . . . very wrong. It all started innocently enough on Christmas morning of my sixth grade year when I received the best present EVER. To me, it was the magnum opus of all Christmas gifts: my very own genuine chemistry set. Other boys my age were asking for autographed footballs, a new leather bomber jacket, or cassette tapes of Guns N' Roses, but who would want such frivolous items when you could have beakers and potent chemicals to mix together?

Upon receipt of the gift, I rushed upstairs to my room that was perfectly sequestered from the rest of the house to mix up some concoctions without any interruptions from my parents. The chemistry set came with a plethora of different chemicals, different-sized beakers, and an instruction book.

As I was the type of kid who never did anything by the book, I think it

is fair to say that the instruction manual was probably never even opened. I mean who needs instruction manuals when you have chemicals, beakers, and a mad-scientist mind?

In the confines of my private laboratory (aka my bathroom), I began to mix different chemicals together. Each time I watched with awe and excitement, wondering what would happen next. Sometimes the different concoctions would voraciously bubble out of the beaker, and other times they would change colors right before my eyes, but nothing had prepared me for the concoction that accidentally turned my beaker into a flying rocket.

I am still not quite sure what I mixed together or why it suddenly turned explosive. All I remember is pouring in the last chemical and the beaker shooting out of my hand and hitting the ceiling. To my horror, I noticed a burning smell and an atrocious stain discoloring the ceiling. I somehow managed to avoid ever telling my parents, because later that same year they decided to have the bathroom painted a different color and the painters painted over the stain without my parents ever seeing. (Sorry. If you are reading this, Mom and Dad . . . please forgive me). Sometime later, after we had moved out of that house, it burned down. I couldn't help wondering if there was a connection to the chemicals on the ceiling from my science experiment gone awry.

Obviously, I can't say all my experiments were successful, but my obsession with science, and discovering why and how things in the natural world worked, continued for the rest of my middle school years. I was a committed explorer of the natural world until I had my first encounter with the supernatural on what was to be my, well, my deathbed.

The Vision, The Word, and The Healing

I will never forget the day I was diagnosed with terminal cancer. As a fifteen-year-old given only six weeks to live, I was petrified, confused, and in disbelief all at the same time. It was a game-changing moment in my life.

The first sign of sickness came during a tennis match at age fourteen. All of a sudden, in the middle of the match, I doubled over in pain and began regurgitating a water-like substance. I visited a myriad of doctors over the next year who tried to find a diagnosis for the painful symptoms I was experiencing. The doctors were baffled as to the cause, but the frequency of the incidents continued to increase until they were happening daily, even sometimes hourly, by the time I turned fifteen.

By this point, I had dropped in weight from 165 pounds to 110, and although we did not know what was wrong with me, we knew it was serious. At the age when most boys are thinking about school dances, sports, and learning to drive, I entered The Ochsner Medical Center in New Orleans for two weeks of intense tests and an examination by a panel of at least twenty different doctors.

After a series of tests—including a liver biopsy, a bone marrow test, and a spinal tap—I was diagnosed with a form of leukemia called eosinophilia, a condition that develops when the bone marrow makes too many eosinophils (a type of white blood cell). The doctors said there was nothing they could do and planned to send me home with a life expectancy of six weeks. The day before I was supposed to leave the hospital, the doctors took one more bone marrow test and a spinal tap, as I lay inthe hospital bed in a state of devastation and disbelief over the prognosis I had received.

Sometime during that day my grandfather, who had been like a second father to me, called the hospital to speak with me. My grandfather was a man whom I deeply respected and loved. As a young boy I spent countless hours with him, visiting his house almost every day, where he helped me with my science experiments and building projects, speaking words of encouragement to me as a mentor.

In his call, Grandfather told me about a vision the Lord had given him where he saw me going up to heaven sickly in a hospital bed and then coming back down from the clouds healthy and dressed in normal clothes. My grandfather spoke with a humble confidence, "You are going to be healed. The Lord told me in prayer."

Although I was not walking with the Lord yet, I immediately clung to those words. My grandfather's words had weight, and what he spoke to me over the phone that afternoon became a source of hope in one of my darkest hours.

Not long after my grandfather shared his vision, as I lay there alone in my hospital bed, I realized that my previous symptoms had dissipated. The vomiting that had occurred like clockwork almost every fifteen minutes had stopped, and the physical weariness that had hung over me like a wet blanket had lifted. I knew the tests would come back clear, but I was still in awe when the doctors came into my room to give me the results of what was to be the last test before I was released to return home to die.

The doctor said, "We can't explain this, but, there is nothing wrong with you." It was a classic response from a medical professional encountering a supernatural healing without basis in science or medicine. Every trace of leukemia had miraculously vanished from my body! I left the hospital that day 100 percent healthy and knowing that God had healed me.

The Apostle Paul reminds us in 1 Corinthians 4:20 that the "kingdom of God is not a matter of talk but of power." My healing was undeniable evidence of the supernatural realm invading the natural. This was my first encounter with the supernatural. I not only experienced complete healing, but I knew beyond a shadow of a doubt that my grandfather had heard a personal message from God. Although it would be a few years until I surrendered my life to God, after that day in the hospital I was marked. At the time, I was very thankful to be healed by God, but I didn't understand what it meant to have a personal relationship with Him. I thought God had intervened in my life as a one-time event because of my grandfather's prayers. All I really knew was I had encountered the supernatural realm, and I was genuinely intrigued to know more.

After I gave my life to God in college, which I will tell you more about in chapter 2, my previous quest to explore science and the natural world became an insatiable search to encounter God and experience more of the supernatural.

Exploring the Supernatural

Scientists are devoting their lives to explore the depths of the natural realm, but who is giving their life to explore the depths of the supernatural? The current proposed budget for the US government to spend on scientific research and development is $143 billion a year.[5] That is just a fraction of what universities and businesses in the private sector spend researching science and the natural world. We often prioritize exploring the natural world, which is a very important search, but I think there is a much greater search waiting for us to begin, and we don't have to be scientists to participate.

The man whose name has become synonymous with science concurs. Albert Einstein once said, "I want to know how God created this world. I am not interested in this or that phenomenon, in the spectrum of this or that element. I want to know His thoughts; the rest are details."[6] Although Einstein never professed personal faith in God, he said God's thoughts are what he wanted to know more than anything else.

When I was younger, I wanted to be like Einstein because of the incredible advances he made in discovering aspects of the natural world, but now I want to be like Einstein because he realized all the scientific discoveries in the world pale in comparison to exploring the supernatural realm of knowing God's thoughts.

THE PRACTICAL SCIENCE OF HEARING FROM GOD

CHAPTER ONE

Questions

The best scientists and explorers have the attributes of kids! They ask questions and have a sense of wonder. They have curiosity. 'Who, what, where, why, when, and how!' They never stop asking questions, and I never stop asking questions, just like a five year old.

—SYLVIA EARLE, MARINE BIOLOGIST, EXPLORER, AUTHOR, AND LECTURER[1]

The art and science of asking questions is the source of all knowledge.

—THOMAS BERGER[2]

If any of you lacks wisdom, you should ask God, who gives generously to all without finding fault, and it will be given to you.

—JAMES 1:5

The first step in the scientific method is asking a question about something that is observed. The question can be a how, what, when, who, which, why, or where type question. It all boils down to what the scientist wants to learn. If the scientist wants to understand the cosmos better, he or she might ask, "How do sun flares affect the Earth?" or "What happens to space debris?"

Do you remember your early years in elementary school, when you planted a bean seed in a disposable cup? You probably didn't realize it at the time, but that was science, and you were being taught the first steps in the scientific method. The questions you might have asked include, "How do plants grow?" or "What happens to a seed when it is stuck deep in dark soil, moistened by water, and warmed by the sun?" As part of your experiment, your teacher probably presented some research on the topic, and you hypothesized that based on the effects of the soil, water,

and sun your little bean seed would eventually sprout and become a bean plant.

The first step for making contact with God begins with a question(s) for Him. As a believer, I know that, as Creator and Lord of the universe, He has all wisdom and certainly has the answers to my questions. Questions similar to those listed above: "What is His will for me in my family, work, ministry, or career?" "Where does He want me to live?" "Which house should I purchase?" "Why is life so difficult during this season?" or "How should I discipline my child about his disobedience?"

As God, He desires to have a relationship with each of us where we have open communication: expressing our hearts and desires and questions to Him, and God expressing His heart and desires back to us, answering our questions with His wisdom and direction. I want that kind of relationship with God, and I'm sure you do, too. The question part is easy; everybody has questions for God. However, hearing the answers from God often seems to elude us. So, how does God answer our questions?

He Clears His Throat

I know I'm not the only one who has wished that God would speak with an audible voice or at least give an occasional message written in the sky when seeking Him for direction. Soon after giving my life to Jesus, I remember thinking many times, *God, I want to follow you and choose what you want me to choose. Why can't you just drop a blueprint from heaven? That would make this so much easier.*

God does not typically speak in an audible voice, and I have yet to receive a blueprint from heaven. However, I have found that He is true to His promise, as spoken through the prophet Jeremiah, "You will seek me and find me when you seek me with all your heart" (Jeremiah 29:13). It is important to note that God does not promise to be found by those who seek Him halfheartedly; but if our hearts are intent on seeking Him and obeying Him, we will find Him. The truth is, God wants to be found by those who really want to find Him.

I think about this truth when I play hide-and-go-seek with my boys. I can typically find where they are hiding in a matter of moments because I hear them giggling, wrestling around, or see their little feet hanging halfway out from under the bed. I think their favorite part of the game is when I find them. They hide in order to be found. I believe the same can be said of God. Meister Eckhart, a thirteenth-century German theologian, expressed this spiritual truth my boys taught me about the delight of being found: "God is like a person who clears His throat when hiding and so gives Himself away."[3]

The Old Testament prophet Isaiah said it like this: "Truly you are a God who has been hiding himself, the God and Savior of Israel" (Isaiah 45:15). Why does God remain hidden to a degree? Why does He not always speak to us in the overt ways we would so prefer? I believe He is looking for those who will look for Him because every true and sincere relationship is always a two-way relationship.

Proverbs 25:2 says, "It is the glory of God to conceal a matter; to search out a matter is the glory of kings." God loves it when we search Him out. He is inviting each one of us on a divine game of hide-and-go-seek, during which He clears His throat so that those who are listening can easily find Him. He wants to teach each of us how to discern His voice and promptings.

The longer you walk with Him and the more you value His voice in your life, the easier it is to discern. Hearing His voice has been compared to a radio picking up airwaves. Radio waves are constantly floating through the air, but you need a radio receiver to pick up the sounds. Like the radio waves, God is always speaking; we just have to learn to tune our frequency to hear what He is saying. Jesus explains in John 10:3–5 that hearing from God is meant to be a reality in every believer's life.

I know some churches teach that we can't hear His voice today. They teach that God only speaks through what is written in His Word: the Bible. God certainly speaks to us through His Word. The whole next chapter focuses on the ways that God speaks through the Bible and that

nothing He speaks will ever contradict His written Word. However, the written Word is certainly not the only way He speaks.

Logos vs. Rhema

There are two Greek New Testament terms pastors often reference that are translated as "word" in the New Testament: *logos* and *rhema*. The first word, *logos*, refers to the written Word of God—the Bible—and also to the living Word, Jesus (see examples in Luke 8:11, John 1:1, Philippians 2:16). The second term, *rhema*, means an utterance or spoken word (found in Luke 1:38; 3:2; 5:5 and Acts 11:16).

For you and me, a *rhema* is the Holy Spirit speaking to us in the present moment, through thoughts, ideas, dreams, visions, and inner knowing or warning, and through the words of others: e.g., a preacher, counselor, friend, or even a total stranger. God's *rhema* word to us will usually deal with specific current circumstances and may give us direction, warning, or confirmation about something God wants us to do. However a *rhema* word will never contradict God's written Word—the Bible—the *logos*. In other words, God will never tell you to do something that is against principles in the Bible.

As you follow the steps outlined in this book, you will see that I encourage you, as you hear from God, to confirm what you believe God is saying to you by referring to the written Word (*logos*) and also share it with a trusted, spiritually mature friend. If God is really speaking to you, His words will stand up to the test and be confirmed by His written Word and His counsel through others.

Listening for the Voice

The one who enters by the gate is the Shepherd of the sheep. The gatekeeper opens the gate for him, and the sheep listen to his

voice. He calls his own sheep by name and leads them out. When he has brought out all his own, he goes on ahead of them, and his sheep follow him because they know his voice. But they will never follow a stranger; in fact, they will run away from him because they do not recognize a stranger's voice. (John 10:2–5)

This passage teaches us that we have an active role to play in listening to His voice. In it, John explains that we follow Him because we know His voice and that we will not follow a stranger's voice.

I love how God speaks to us through metaphors so that we can understand spiritual truth through natural symbolism. One of the interesting facts I learned when I was studying about sheep for a weekend message is that they really do learn the voice of their particular shepherd. If there are a thousand sheep all together in a pasture and five hundred of the sheep belong to one shepherd, only five hundred sheep will respond to his call. The other five hundred will stay in the pasture because to them it is a stranger's voice calling and they have learned not to respond.

John 10:27 reiterates this same principle: "My sheep listen to my voice; I know them, and they follow me." Notice the passage does not say "my super-spiritual sheep" or "my full-time ministry sheep" will know my voice. It simply says my sheep will know my voice. This is a promise for all believers.

We learn to quickly recognize the voice of the ones we love and those whose voices have weight in our lives. I remember when my wife, Taryn, and I were dating in the days before cell phones and caller ID; I could recognize it was her voice as soon as the first word was out of her mouth. After thirteen years of marriage, her voice has become even more familiar to me. Let's say she calls and says, "Hey, babe!" and I say, "Who is this?" If she replies, "It's me," and I say, "Me who?" I don't have to be a prophet to know that I am going to be sleeping on the sofa that night.

Although I can't always recognize God's voice with the same clarity or certainty that I can recognize Taryn's, I have placed focus and effort into discerning and obeying His voice because I love Him and His words have weight in my life.

Discerning His Voice

How can we know we are hearing the voice of God versus the voice of the enemy or the voice of our personal desires? Ask yourself the following questions:

+ Is what I am hearing unclear or confusing?
+ Does what I hear contradict the Bible?
+ If I act on what I am hearing, will it lead me to compromise my values?

The voice of the enemy is often unclear and confusing, it frequently contradicts biblical truths, and it ultimately leads you into sin and compromise. In the Garden of Eden, the serpent deceived Eve by adding to, omitting, twisting, and questioning what God said. The confusion in his words contradicted the simple directions that God had given Adam and eventually led Adam and Eve into sin.

Satan did the same when he tempted Jesus in the wilderness. He quoted Scripture to Jesus, but the motive was to tempt Jesus toward selfishness so he would disobey the call of God. Satan pulled on the human desires that Jesus likely had for food and authority, but the offering was outside the will of God.

The key to discerning between God, the enemy, and our own voice comes by familiarity through practice. The longer you walk with God, the easier it becomes to distinguish between the three. It is often easiest to recognize the difference between God's voice and the enemy's voice; it is more difficult to distinguish between your human voice and God's.

It's okay if you can't readily discern God's voice at first. Don't let that uncertainty paralyze you. If what you're hearing seems like something that would be pleasing to God and agrees with His character and Word, take a step toward it as you remain in dialogue with the Lord, asking Him to redirect you if it is not the best path for you. God looks at the intention of the heart. If your

heart's desire is to please Him, you can trust He will not let you miss anything.

Based on the three questions I asked above, if what you are hearing is unclear or confusing, wait until the direction is clear. If what you are hearing contradicts the Bible in any way, even if it seems clear, do not act on it. If what you are hearing will lead you into sin in your actions, attitude, or speech, it is not coming from God.

God is not a God of confusion, but of peace (see I Corinthians 14:33). God will never contradict His Word, and if He is speaking to you and leading you by His Spirit, He will never direct you into gratifying the desires of your flesh (see Galatians 5:16). Isaiah 30:21 says, "Whether you turn to the right or to the left, your ears will hear a voice behind you, saying, 'This is the way; walk in it.'" I have found that this voice brings joy, clarity, and further revelation, and even when I am not 100 percent sure of the origin of a thought, I can trust that as I continue to seek Him, He will guide me in the way I should walk, just as this verse promises.

There is a great story in 1 Kings Chapter 19. The great prophet Elijah had just come through a season of powerful ministry—he was physically, emotionally, and spiritually exhausted, and he was running in fear after being threatened by his enemy, Jezebel. In his exhaustion, Elijah's perspective becomes one of self-pity, but the Lord continues to minister to him, feeding him, providing water, and allowing him to sleep. God's desire is to restore his servant so he can continue with the call and purpose that God has for his life.

In verse 11, Elijah is hiding in a cave and God tells him to stand outside on the mountain because He is going to pass by. Then three dramatic signs happen. First, there is a wind that tore apart the mountain, but the Lord was not in the wind. Second, there was a great earthquake, but the

Lord was not in the earthquake. Third, there was a fire, but the Lord was not in the fire. After the fire there was a "still, small voice."

Although the wind, earthquake and fire were probably creation's dramatic response to the presence of the Lord, Elijah did not respond to any of these signs. It was when he heard the still, small voice of the Lord that the Bible says he put his cloak over his face and stood at the mouth of the cave to hear what God wanted to say. As Elijah responded to God's voice, he received his next set of directions.

As you learn to attune your ears to hear the voice of the Lord, there are a few things that can be produced or evidenced, so I encourage you to look for the following six occurrences:

1. **Strong Recurring Thought:** One of the most common ways I hear His voice is through a recurring thought or idea. As explained earlier, this is often a *rhema* word from God that comes through our thoughts. I have learned to pay close attention to my thoughts, especially recurring ones, and ask God if these are ideas from Him.

2. **An Idea with Genuine Excitement:** Generally when God is calling you to do something, there is an excitement about that area. But there are times when He calls you to do something difficult, so there is not a natural excitement about following through, but it is still typically superseded by the excitement of knowing that He is actively calling you and providing direction, and that He will be with you.

3. **Deep, Calming Peace:** Colossians 3:15 explains that God's peace will rule in our hearts—it is a gift He gives that helps guide us. His peace is a supernatural confirmation of His presence with us and a way He confirms where He is leading. We will explore this topic more thoroughly in chapter 4.

4. **An Inner Warning, Caution, or Check:** God in His kindness allows us to discern that certain decisions are not the wisest or best, or the direction may be right, but not the timing. It is up to us to heed these warnings and choose to go a different path or wait when we sense an inner check or caution.

5. **A Supernatural Knowing:** This is when you have a strong inclination about something that feels certain deep down, but that certainty is too deep to have a logical, natural understanding. This is more than intuition, as it is a supernatural understanding from the Lord. However, because of the subjective nature of our inclinations, we must test it, just as we test the other ways we hear from God.

6. **Open Doors:** Revelation 3:7 says that God will open doors that no man can shut and shut doors no man can open. We will explore this idea further in this chapter, but I encourage you to be looking for open doors of opportunity and to ask God if He is leading you through those doors. Obviously, not every door that opens before you is God leading you in that direction, but I have learned to look for open doors as a way that God leads and provides direction.

The Seeds of Vision

God subtly speaks to me every day through His still, small voice as well as little nudges and ideas that I know did not come from me or even through my desires. However, there have also been monumental times God has spoken to me that I would place in the game-changer category. I have documented each of these milestone moments in the back of my Bible with their corresponding date. One of the most significant game-changing moments came on April 22, 2005.

I was at a retreat center in the Shenandoah Valley for a doctoral course. Our professor, Dr. Mara Crabtree, taught the class about stewarding the dreams God had placed in our hearts. She shared a passage in Genesis explaining that there were many years between the time when Joseph first received the dream God had for his life and the time that the dream was fulfilled. She then gave us a handful of seeds that were supposed to represent the dreams God had placed in our hearts. Planting the seeds was meant to be symbolic of the season of stewarding our dreams before they came to fruition. With the rest of the class, I planted my seeds outside the chapel at the retreat center. I knew my seeds represented the church Taryn and I had long felt called by God to plant in the Washington, D.C., area.

Planting a church had been a dream in my heart since 1998, but the dream felt vague and seemed way too big for me. (This is actually a great litmus test to show that it is a God-sized dream. As Ephesians 3:20, says, He doesn't want to give us dreams we can accomplish with our own strengths or talents because He wants to show us that He can do immeasurably more through us than we could ask or even imagine.)

I had actually shared this dream with Taryn on our first date. Some guys may stick to the light stuff on the first date, like asking about the girl's favorite food or where she grew up, but evidently not me. I knew there was a call on both of our lives to do something great for God, and I began to pursue her to see if we were meant to walk together in the dream of planting a church in D.C. After I felt God's yes, I asked Taryn to marry me in the spring of 2002 (after a few obstacles and course corrections from God, which I will share in more detail in chapter 5). We were married that summer, and we both knew we were called to plant a life-giving, multicultural church in the Washington, D.C., area. What we didn't know was when or how it would happen.

After I planted the seeds my professor had given me, I looked down at the formation in which the seeds were planted—I noticed there were seventeen seeds planted in a circle and three above it to the side. At that moment, I sensed the Holy Spirit whisper, "You will plant seventeen

churches in the D.C. metro area (the seventeen seeds represented the seventeen campuses we would plant around the D.C. area) and three up in New York (represented by the three seeds off to the side)." This was one of the clearest voices I have heard in my life, and I know that it was the Living God speaking to me. For the next two years Taryn and I continued to seek God and wait on His timing for how and when we should launch the church.

Look Expectantly

The Hebrew word for "wait" is *qavah*, meaning to "look expectantly." The definition demonstrates that waiting on the Lord is not a passive activity. Rather, it is actively seeking where He is moving, so we are ready to step forward when God says it's time.

Waiting on the Lord has been a significant theme in DC Metro Church's story. The spring before we launched in 2007, two of my closest friends from graduate school who would help me plant the church, Matt Stroia and Julie Reams, and I visited the D.C. area to fast, pray, and walk the streets asking God to reveal to us the location He had for what would become DC Metro Church. We investigated over twenty-five locations, knocked on countless doors, and even sent chocolates and flowers to one of the school superintendents, hoping the gesture would gain her favor and possibly an opportunity to use one of the area schools. All twenty-five-plus doors were closed—very humbling!

One day Matt was lying on his bed thinking about the future church when a Middle Eastern restaurant he had visited in Alexandria, Virginia, popped into his mind. He was puzzled as to why he was thinking about food. He was about to attribute it to random, wandering thoughts or hunger, when he decided to ask God if this thought was somehow connected to the church. He immediately thought about the movie theater, the Regal Potomac Yard Theater, down the street from the restaurant. Was this God's voice speaking through a picture in his mind's eye?

Thoughts and Ideas

Just as Matt experienced the thought of the Middle Eastern restaurant popping into his head, God will sometimes speak to us through thoughts, ideas, or a picture in our imaginations. In February 2014, I experienced God speaking to me through a **recurring thought**. DC Metro Church was close to making an offer on a large church facility in Maryland that was in foreclosure (the building was the size of one-and-a-half Walmart Supercenters). Our board had signed off on making an offer, and although I still didn't have complete peace about it, we were moving forward with an offer that we expected would be accepted.

A short time before the offer was to be made, I was sitting in a local pastors' gathering called City Fathers. Pastor Mark Batterson, who was leading the gathering, said he believed God was going to speak to each of us that day about our area of greatest need. As I bowed my head and was thinking about that potential property, a thought came to my mind: *Take Virginia first!* It was a thought that I heard over and over again that day at the gathering and many times over the following weeks. For me and the church, it was God's direction that we not purchase the property in Maryland but focus future expansion in Virginia—something that is happening as I write.

Another time I experienced Him speaking to me through a **great idea**. I was on my way home to spend a date night with my wife. The church was in the middle of a fast from food and media, so I couldn't take her to a restaurant or to a movie. I wanted to have a special date night with my wife and asked the Lord if He had any ideas of what we could do together. I had a thought that was too good to be mine: take Taryn to all the houses God had provided for us to live in during our time in D.C., and other places significant to what He had done through DC Metro Church. As we stopped in front of each location, we took time to pray a prayer of thanks for God's blessings. The God-inspired idea was both spiritual and romantic!

God can speak to us through thoughts, ideas, and through pic-

tures in our imaginations in which, instead of hearing words or thoughts, we see an image. Similar to the other ways that God speaks to us, you should validate these thoughts, ideas, and images to what is in the written Word (the Bible) and, when necessary, submit to godly counsel. The source of our thoughts can be God, self, or even the enemy, so it is important to test them. Remember, nothing from God will contradict the Bible. If you are unclear of the source or interpretation of a thought, it can be tested and weighed with the help of some spiritually mature friends.

The absolutely incredible part of the story is that while Matt was having this interaction with God, God was also speaking to me about the movie theater. I had just heard about a church in Florida that had started in a movie theater, so I began to research theaters in the Alexandria area. I had the Regal movie theater website still open on my computer when Matt called me that afternoon to ask me my thoughts on starting the church in the Potomac Yard Theater. Talk about an incredible confirmation that this was the location we were to pursue! Needless to say, I immediately contacted the theater to see if they would be open to a church meeting in one of the theaters. After a ton of discouraging closed doors, this door essentially flew open . . . and the rest, as they say, is history. The moment we secured the theater, I was overwhelmingly thankful for all the closed doors, knowing that all twenty-five-plus facilities that rejected us paled in comparison to the theater.

We had a similar journey while searching for our first campus location. Because the Lord had so clearly spoken to me in 2005 that the church would have seventeen campuses throughout the D.C. area and three in the New York area, becoming a multisite church had been in our hearts from the beginning. What the Lord did not tell me was when or

how. During the third year of the church, we began seeking God to see if it was time to start the first campus. Over the next two years we went to go see more than thirty potential campus locations. Similar to our search five years earlier, we encountered closed door after closed door . . . until—you guessed it—we approached another Regal movie theater, this time in Fairfax, Virginia.

Throughout the process, we had been praying the prayer from Revelation 3:7 that says, "These are the words of him who is holy and true, who holds the key of David. What he opens no one can shut, and what he shuts no one can open." The Fairfax area was already on the radar of our leadership team as a strategic area to start our first campus, so we were thrilled when this location opened up. We saw God's fingerprints in this choice, as our first sanctuary was a Regal movie theater in Potomac Yard. Somehow it seemed right in step that the door God chose to open for our first campus would bring us back to our roots in a Regal theater. Thus, we officially became one church in two locations on January 13, 2013, as we launched our Fairfax campus.

When God Says No!

The number of closed doors we experienced before we initially launched the church and the first campus illustrates an important principle we find in the Apostle Paul's life in Acts 16. God often speaks through a no before He says yes to what is actually the very best choice for us. I am not always the biggest fan of hearing God say no because I am so ready for Him to say yes, but I have seen time and time again how the no is actually a gift, as He is at work to bring into alignment His best and highest for me.

Modern day amateur theologian Garth Brooks had this same revelation in his song "Unanswered Prayer," which hit number one on the Country Billboards in the 1990s. Brooks talks about taking his wife to a hometown football game and running into his girlfriend from high school. As he introduces the two women, he begins to remember how much he had desired his girlfriend back in the day, praying each night that

if God would give her to him for all time, he would never ask for anything again.

Although he doesn't tell us what had happened to the old girlfriend over the years, Brooks ends the song thanking God for unanswered prayers, reminding us that God still cares even if He doesn't answer prayers the way we want Him to—and that some of His greatest gifts are those unwanted answers. God always answers, but sometimes His answer is "in a different way" or "in a different time" because He sees from a perspective we cannot and He can be trusted to work all things together for good, even when it is not what we would have chosen at the time. I think all of us in hindsight can thank God for His no's to some of the prayers in our lives. As author Tim Keller says, "God will either give us what we ask or give us what we would have asked if we knew everything he knows."[4]

We see this same principle of God saying no before He says yes to direct the Apostle Paul where to go in Acts 16. When teaching others to hear God's voice, I often choose the Apostle Paul as my biblical example because he did not walk with Jesus while Jesus was on the earth. The other apostles had the advantage of hearing His voice before His ascension, but Paul had his first encounter with the ascended Jesus on the road to Damascus in Acts 9. Like you and me, he had to learn to discern the promptings and leadings of the Holy Spirit. From the start of Paul's ministry in Acts 9 until Acts 16, we see that he received very distinct direction on where to go and what to do, but it does not clearly explain how he determined where to go until Acts 16. In fact, I believe Acts 16 reveals his grid for how you and I can discern His voice.

In Acts 16:6–10, there is a process that Paul is taken through that gives much insight on how to discern the guidance of the Holy Spirit for our own lives.

They passed through the Phrygian and Galatian region, having been forbidden by the Holy Spirit to speak the word in Asia; and after they came to Mysia they were trying to go into Bithynia and the Spirit of Jesus did not permit them; and passing by Mysia,

they came down to Troas. A vision appeared to Paul in the night, a man of Macedonia was standing and appealing to him and saying, "Come over to Macedonia and help us." When he had seen the vision, immediately we sought to go into Macedonia concluding that God had called us to preach the gospel to them.

In Acts 16:6 we see Paul learning where he is not to go. It seems to reveal that if there is a place that we specifically should not go, then we can infer that there is a place that we are to go. It is significant to observe that the passage says the Spirit of Jesus would not let them go. I don't know about you, but I had to learn the hard way that it is not worth it to push ahead if God does not want me to go somewhere. Now when I feel a hesitation in my spirit or a check from the Lord about a certain direction, I have learned to more quickly say, "I'm not going."

The next thing we observe from the text is that Paul comes to the end of the road in Troas. It seems highly probable that Paul came to a point here where he started to doubt. He had just tried to go two other places, and they were both obviously blocked by the hand of God—let's call them closed doors. Perhaps he thought God was going to block everywhere and anywhere he wanted to go, or perhaps he wondered if he was listening more closely to his own voice rather than God's.

This is helpful to remember when we are having trouble discerning the will of God. Even Paul, the man God used to change the course of history in the Roman world, could not always immediately know God's direction. I've learned that to enjoy this process with God, I have to focus on the outcome or reward rather than on any delays or setbacks. It's similar to eating a Cadbury Creme Egg. You have to unwrap it and break through the chocolate "shell" in order to get to the center—a tasty surprise better than you could even imagine. God delights in the relationship and trust that is formed when we have to continue to look to and depend on Him for each step of the journey.

I like to call this "progressive revelation" where He gives us just what we need to know exactly when we need to know it. I naturally prefer to

know where the path is going to lead before I start my journey, but God kindly reminds me that He is walking with me and that it's His path, not mine. He invites me to enjoy the adventures we will go on together and promises to help me navigate every twist and turn along the way—and at the end of the day that is all I need to know.

In verse 9, we see that in the night, in what may have been Paul's moment of despair, a vision came to him. All Scripture tells us is that it came to him "in the night." It is not stated whether he was sleeping and he woke up or if the vision came to him as he walked along the road. However, the most important thing is the content of his vision—it was of a man that needed his help in Macedonia.

Dreams and Visions

Two additional ways God will speak to us is through dreams and visions. There is a prophetic word that appears in the Old Testament book of Joel and later in Acts 2:17. The word talks about God pouring out His Spirit on all mankind in the last days. One of the results of this outpouring will be that "Your old men will dream dreams, your young men will see visions" (Joel 2:28). The difference between a dream and a vision is that a dream takes place while you are asleep and a vision occurs while you are awake.

In a dream, God's Spirit often speaks to you through images. Sometimes the meaning of a God-inspired dream is very clear—a warning, a blessing, or a sense of direction for something you had asked God about earlier. Other times the meaning is not so clear and will need some interpretation.

As a disclaimer, not all dreams are God inspired. Our dreams can be influenced by different stimuli: random people and events strung together through subconscious thoughts, a mind that is racing with thoughts from your busy day, or even from the enemy. When in doubt if a dream is from God, or when you don't understand the meaning of a dream you believe is from Him, ask Him

for the wisdom to understand. James 1:5 affirms that God wants to give us wisdom if we ask.

A vision is like a spiritual movie playing in front of us or in our heads while we are awake and conscious. Like a dream, the vision may be clear in meaning, or it may need some additional interpretation and understanding from God. If you do experience dreams or visions, submit them to the process we are introducing in this book. See if the dream or vision's message is supported by the Bible (God will never contradict His written Word) and submit it to someone who is spiritually mature and whose counsel you trust.

Paul's night vision reveals something about the way God guides, but it also reveals something about Paul's heart. Paul was partnered with God. It seems to reveal that he sincerely wanted to go where he could help people. Why else would the Lord give him a vision of someone needing help? The Lord did this because He knew that Paul wanted to go where he would be used to help people. Here we see God's sovereignty in choosing to guide Paul in a way that would relate to desires in his heart. Once we submit our hearts and lives to Christ and begin growing closer to Him, God often uses the desires of our heart to guide us into His will. Psalm 37:4 says, "Take delight in the Lord, and He will give you the desires in your heart," but we must remember to look at Psalm 37:4–5, which says, "Commit everything you do to the Lord, trust in Him, and He will do this." These verses are a great reminder that although the Lord directs us through our desires when we are surrendered to Him, our role is to commit everything to Him, trust Him, and receive His help, just as we see modeled in Paul's life in Acts 16.

In verse 9, the Greek word *parakaleo* is translated into the English as "appealing to him" in reference to the man from Macedonia. This word

means, "To call to, to beseech, and to exhort."[5] This brings us to a greater depth of understanding on what the passage is really stating. Further insight is gained by noting that the use of this word is "to call someone to oneself," not "to call to someone." It is evident from the Greek word chosen that this man in Macedonia needed help and that it did not matter where the help came from; it just mattered that the help came to him.

It is also significant to note that once Paul received guidance from the Lord, he was confident in putting that guidance into motion immediately. This word is derived from the Greek word *eutheos*, which means, "suddenly and straightway."[6] Thoralf Gilbrant explains in *The New Testament Greek-English Dictionary*, "Paul and his company did not hesitate once this positive guidance was given. They concluded that God had called them, therefore they acted."[7] It is said that slow obedience is no obedience. Paul's expedient obedience should be a model to all believers, that when we do receive guidance from the Lord, we are to act upon it quickly.

As we take a closer look, we can begin to see a pattern of guidance that the Lord used in Paul's life, especially concerning the geographic location of ministry. It is interesting to note that Paul's discernment came in two steps. First, God told Paul where not to go. Only after Paul was obedient to those instructions, God told him where he was to go. This is not always the pattern, but as we discussed earlier, one of the ways in which God often speaks is that He closes wrong doors before He opens the right one.

God wants the type of relationship with us where we speak to Him and He speaks to us. His speaking to us can happen in many different ways: through His written Word—the Bible, a rhema word, thoughts and ideas, pictures and images, dreams and visions, an inner knowing, or even through closed or open doors. As you experience God in Step One of the 40-Day Challenge, get ready to submit your questions to Him. You will then have the opportunity to record the preliminary answers you think you have received in Step Two of the process: The Research.

Research

"Research is to see what everybody else has seen, and to think what nobody else has thought."

—ALBERT SZENT-GYORGYI, HUNGARIAN BIOCHEMIST[1]

"Somewhere, something incredible is waiting to be known."

—DR. CARL SAGAN, AMERICAN ASTRONOMER, WRITER, AND SCIENTIST[2]

"Study to shew thyself approved unto God, a workman that needeth not to be ashamed, rightly dividing the word of truth."

—2 TIMOTHY 2:15 KJV[3]

The second step in the scientific method is research. For the scientist, this means using all the available tools—scientific journals, the internet, other scientists—to gain the most information about how to answer the question being researched. Researching and collecting as much information as possible before starting to experiment helps the scientist create his or her plan for answering the question and for making sure mistakes from the past aren't repeated.

Likewise, in this book the second step to hearing from God consists of research that helps to either answer the question we just asked in Step One, or to confirm the answer we think we've already received from God. As I've mentioned, I have asked God to speak to me in dramatic ways, and I love it when He does. However, I have found I often seek a spectacular outward sign from Him instead of spending my time in Scripture— in research, "rightly dividing the word of truth" (2 Timothy 2:15 NKJV)[4] and asking Him to speak to me through His Word.

He Speaks through His Word

God loves to reveal Himself to those who are seeking Him—digging deeper—through His Word. Jeremiah 29:13 says, "You will seek me and find me when you seek me with all your heart." In applying this verse, I have found that the more I seek Him in His Word, the more He will speak.

When I was growing up, I had a distant respect for God's Word, but I also thought reading it was extremely boring and best suited for those in the retirement community. I viewed the Bible as a book with antiquated stories and as a manual on how to be good. Being good seemed quite dull, and I felt a certain cognitive dissonance (believing in the truth of Scripture but also feeling a distancing ennui) whenever I heard someone read from the Bible. I went to church every Sunday, but I definitely did not love His Word.

In my high school and college years I drifted further from Jesus. During my junior year in college, I decided to spend a semester in Utah, away from all my LSU fraternity brothers, in an attempt to get a fresh start. After a semester of searching for the meaning of life to no avail, taking a myriad of drugs, and essentially living my same hedonistic lifestyle, I reached a low point. My move was an attempt to escape, but change seemed elusive. I could not escape myself.

However, while waiting for my parents at the airport when they were coming to visit me, a man handed me a little book—an orange Gideons Bible containing the New Testament, Psalms, and Proverbs. My first thought was to tuck it away in my junk drawer, but my curiosity got the best of me. I opened to the book of Proverbs, and I could not put it down. Little did I know that the content in that little orange book would change the trajectory of my life. The wisdom and insight found in the verses of Proverbs seemed to leap off the page. How could this be the same book I had written off as obsolete and irrelevant years before?

This began my journey into reading through the New Testament and surrendering my life to this man named Jesus who fascinated me. Over the years I can honestly say that I have fallen in love with the Bible. The

more I love God's Word and revere it, digging into it, researching the truth between its covers, and meditating on its meaning, the more I recognize Him speaking to me. The same can happen for you, too. God wants all believers to truly love His Word and to hear Him speak with specific and personal clarity.

It's Alive!

One of my favorite passages in the Bible is Hebrews 4:12 because it reminds us that God desires to speak to us and shape us through His Word: "For the Word of God is *alive* and active (emphasis mine). Sharper than any double-edged sword, it penetrates even to dividing soul and spirit, joints and marrow; it judges the thoughts and attitudes of the heart." Do you know of any other book that claims to be alive?

The Holy Spirit causes God's Word to come alive so that we are pierced, or penetrated, to the core and empowered supernaturally to apply what we read to our lives. The Bible was written to be an invitation into an interactive conversation with God rather than just another book containing some stories, wise sayings, and principles. This means that although I can read the same passage again and again, the Holy Spirit will highlight new aspects each time or teach me how the passage applies to a particular circumstance. I love how specific and personal the Lord is and never tire of it.

For example, I was reading through Psalm 78 one morning before we moved my family across town into a new home. Taryn and I were already a little nervous for the kids and us, as it was a bit outside of town—we were moving to "the country." While reading Psalm 78, I felt the Holy Spirit highlight verse 55, "He drove out nations before them and allotted their lands to them as an inheritance; he settled the tribes of Israel in their homes." A wave of peace came over me as I felt God speak a promise to me through His Word, *David, just as I settled the Israelites in their home, so I will settle you, Taryn, and your boys in your home.*

That Word from the Lord came at the perfect time. I have found that

no matter how much we plan and prepare, moving is an unsettling ordeal. What encouraged me most was that I felt like He was saying that He would turn our house into a home—that He would truly settle us. I wrote "January 2012—Psalm 78:55" in the back of my Bible. I wanted to remember this promise from God and claim it as we transitioned. I can say now, this Word truly came to pass as we made the move. The boys love our new place because of all the surrounding woods for them to explore, and it has become a respite to create memories together as a family. We feel truly settled.

Not long after our move, I was reading in Jeremiah 30 and verse 2 stood out to me: "This is what the Lord, the God of Israel, says: 'Write in a book all the words I have spoken to you.'" I've always dreamed of writing a book, but I needed some momentum and direction from God as to when to start. As I read this verse, I felt God giving me the green light to begin writing. From this, I also realized His hand would be upon it as I recorded the words He had spoken to me. I wrote "April 2012—Jeremiah 30:2-3" in the back of my Bible because it was my word from the Lord to begin the book you are reading now.

Confirmation Through the Word

On the morning of June 15, 2010, I saw a vision—an animated picture in my mind's eye—during my time with God. In the vision I was standing on the bridge that is adjacent to our current church facility and looking at our new building. I saw not only our current building but another large facility next door, as plain as day. Next, I saw myself in the facility in what I understood to be a several-stories-high prayer tower overlooking Washington, D.C., and the monuments. I was surrounded by my four kids, who looked like they were teenagers, and they were praying with me for the city of D.C. I began to scribble the vision of what I saw on a nearby napkin. I sensed in my spirit that God was calling us to take steps toward acquiring the building and land next door to our facility, but I was not sure when or how it would happen.

We had just gone through an arduous year-and-a-half process of acquiring permits and renovating our current facility to be able to move in just two months prior. It was a significant step in faith because our budget had to double to pay the bills in the new facility. I heard the still, small voice of God telling us to acquire that first facility, confirmed it with DC Metro Church's Lead Team and Overseers, and stepped out in faith. (In chapter 3 we will talk about the importance of seeking counsel when you are making important decisions.) God was completely true to His Word. In one month the budget of DC Metro doubled, which had not happened before and has not happened since. After that season of being stretched in the area of faith, the last thing on my mind was trying to acquire more property. I thought it might be time to have a relaxing, low-key summer, but evidently God had other plans.

During that time, I was studying the book of Joshua. The theme of the passages I was reading was about the Israelites possessing the Promised Land. As I read, I felt Him stirring my heart about the call that He has on DC Metro not only to possess physical land, but to partner with Him in repossessing the land spiritually. There is a rich spiritual heritage upon which our country was founded, a godly foundation that our forefathers sought to implement. Unfortunately, we have veered away from that foundation, but God, in His mercy, is calling us to help restore a God-first culture throughout the D.C. metro area.

In Joshua 6, Joshua leads the Israelites to march and pray around the city of Jericho as a prophetic declaration of the land they would possess. After reading this and praying about the vision God had given me of the property next door, I felt led to go do my own Jericho march around the property. But there was one significant obstacle: a gate around the property and a security guard in front of the building. I figured that if the Israelites could go boldly into Jericho to possess the Promised Land that was filled with their enemies, then I could take down the security guard. (I am only kidding!)

As a pastor, I decided it might be wise to try a different approach. I convinced Dana Sorensen, a staff member who has been a part of the

church since the beginning, to go with me to try and convince the security guard to let us walk around the building. I was sure the guard was going to think we were crazy and was ready for her to turn us down, when she said (to my surprise), "Sure, you can walk around the building, as long as I walk with you." The three of us began to circumnavigate the building. Pamela, the security guard, began to tell us her story. It happened to be her first night on the job, and she shared how she was a believer who had recently returned to the Lord. When we were halfway around the building she blurted out, "This may sound strange to you, but I feel like Rahab in the Bible who allowed Joshua and Caleb to spy out the land." Dana and I couldn't believe our ears. Did she just compare us to Joshua and Caleb? She had no idea that I had been studying the book of Joshua or that God had just given me a vision about possessing the land.

I believed in divine appointments before that night, but this further confirmed my belief that God absolutely is in the details of our life and that He strategically places certain people in our lives for a specific purpose. As if that were not enough, God in His kindness wanted to bring me further confirmation. Two nights later, on June 19, we had the incredible privilege of Christine Caine coming to speak at our church. Chris Caine is one of the most passionate, dynamic preachers I know, as she has acquired a reputation for speaking prophetic word through the message she brings to each particular church. I felt especially excited about what Chris would preach that night. Believe it or not, her message was the story of Joshua and Caleb spying out the land from the same passage in Joshua I had been studying. At one point in the message, she pointed in the direction of the property next door and loudly proclaimed, "God is calling you to possess the land!" Dana and I were having trouble containing ourselves as we looked at each other with wide eyes and knowing smiles. God was confirming through His Word what He had shown me earlier in a vision.

Holy Txt Challenge

A few years after we planted DC Metro Church, God spoke to me to help the church learn what it means to fall in love with the Bible. In a still, small voice I heard the instruction *Read my Word.* I realized that God was leading me to read His Word aloud to the church to awaken their hearts to Scripture in a greater way. "Read my Word" was the game changer that inspired what I aptly called the Holy Txt Challenge.

The challenge was, if one thousand people committed to reading their Bibles for twenty minutes a day for forty days, I would read the entire New Testament straight through, out loud, in one consecutive reading. They unabashedly rose to the challenge. On Friday, May 11, 2012, at 7 p.m., the marathon began—I sat in the front of the sanctuary and began reading from Matthew. I had excitement in my heart and expectancy in my spirit because I know that something significant happens as we declare His powerful Word aloud.

The most exhilarating part of the challenge was reading the last book—Revelation. The sanctuary was filled with a tangible faith and a palpable electricity, as so many members joined us for the reading of the final book of the New Testament. On Saturday, May 12, a little after 5 p.m., I completed approximately twenty-two hours of reading 260 chapters, 7,956 verses, and 138,020 words (and I consumed twenty cups of tea, twenty-four bottles of water, and three-and-a-half bears of honey). My part of the Holy Txt Challenge was finished, but the catalytic effects were just beginning.

One member shared, "During the Holy Txt Challenge, I felt the Word of God come alive for me like never before. My goodness! It was like all the cogs to an engine were coming into place in my head and heart as different pieces of the New Testament were being read, and then that engine started to turn, and revelation after revelation starting forming and gaining traction."

Another member explained, "After hearing the reading of the whole New Testament, the Word became so much more approach-

able for me. I never realized that the whole book of Matthew could be read in approximately two hours. The Holy Txt Challenge created a desire for me to read and study the Bible more on my own, so that I can unlock its treasures."

Reflecting back to when God told me that He wanted the people of our church to fall even more in love with His Word, I am encouraged to see how their desire to read and know its promises has increased. I am convinced that your love for it will grow, too, as you are faithful to read, study, and obey what it says. As A. W. Tozer said, "The Bible is not an end in itself, but a means to bring men to an intimate and satisfying knowledge of God, that they may enter into Him and delight in His Presence . . ."[5]

S-O-A-P

Oftentimes people ask me how I study the Bible. They want to know what research methods I use as I seek to answer my questions. My devotional times are very simple. I begin with a formula I learned years ago called S-O-A-P, created by Wayne Cordeiro. S-O-A-P stands for Scripture, Observation, Application, and Prayer.[6]

Scripture

The first step is simply to decide which passage you are going to study and then begin reading it. In the 40-Day Challenge at the back of the book, I've provided one scripture passage for each day. After completing the forty days, I recommend choosing a book of the Bible that you want to read, or doing a topical study with the help of a concordance. Some good books in the Bible to start with are the Gospel of John, any of Paul's letters in the New Testament, such as Ephesians or Philippians, or Psalms in the Old

Testament. Proverbs is great as well, as it has thirty-one chapters, providing a solid chapter a day for a month.

If you are interested in reading narratives about the lives of great men and women, I recommend tracing the story of the patriarchs in Genesis, Moses and the Israelites' escape from Egypt in the book of Exodus, the adventures of King David in 1 and 2 Samuel, or Peter and Paul in the book of Acts.

If you prefer a topical study, you can use a concordance to find what you are interested in and follow the passages and verses provided about that topic. Many study Bibles have concordances in the back, or you can find incredible concordances online at locations such as biblestudytools .com. Another good website is BibleGateway.com. There you can type the keyword you want to learn more about, and it will list all of the places that word appears in the Bible.

For example, if I am studying about purpose, I would look up the word *purpose*, and it would lead me to verses such as Psalm 138:7–8a, "Though I walk in the midst of trouble, you preserve my life; you stretch out your hand against the anger of my foes, with your right hand you save me [NIV]. The Lord will fulfill [His purpose] for me, [ESV]" or Proverbs 19:21, "Many are the plans in a person's heart, but it is the Lord's purpose that prevails." I recommend choosing a chapter, if you are studying a book, or a few verses if you are doing a topical study. Once you have your chapter or verses selected, you are ready to move to the O, or observation stage.

Observation

As you read Scripture, ask yourself, *What stands out?* Ask God, *What are you highlighting to me today?* For example, when I was studying the book of Joshua, the verse found in Joshua 1:8 stood out to me, "Keep this Book of the Law always on your lips; meditate on it day and night, so that you may be careful to do everything written in it. Then you will be prosperous and successful."

Here are some questions you can ask in the observation stage:

- ✦ What is the historical/contextual situation?

- ✦ When was it written?

- ✦ To whom is it speaking?

- ✦ Why was it written?

- ✦ What kind of literary genre is it (narrative, command, poetry, or prophecy)?

- ✦ How does the author arrange the text? Look for repeated words or phrases and theological words. (You can look these up if you do not know a definition or want to explore further.)

- ✦ What does the passage say about God, Jesus, and the Holy Spirit?

- ✦ What does the passage say about the believer?

- ✦ What is the theme of the passage (the big idea)?

- ✦ What are the main principles you learn from this text (timeless truths)?

- ✦ What does the commentary or study Bible say about this passage, and how does that add to your understanding?

A few observations I wrote about Joshua 1:8:

1. This passage is a command to "Keep this book of the law always."

2. There are three things we are commanded to do with the book of the law: speak about it ("on your lips"); continually think about it ("meditate on it day and night"); and, act on it ("do everything written in it").

3. The result of us fulfilling this command is biblical prosperity and success.

After you finish writing down some observations, you can move to the A, or the Application step, where you try to determine how the passage applies to your personal life.

Application

For the Application step, I made up my own acronym, GOD SPA, which helps me ask intentional questions in order to apply the passage to my life. Besides, who doesn't like a little spa action? I want not only to read the Word, I also want to let it read me. When you let the Word read you, you are allowing God to speak to you through His Word so that you can apply its teachings to your life rather than just reading the words for cognitive knowledge. James 1:23–24 says: "Anyone who listens to the word but does not do what it says is like someone who looks at his face in a mirror and, after looking at himself, goes away and immediately forgets what he looks like."

Here are the six questions for you to ask to help you apply James 1:23–24:

1. G (Growth)—Is there an area where God is calling you to grow?

Is there a part of God's Word that you know you are not walking in the fullness of what God has for you? Perhaps God is revealing something in your heart. Maybe He is highlighting a relationship or an area in your marriage that needs work. Perhaps it is in your finances, your health, or something going on at work. Whichever area you feel Him revealing, I encourage you to surrender it to Him and ask Him to help you give Him full leadership.

2. O (Obedience)—Is there an area where God is calling you to obey?

Is there an area in your life that you are not obeying God right now? This can be similar and even overlapping with a growth area, but it is generally

focused either on a specific action that you feel the Holy Spirit is asking you to take or a particular command in His Word that you know you have not been following.

As I often tell my boys, delayed obedience is not really obedience. Like any good parent, God wants our wholehearted obedience, so we should honestly be asking the Holy Spirit if there is any area where we are not walking in full obedience. God will graciously meet us in that place to give us His strength to help us turn from these areas, as we are honest and authentic before Him.

3. D (Direction)—Is there a direction God is speaking to you through this passage?

We all desire God's perspective on what we should do next in life. One of my favorite verses on direction is Psalm 32:8, which says, "I will instruct you and teach you in the way you should go." I have found one of the most common ways that God gives me direction is through my time in the Bible. When I have a decision coming up, I will allow myself some private time to pray and read, giving myself the space and quiet to see if God highlights anything through Scripture. I find that, time and again, He leads me to just the right passage, whether it be through my daily reading, a verse someone shares with me, or through one of my topical studies I explained earlier. God loves to guide us through His Word.

4. S (Sin)—Is there a sin God wants you to confess and turn from in this passage?

Sin sometimes sounds like a really religious word, but the Greek definition of sin is actually an archery term that means to "miss the mark." Often when I am reading the Word, God will bring to mind a certain area of my life, and I will realize that I haven't hit the mark in that area.

If God points out an area in your life where you have missed the mark, you need to do two things: repent and confess. The Greek word for repentance, *metanoia,* means changing your mind about a former attitude or action. You repent by recognizing that that attitude or action was

wrong toward God or other people and choosing to change your mind and turn away from it. Confession is a part of repentance. It is telling God you are sorry for missing the mark. And not just saying the words, but really meaning them in your heart. The beauty is that 1 John 1:9 tells us that "If we confess our sins, he is faithful and just and will forgive us our sins and purify us from all unrighteousness."

Conviction vs. Condemnation

I have found it extremely helpful to know the difference between conviction and condemnation. Conviction is when God points out sin in your life because He wants you to know that He has something better for you and that He will help empower you to choose His path. It is often an action that God wants you to take such as, "Apologize to your co-worker for being selfish when you took the last sandwich at the luncheon without checking to see if he had eaten."

Condemnation is altogether different and from a different source. Condemnation is an attack from the enemy on your identity where he makes you feel guilty and weighed down. It is typically an accusation about who he says you are instead of a particular action you have done. For example, "You are a selfish person who is always looking out for yourself at the expense of others, and you'll never change."

As believers, we need to know how to discern between conviction and condemnation. Conviction is life-giving and empowering. It is never easy to face up to the mistakes in our lives, but when God highlights an area where we have missed the mark, He does it because He loves us and will give us the power to change as we surrender it to Him. Simply put, condemnation attacks your identity or character and often leaves you feeling hopeless and shameful while conviction guides you back to God's highest path for you and seeks to empower you for change.

5. P (Promise)—Is there a promise from this passage you can claim for your life?

Did you know that there are over six thousand promises in God's Word? For example, the passage Joshua 1:8 that we discussed earlier contains a clear promise: God promises that as I meditate and walk in the truths of His Word, He will make my way prosperous and successful. This is an example of a conditional promise, meaning God will fulfill His part on the condition that you fulfill your part.

We all would like to have what I call "God success" in our lives. In fact, the Hebrew translation of the word *prosper* means "to be pushed forward in life." How exciting is it to know that if we commit to read God's Word, He will push us forward in life? God's Word is filled with promises that we can cling to and pray over ourselves when we are in a hard situation or when we need to be reminded of His truth.

6. A (Accountability)—Is there any area where you need accountability?

Accountability is a key to success, because whenever you come across one of the five application areas in your Bible study, there is probably an area where you're thinking to yourself, *You know what? I don't know if I'm going to be able to walk this out on my own. I know I've got God's help, but I think it would be wise to call someone to hold me accountable in this area.*

Many times, after spending time in the Word, I've picked up the phone to call one of my accountability partners. I have three men whom I can call and say, "God is dealing with me, and I need you to regularly ask me about this area of my life."

By the way, no one can hold you accountable unless you tell that person where you're tempted or struggling. If they don't know your weakness, they're just going to ask you a general question, such as "Hey, how are you doing?" and we are most likely to answer, "Fine." I'm fine because I don't want to talk to you about my real issues. Did you know that when we avoid accountability, what we're actually saying is we don't really want to change? Because it is so important to be transparent in your account-

ability, having safe friendships where there is mutual trust is paramount. In chapter 3, I will share with you how to find and develop these types of relationships.

I ask all six of these GOD SPA questions for each passage I study. Typically, God will lead me to focus on a couple of these areas to highlight how He wants me to apply its message.

For example, from Joshua 1:8, I felt led to focus on Growth, Promise, and Accountability. I was challenged to increase my time in meditating on the Word (Growth) so that I can experience true success (Promise). I shared this challenge I was sensing with a few close friends who hold me accountable. After some dialogue with them and processing how I could implement this, I felt encouraged and empowered to increase my time of intentionally studying and meditating on God's Word.

Prayer

Using our S-O-A-P acrostic, we've discussed Scripture, Observation, and Application. The final *P* in S-O-A-P is Prayer. Prayer is actually the most important step and one of the most overlooked. This is simply taking whatever God has spoken to you and bringing it back to Him, asking Him to help you. You might pray, "God I'm going to need some help with this. I'm going to try to walk this out today."

A great support for this step is two-way prayer journaling: writing down your thoughts to God and then writing what you believe God is speaking to you. King David was one of the toughest, fiercest warriors in Scripture, and he was a voracious journal-er. A good portion of the book of Psalms is essentially David's journals crying out to the Lord and then listening and responding to what he hears. David received the plans for rebuilding the temple during one of his times of journaling. "'All this,' David said [in 1 Chronicles 28:19], 'I have in writing as a result of the Lord's hand on me, and he enabled me to understand all the details of the plan.'"

The prophet Habakkuk was no stranger to journaling. The first chapter of Habakkuk is essentially Habakkuk complaining to the Lord—which is a good reminder that we can be totally authentic with God when we are praying. Habakkuk asks God why it is taking Him so long to move regarding Habakkuk's situation. Before God answers, He instructs Habakkuk to write down his answer. Habakkuk 2:2 says, "Write down this vision; clearly inscribe it on tablets so one may easily read it" (HCSB).

In my first decade of walking with God, I definitely did not love journaling. I watched Taryn pour her heart out in journal after journal during the years we were dating and the first years of marriage, but I just couldn't get into it. Several years ago, at a retreat, my seminary professor challenged us to journal to God and then write what we were sensing He was saying to us. I had previously thought of journaling as just writing to myself, so writing to God felt a little strange, but when I realized I could write prayers to God and then listen for His reply, it became an entirely new experience for me.

I now love journaling and average about eight journals a year. As I have coached others in journaling, the method I teach is to write a letter to God and then write a letter back from God. I have heard countless others say that this brought a breakthrough in hearing from Him. One lady recently shared that as she practiced this technique of writing to herself from God, she was getting so many responses in her mind that she had trouble writing fast enough.

I am confident that God wants to bring a breakthrough in your walk with Him, too, and I encourage you to give it a try. To break it down, I first write God a letter where I am very honest and authentic before Him. I might include what I read in Scripture that day and if there were any challenges, revelations, or insights I want to remember. I thank Him for who He is and how good He is to me. I try to release any burdens I am still carrying and invite Him to speak into any of the problems or situations that are concerning me. I typically ask the Lord some questions about direction I am seeking or whatever is on my

mind that day. I lift up my family, the church, and the people who are in my heart, asking Him to move in their lives and allowing space for Him to speak to me about any messages I should be conveying to others.

Next comes the fun part, where you write a letter to yourself from God. The first time I did this, I will admit it felt a little odd because I wasn't sure if God would speak or if it would feel like me making up something to say to myself. My seminary professor encouraged us just to try it with an open mind and ask God to speak, so I decided to go for it. I started with my name at the top of the paper and then just asked the Lord what He wanted to say to me that day.

I was surprised at how natural it felt to write what I believed God was saying to me and how I even felt it came in a different tone than the one I typically write in. A good portion of the letter is often encouragement from God about how much He loves me or how He is with me in whatever circumstance I am experiencing. He will often bring to mind scriptures that apply directly to my current struggles or questions. Sometimes I will hear a specific answer to something I have been asking Him. But my primary purpose in spending time with God is not to receive information or get answers; my principal reason is to know Him and to walk with Him. Out of this relationship will come all that I need to know for each day, including where He is leading me.

After you finish journaling, it is important to remember to submit everything back to God. To be sure, I always ask Him if I misheard or wrote anything that was not from Him and, if so, to redirect me. Just like anything else you hear from God, no matter how you hear it, it is important to test the word you've received and run it through filters, such as seeing if it lines up with Scripture, testing it through the godly counsel in your life, and examining whether you feel the peace of God about the direction you heard. I will address all these steps in more detail in the following chapters of the book. You will also have an opportunity to try two-way journaling as a part of the 40-Day Challenge.

Devo Time

A "devo time" is what I call my daily devotional time with God. That is a block of time I set aside to spend in worship, prayer, and Bible study. The simple steps I outlined in this chapter will be a core part of your devo time and help you download God's specific message for you. We will talk more about having a devo time throughout this book and give you more detailed instructions and a structure to follow in The Experiment.

The Bible is meant to propel you into conversation with God, so keep the conversation going even after your official devo time is over. Some of my best revelations have come in the middle of my day, when God drops an idea in my mind or speaks something to me in reply to what I asked Him earlier or what I read in Scripture. As you keep the communication lines open, He shows up and delights to speak!

Mark it Up!

I once heard that a Bible that is falling apart usually belongs to a person who is not, so I make it my personal goal to mark up my Bibles by highlighting, writing, and poring over their pages. In fact, every year I write my annual goals on a piece of paper and tape it in the front cover of my Bible. Every time God speaks something really specific to me or gives significant direction for my life, I write it on the back cover of my Bible.

I recommend marking up your Bibles because you can look back through the pages and see all the ways God has met you and worked in your life. God wants to build a personal history with you through His Word. When He highlights a verse or a promise, it comes alive. I like to write the date next to a passage or write down what God spoke to me through the passage so that I can remember each encounter with Him.

When I am having a difficult day or feeling distant from God, I can go back to these passages where I have already met with God and experienced triumphs. These verses often become a springboard that propels me back to Him. This takes any Bible from being God's Word and turns it into God's Word for you!

If you have not encountered God in this way, ask Him. He loves to reveal Himself to those who are hungry and speak to those who desire to hear Him. God's Word is never meant to be merely a theological book to be studied. Its primary role is to draw you closer to the Author so that you can know Him and be led by Him. Remember the story of Elijah I referenced earlier? God did not speak to Elijah in an earthquake, mighty wind, or a fire but, rather, a still, small voice. The reason why He uses a still, small voice is because He is close, and when you're close, you only need to whisper. Get to know the Word and you will draw close to the Author.

One of the analogies that God uses to explain the importance of His Word is when He compares it to bread. The children of Israel walked in the desert for forty years, and there were some pretty amazing things going on out in that desert. First, God led them with a cloud by day and a pillar of fire by night. In addition, He miraculously provided food because there's not a lot to eat in the desert. So He caused it to rain bread—manna from heaven—every day.

Exodus 16:4 says, "Then the Lord said to Moses, 'I will rain down bread from heaven for you. The people are to go out each day and gather enough for that day. In this way I will test them and see whether they will follow my instructions.'" He explained that He would do this every day to test them and see whether or not they would follow Him.

God's role was to provide, but the Israelites had a role to play: they were to gather new manna every day because it would rot if they tried to keep it overnight. God's test was simple: Either they were going to be full that day or they were going to be hungry. Either they were going to gather and consume the manna or they were going to find themselves weak, tired, and frustrated.

I believe this passage foreshadows the relationship God invites us to

have with His Word. He promises to provide spiritual food for us, but there is a significant responsibility on our parts. We have to literally make the steps to research and seek God through His Word daily so that we can apply His message to our lives. The test is simple. If we get to Wednesday and we're feeling a little bit overwhelmed by life, a bit frustrated by our circumstances, or perhaps a little weary and anxious, we should honestly evaluate if we have been seeking out and applying God's message to our circumstances every day.

God's Word has sustenance that provides exactly what we need at the right time and in the right way, but we have to set aside time to seek out His message in order to find it and to receive it.

Once you have asked your questions and done your research, you are ready to move on to Steps Three and Four in the scientific method: constructing and testing your hypothesis.

Constructing and Testing the Hypothesis

There are two possible outcomes: if the result confirms the hypothesis, then you've made a measurement. If the result is contrary to the hypothesis, then you've made a discovery.

—ENRICO FERMI, ITALIAN PHYSICIST [1]

Let the wise listen and add to their learning, and let the discerning get guidance.

—PROVERBS 1:5

In the scientific method, Step Three is to construct a hypothesis—an educated guess about how something will work. It is based on the question(s) asked in Step One and the research gleaned in Step Two. It is an educated guess because it is merely a prediction of the answer to the question based on your research. In your elementary school bean experiment, the hypothesis was that if you stuck a seed in some dirt, watered it daily, and exposed it to the warmth of a heat lamp, the seed would sprout and become a bean plant.

The hypothesis here is what you believe God is speaking to you. As you posed your question(s) to the Lord, listened for His voice and direction, and further discovered His direction through your research into the written Word of God, you came up with an idea of what He is speaking to you and what He desires you to do—with the expectation that your obedience to His direction will result in certain outcomes.

Before you launch out on what you believe God is speaking to you, or if you still remain uncertain of His direction—even after following Steps One and Two—I encourage you to share your hypothesis with one or

two close friends. In addition to speaking through the still, small voice and His Word, another primary way God speaks is through other people. Sharing with others what you believe God is speaking to you and allowing them to give you feedback correlates with Step Four in the scientific method, which is to test your hypothesis by doing an experiment. This step is absolutely key and is one of the most missed steps in the process of hearing from God.

A scientist would never stop a science experiment at Step Three with just a hypothesis, so why do we stop here when we think we have heard from God? There are still steps left in the process that I believe help to build our confidence in what God is saying!

A Prophetic Word

My first job out of college was as youth pastor in the little town of DeRidder, Louisiana. I knew I was called to full-time ministry and desired to go to seminary, but I had no idea how I would ever pay for it. An opportunity presented itself for me to build a house, although there was no way I could afford to build a house on my $12,000-a-year youth-pastor salary, but my dad offered to cosign the loan with me.

I kept praying that God would clearly show me if it was something I should move forward with and to shut the door if it was not. On the Sunday before I needed to decide, I prayed the whole forty-five-minute drive to church about whether I was supposed to take out the loan and build the house.

I was actually leaning against doing so because I started wondering if it was wise to borrow all that money. As it turned out, the title of the sermon was "There is a Miracle in Your House." Through that message I was flooded with peace and knew that God was giving me His go-ahead to build the house. I had no idea that it would be Taryn's and my first home. The house also provided the finances for us to afford a home when we responded to God's call to move to D.C. There truly was a miracle in my house.

I knew God had clearly spoken to me through the message about something the pastor didn't even know I was asking God.

I love it when God speaks so definitively through someone else to answer a specific question I have asked Him. There have been numerous times similar to this when I have received an answer to something I was praying about through someone else. At first glance these incidences appear to be coincidences, but each time I knew it was actually God speaking directly to me and confirming His voice.

Other times God has spoken to me through someone else who's received a Word from Him for me. These are often called prophetic words, and I absolutely love it when I receive one that resonates or speaks to me right where I am. However, prophetic words are not the primary way we should seek to hear God through other people. They are usually encouraging words of affirmation of either what God is speaking or what else God could be saying.

Counsel

The most frequent and reliable way God speaks to us through others is through relationships in our lives that Scripture calls counsel or advisors. For example, Proverbs 15:22 says, "Plans fail for lack of counsel, but with many advisors they succeed." The focus of this chapter is going to be on the importance of having counsel in our lives and how we can best position ourselves to hear from Him through these intentional and God-first relationships. One of the primary roles of counsel is to test what we believe we have heard from God to see if it resonates with others.

Why do so few people prioritize seeking out counsel as a way for God to speak to them or to confirm what they believe He has already spoken? One reason is because people are afraid that their hypothesis

will be proven wrong when tested. They would rather not submit the message to trusted counsel because they want to do what they want to do without other people's input. These people tend to use the phrase "God told me to do this" at alarmingly frequent rates and are not open to hearing another person's perspective if he or she disagrees with theirs. I do not think I need to elaborate on why these people are placing themselves in an unhealthy, dangerous position. Proverbs 12:15 describes them as fools because they are not seeking or heeding counsel, "The way of a fool *is* right in his own eyes but he who heeds counsel *is* wise."[2]

I had an individual come to my office a few years ago claiming to be seeking counsel. After entering the room, he sat down on my couch and proceeded to tell me God had spoken to him and that he knew what he was going to do in the situation—even though he was supposedly coming to me to seek my advice. When I asked him why he made the appointment, he said, "Well, the Bible says I am supposed to seek counsel." I asked him, "If I told you I didn't think you should move forward in the situation, would you change your mind or course of action?" He answered with a frank but adamant "no." This man was not coming to seek counsel. He was coming to communicate information in hopes that I would agree with him and he could check off what he felt was the obligatory command from God to "seek counsel."

There are many like this man who honestly do not want counsel. However, I believe the most common reason people don't seek counsel is that they have never chosen anyone to play this role in their lives. They either skip this step entirely or they end up asking a plethora of people whom they are not in a close relationship with or who do not have a biblical worldview. It is no surprise that they end up getting confused when their counsel gives different advice. They often misuse Proverbs 11:14, which says, "Where there is no counsel, the people fall; but in the multitude of counselors there is safety."[3]

Wise Counsel

Proverbs 11:14 says to seek counsel through a multitude of counselors, but when we look at the Hebrew word for counsel, we receive a vital barometer to use when selecting the people we ask. The Hebrew word for counsel translates to "wise counsel or good advice and direction," and the Hebrew word for counselors means those who "counsel or give wise advice." This verse is saying not to choose just any group of counselors, but those who give wise advice.

The Hebrew word for counsel is also a nautical term, conveying that receiving and following wise advice will help steer us in the right direction. Therefore, it is paramount to make the right choice regarding whom we choose to speak to about our lives because, as this verse reminds us, when we choose well, we will find safety.

So how do we find wise counsel? I have three preliminary questions I use as a litmus test:

Are they walking closely with God?

The first question I ask: "Are they walking closely with God?" is the most important question. Proverbs 11:14 says we need to have those who will give us wise advice, and this comes best from those who have a vibrant relationship with God and make decisions with a biblical worldview.

Having a vibrant relationship with God means they spend time with God and hear from Him. I want to receive counsel from someone who is listening to His leading, both for their lives and for my life.

I define someone with a biblical worldview as one who looks to the Word of God as their ultimate truth and authority, which means that their value system lines up with God's value system. This manifests in their lives through their personal character, their genuine love for people, and their desire to live life for what ultimately matters—eternity.

Are they walking closely with me?

The second question, "Are they walking closely with me?" is also very im-

portant because I have found that the people who can give me the best advice are the people who know me the very best. They know my strengths, weaknesses, fears, dreams, and insecurities, so they have insight into my life that others would miss. They also are praying for me on a regular basis and have a vested interest in my life, so they are trusted counselors whose words have weight and authority.

Are they able to tell me no?

The third question, "Are they able to tell me no?" is one that is often missed. If you surround yourself with those who automatically agree with you, often referred to as yes men, you are missing the whole point of seeking counsel. You need to give people permission to tell you no and take the time to listen to why they disagree with you or have reservations about your ideas. Those closest to you often have a different vantage point that is able to bring to light something you missed seeing and even save you from future trouble. Proverbs 19:20 says, "Listen to advice and accept discipline, and at the end you will be counted among the wise." Are you willing to hear advice or discipline, even when it is not what you want to hear, and take time to seriously weigh what has been shared?

Someone who was not afraid to give me straightforward advice and even provide some needed discipline in my life was Billy Hornsby. Billy was one of the founders of the Association of Related Churches (ARC), an organization that helps plant churches all over the world, who became a mentor and personal friend. He was one of the kindest, most fun-loving men you could ever meet, but he was also not afraid to speak the truth. I learned this firsthand when he came to visit DC Metro about a year after we planted the church. He evaluated every aspect of our services and of the DC Metro experience, and he gave us a C-minus. Yes, only slightly better than a D. Ouch! I admit this was a tough pill to swallow because he was a man I deeply respected and I wanted him to be impressed with the ministry we were developing in our nation's capital.

However, looking back, I am thankful for his brutal honesty, because he gave me a list of ten things he would change. For example, he said we

needed to train our leaders on how to host guests because his experience of being hosted was subpar. He advised us to remove superfluous parts of the service, such as long prayers and any language that non-Christians and new believers would not understand. He also recommended adding a ten-minute guest reception at the end of each service to be able to connect with those who were new to the church.

We implemented every one of his recommendations and saw immediate fruit, especially in our guest relations. After his assessment, we were compelled to study the organizations with the best guest relations in the world to find the ones we would model ourselves after: the Ritz-Carlton, Nordstrom, and Starbucks. For example, from the Ritz we learned that you should always walk your guests to wherever they are asking directions to rather than just pointing them in the right direction. Nordstrom trains their employees to answer any question related to any department, and if they cannot answer, they will personally escort you to someone who can answer your question. After learning this, we started to train our different serving teams at church to be able to answer basic questions about other serving teams and if they could not answer the guest's questions, they were instructed to take the person to a leader on the serving team. Finally, Starbucks desires to be your "third place," where you hang out other than work and home, and after learning this we intentionally created environments and places for people to connect with one another because we want church to be their third place.

I am happy to say that when Billy returned a year later, he gave his experience at DC Metro an A. The only significant feedback he recommended on his second visit was that I take my family on a vacation because we needed some rest and quality time together. He also challenged me to intentionally invest in a relationship with another ARC church planter whose church was at a similar stage as DC Metro.

My first thought was Pastor Rob Brendle from Denver United Church. What I didn't know is that Billy had told Pastor Rob something similar. At Billy's bidding, we both began to invest in our relationship, and Rob quickly became a close friend. He actually took Billy's place on our

board, as one of DC Metro's Overseers when Billy passed away. I am incredibly thankful for Billy's willingness to give me honest feedback and to challenge me because it is still bearing fruit in my life and in DC Metro today. Do you have these types of relationships in your life? If not, I believe it is God's desire to help you find them.

S.A.F.E. Relationships

A recent study indicated that the greatest statistical predictor of spiritual growth is the quantity of close Christian friends a person has in any given season of his or her life. In other words, from a statistical growth standpoint, having healthy, God-first friendships is far more important than any other Christian behavior or discipline. Peter Haas, founder and lead pastor of Substance Church in Minneapolis, elaborates on these findings, "In fact, you can preach the same quantity of God's Word at two different people, and studies show that the 'person with more friends' is the one who is 'most likely to apply it.' "[4]

This study reinforces our DC Metro small group motto: "Transformation happens best in the context of healthy, God-first relationships." We believe healthy, God-first relationships are S.A.F.E. relationships, meaning that they are:

Supportive—We are called to support and encourage one another. After all, we all need friends who will be there for us in both the good times and the hard times.

Accountable—We need people in our lives who we can be totally authentic with, who sharpen us and, no matter what, point us back to Christ.

Fun—We need people in our lives who we can enjoy and who help us live the abundant life God calls us to enjoy together.

Empowering—We are called to speak into one another's lives and help each other fulfill our God-given purpose and potential in life.

I intentionally place S.A.F.E. relationships in my life not only because they enrich my life and have helped me become who I am called to be, but also because they play the vital role of providing me trusted, godly counsel.

Supportive

The people you place as counsel should play a supportive, encouraging role in the narrative of your life. As I mentioned when I shared the three questions I ask when choosing counsel, they are people who should know you well and love you, because this gives them more authority and insight to speak into your life. They will sacrifice for you and help support you so that you can accomplish more together than you could possibly accomplish apart.

Ecclesiastes 4:9–12 describes the advantages of this type of unified, synergistic relationship:

> Two are better than one, because they have a good return for their labor. If either of them falls down, one can help the other up. But pity anyone who falls and has no one to help them up. Also, if two lie down together, they will keep warm. But how can one keep warm alone? Though one may be overpowered, two can defend themselves. A cord of three strands is not quickly broken.

This passage reminds me of Bubba's relationship with Forrest Gump when he stated, "I'm gonna lean up against you, you just lean right back against me. This way, we don't have to sleep with our heads in the mud. You know why we a good partnership, Forrest? 'Cause we be watchin' out for one another. Like brothers and stuff."[5] Our lives get real muddy when we attempt to go it alone. Jethro modeled this type of supportive relationship to Moses in Exodus 18. Even though Moses had received the best education available in Egypt, I believe he learned even more from Jethro about practical leadership. Jethro taught Moses how he could serve the

people more strategically. After heeding Jethro's advice, Moses became a much better leader of the people, and a better sustainer of his own life.

Jethro knew Moses had a tendency to try to please people because Jethro understood Moses's weaknesses. Jethro told Moses there was no way Moses could continue to handle the number of people who wanted to see him every day without his growing too weary. Jethro played a vital role by speaking into Moses's life and coming up with a practical solution to an issue affecting his success as a leader. We all need people in our lives who help us know our blind spots and support us by figuring out practical ways we can overcome our current obstacles.

Accountable

The people we place as counsel also have a role of accountability. As we agree to be authentic with them and give them permission to speak into our lives, they bring great affirmation of the road ahead. The Overseers of DC Metro are some who play this role in my life because I openly share with them when I am walking through a challenge. However, the two people who play this role in the greatest way are my wife, Taryn, and my best friend, Matt. I have allowed them access to every area of my life, and have agreed to be transparent with them in any area of struggle. Although sometimes a bit humbling and even embarrassing, I have found it to also be one of the most freeing disciplines in life.

When we confess our sins to each other and share our insecurities and fears, we are actually deepening our relationship with the other person. We are showing them that they are someone we value and trust enough to share the parts of our selves that are not open to the public. I have found that transparency begets transparency, so if I open up and share first, I am also providing a safe place where they can be themselves and share openly about their shortcomings and insecurities. No matter how embarrassing or how revealing, this type of open transparency brings safety.

James 5:16 instructs, "Therefore confess your sins to each other and pray for each other so that you may be healed. The prayer of a righteous

person is powerful and effective." The Greek word for "healed" in this passage can be translated as "physical healing," but it can also mean "healing of the soul." I have found both to be true in my own life, especially the healing of the soul, which is comprised of our mind, will, and emotions.

In James 5:16, we are instructed to "pray for each other," which is written in the present imperative and translates as "pray and keep on praying for each other." We are able to serve one another by being a reflection of God's heart in the midst of our brokenness and by praying for one another when we share our failures. There is something powerful that takes place as you show yourself as you really are, which leads to receiving unconditional love.

Recently, my son Isaac grabbed a book from my seminary days off my bookshelf. It was about the healing power of community called *The Safest Place on Earth*. As I began reading it again, I began to see how timely it was that Isaac should "happen" to pick up this particular book, because this action confirmed what God had been teaching me. This book provoked me to be even more transparent in my closest relationships.

In this book, Larry Crabb explains, "A central task of community is to create a safe enough place for walls to be torn down. . . . In spiritual community, people reach deep places in each other's hearts that are not often or easily reached. They openly express love and reveal fear even though they are not accustomed to that level of intimacy. When they reach a sacred place of vulnerability and authenticity, something is released. Something good begins to happen."[6]

It's amazing when we experience true Christian friendship the way Christ intended it to be. The results are altogether transformative to our souls. If you have yet to experience this—I challenge you—be vulnerable and open up to a safe person: the results will leave you desiring more.

Fun

I personally believe that the people who you place as closest counsel in your life should be those you have fun with and enjoy. I will be the first to admit that, at first glance, many pastors would not consider fun as one

of their top qualifications for counsel, but I definitely recommend this quality. Most Americans have a tendency to overwork and, consequently, their lives becomes unbalanced, with their personal lives and having fun taking a backseat to their careers. I don't believe this is God's design for us, as He desires us to make life-giving relationships a top priority in our lives.

First of all, I believe you should sincerely enjoy the people you have in the closest places in your life. I have had the same best friends for almost fifteen years. We vacation together, we have dinner parties together, and we celebrate birthdays and life's other milestones together. Simply put, we have a ridiculous amount of fun together. Just as in a marriage, I believe you need to be intentional about doing activities that you enjoy together and that you need to be purposeful about having fun. I want those who are speaking into my life to know what makes my heart come alive, what makes me laugh, and what brings me the deepest joy. After all, as C. S. Lewis wrote, "Joy is the serious business of heaven."[7]

Second, I want to receive from people who are living the life that Jesus promised in John 10:10, "I have come that they may have life, and have it to the full." I purposefully seek out those who know how to live to the fullest and who help me live this carpe-diem lifestyle. Whoever said God is boring and that our lives as Christians have to be dull has not had a true revelation of Him. God is the most enjoyable being that has ever existed, and I want to be around those who remind me of this reality. After all, life and ministry are meant to be fun and fulfilling adventures with God.

Some may argue that fun is too hedonistic of a barometer, but I have found the most profound joy actually comes from serving Jesus, doing life with other believers, and being a part of others' lives being transformed. This is the type of fun I am talking about and what I seek to share with those who play the role of my closest friends and advisors. I think we could all use a little more fun in our lives. After all, walking out God's call is meant to be an enjoyable group project.

Empowering

The counsel in your life should also be empowering. We talked about biblical accountability earlier. We tend to focus on areas of sin or weakness when we think of accountability, but true biblical accountability also includes empowerment. You hold the people closest in your life accountable to the dreams that are in their hearts and to living out the gifts and passions you see in their lives. You hold them accountable to be who God has called them to be, and you will do anything you can to empower them or to help them fulfill their calling.

Empowering is one of my favorite roles to play with those who are on our executive leadership team. A couple of years ago we went out to lunch as a lead team. Dr. Joseph Umidi, the current dean of Regent University's School of Divinity and one of our DC Metro Overseers, shared with us what he believed was the main reason why DC Metro had grown at a significant rate yet remained spiritually healthy: our relationships with each other. Dr. Umidi called our relationships our secret sauce because they are what the Holy Spirit flows through to reveal the deep, unconditional love of God.

I began to unpack Dr. Umidi's statement as I looked at the people around the table. I have known most of the members of the lead team for over a decade. We have walked together both through each other's trials as well as our victories. We know each other's weaknesses and vulnerabilities, but we also know how to call forth the best in each other. We know beyond a shadow of a doubt that we are for each other and that we are better together than we would be apart. I believe that God desires these types of relationships in each of our lives. C. S. Lewis explains:

In friendship . . . we think we have chosen our peers. In reality a few years' difference in the dates of our births, a few more miles between certain houses, the choice of one university instead of another . . . the accident of a topic being raised or not raised at a first meeting—any of these chances might have kept us apart. But,

for a Christian, there are, strictly speaking, no chances. A secret master of ceremonies has been at work. Christ, who said to the disciples, "You have not chosen me, but I have chosen you," can truly say to every group of Christian friends, "You have not chosen one another but I have chosen you for one another."[8]

I know God strategically placed each of the people who are in the closest places in my life, but it has taken intentionality on my part to invest in these relationships. If you do not already have these S.A.F.E relationships in your life, I believe God wants to help you develop them. It is a strategic way that He wants to speak to you. If you do have these relationships, I encourage you to continue to invest in them and ask God to help you recognize His voice through them. They are truly your greatest assets in this life.

Bonds and Boats

When I was in seminary, I was honored when my dad, someone I deeply respect, asked me for counsel when he told me he found a sailboat he wanted to buy. After many years of casually looking at boats, this particular boat had captured his attention enough that he asked me to pray about whether he should buy it—he was unsure if he should spend a large amount of money on a recreational expense.

It is important to mention that my dad is extremely thrifty, and he actually had the money in a savings account from an insurance reimbursement he had received years earlier when his old boat was destroyed in a Louisiana hurricane. In my mind, I thought he should buy the boat because he has always had a passion for sailing, and he had the money sitting in a bank account. However, because I knew how unlikely it was for my frugal dad to buy anything he considered frivolous, I told him I would pray that God would confirm whether or not he should buy the boat. Little did I know how incredibly God would answer that prayer.

When I entered the campus prayer chapel—a routine of mine each

day before hitting the books in the library—I had two main requests to lift up to God. The first was my dad's boat, and the second was my need for additional finances for living expenses while I was in seminary. At the time I had a series of part-time jobs, but it was still a stretch each month to pay all my bills. My roommate, Matt, and I were living off of hot dogs and mac and cheese, so I decided I would ask God for help.

After about half an hour talking with God, and right before I was getting ready to leave, I heard God say, *Sell the bonds and I'll give him the boat.* This phrase was honestly baffling to me because I did not know what bonds He was talking about—even though I knew it was His voice.

While I was asking God what He meant, I suddenly remembered that my parents had told me years earlier that they had purchased savings bonds for me when I was born. I also remembered that a week earlier my mom had sent me an old accordion file containing papers and documents from my childhood. When I'd received this file, I'd stuck it in my closet and given no thought to what it contained.

I decided to skip my time in the library that afternoon to go on a little adventure with God. On my drive home, I wondered if that old file could possibly contain the savings bonds my parents had bought for me a quarter of a century ago. I was thrilled when I pulled the accordion file from the closet to find a dusty manila envelope with the savings bonds that had matured only one month prior. However, nothing could have prepared me for what else I pulled out of that same envelope: there was a brochure for a sailboat that I had picked up at a marina in Louisiana and placed in the file years earlier. I know . . . what are the odds? Well, it gets even better. I pulled out the brochure for the sailboat to find out it was for a 1997 Hunter twenty-five-foot sailboat, which was the exact make, model, and year that my dad was looking at! In my left hand, I was holding the savings bonds, and in my right hand, I was holding the brochure. I was so blown away I could hardly contain myself at the specificity and goodness of God.

The phrase "Sell the bonds and I'll give him the boat" reverberated in my head, as now it made perfect sense. Of course, I immediately called

my dad and told him I felt very confident that God wanted him to buy the boat. God knew it was hard for my dad to buy things for himself, so He wanted to do something so overt that no one could doubt—not even my dad—that God wanted him to buy a boat. God knew I was struggling financially and led me to the bonds right after they matured at the exact time I was in need of finances.

As my father sought out my counsel on his desire to purchase a boat, God confirmed his decision to me as I prayed and through the unique circumstances of the bonds and the boat brochure. Not only was I able to affirm his decision in my counsel, but God used the situation to meet my financial needs.

As incredible as it was for my dad to get the sailboat he had been dreaming about and for me to get the financial resources I needed, we received something far more valuable that day. We heard the voice of God in an undeniable way, which became a powerful reminder of how much He loves us and how He is involved in the intricate details of our lives. We still marvel at the kindness of God and how we believe He had been planning that surprise for us since my parents had first bought the bonds twenty-five years earlier.

Choosing Your Counsel

By seeking counsel in life as you attempt to hear from God, you will truly fulfill the scientific method of the practical science of hearing God's voice. Testing your hypothesis by inviting others to weigh in on what you believe God is speaking to you will prove to be a final confirmation or a S.A.F.E. redirection as His voice is clarified.

In the 40-Day Challenge, we are going to ask you to share what God speaks to you as you spend thirty minutes with Him each day for forty days. In preparation, think of one relationship you have that is a good candidate for being your wise counsel. Remember, I define wise counsel as a person who is walking closely with God and with you, and who will not be afraid to tell you no if they do not agree with what you believe God is saying.

Is the individual you have in mind a S.A.F.E. relationship? Are they supportive, will they provide accountability, are they fun and empowering? If your answer to all the above questions is yes, give them a call and schedule a time to meet.

During your meeting, share with your friend the purpose of The Experiment.

+ Give them a summary of *Hearing from God* (or, better yet, give them a copy) and share how you are applying the steps of the scientific method to learning to hear and discern the voice of God.

+ Explain where they fit into the process and, as a person you trust, you can share what you believe God is speaking to you.

+ Tell them the definition you learned of wise counsel and what a S.A.F.E. relationship is. Tell them why you picked them for the role.

+ If they agree to fill the role, pray together for God to bless the relationship, and give them wisdom and discernment.

+ Share with them what you have been asking God and the answers you believe God has spoken to you through your prayer and study.

+ Remember, no counsel you choose will give you perfect advice or hear from the Lord perfectly. If your counsel does not believe you should move forward in what you shared, it is worth investing some significant time in prayer and asking them to continue to pray, too.

+ Don't do all the talking. After you have spoken, allow your friend the freedom to ask questions and share their ideas and counsel.

You have asked God your question(s) and done research in the Word of God—looking for answers to your questions or confirmation of the answers you already received. You have submitted your hypothesis of what you believe God is speaking to you to trusted counsel from other individuals. Now it's time to move on to Step Five of the scientific method: analyzing and drawing a conclusion about what you believe God has spoken.

CHAPTER FOUR

Analysis and Conclusion

The only relevant test of the validity of a hypothesis is comparison of prediction with experience.

—MILTON FRIEDMAN, ECONOMIST[1]

Do not be anxious about anything, but in every situation, by prayer and petition, with thanksgiving, present your requests to God. And the peace of God, which transcends all understanding, will guard your hearts and your minds in Christ Jesus.

—PHILIPPIANS 4:6–7

Step Five of the scientific method is to analyze the data and draw a conclusion. The data is the record of what happened during the experiment. Once a scientist has completed his or her experiment, they collect and analyze the data to see if it supports the original hypothesis. Many times scientists find that their original hypothesis could not be supported by the data. Based on what they have learned from their experiments, the scientists will develop a new hypothesis. This starts the scientific method process over again.

Thomas Edison had a hypothesis of what it would take to create the lightbulb. He made over a thousand attempts and filled over forty thousand pages of notes before he found the missing piece that led him to his invention. Edison was searching for the right material for the filament, the little wire inside the lightbulb. " 'Before I got through,' Edison recalled, 'I tested no fewer than 6,000 vegetable growths, and ransacked the world for the most suitable filament material.' "[2] His attempts included coconut fiber, fishing line, and even hairs from a friend's beard, before Edison finally figured out to use carbonized bamboo for the filament.[3]

Patent number 223,898 was given to Edison's electric bulb, which was

one of 1,093 patents accredited to him.[4] Edison reflected on his pièce de résistance, "The electric light has caused me the greatest amount of study and has required the most elaborate experiments. . . . We are striking it big in the electric light, better than my vivid imagination first conceived. Where this thing is going to stop, Lord only knows."[5] Thankfully Edison did not give up on searching for the missing piece.

Edison was one of my middle-school heroes. As I shared earlier, I incessantly dreamed of one day having a patent in my name. In fact, in my quest to win at a science fair, I entered four different fairs over the course of four years trying the same experiment with magnets. Each time, I attempted to make a metal ball levitate by wrapping coils around nails to create a magnetic pull strong enough to keep the ball floating in midair.

Each year it was an epic fail, so I hypothesized that I needed more power and tried to add a stronger magnetic pull each successive year. Ironically, even though my science experiment failed again and again, my final year I still won the science fair for explaining why my hypothesis was wrong. My missing piece was power. I am sorry to say that, unlike Edison, I did not have the tenacity to keep trying after the fourth failed attempt, so the missing piece remained missing.

Finding the "Missing Peace"

Have you ever had a missing piece that you desperately needed to make something work? Nothing can be more frustrating than missing a piece to a puzzle or the final part of a solution to an issue.

When it comes to hearing the voice of God and discerning which direction to step, I have found that there is a final piece that simply cannot remain missing, which is the peace of God. One of the first questions I ask myself when I am contemplating taking a step in a certain direction is: "Do I have peace?" If I believe I have heard God through His still, small voice, His Word, or through counsel, I always test it by asking myself whether or not I feel peace.

At first the litmus test of whether or not I feel peace about the situa-

tion or direction can seem too subjective or too dependent on mood. That is, until you understand that the biblical definition of peace is much more than a feeling and is one of the primary ways He confirms where He is leading you. As the next step, analyzing the data and drawing a conclusion is used to evaluate the direction we have received from the Lord, but at the end of the day I do not move forward without His peace.

A Biblical Understanding of Peace

The word *peace* is mentioned four hundred times throughout Scripture and has several different connotations. The first connotation describes a believer's state of reconciliation with God because of what Jesus did on the cross. Romans 5:1 says, "Therefore, since we have been justified through faith, we have peace with God through our Lord Jesus Christ."

The second connotation of peace describes the type of relationship God desires us to have with others. Talking about this type of relational peace, Romans 12:18 states "as far as it depends on you, live at peace with everyone."

The third connotation of peace is the one that we are going to be focusing on in this chapter. It is listed as the third fruit of the Spirit in Galatians 5:22 and is described in Philippians 4:7: "The peace of God, which transcends all understanding, will guard your hearts and your minds in Christ Jesus."

The Greek word for peace means "harmony or tranquility." But as Philippians 4:7 explains, this peace is supernatural and beyond rational comprehension. This Greek word should be understood as "not just freedom from trouble, but everything that makes for a man's highest good,"[6] and relates to the Hebrew word for peace, *shalom*, which has a basic meaning of "totality or completeness including fulfillment, maturity, soundness, and wholeness."[7]

Let's look at a few other verses that describe this supernatural peace to further understand this gift that God gives to believers as we submit ourselves to His leadership. Isaiah 26:3 says: "You will keep in perfect

peace those whose minds are steadfast, because they trust in you." In other words, peace is promised for those who trust in Him. Isaiah 55:12 explains "you shall go out in joy, and be led forth in peace." Joy and peace are gifts from the Lord as we follow Him. In John 14:27, Jesus again promises His supernatural peace to believers, "Peace I leave with you; my peace I give you. I do not give you as the world gives. Do not let your hearts be troubled and do not be afraid." It is evident that this peace does not come from the absence of trials or problems but, rather, comes from the presence of God no matter what you are walking through or where you are going.

What about my emotions?

Have you noticed that your emotions are not particularly trustworthy? In fact, depending on what is happening in your life, your emotions can be like a roller coaster—way up one moment and way down the next, not to mention when they take you on a ride around in loops. While your feelings are a normal part of your human nature, and not to be suppressed or denied, be careful that you don't let them take the lead in your life, as they can take you places you don't want to go.

When I talk about the peace of God, I am not talking about your feelings. The peace of God is something that transcends your human emotions and rational comprehension. There is an old gospel song that talks about God giving peace in the midst of the storm. The idea is that in the middle of turmoil and chaos (the storm) God can give a supernatural peace that everything will somehow be all right. Your rollercoaster of emotions in the storm may include fear, anxiety, or dread, but somehow the peace of God overrides all the emotions and gives you the grace to trust in Him.

While the peace of God can have a calming effect on your emotions, it is not given to you through your emotions, but by the Holy Spirit to your human spirit. That's why Philippians 4:6-7 tells us not to be anxious about anything (emotion), but to tell God our

needs and thank Him for meeting our needs (spirit to Spirit communication with God). The result will be His peace—deposited in our human spirit—guarding our hearts and minds.

If you haven't completely sorted out the difference between your emotions and His peace, don't worry. Your ability to discern between them will increase as you grow in your relationship to Him.

The Peace of God Guides Us

So how does peace relate to God's guidance? Colossians 3:15 gives us further insight: "let the peace of God rule in your hearts."[8] In the Amplified Bible, the word rule is defined as "act as an umpire." Just as an umpire decides whether a play is safe, fair, or good, so the peace of God is to act as an umpire in the decisions we make. The Good News Translation of this same verse says, "The peace that Christ gives is to guide you in the decisions you make."

Sometimes I know God has been leading me to make decisions that do not seem completely logical, but they are accompanied by what I can only describe as supernatural peace. I felt God's presence strongly with me, which manifested as the peace that passes all understanding that Paul referred to in Philippians 4:7.

One of these times was when God called Taryn and me to move across the country to start DC Metro Church. I was an associate pastor at an incredible church I loved: Celebration Church in Jacksonville, Florida. Taryn was also on staff working in the women's ministry. We thoroughly enjoyed our roles and relationships in the church. We had known for many years that God was calling us to plant a church in the D.C. metro area one day in the future, but we did not know when He would send us, so we became very rooted in Celebration.

In November 2006, Taryn and I both began to strongly feel it was time. We met with our lead pastors and dear friends, Stovall and Kerri Weems, who agreed with us. We all felt God's indescribable peace, even though it made us sad to think about not doing life and ministry together. It certainly did not seem logical to leave. Our son Isaac was only a year old at the time of our move, and we had just found out that Taryn was pregnant with our second son Josiah.

We were also leaving people we loved and secure jobs in a phenomenal church—and for what—to launch out into the unknown with no income and a growing family to support? Not exactly what most financial advisors would recommend, but the remarkable part is that we felt an unwavering, supernatural peace along with the peace that came through my pastor's counsel and support. Now don't get me wrong—Taryn and I would look at each other sometimes and ask if we were crazy. However, even in the midst of our questioning, we felt an undeniable peace—a peace that truly passed all our understanding.

I have learned that unless God's presence goes with me, I do not want to go; and if His presence is leading me, then I do not want to stay. I have found that His peace is a very helpful litmus test to see if He is initiating a move, ultimately because I want to know that He is going with me.

In Exodus 33:15, Moses expressed a similar desire when God was calling him to a foreign land. He wanted to make sure the Lord understood that the only way he was going was if God went with him: "If your presence does not go with us, do not send us up from here." I felt the exact same way when we were leaving Florida, but the peace both Taryn and I felt was confirmation that God's presence was with us and that it was He who was sending us. As we stepped out in obedience, God proved to be faithful every step of the way, and He met all our needs as we responded to His leading.

Another time God called us to step out in faith prompted by His peace was when DC Metro was moving into our first permanent facility, 1100 N Fayette Street in Alexandria, Virginia. We had been meeting in the movie theater for more than two years, and we really wanted to find a

building that could become our permanent church home. On Easter Sunday morning in 2009, I was driving my normal route from Starbucks to the movie theater that we called home, when directly in my path I stumbled upon a building that was for lease. I immediately fell in love with the building, as I could picture it as a church where thousands of people would encounter God and be changed in His presence.

I began to pursue leasing this building, but I was extremely discouraged when I heard the price. After some quick mental math, I realized that our church income would have to double to afford the building. In my rational, business mind, that was an immediate no. However, to my surprise, I had an incredibly strong peace about the building. I began to seek counsel with our Overseers and our leadership team. To my astonishment again, every single one said they felt peace, too, and thought we should lease the building.

Even though part of me was quite nervous, the peace we felt was stronger, so we signed the lease to move into the building. I shared in an earlier chapter that the month we signed the lease, our church income doubled! God came through for us in a way that confirmed that His hand was definitely upon our bold step of faith. We experienced firsthand what Paul was referring to in Romans 15:13: "May the God of hope fill you with all joy and peace as you trust in him, so that you may overflow with hope by the power of the Holy Spirit."

When God is guiding you in a decision or path that does not seem logical or causes you to step outside of your comfort zone, He gives you His peace to remind you, just as He told Moses in Exodus 33:14, "My presence will go with you."

What about the really tough times?

Life is often difficult. God never promised us that every day would be easy. We face circumstances where our world is being shaken, where challenges and conflicts leave us numb and without peace, and the human emotional response is fear, sorrow, pain, or any number of other feelings. Sometimes the tough seasons in life are due to our bad choices, other people's bad choices, or even the devil's attack, but regardless of the cause of the trial, God promises to walk through those times with us.

Jesus is our best example of someone who endured tremendous difficulties. The will of God for His life was full of conflict—with religious and political leaders, in confrontations with demons, and, the ultimate, His death on the Cross. We know that His humanity caused Him to experience the full range of our human emotions—and He struggled. In the garden of Gethsemane, He told the disciples that He was "deeply distressed and troubled. 'My soul is overwhelmed with sorrow to the point of death'" (Mark 14:33–34). He prayed three separate times, asking God to remove the cup of suffering that He was about to experience. Luke's version of the story tells us that Jesus was in anguish, praying so hard His sweat was like drops of blood falling to the ground (Luke 22:44). That is some serious praying. But while Jesus was honest with His emotions, His prayer was ultimately one of submission to the will of His Father: "yet not my will, but yours be done" (Luke 22:42).

Did Jesus experience a supernatural peace that surpassed His raging emotions? The Bible is silent about that. What we do know is that after He had wrestled with His emotions in prayer—three times—He was ready to move forward in the will of God (the scourging, mocking, and the agony of the Cross). My point? When you are called to difficult circumstances in life where a natural peace is lacking, deal honestly with your emotions before God, submit yourself fully to the will of God, and move forward in the will of God. As you do that, trust that God

> can and will deposit a supernatural peace in your spirit that will surpass the thoughts in your mind and your roller-coaster emotions.

Losing and Regaining Your Peace

One question I am often asked is what to do if you had peace at one point, and then you lose it. Peace gives us an initial green light to take a first step, but sometimes we lose our peace along the way. There are different reasons we can lose our peace. We may have let fear creep in so that we are no longer being led by faith but rather by our emotions and insecurities. If this is the case, don't derail the process but, instead, go back to the place you first had peace.

This is exactly what happened to me when we were buying our first house in the D.C. area. We found a neighborhood we loved in the school district we wanted for our kids, so we began the search. One morning during that season, I was reading Ephesians 5, when I felt the Holy Spirit highlight verse 25: "Husbands, love your wives, just as Christ loved the church and gave Himself up for her." This is a sweet, sentimental-sounding verse that is read at many weddings, but I have been walking with the Lord long enough to know that when God highlights a verse like this, it is often because He is going to give me an opportunity to walk it out.

I was right. Almost immediately after reading that verse, I sensed the still, small voice of God whisper to let Taryn pick out the house we would buy. I consented to this prompting, but I must admit I was feeling rather prideful about what a good husband I was to let her choose the house. I felt like I deserved a big pat on the back. One of my passions is picking, purchasing, and renovating houses, but I was going to obey the passage in Ephesians and lay down my life and choices for my wife.

Taryn was elated when I told her she could pick the house. She quickly found a ranch-style house in our favorite neighborhood, but as soon as we pulled up to tour the house, I completely lost my peace. The landscaping was ridiculously overgrown. When we stepped inside, the house reeked of a foul odor. I am still not quite sure what to say about the seventies wallpaper or decor. Not to mention there was a dripping sound coming from the basement. I went downstairs to check it out only to find chains hanging from the ceiling. My immediate thought was we must have stumbled upon an ax-murderer hangout!

I looked over at Taryn to give her the *let's get out of here* look only to find my wife's eyes lit up. I thought, *Uh-oh, I know that look . . . she likes it.* My wife is an incredible visionary, and she began to envision our future home, saying, "David, we can blow this wall out and this wall out and we can renovate this area." I must confess, at that point all I could see were dollar signs flashing before my eyes. With each new project she proposed, my peace seemed to dissipate further and further at an alarming rate.

I began to dialogue with the Lord. *I can't believe she likes this house! The renovations she wants to do will cost a small fortune, and the house already costs more than it is worth, in my opinion. This does not feel peaceful!* The Lord asked me when the last time I had peace was. I thought back to when God spoke to me though Ephesians 5 and I then told Taryn she could pick the house. I quickly realized that I had tried to take control of picking the house again, when the last time God had spoken to me was to let Taryn choose. I repented and released the decision back to Taryn, and immediately my peace came rushing back. I was still not happy about the house and did not think it was the best deal, but I had peace that God was with us in the decision.

Taryn had no idea of the internal dialogue I had just had with the Lord, but she turned to me and said, "I don't think we should buy this house." My wife is a savvy businesswoman, and when she crunched the numbers, she concluded that it was overpriced. "I love the house. I have a vision for it, but I don't think the numbers make sense," she said. Secretly, I was thrilled. End of story . . . or so I thought.

The next day Taryn was back on the multiple listing service, and she realized the owners of the ranch-style house had dropped the price by seventy thousand dollars. We prayed about it again and both felt a green light and tremendous peace. All the qualities I hadn't liked about the house at first were cosmetic and easily altered, particularly because we were able to invest the money from the price drop into the needed renovations. A number of blessings resulted in following God's direction in Ephesians 5:25, but one of my favorites is how Taryn and I discovered renovating houses was a new hobby we could enjoy together. We had previously struggled to find a joint hobby, as she loves to work out and cook delicious meals from scratch (which I enjoy eating), and my hobbies are more outdoorsy, like hunting and fishing. While we were pretending to be Chip and Joanna Gaines from one of our favorite HGTV shows, *Fixer Upper,* we connected with each other in a new way, and our marriage was strengthened as a result. The house became a home where we had many happy memories. When we sold it, we even gained a significant profit. In the end, this became yet another personal testimony of the wisdom of following God's peace and how to regain it even when you lose it.

God's Redemption

I have had to follow this process of restoring peace in my own life countless times, but I have found that even when we step off course, God loves to draw us back and brings the needed redemption. There is no place that I have seen this more clearly than in my relationship with my wife. We were engaged—twice.

I met Taryn at a college conference in Baton Rouge, Louisiana, and was immediately drawn to her. I prayed with my prayer partner for six weeks for the opportunity to run into her again and ask her out. When I saw her at the business school, my fraternity brother asked whom she was dating. I thought to myself, *me.* Okay, maybe I really wasn't there at that moment, but when my fraternity brother left, I went over to her and asked her out, and to my surprise she said yes. On our first date, I talked

to her about my dream of one day starting a church in the D.C. area. She shared that she, too, had dreams of doing something great for God. My heart felt an abundance of peace, as I sensed that she could be the one.

Fast-forward three years later to a broken engagement with Taryn. Confusion and hurt usurped the peace that had previously filled my heart. Hindsight is always 20/20, but I now see that I had allowed myself to be too influenced by the counsel of one person, who was against us getting married. This person was not close to either of us—hence the need for my counsel in the previous chapter. This person's perspective had triggered my own doubts as well as Taryn's, which caused both of us to pull away from each other and ultimately call off our wedding.

After we ended our engagement, I didn't talk with Taryn for almost a year, until I decided to call and check on her after the 9/11 tragedy. She then came to visit the graduate school I was attending in Virginia Beach as a prospective student, and we quickly realized we still had feelings for each other. Peace came flooding back, and within a few months we were engaged again.

Testing Counsel

Taryn and I got some negative counsel from a source that we didn't have a S.A.F.E. relationship with, bringing doubts about our relationship and leading us to break off our engagement—the first time. Unfortunately, we did not weigh the advice we were receiving and allowed it to influence our decisions.

Even when you have the most trusted counselors in your life and you receive the best counsel—you are still responsible to weigh their advice. Thessalonians 5:20-21 says: "Do not treat prophecies with contempt, but test them all and hold onto that which is good." All prophecies (words of encouragement, comfort, or direction) and advice from others need to be weighed. What is the spirit in which the advice is given? What are the consequences of following the advice—where will it lead?

> Sometimes the only way to weigh the counsel of others is the test of time. Not discounting what has been spoken to you, but holding it lightly before God until He confirms the advice, or proves it wrong. You and I are to be open to counsel, but we are not to roll over and accept everything someone speaks over us, or to us—even godly people. God calls us to be responsible, testing words and holding to that which is good.

We now understand that the confusion we were feeling that had caused us to break off our engagement was not actually the lack of God's peace. The peace was just buried underneath all of the other soulful emotions that we allowed to dictate our choices. God, in His mercy, allowed us to be reunited, and we were married the next summer. One of Taryn's favorite parts of our story is that when she went to a bridal boutique in Baton Rouge to pick out a second dress, they told her they still had her original dress in the back with her name on it. The dress should have been returned over a year earlier, but the lady in the store forgot to send it back. We truly believe that God was saving the dress because He knew that our story was not over, only delayed.

I share this part of our story to remind you that we don't always hear God perfectly and sometimes we inadvertently step off course. We can trust that when we do, God will draw us back. I will say that as Romans 8:28 reminds us, God redeems and works all things together for good. During our year apart, we both drew even closer to God, which not only deepened our walk with Him but also gave us a stronger foundation for our marriage. Hearing God and walking with Him is first and foremost about having a willing heart that is seeking to follow Him. As we seek to follow Him, we analyze the data He gives us through His voice, His Word, His counsel through others, and His peace in order to draw a conclusion on what He is saying and where He is leading.

What if God doesn't answer my questions?

I have learned over the years that although God desires a relationship with each of us and wants us to continually approach Him with our questions and requests, He doesn't always give us the answers in the exact moment we ask. There are a few reasons why He may delay:

- ✦ *You ask amiss.* James 4:3 says: "You ask and do not receive, because you ask amiss, that you may spend it on your pleasures." Why would a loving heavenly Father give you something, or answer a question about something that is not ultimately good for you? Oftentimes we don't even realize we are asking amiss and that what we are asking for is actually not God's best for us.

- ✦ *The timing is not right.* I believe this is the most common reason we don't get answers to our requests. God sees the bigger picture of the universe and your life. In theological terms we call that His omniscience—He sees and knows all! Your pleas for something are based on your limited perspective. While your motives may be valid, there may be other factors that you do not presently understand that need to fall in place before God answers.

- ✦ *God reserves His answers to some questions.* We need to trust the mystery and sovereignty of God. Sometimes we ask great questions like "Why won't you heal my friend of cancer?," yet we don't get a clear response. I encourage you to continue to seek God while trying not to get frustrated about the apparent lack of an answer. Deuteronomy 29:29 says: "The secret things belong to the Lord our God, but the things revealed belong to us and to our children forever, that we may follow all the words of this law."

> We can trust that God will make known to us what
> we need to know when we need to know it.

If He doesn't answer your specific question, ask Him to give you a word—any word, idea, thought, or verse. Keep an open mind so that He can speak to you about any topic that is on His heart. Be willing to have Him reveal if you are asking amiss, or the timing is not right, or if He's waiting for you to ask a different question first. Be open to the sources through which God will speak to you. He may be trying to answer your question, but He might be doing so in a way that is new to you. Remember, as Amos 3:7 says: He loves to share His secrets with His people, so keep seeking Him and trusting that He will reveal what you need to know when you need to know it. I have found that hearing from God is like an incredible treasure hunt where He gives you the next "clue" in His perfect timing.

How to Find Peace

If you are in a place where you are in need of peace, or if you once had peace but you lost it, here are a few actions that will help you find the supernatural peace God desires to give you.

Pray

Be completely honest before God. He wants you to tell Him what you are feeling anxious or unsure about and present your requests to Him. This is a necessary catalyst for the peace that Paul refers to in Philippians 4:6–7: "Do not be *anxious* about anything, but in every situation, by prayer and petition, with thanksgiving, present your requests to God. And the peace of God, which transcends all understanding, will guard your hearts and

your minds in Christ Jesus" (emphasis mine). If you previously had peace, ask Him to help you retrace your steps back to that place, so you can release whatever you have picked up in the process that has made you question his guidance.

Release to God

This is typically the hardest but most important step. Sometimes it is called laying it on the altar, because you are fully releasing it to the Lord. When you have anxiety, pressure, or stress, it is typically because you are still trying to be in control. A good litmus test to see if you have fully given something over to God is if you sense His peace after the release. If you are still experiencing restless nights and confusion, you are most likely still holding on to the burden. 1 Peter 5:6–7 instructs, "Humble yourselves, therefore, under God's mighty hand, that He may lift you up in due time. Cast all your anxiety on him because he cares for you." His care is always most obvious when your trust is at its fullest.

Trust God's Leadership

When you have given God full control, it is then important to fully trust His leadership and His timing. God promises throughout His Word that He will guide you. Proverbs 3:5–6 says, "Trust in the Lord with all your heart and lean not on your own understanding. In all your ways submit to him, and He will make your paths straight." When you release what you had previously been holding on to, you will find not only does He flood you with His peace, but new doors of opportunity open. Why? Because He knows you can be trusted to trust Him again and again.

If you've asked God the questions on your heart, searched in His Word for answers or confirmation of what you believe He has spoken to you, and shared those answers with trusted counsel, hopefully you have experienced the final confirmation He gives through His peace about what He is saying. If not, don't be discouraged. Check out the text box in

this chapter entitled "What if God Doesn't Answer My Questions?" Then wait until all the confirmations line up: His voice, His Word, His confirmation through trusted counsel, and His peace.

If all the confirmations did line up, then you are ready for Step Six in the practical science: Communicating Your Results.

Communicating Your Results

If you can't explain it simply, you don't understand it well enough.

—ALBERT EINSTEIN

Come! Listen, all you who are loyal to God! I will declare what He has done for me.

PSALM 66:16 NET

No experiment is complete without Step Six of the scientific method: communicating your results. For my science fair projects I created display boards that showed my hypothesis, research, experiments, and the results. Professional scientists will publish their final reports in scientific journals or present their findings at scientific symposiums.

In our practice of hearing God's voice, the final step is to tell someone what God has done in your life. As you listen for His voice, research His Word, listen to His counsel through others, and experience His peace (or lack thereof), confirming what God was saying, tell somebody! Let them know what God has done in your life, and encourage them that He can and will do the same in theirs. This is a critical part that is often missed.

Your Testimony

One of the primary reasons I wrote this book was to remind you that God wants to speak to you and that He wants to move in your life. In the Old Testament the word *testimony* comes from the Hebrew root word *uwd,* which means "to repeat, return, or do it again." As you hear other people's testimonies of how God has moved in their lives, you are reminded that your God

is a God who loves to repeat Himself. As you hear stories of God moving and bringing breakthrough in someone's life, your faith is strengthened to believe God is going to move and bring breakthrough in your life, too.

Revelation 19:10 states: "the testimony of Jesus is the Spirit of prophecy."[1] I believe every time we testify of God's goodness or share a testimony of how He has spoken to us or moved in our lives, we are essentially prophesying to others what He wants to do in their lives as they partner with Him. We are preparing the atmosphere for another move of God because testimony carries with it the power of hope and change. If we speak out of our experience in God, we are not just giving information, we are providing proof that He is true to His promises, He sincerely cares about the details of our lives, and He wants to bless us. It seems only natural that we would invite others to believe that God will move again and that they, too, can experience the power of transformation!

This book contains numerous stories of how God has moved in my life and how hearing His voice has profoundly shaped and directed its course. These testimonies continue to be a catalyst for faith and trust in my own walk with God because I am reminded how He has showed up for me time and time again. As I was writing these stories, I realized there are some updates to communicate about DC Metro's story, which I've done in the next section. I am reminded of the wisdom of following His voice and how one step of obedience can set the course for years and years of good fruit if we stay connected to Him. This is the economy of God in action—any step of obedience on our part can be used to position us for the "immeasurably more" (Ephesians 3:20) He wants to do in and through us, as we align with His bigger purpose. So let me communicate the results of what God has done!

DC Metro's Testimony

Little did I know that saying yes to the vision to plant a life-giving church in the D.C. metro area in 1998 would set the trajectory of my life to be a part of all the incredible blessings we have received as a church family. The

ripple effect of that original yes has included: over ten thousand people committing their lives to the Lord since 2007; countless lives encountering God's goodness as marriages have been restored; people finding authentic community in what has been called one of the loneliest cities in America; and many discovering how to hear His voice more clearly as they walk with Him toward their destinies.

As I have shared, it has not always been easy, because God's timing has been very different from mine. In my mind, I was ready to move to D.C. to start a church in 1998. Looking back, I'm very thankful that was not God's timing because, in reality, I wasn't ready. I have found that God will often give you a vision years before He gives you the green light for the vision.

For example, I shared with you in chapter 2 that God gave me a vision for the property next door in 2010, but it has taken nearly five years for that door to open. It took almost two years for the car rental company that was leasing the building to move out—a move of God because they had been in the building for thirty years. It took another year and a half for our plans to be approved, and there were many times along the way where it looked as though we were going to be denied access. All the while, I kept believing that God was going to bring it to pass at "an appointed time" and reminding myself "though it linger, wait for it, it will certainly come and not delay" (Habakkuk 2:3).

I am encouraged to share with you that DC Metro moved into this building located next door in December 2015. This building allowed us to double the number of seats available at our weekend services, allowing twice as many people the opportunity to encounter God in a real, relevant, and enjoyable environment. This also allowed us to turn our previous sanctuary into what we call the Metro Kids building, doubling our capacity to reach the next generation.

In chapter 1, I told you about the vision God gave me in 2005 for seventeen campuses in the D.C. metro area. I am excited to tell you we recently launched our third campus in Woodbridge, Virginia. God had clearly instructed us to take Virginia first. As we sought God on that phrase *Take Virginia first,* He helped me understand it further. I thought about the

connotation of the word *take* and how it typically implies that it will not be an arduous battle. For example, when I hold a Lego car in my hand and tell my son Josiah to take it, all he has to do is step forward and grab it. Once I have instructed him to take it, he does not have to wrestle it out of my hands or convince me to give it to him. I had a similar sense about what God was saying for the next several campuses we would launch in Virginia. I believe God was telling us that as we continued to walk with Him, these campuses in Virginia would have His favor resting upon them. He would provide the finances, the right location, the right leaders, and He would draw the people He desired to be a part of each campus.

Launching the first two campuses in Alexandria and Fairfax were more taxing and felt like an uphill battle, but we felt like we had the wind at our backs when we launched the Woodbridge campus. I believe this will be the case for the next several campuses we launch in Virginia, as we continue to heed His direction. This is a reminder that there are different seasons in God's workings, and some are more challenging than others. But no matter what season you are in, it is important to stand on the Word God has spoken to you.

In the beginning seasons of my church, I stood on the Word I first received in 1998 and reminded God that He called us to D.C. to plant a life-giving, multicultural church in the nation's capital. When we were experiencing difficulties finding a location to launch our second campus, year after year, I stood on God's Word to me that there would be seventeen campuses in the area and reminded Him that a multisite church was His idea. As we launched our third campus and now are in the process of looking for our fourth campus in Virginia, I regularly remind myself that He has commissioned us to take Virginia first and where He guides, He provides. The multisite vision is becoming a reality as we follow God's voice where He leads.

What has God spoken to you in previous seasons that you can stand on in this season? If you do not have anything that you know He spoke, spend some time this week listening for His voice and asking Him to lead you where He wants you to go. If it is still unclear, look at the desires that

are in your heart, and if they line up with God's Word and what you believe would please Him, I encourage you to walk in that direction. As I mentioned earlier, if you keep your heart humble and your ear listening for His voice, He will redirect you if you ever step off course. I believe as you step out in faith with God, you are going to be amazed at His goodness. I am still astounded that He chose to use my life to plant DC Metro Church, and I believe as you continue to surrender to Him, He wants to do something through your life that is even better than you can imagine.

My Personal Testimony

At the beginning of this book I shared with you the story of miraculously being healed of cancer when I was a teenager. This year marks twenty-five years of being cancer free! I hope that my testimony here encourages you to always seek God for any area of your life that needs healing or for anyone you love who needs healing. I fully believe that God is a God who still heals today, and I pray that my testimony will be your catalyst to continue to contend for full healing and wholeness in every area of life.

I share all of this to encourage you to pray for a breakthrough in whatever ailment, illness, or disease in your body or of someone you love. I am often asked why God does not heal in every situation, and while I cannot fully answer that question, I can tell you that those who choose to believe and pray for healing see breakthroughs at a much higher rate than those who don't. We are wise to choose to focus on what God is doing rather than focusing on what He is not doing. God is a God of hope, and you never know when your breakthrough could come, so I encourage you to keep seeking Him and to keep your heart alive to Him.

I have also seen incredible breakthroughs in my marriage and family. Although Taryn and I have been in love since we first started dating seventeen years ago, we have walked through some challenging seasons in our marriage and in our calling. The pressure of leading a growing church and family is real, and we were not immune to the weight of these struggles. Taryn received a prophetic word years before we were married that

although she had grown up in a broken home, she would have a happy marriage and a happy family life. We named our home the Happy Nest as a prophetic declaration of the Word that had been given to her years earlier. We have stood upon this Word as we both worked hard to have a happy, healthy marriage and to raise our kids to have an authentic love for Jesus in a home where they can grow into who God is calling them to be.

Taryn threw me a surprise birthday party for my fortieth birthday. During the party, I was reflecting on God's goodness in our lives. I am encouraged to share with you that our marriage is as strong as it has ever been, and I am more in love with my wife than I was when she walked down the aisle to me thirteen years ago. Our three boys, Isaac, Josiah, and Asher, are full of energy and life, and Karis is our little princess. They have each brought us indescribable joy, as they, along with Taryn, are the best presents Jesus has ever given me. I am excited to see what God has for us as a family as we continue the incredible adventure of following His voice.

Is there a relationship in your life you are praying for? Maybe you are single and wondering if you are ever going to meet the right person. Perhaps you are in a difficult season in your marriage or one of your children is walking through a significant struggle. Maybe there is relational discord with someone you love and you do not know how to reconcile the relationship. Whatever the relational challenge you are experiencing, know that God wants to walk through the challenge with you. I encourage you to be one who chooses hope in each of these situations and believes these relationships can be restored.

This book contains testimonies about what happened when Taryn and I surrendered our lives to the Lord. The testimonies are of different ways God has spoken to me, Taryn, and others about our personal decisions and about the greater vision that He had for us and our church. You may not be called to do the same things I have done, but be assured God has a purpose for your life. Your sphere of influence may be different from mine, but God can do incredible things through your surrendered life as you continue to say yes to the adventure of being led by the Lord's voice!

As you position yourself to hear from Him, preparing to enter into

the 40-Day Challenge, remember to communicate your results as you hear God's voice and experience Him moving in your life. I hope the results I've experienced have been an encouragement to you. God wants to use you to encourage someone else and invite them on a similar journey to know Him more!

THE EXPERIMENT— A 40-DAY GUIDE TO HEARING GOD'S VOICE

I n part one, I said that this book was written to help believers discover and apply specific knowledge to the practical dilemma of wanting to hear clearly from Him so that we can experience more depth in our relationship with Him. Throughout this book, I have explored ways you can position yourself to encounter the supernatural voice and leadings of God, and make contact with Him.

You started by asking God a question(or questions), and creating space and time in your life to hear from Him (Step One of the scientific method: Ask a Question). You learned about the still, small voice of God and of some of the different ways He will communicate with you.

You learned how to do background research, taking your question(s) and researching what the Word of God says about the topic (Step Two of the scientific method: Do Background Research). You are now familiar with the SOAP method of Bible study and the GOD SPA.

As you listen for His still, small voice and research the Word of God, you should discover a hypothesis of what you believe God is speaking to you (Step Three of the scientific method: Construct a Hypothesis). Next, you share what you believe God is speaking to you with trusted friends or counselors—testing to see if they confirm what you are hearing (Step Four of the scientific method: Test Your Hypothesis).

After this, you analyze what you have heard through His voice, His Word, and His counsel through others and see if your conclusion is confirmed by His peace (Step Five of the scientific method: Analyze Your Data and Draw a Conclusion). Finally, you tell others what you have learned through this process and what God has done in your life (Step Six of the scientific process: Communicate Your Results).

I have shared different ways that God speaks and how to recognize His voice, but the real purpose of this book is for you to hear God for yourself.

The Experiment

I challenge you to commit to the experiment I mentioned in the beginning of the book—a forty-day challenge designed to help you hear God and grow closer to Him. To that end I have created a guide that contains a forty-day devotional to help you implement the practices in this book and position yourself to hear from God.

The experiment's challenge is for you to practically apply what you have learned by spending thirty minutes each day in prayer and Bible study for the next forty days. I believe that God will meet you as you step out to seek Him. The promise of His guidance is stated in Psalm 32:8, "I will instruct you and teach you in the way you should go. I will guide you with my eye"[1] NKJV. There is no more important skill to gain than learning to recognize and follow His voice.

Before you jump into the actual devotional, I want to share some practical instructions on how to have a devo time. Whenever I am coaching anyone on how to hear from God, I encourage them to focus on five things, which I'll explain. I have yet to have someone come back to me later and say that they have not experienced a significant increase in being able to hear and discern His voice in their lives. At the end of the instructions is a short commitment for you to read and sign, acknowledging your desire to commit to the forty-day experiment.

Step One: Pick a time and a place to meet with God.

Before Taryn and I moved to Washington, D.C., to plant the church, I had been drawn to this area for many years because I knew it was a city of influence. If you can influence the D.C. area for Christ, you can influence the nation, and ultimately you will influence the world. Movers and shakers are attracted to D.C., and the people here tend to have an obsession with

schedules and appointments. On more than one occasion I have heard someone say something to the effect of, "I have an opening three weeks from now for thirty minutes. Sorry, everything else is booked solid."

I have heard these same people confess that they struggle to find time to meet with God. My thought in pastoring them has been simple: How is it that we prioritize meetings with people we don't even like and neglect to meet with the God we love? I don't say this in a critical way but rather as a wakeup call and a reminder that we prioritize what we value. I challenge you to pull out your iPhone or your Day-Timer right now and literally schedule daily time with God.

This sounds simple, but it is all too easy to let the appointment slip if you do not tenaciously guard it. In my earlier years I was more sporadic in my devo times, but I found that missed appointments with God led to dis-appointments in life. How can I expect to find the abundant life He offers if I am not seeking Him each day to guide me into His fullness?

THE TIME:

I recommend that you choose the time when you are at your very best. I believe that God always gives us His very best, so I want to respond in suit by spending time with Him when I am most alert and ready to receive. Some people like getting up early, like 5 a.m.—that's great for them, but I am not at my best that early. I have found that God does not speak to me at that hour because . . . well, I am asleep (He can speak to me in my dreams if He wants to say anything to me before the sun rises). God is happy to meet with you any time of day, so what time works for you?

THE PLACE:

Next, find a place for you and God to meet. I recommend going some-where you love. When I take Taryn out on a date, I do not choose a fast-food place because I want us to be somewhere we both love and enjoy. My organic, gluten-free-loving wife's love language is most certainly not some greasy french fries or being in an environment with screaming kids

and dirty booths. Instead, I try to choose a healthy restaurant that has an atmosphere where we are able to connect with each other.

In a similar way, I recommend choosing a place for your time with God that you are excited to go to and a place that is conducive to connecting with Him. When I lived in my previous house, I would walk the neighborhood streets and pray. I am sure my neighbors wondered, *Who is this guy who paces the streets late at night in dark clothing talking to himself?*

When we moved to our new house, I decided that I didn't want to scare my neighbors or make them think I am any crazier than they probably already think I am, so I chose a new prayer strategy. Now I meet with God every day in my basement or in a special chair on my back porch overlooking the water, rolling hills, and the beautiful country landscape. It reminds me of where I grew up as a boy in Louisiana and helps me disconnect from the fast pace of the city so I can hear from Him.

If you are not able to be out in nature, I recommend preparing a place that you can make sacred. It could be a chair in a quiet room. It could even be your bed (if you can resist the temptation of dozing off). The most important part of choosing a place is that when you are there for your appointment with God, you can be fully present. Whenever I sit in my chair, I don't look at my phone or answer emails. It is time solely focused on Him and what He has to say. It is my best and my favorite meeting of the day.

I believe that God loves to come to places that are especially prepared for Him. It is our way to honor Him and demonstrate how excited we are for Him to come. In Exodus, the Lord tells Moses to tell the people to prepare for His coming. Exodus 19:10–11 says, "Go to the people and consecrate them today and tomorrow. Have them wash their clothes and be ready by the third day, because on that day the Lord will come down on Mount Sinai in the sight of all the people."

On the third morning there was thunder, lightning, and a thick cloud over the mountain. God showed up in a spectacular way in response to His people's preparation to hear from Him. There was a trumpet blast be-

fore Moses spoke. Then God answered. I don't know about you, but my devo times are not usually quite this dramatic. But I have found that when I prepare a time and a place to meet with Him, He shows up.

There is a classic eighties flick that I love called *Field of Dreams*. The movie is about an Iowa farmer who hears a voice telling him, "If you build it, he will come." Although in the movie it is referring to building a baseball field for the Chicago Black Sox, I have found this principle to be true in my relationship with God. If you prepare a place for Him and build in a time to be with Him, He will show up. If you build it, He will come!

Once you have picked a time and a place, what do you do next?

Step Two: Be still and worship.

Psalm 46:10 says to "be still and know that I am God." Honestly, I am not always good at being still. I would definitely rather be moving, preferably at a very high speed. Fortunately, the Hebrew word for the phrase "be still" is *raphah*, which is not necessarily a literal stillness but more of a stillness of the soul. Psalm 46:10 can be translated as: "Stop striving and know that I am God." The context of this passage was at a time when Israel was being threatened by other nations. In the midst of these threats, the Israelites could trust in the covenant that God made with them and know that He would be their very present help, refuge, and strength (see Psalm 46:1).

There is something about being still before God that reminds us we are not in charge—He is. Once we are still before Him, we can enter into true worship. I have found that when I worship, everything shifts. If my perspective was off, I see rightly once again. I am reminded of the bigness of God and of how much He loves me and how much I love Him. I am also reminded again of how much I need Him and how trustworthy He is.

I have not always begun my devo times with worship, but I highly recommend taking some time to worship before you jump into reading the Word. Worship helps you release burdens you are carrying and shifts your perspective so you see rightly again. Sometimes I will put a song on

repeat so that the words wash over me again and again. Our hearts become more surrendered and tenderized in His presence. We were made to worship.

It is during my time of being still and worshipping that I often bring my questions and requests to God (Step One of the scientific method). As I am still before Him and aware of His presence, my heart opens to Him—I share with Him what is in my heart.

Step Three: *Read and pray.*

God has written down His opinions and wisdom regarding the most common problems we face, so I recommend spending time looking at what He says in His Word—Step Two of the scientific method. There is an integral partnership between the Word and the Spirit when it comes to God speaking. As you open your Bible and read, you are hearing what God has already spoken and asking the Holy Spirit to make those words come alive so you can discern what God is speaking to you.

In chapter 2, I gave you some basic Bible study tools that have worked in my personal devos. We have included a daily passage from the Bible for each of your forty days in the 40-Day Challenge. After you complete the experiment, we recommend you try one of the following options:

1. **A topical study:** Take one of the questions that you have been asking God or a question that He has already answered. Look for what the Bible has to say around that question or issue. For example: if you are asking God's direction on marriage, search out in a concordance or in an online search (on websites such as BibleGateway.com) those passages in the Bible that deal with marriage. If you are asking Him for wisdom on some decisions you have to make, what does the Bible say about wisdom? Your study will often either confirm something He has already spoken or direct you to your question's answer.

2. ***A book or character study:*** Choose a book of the Bible to study, or choose a person from the Bible to study.

Since the experiment is to spend thirty minutes a day with God, I recommend you start by spending ten to fifteen of those minutes in study after you worship. As you get into the Word, that time will likely increase. Sometimes I study for hours, looking up Greek and Hebrew words and cross-referencing passages in the Bible. Other times I spend just a few minutes reading a few verses.

Sometimes I feel as though God is speaking directly to me through His Word, and I understand exactly what He is asking me to do next through something I read. Other times, when I read, God feels abstract and I struggle to understand how the passage has any correlation to my life whatsoever. This is very normal. Keep reading. As you continue to read with your ears and heart open, He will speak to you.

I believe that reading the Bible is meant to be an interactive experience—God wants you to dialogue with Him as you are reading, so I recommend praying as you are reading and again after you read. I often ask Him what He means in certain passages or how I can apply certain words of wisdom that I read to my current situations. The Word of God was never meant to be mere moral instructions but a launchpad into an interaction with God, so if you are not talking to God as you read, you are missing the point.

After you finish reading, take a few minutes to respond in prayer to what you read. Pray about whatever is on your heart—those questions from Step One of the scientific method. Many people lose traction in prayer because they think they need to be praying about major world issues. If those big topics are on your heart, go for it, but if you are distracted by the fight you just had with your significant other or your friend, pray about that first. Maybe you are struggling with feeling overwhelmed by all your responsibilities at work or home and the weight you have gained recently from stress eating or with feeling like you can't make traction in your finances. Pray about what is in your heart. God desires authenticity more than manufactured piety.

Often when I am trying to pray for more than a minute or two, my mind starts to wander. When that happens, I have found it extremely helpful to write down my prayers, or sometimes I pray out loud as I pace back and forth in my basement. This brings us to the next step in how we can practically position ourselves to hear the supernatural voice of God.

Step Four: *Listen and write.*

I recently heard that the above average person only listens for approximately seventeen seconds before diverting the conversation back to themselves. It seems that we are just naturally egocentric unless we intentionally guard against it. To illustrate this point, when you see a group picture, who is the first person you look at? What criteria do you use to determine if you like the picture—how your friend looks or whether the angle is flattering for the person next to you? I didn't think so.

In our relationship with God and with others, most of us struggle with being good listeners, but we will miss many important promptings from God if we do not take the time to listen for the still, small voice of God.[2] Do you pause to listen to God, or do you spend most of your time rattling off prayer requests?

Prayer is meant to be a two-way conversation. I know some people get frustrated when they hear pastors and teachers say that because they struggle to hear from God when they stop to listen, so they just keep talking.

This wrestling can come from many places, and it is important to discern its root so that you can address it. It could be from a place of doubt—some people don't believe He is really going to speak to them or trust that they can discern His voice. Other times it can come from wrong teaching—some people today have been taught in Christian churches that He does not speak to us personally, so they don't even try. It can also come from fear—some people have stopped trying to listen to what He is saying because they are fearful of what He might ask them to do. It could even be busyness—some of us don't stop and listen simply because we are always on the run.

If you struggle to listen, what is the root motive? Confess this to God and ask Him to help you take time to listen, believing that He wants to talk with you and that whatever He asks is for your ultimate good.

TWO-WAY JOURNALING:

As I shared in chapter 2, the single most revolutionary step I have taken in the past several years to dramatically increase both the amount of time I spend listening and the frequency I hear from God is something I call two-way journaling. To refresh your memory, go back and review that section in chapter 2.

You first write God an honest and authentic letter, thank Him for who He is, release any burdens, ask Him questions, lift up your requests, or invite Him to speak into your life situations or problems. Then write yourself a letter from God. He may encourage you, or bring scriptures to your mind that deal with your struggles or questions. When you finish journaling, submit everything back to God and ask Him to make clear or redirect you in what you heard. Test everything with the same filters you do any time you are attempting to hear from God.

You will have an opportunity to try two-way journaling as a part of your devotional time in the 40-Day Challenge. If this is a new exercise for you, I believe you will enjoy this focused way of processing with the Lord and hearing what He says as you write!

Step Five: *Share and obey.*

With whom can you share what God spoke to you? If it is direction you received, it is wise to share this with the godly counsel in your life. As I shared in chapter 3, I am committed to always having close, godly counsel and have given them permission to speak into my life and hold me accountable.

After you have shared with godly counsel in your life in order to seek their direction and accountability, ask God if there is anyone else He

wants you to tell about what He has done or how He has met you. If it is a revelation or insight He has showed you, think about who could benefit from hearing what God has been teaching you. Is there someone in your life going through something similar that might be encouraged by your story or what God has spoken to you?

I encourage you to be ready to tell whomever God brings in your path, even if it is a stranger you meet on an airplane or someone who is a casual acquaintance. Dr. Umidi, one of DC Metro's Overseers, talks about how God loves to use us as "UPS men" because He has special-delivery packages for divine appointments in our lives. This special-delivery package could be you telling the story of something God just walked you through or a revelation God shared with you in your devo time. As you walk in step with the Holy Spirit, He will highlight exactly who and what to share. Will you step out in obedience?

As a final step in the process, spend some time asking God if there are any additional steps of obedience or action steps He would like you to take. Or if there is something He has already showed you to do, commit to walking that out and commit to the time frame you will need to complete it. Colossians 3:15 instructs us to let God's peace lead us. This is a helpful reminder when we feel challenged to obey or step out because His peace is a tangible reminder of His presence with us.

As you begin the 40-Day Challenge, note that I structured it after the devo format above that I personally follow. For me, the scientific method steps that I talked about in the earlier chapters fit well into the devo format.

The Commitment

I included this simple commitment between you and God, because I believe your commitment to the experiment will radically change your life. Read it, decide if you are ready to take the plunge, sign, and date.

My Commitment to God

I have read and understand the basic steps for hearing the voice of God introduced in *Hearing from God*. I am excited about the opportunity to develop my relationship with God, learning how to spend time in His presence and Word, and growing in my ability to hear from Him. I consider it an honor that God desires to communicate with me and an adventure to learn how to make contact with Him!

I recognize that my desire to know him needs an investment of my time and discipline. Therefore, for the next forty days, I commit to the following:

1. I will purposely position myself to hear from God, scheduling a time and place to daily meet with Him.

2. I will follow the suggested devo format Pastor David introduced: spending time in stillness and worship, reading the Word of God, praying, and two-way journaling.

3. I will find a trusted friend or friends to serve as godly counsel and share what I am learning and believe God is speaking to me.

4. Finally, I will step out in obedience and do whatever He calls me to do, including sharing with others what God is doing in my life.

I recognize that my commitment for the next forty days is the start of a new dimension in my relationship with God, and the principles that I put into practice during this time will lay the foundation for a lifelong experience of making contact with God!

_____   _____
My Signature   Date

The 40-Day Challenge

The 40-Day Challenge

Now that you have read about how to position yourself to hear from God through the steps that correlate to the scientific method, it is your turn! The whole purpose of the scientific method is to prove or disprove a hypothesis. My hypothesis is not just that God speaks but that God wants to speak to you personally. The only way to find out if this is true is to perform the experiment on yourself.

You have read about my stories of success, my adventures, and my supernatural breakthroughs that came from following His voice. I now challenge you to come on this forty-day journey with God I have called "The Experiment." I believe you will love this process and I am praying that it will become a lifestyle of hearing from God. I am excited for you to experience your own stories of success, adventures with God, and supernatural breakthroughs in your life. I believe you will have success in hearing from God, adventures in obeying what He says, and supernatural breakthroughs in whatever area of spiritual growth you are seeking Him.

On page 119, you will find a sample entry of someone named Susan on the first day of her forty-day journey. As you read her entry, you will notice her realness and transparency. I believe it is absolutely critical that you are completely authentic with God (remember, yours will not be published in a book!).

Here are a few tips I have found to be helpful in each step:

1. **Pick a Time and a Place:** Pick a time where you are at your best and a place where you will not be distracted.

2. **Be Still and Worship:** Worship until you sense God is in the room because He is. I encourage you to talk with God as though He is right in front of you. There is a big difference between knowing that He is an ever-present help and believing that He is an ever-present help for you.

3. **Read and Pray:** As you go through the experiment, I have selected scriptures that I believe will help you hear from God with ease. Remember that this is something His voice has said, is saying, and will be saying for all of eternity. You can keep an open notebook by you to jot down anything that comes to mind—such as your to-do list—while you are praying so you won't get sidetracked.

4. **Listen and Write:** Take a moment to listen for anything God may be saying after you pray. When you begin to write your letter to God, write about whatever is on your mind and, remember, you can be raw and real—don't hold back. After you have finished writing to God, ask Him what He wants to say to you. When you write the letter to yourself from God, don't worry about questioning whether each word is from God because you can test it later through Scripture and godly counsel. Focus on what you believe God is saying to you and write freely.

5. **Share and Obey:** If you have received specific direction from God, focus on sharing and processing it with your SAFE people. Then, by obeying God, you will experience adventures, success, and supernatural breakthroughs that bring victory by following where He leads!

Welcome to what I believe could be one of the best seasons of your life as you follow Him. I am praying for you as you embark on this incredible journey!

SAMPLE DEVO PAGE

Here is a sample devo page from a woman named Susan. It will give you an idea of what a completed devo time looks like. Note, Susan didn't fill out all the points in GOD SPA. She only responded to those that were relevant to what God was dealing with her on that specific day.

Sample Day

   Romans 12:1–10

1. **Time and Place**—When and where did you meet with God?

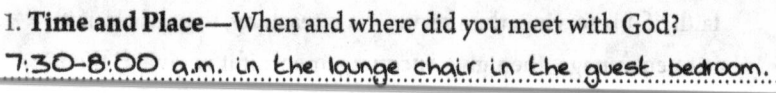

7:30–8:00 a.m. in the lounge chair in the guest bedroom.

2. **Be Still and Worship** (5–10 minutes)—Turn on worship music and ask God to help you connect to Him. Start by telling Him how wonderful He is and thanking Him for ways He's blessed your life. Ask if there is any burden you need to release to Him. After you are finished, write down any impressions, thoughts, or themes you felt during your time of worship.

Quickly recognized that I have been feeling heavy about the lack of work the past couple weeks. Told Him I was sorry for not trusting Him, and asked Him to take the burden I've been carrying. I was reminded that He is always faithful, even when I can't see what He is doing.

3. **Read and Pray** (10–15 minutes)—Read the following passage and use the SOAP method and the GOD SPA questions:

> "Therefore, I urge you, brothers and sisters, in view of God's mercy, to offer your bodies as a living sacrifice, holy and pleasing to God—this is your true and proper worship. Do not conform to the pattern of this world, but be transformed by the renewing of your mind. Then you will be able to test and ap-

prove what God's will is—his good, pleasing and perfect will. For by the grace given me I say to every one of you: Do not think of yourself more highly than you ought, but rather think of yourself with sober judgment, in accordance with the faith God has distributed to each of you. For just as each of us has one body with many members, and these members do not all have the same function, so in Christ we, though many, form one body, and each member belongs to all the others. We have different gifts, according to the grace given to each of us. If your gift is prophesying, then prophesy in accordance with your faith; if it is serving, then serve; if it is teaching, then teach; if it is to encourage, then give encouragement; if it is giving, then give generously; if it is to lead, do it diligently; if it is to show mercy, do it cheerfully. Love must be sincere. Hate what is evil; cling to what is good. Be devoted to one another in love. Honor one another above yourselves." (Romans 12:1–10)

Observation—What stands out to you in this passage?

That worship is not just what we do on Sunday at church! It is giving my whole life to God as a sacrifice. This is the kind of devotion that pleases God. Also, it seems that the idea of giving our bodies as a living sacrifice is explained in verse 2: not conforming to the world, getting a new mind, and figuring out what God's will is for me.

Application—How can you apply this passage to your life? (You may not have all of these answered for every passage, but it is helpful to ask the following questions.) Is there a/an:

Growth Area?

I need to work on the not conforming part, and renewing my mind. It kind of fits with my feeling

heavy about no work.....Instead of trusting God with my whole life, I tend to try to take control when I don't think He has me covered. I get pushy, bossy, and manipulative and think negative thoughts about everything and everyone.

Obedience Needed?

Recommit my life to Him. I will ask Him to show me what His will is for my life concerning work-and needing to pay my bills! What do I need to do that I'm not doing?

Direction to Follow?

Sin to Confess?

Already did this!

Promise to Claim?

I can know God's will if I live my life as a living sacrifice to Him!

Accountability?

Getting rid of the negative and critical thinking about circumstances and people.

Prayer—Spend a minute in prayer asking God to help you apply these truths to your life.

4. **Write and Listen** (10–15 minutes)—Write a letter to God. This can be in response to what He was saying to you through Scripture, or you can write Him about anything that is on your mind.

Dear God,

Thanks for taking care of me, even when I don't see or understand what you are doing in my life. I belong to you, so keep on working on my character and my thoughts so that they will be pleasing to you. I do trust you in my head; help me trust you in my heart and experience.

The work situation has been difficult. And I've had a hard time not carrying the burden of my financial needs. I see the pile of bills each morning. The past couple weeks I haven't seen where the money to pay those bills is coming from. I'm sorry because I know that you see the bills, too, and probably have a great plan to meet my needs—if I only chill a little and let you take the burden. Show me what I need to do about work and the bills!

I'm not sure I'm totally comfortable with the image of being a sacrifice. I guess that means some desires and other things in my life have to die. More than any discomfort I might feel, I want to be pleasing to you, so here I am. Help me so I won't be pushed and molded into what the world wants me to be. Also, help me with my negative and critical thoughts. I'm going to work on that, but I sure need you to help keep me in check. I love you!

Susan

Listen for what God is saying to you. Write a letter to yourself from God with what you believe He is saying in response to you.

Dear Susan,

Your desire to know me and my purposes in your life makes me happy. I've promised to meet your physical needs, so relax and I will help you grow in your ability to trust. I do see what you need, and see it long before you are even aware. When you take control and worry, you lose sight of who I am and overlook the many ways I am at work in your situation. I will meet your needs when you have a job and are working hard, and I will meet your needs when you are unemployed and work is slow. Ultimately, I am your provider—depend on and trust me, instead of putting your trust in a biweekly paycheck. I love to show up for you and surprise you with my goodness. Get ready!

I will help you to grow in your relationship with me. I desire that you know me and my ways even more than you desire it. I see your desire to be pleasing to me, and that means so much to me. As you lay your life down as a living sacrifice, I will work in you to help you conform to my will and purposes for you. Trust me and obey me and see what I am able to do in your heart, mind, and your circumstances.

Love, your Father

5. **Share and Obey** (After devo is completed)—With whom can you share what God spoke to you? If it is direction you received, it is wise to share this with the godly counsel in your life, and if it is revelation or insight, think about who would be encouraged to hear what God has been teaching you and who can hold you accountable to what He spoke.

I want to tell Katie all about the trust issues that

I have been dealing with about no work, and that I am recommitting myself as that living sacrifice.

What steps of obedience or action steps are you going to take? Colossians 3:15 reminds us to let God's peace lead us when we feel challenged to obey or step out because His peace is a tangible reminder of His presence with us.

Talk to Katie. Continue to ask God what I need to be doing differently, until I get some specific direction.

DAILY DEVO PAGES

John 10:1–10

1. **Time and Place**—When and where did you meet with God?

....

....

....

2. **Be Still and Worship** (5–10 minutes)—Turn on worship music and ask God to help you connect to Him. Start by telling Him how wonderful He is and ask if there is any burden you need to release to Him. After you are finished, write down any impressions, thoughts, or themes you felt during your time of worship.

....

....

3. **Read and Pray** (10–15 minutes)—Read the following passage and use the SOAP method and the GOD SPA questions:

"'Very truly I tell you Pharisees, anyone who does not enter the sheep pen by the gate, but climbs in by some other way, is a thief and a robber. The one who enters by the gate is the shepherd of the sheep. The gatekeeper opens the gate for him, and the sheep listen to his voice. He calls his own sheep by name and leads them out. When he has brought out all his own, he goes on ahead of them, and his sheep follow him because they know his voice. But they will never follow a stranger; in fact, they will run away from him because they do not recognize a stranger's voice.' Jesus used this figure of speech, but the Pharisees did not understand what he was telling them. Therefore Jesus said again, 'Very truly I tell you, I am the gate for the sheep. All who have come before me are thieves and robbers,

but the sheep have not listened to them. I am the gate; whoever enters through me will be saved. They will come in and go out, and find pasture. The thief comes only to steal and kill and destroy; I have come that they may have life, and have it to the full.'" (John 10:1–10)

Observation—What stands out to you in this passage?

....

....

....

Application—(You may not have all of these answered for every passage, but it is helpful to ask the following questions). Is there a/an:

Growth Area?

....

....

....

Obedience Needed?

....

....

....

Direction to Follow?

....

....

....

Sin to Confess?

....

....

....

Promise to Claim?

....

....

....

Accountability?

....

....

....

Prayer—Spend a minute in prayer asking God to help you apply these truths to your life.

4. **Write and Listen** (10–15 minutes)—Write a letter to God. This can be in response to what He was saying to you through Scripture or you can write Him about anything that is on your mind.

....

....

....

....

....

....

....

....

....

....

....

....

....

....

....

Listen for what God is saying to you. Write a letter to yourself from God with what you believe He is saying in response to you.

....

....

....

....

....

....

....

....

....

....

....

....

....

....

....

5. **Share and Obey** (After devo is completed)—With whom can you share what God spoke to you? If it is direction you received, it is wise to share this with the godly counsel in your life, and if it is revelation or insight, think about who would be encouraged to hear what God has been teaching you and who can hold you accountable to what He spoke.

....

....

....

What steps of obedience or action steps are you going to take?

....

....

....

1. **Time and Place**—When and where did you meet with God?

....

....

....

2. **Be Still and Worship** (5–10 minutes)—Turn on worship music and ask God to help you connect to Him. Start by telling Him how wonderful He is and ask if there is any burden you need to release to Him. After you are finished, write down any impressions, thoughts, or themes you felt during your time of worship.

....

....

....

....

3. **Read and Pray** (10–15 minutes)—Read the following passage and use the SOAP method and the GOD SPA questions:

> "You are my hiding place; you will protect me from trouble and surround me with songs of deliverance. I will instruct you and teach you in the way you should go; I will counsel you with my loving eye on you. Do not be like the horse or the mule, which have no understanding but must be controlled by bit and bridle or they will not come to you. Many are the woes of the wicked, but the Lord's unfailing love surrounds the one who trusts in him. Rejoice in the Lord and be glad, you righteous; sing, all you who are upright in heart!" (Psalm 32:7–11)

Observation—What stands out to you in this passage?

....

....

....

....

Application—How can you apply this passage to your life? (You may not have all of these answered for every passage, but it is helpful to ask the following questions.) Is there a/an:

Growth Area?

....

....

....

Obedience Needed?

....

....

....

Direction to Follow?

....

....

....

Sin to Confess?

....

....

....

Promise to Claim?

....

....

....

Accountability?

....
....
....

Prayer—Spend a minute in prayer asking God to help you apply these truths to your life.

4. **Write and Listen** (10–15 minutes)—Write a letter to God. This can be in response to what He was saying to you through Scripture, or you can write Him about anything that is on your mind.

....
....
....
....
....
....
....
....
....
....
....
....
....
....
....
....
....
....
....
....
....

Listen for what God is saying to you. Write a letter to yourself from God with what you believe He is saying in response to you.

....
....
....
....
....
....
....
....
....
....
....
....
....
....
....
....
....

5. **Share and Obey** (After devo is completed)—With whom can you share what God spoke to you? If it is direction you received, it is wise to share this with the godly counsel in your life, and if it is revelation or insight, think about who would be encouraged to hear what God has been teaching you and who can hold you accountable to what He spoke.

....
....
....

What steps of obedience or action steps are you going to take?

....
....
....

Ephesians 3:14–21

1. **Time and Place**—When and where did you meet with God?

....
....
....

2. **Be Still and Worship** (5–10 minutes)—Turn on worship music and ask God to help you connect to Him. Start by telling Him how wonderful He is and ask if there is any burden you need to release to Him. After you are finished, write down any impressions, thoughts, or themes you felt during your time of worship.

....
....
....

3. **Read and Pray** (10–15 minutes)—Read the following passage and use the SOAP method and the GOD SPA questions:

> "For this reason I kneel before the Father, from whom every family in heaven and on earth derives its name. I pray that out of his glorious riches he may strengthen you with power through his Spirit in your inner being, so that Christ may dwell in your hearts through faith. And I pray that you, being rooted and established in love, may have power, together with all the Lord's holy people, to grasp how wide and long and high and deep is the love of Christ, and to know this love that surpasses knowledge—that you may be filled to the measure of all the fullness of God. Now to Him who is able to do immeasurably more than all we ask or imagine, according to His power that is at work within us, to Him be glory in the church and in Christ

Jesus throughout all generations, for ever and ever! Amen." (Ephesians 3:14–21)

Observation—What stands out to you in this passage?

....
....
....

Application—How can you apply this passage to your life? (You may not have all of these answered for every passage, but it is helpful to ask the following questions.) Is there a/an:

Growth Area?

....
....
....

Obedience Needed?

....
....
....

Direction to Follow?

....
....
....

Sin to Confess?

....
....
....

Promise to Claim?

....
....

Accountability?

....

....

....

Prayer—Spend a minute in prayer asking God to help you apply these truths to your life.

4. **Write and Listen** (10–15 minutes)—Write a letter to God. This can be in response to what He was saying to you through Scripture, or you can write Him about anything that is on your mind.

....

....

....

....

....

....

....

....

....

....

....

....

....

....

....

....

....

....

....

....

Listen for what God is saying to you. Write a letter to yourself from God with what you believe He is saying in response to you.

....
....
....
....
....
....
....
....
....
....
....
....
....
....
....
....

5. **Share and Obey** (After devo is completed)—With whom can you share what God spoke to you? If it is direction you received, it is wise to share this with the godly counsel in your life, and if it is revelation or insight, think about who would be encouraged to hear what God has been teaching you and who can hold you accountable to what He spoke.

....
....
....

What steps of obedience or action steps are you going to take?

....
....
....

John 6:5–15

1. **Time and Place**—When and where did you meet with God?

....

....

....

2. **Be Still and Worship** (5–10 minutes)—Turn on worship music and ask God to help you connect to Him. Start by telling Him how wonderful He is and ask if there is any burden you need to release to Him. After you are finished, write down any impressions, thoughts, or themes you felt during your time of worship.

....

....

....

3. **Read and Pray** (10–15 minutes)—Read the following passage and use the SOAP method and the GOD SPA questions:

> "When Jesus looked up and saw a great crowd coming toward him, he said to Philip, 'Where shall we buy bread for these people to eat?' He asked this only to test him, for he already had in mind what he was going to do. Philip answered him, 'It would take more than half a year's wages to buy enough bread for each one to have a bite!' Another of his disciples, Andrew, Simon Peter's brother, spoke up, 'Here is a boy with five small barley loaves and two small fish, but how far will they go among so many?' Jesus said, 'Have the people sit down.' There was plenty of grass in that place, and they sat down (about five thousand men were there). Jesus then took the loaves, gave thanks, and distributed to those who were seated as much as they wanted.

He did the same with the fish. When they had all had enough to eat, He said to His disciples, 'Gather the pieces that are left over. Let nothing be wasted.' So they gathered them and filled twelve baskets with the pieces of the five barley loaves left over by those who had eaten. After the people saw the sign Jesus performed, they began to say, 'Surely this is the Prophet who is to come into the world.' Jesus, knowing that they intended to come and make Him king by force, withdrew again to a mountain by Himself." (John 6:5–15)

Observation—What stands out to you in this passage?

....

....

....

....

Application—How can you apply this passage to your life? (You may not have all of these answered for every passage, but it is helpful to ask the following questions.) Is there a/an:

Growth Area?

....

....

....

Obedience Needed?

....

....

....

Direction to Follow?

....

....

....

Sin to Confess?

....

....

....

Promise to Claim?

....

....

....

Accountability?

....

....

....

Prayer—Spend a minute in prayer asking God to help you apply these truths to your life.

4. **Write and Listen** (10–15 minutes)—Write a letter to God. This can be in response to what He was saying to you through Scripture, or you can write Him about anything that is on your mind.

....

....

....

....

....

....

....

....

....

....

....

Listen for what God is saying to you. Write a letter to yourself from God with what you believe He is saying in response to you.

....
....
....
....
....
....
....
....
....
....
....
....
....
....
....

5. **Share and Obey** (After devo is completed)—With whom can you share what God spoke to you? If it is direction you received, it is wise to share this with the godly counsel in your life, and if it is revelation or insight, think about who would be encouraged to hear what God has been teaching you and who can hold you accountable to what He spoke.

....
....
....
....

What steps of obedience or action steps are you going to take?

....
....
....

1. **Time and Place**—When and where did you meet with God?

....

....

....

2. **Be Still and Worship** (5–10 minutes)—Turn on worship music and ask God to help you connect to Him. Start by telling Him how wonderful He is and ask if there is any burden you need to release to Him. After you are finished, write down any impressions, thoughts, or themes you felt during your time of worship.

....

....

....

3. **Read and Pray** (10–15 minutes)—Read the following passage and use the SOAP method and the GOD SPA questions:

"Create in me a pure heart, O God, and renew a steadfast spirit within me. Do not cast me from your presence or take your Holy Spirit from me. Restore to me the joy of your salvation and grant me a willing spirit, to sustain me. Then I will teach transgressors your ways, so that sinners will turn back to you. Deliver me from the guilt of bloodshed, O God, you who are God my Savior, and my tongue will sing of your righteousness. Open my lips, Lord, and my mouth will declare your praise. You do not delight in sacrifice, or I would bring it; you do not take pleasure in burnt offerings. My sacrifice, O God, is a broken spirit; a broken and contrite heart, you, God, will not despise." (Psalm 51:10–17)

Observation—What stands out to you in this passage?

....

....

....

....

Application—How can you apply this passage to your life? (You may not have all of these answered for every passage, but it is helpful to ask the following questions.) Is there a/an:

Growth Area?

....

....

....

Obedience Needed?

....

....

....

Direction to Follow?

....

....

....

Sin to Confess?

....

....

....

Promise to Claim?

....

....

....

Accountability?

....

....

....

Prayer—Spend a minute in prayer asking God to help you apply these truths to your life.

4. **Write and Listen** (10–15 minutes)—Write a letter to God. This can be in response to what He was saying to you through Scripture, or you can write Him about anything that is on your mind.

....

....

....

....

....

....

....

....

....

....

....

....

....

....

....

....

....

Listen for what God is saying to you. Write a letter to yourself from God with what you believe He is saying in response to you.

....
....
....
....
....
....
....
....
....
....
....
....
....
....
....
....
....

5. **Share and Obey** (After devo is completed)—With whom can you share what God spoke to you? If it is direction you received, it is wise to share this with the godly counsel in your life, and if it is revelation or insight, think about who would be encouraged to hear what God has been teaching you and who can hold you accountable to what He spoke.

....
....
....

What steps of obedience or action steps are you going to take?

....
....
....

Philippians 2:1–11

1. **Time and Place**—When and where did you meet with God?

....

....

....

2. **Be Still and Worship** (5–10 minutes)—Turn on worship music and ask God to help you connect to Him. Start by telling Him how wonderful He is and ask if there is any burden you need to release to Him. After you are finished, write down any impressions, thoughts, or themes you felt during your time of worship.

....

....

....

3. **Read and Pray** (10–15 minutes)—Read the following passage and use the SOAP method and the GOD SPA questions:

> "Therefore if you have any encouragement from being united with Christ, if any comfort from his love, if any common sharing in the Spirit, if any tenderness and compassion, then make my joy complete by being like-minded, having the same love, being one in spirit and of one mind. Do nothing out of self-ish ambition or vain conceit. Rather, in humility value others above yourselves, not looking to your own interests but each of you to the interests of the others. In your relationships with one another, have the same mindset as Christ Jesus: Who, being in very nature God, did not consider equality with God something to be used to his own advantage; rather, he made himself nothing by taking the very nature of a servant, being

made in human likeness. And being found in appearance as a man, He humbled Himself by becoming obedient to death—even death on a cross! Therefore God exalted him to the highest place and gave him the name that is above every name, that at the name of Jesus every knee should bow, in heaven and on earth and under the earth, and every tongue acknowledge that Jesus Christ is Lord, to the glory of God the Father." (Philippians 2:1–11)

Observation—What stands out to you in this passage?

....
....
....
....
....

Application—How can you apply this passage to your life? (You may not have all of these answered for every passage, but it is helpful to ask the following questions.) Is there a/an:

Growth Area?

....
....
....

Obedience Needed?

....
....
....

Direction to Follow?

....
....
....

Sin to Confess?

....

....

....

Promise to Claim?

....

....

....

Accountability?

....

....

....

Prayer—Spend a minute in prayer asking God to help you apply these truths to your life.

4. **Write and Listen** (10–15 minutes)—Write a letter to God. This can be in response to what He was saying to you through Scripture, or you can write Him about anything that is on your mind.

....

....

....

....

....

....

....

....

....

....

....

....

Listen for what God is saying to you. Write a letter to yourself from God with what you believe He is saying in response to you.

....

....

....

....

....

....

....

....

....

....

....

....

....

....

....

....

5. **Share and Obey** (After devo is completed)—With whom can you share what God spoke to you? If it is direction you received, it is wise to share this with the godly counsel in your life, and if it is revelation or insight, think about who would be encouraged to hear what God has been teaching you and who can hold you accountable to what He spoke.

....

....

....

What steps of obedience or action steps are you going to take?

....

....

....

Joshua 1:1–9

1. **Time and Place**—When and where did you meet with God?

....

....

....

2. **Be Still and Worship** (5–10 minutes)—Turn on worship music and ask God to help you connect to Him. Start by telling Him how wonderful He is and ask if there is any burden you need to release to Him. After you are finished, write down any impressions, thoughts, or themes you felt during your time of worship.

....

....

....

3. **Read and Pray** (10–15 minutes)—Read the following passage and use the SOAP method and the GOD SPA questions:

"After the death of Moses the servant of the Lord, the Lord said to Joshua son of Nun, Moses' aide: 'Moses my servant is dead. Now then, you and all these people, get ready to cross the Jordan River into the land I am about to give to them—to the Israelites. I will give you every place where you set your foot, as I promised Moses. Your territory will extend from the desert to Lebanon, and from the great river, the Euphrates—all the Hittite country—to the Mediterranean Sea in the west. No one will be able to stand against you all the days of your life. As I was with Moses, so I will be with you; I will never leave you nor forsake you. Be strong and courageous, because you will lead these people to inherit the land I swore to their ancestors

to give them. Be strong and very courageous. Be careful to obey all the law my servant Moses gave you; do not turn from it to the right or to the left, that you may be successful wherever you go. Keep this Book of the Law always on your lips; meditate on it day and night, so that you may be careful to do everything written in it. Then you will be prosperous and successful. Have I not commanded you? Be strong and courageous. Do not be afraid; do not be discouraged, for the Lord your God will be with you wherever you go.'" (Joshua 1:1–9)

Observation—What stands out to you in this passage?

....

....

....

....

Application—How can you apply this passage to your life? (You may not have all of these answered for every passage, but it is helpful to ask the following questions.) Is there a/an:

Growth Area?

....

....

....

Obedience Needed?

....

....

....

Direction to Follow?

....

....

....

Sin to Confess?

....

....

....

Promise to Claim?

....

....

....

Accountability?

....

....

....

Prayer—Spend a minute in prayer asking God to help you apply these truths to your life.

4. **Write and Listen** (10–15 minutes)—Write a letter to God. This can be in response to what He was saying to you through Scripture, or you can write Him about anything that is on your mind.

....

....

....

....

....

....

....

....

....

....

....

Listen for what God is saying to you. Write a letter to yourself from God with what you believe He is saying in response to you.

....
....
....
....
....
....
....
....
....
....
....
....
....
....
....
....
....

5. **Share and Obey** (After devo is completed)—With whom can you share what God spoke to you? If it is direction you received, it is wise to share this with the godly counsel in your life, and if it is revelation or insight, think about who would be encouraged to hear what God has been teaching you and who can hold you accountable to what He spoke.

....
....
....

What steps of obedience or action steps are you going to take?

....
....
....

1. **Time and Place**—When and where did you meet with God?

....

....

....

2. **Be Still and Worship** (5–10 minutes)—Turn on worship music and ask God to help you connect to Him. Start by telling Him how wonderful He is and ask if there is any burden you need to release to Him. After you are finished, write down any impressions, thoughts, or themes you felt during your time of worship.

....

....

....

3. **Read and Pray** (10–15 minutes)—Read the following passage and use the SOAP method and the GOD SPA questions:

> "Moses answered the people, 'Do not be afraid. Stand firm and you will see the deliverance the Lord will bring you today. The Egyptians you see today you will never see again. The Lord will fight for you; you need only to be still.' Then the Lord said to Moses, 'Why are you crying out to me? Tell the Israelites to move on. Raise your staff and stretch out your hand over the sea to divide the water so that the Israelites can go through the sea on dry ground. I will harden the hearts of the Egyptians so that they will go in after them. And I will gain glory through Pharaoh and all his army, through his chariots and his horsemen. The Egyptians will know that I am the Lord when I gain glory through Pharaoh, his chariots and his horsemen.' Then

the angel of God, who had been traveling in front of Israel's army, withdrew and went behind them. The pillar of cloud also moved from in front and stood behind them, coming between the armies of Egypt and Israel. Throughout the night the cloud brought darkness to the one side and light to the other side; so neither went near the other all night long. Then Moses stretched out his hand over the sea, and all that night the Lord drove the sea back with a strong east wind and turned it into dry land. The waters were divided, and the Israelites went through the sea on dry ground, with a wall of water on their right and on their left." (Exodus 14:13–22)

Observation—What stands out to you in this passage?

....

....

....

Application—How can you apply this passage to your life? (You may not have all of these answered for every passage, but it is helpful to ask the following questions.) Is there a/an:

Growth Area?

....

....

....

Obedience Needed?

....

....

....

Direction to Follow?

....

....

Sin to Confess?

....
....
....

Promise to Claim?

....
....
....

Accountability?

....
....
....

Prayer—Spend a minute in prayer asking God to help you apply these truths to your life.

4. **Write and Listen** (10–15 minutes)—Write a letter to God. This can be in response to what He was saying to you through Scripture, or you can write Him about anything that is on your mind.

....
....
....
....
....
....
....
....
....
....
....
....

Listen for what God is saying to you. Write a letter to yourself from God with what you believe He is saying in response to you.

....
....
....
....
....
....
....
....
....
....
....
....
....
....
....
....
....

5. **Share and Obey** (After devo is completed)—With whom can you share what God spoke to you? If it is direction you received, it is wise to share this with the godly counsel in your life, and if it is revelation or insight, think about who would be encouraged to hear what God has been teaching you and who can hold you accountable to what He spoke.

....
....
....

What steps of obedience or action steps are you going to take?

....
....
....

Romans 8:31–39

1. **Time and Place**—When and where did you meet with God?

....

....

....

2. **Be Still and Worship** (5–10 minutes)—Turn on worship music and ask God to help you connect to Him. Start by telling Him how wonderful He is and ask if there is any burden you need to release to Him. After you are finished, write down any impressions, thoughts, or themes you felt during your time of worship.

....

....

....

3. **Read and Pray** (10–15 minutes)—Read the following passage and use the SOAP method and the GOD SPA questions:

"What, then, shall we say in response to these things? If God is for us, who can be against us? He who did not spare his own Son, but gave him up for us all—how will he not also, along with him, graciously give us all things? Who will bring any charge against those whom God has chosen? It is God who justifies. Who then is the one who condemns? No one. Christ Jesus who died—more than that, who was raised to life—is at the right hand of God and is also interceding for us. Who shall separate us from the love of Christ? Shall trouble or hardship or persecution or famine or nakedness or danger or sword? As it is written: 'For your sake we face death all day long; we are considered as sheep to be slaughtered.' No, in all these things

we are more than conquerors through him who loved us. For I am convinced that neither death nor life, neither angels nor demons, neither the present nor the future, nor any powers, neither height nor depth, nor anything else in all creation, will be able to separate us from the love of God that is in Christ Jesus our Lord." (Romans 8:31–39)

Observation—What stands out to you in this passage?

....

....

....

Application—How can you apply this passage to your life? (You may not have all of these answered for every passage, but it is helpful to ask the following questions.) Is there a/an:

Growth Area?

....

....

....

Obedience Needed?

....

....

....

Direction to Follow?

....

....

....

Sin to Confess?

....

....

....

Promise to Claim?

....

....

....

Accountability?

....

....

....

Prayer—Spend a minute in prayer asking God to help you apply these truths to your life.

4. **Write and Listen** (10–15 minutes)—Write a letter to God. This can be in response to what He was saying to you through Scripture, or you can write Him about anything that is on your mind.

....
....
....
....
....
....
....
....
....
....
....
....
....
....
....
....

Listen for what God is saying to you. Write a letter to yourself from God with what you believe He is saying in response to you.

....
....
....
....
....
....
....
....
....
....
....
....
....
....
....
....
....

5. **Share and Obey** (After devo is completed)—With whom can you share what God spoke to you? If it is direction you received, it is wise to share this with the godly counsel in your life, and if it is revelation or insight, think about who would be encouraged to hear what God has been teaching you and who can hold you accountable to what He spoke.

....
....
....

What steps of obedience or action steps are you going to take?

....
....
....

Judges 7:1–8

1. **Time and Place**—When and where did you meet with God?

....

....

....

2. **Be Still and Worship** (5–10 minutes)—Turn on worship music and ask God to help you connect to Him. Start by telling Him how wonderful He is and ask if there is any burden you need to release to Him. After you are finished, write down any impressions, thoughts, or themes you felt during your time of worship.

....

....

....

3. **Read and Pray** (10–15 minutes)—Read the following passage and use the SOAP method and the GOD SPA questions:

"Early in the morning, Jerub-Baal (that is, Gideon) and all his men camped at the spring of Harod. The camp of Midian was north of them in the valley near the hill of Moreh. The Lord said to Gideon, 'You have too many men. I cannot deliver Midian into their hands, or Israel would boast against me, 'My own strength has saved me.' Now announce to the army, 'Anyone who trembles with fear may turn back and leave Mount Gilead.' So twenty-two thousand men left, while ten thousand remained. But the Lord said to Gideon, 'There are still too many men. Take them down to the water, and I will thin them out for you there. If I say, 'This one shall go with you,' he shall go; but if I say, 'This one shall not go with you,' he shall not go.' So

Gideon took the men down to the water. There the Lord told him, 'Separate those who lap the water with their tongues as a dog laps from those who kneel down to drink.' Three hundred of them drank from cupped hands, lapping like dogs. All the rest got down on their knees to drink. The Lord said to Gideon, 'With the three hundred men that lapped I will save you and give the Midianites into your hands. Let all the others go home.' So Gideon sent the rest of the Israelites home but kept the three hundred, who took over the provisions and trumpets of the others." (Judges 7:1–8)

Observation—What stands out to you in this passage?

....

....

....

Application—How can you apply this passage to your life? (You may not have all of these answered for every passage, but it is helpful to ask the following questions.) Is there a/an:

Growth Area?

....

....

....

Obedience Needed?

....

....

....

Direction to Follow?

....

....

....

Sin to Confess?

....

....

....

Promise to Claim?

....

....

....

Accountability?

....

....

....

Prayer—Spend a minute in prayer asking God to help you apply these truths to your life.

4. **Write and Listen** (10–15 minutes)—Write a letter to God. This can be in response to what He was saying to you through Scripture, or you can write Him about anything that is on your mind.

....

....

....

....

....

....

....

....

....

....

....

....

Listen for what God is saying to you. Write a letter to yourself from God with what you believe He is saying in response to you.

....
....
....
....
....
....
....
....
....
....
....
....
....
....
....
....

5. **Share and Obey** (After devo is completed)—With whom can you share what God spoke to you? If it is direction you received, it is wise to share this with the godly counsel in your life, and if it is revelation or insight, think about who would be encouraged to hear what God has been teaching you and who can hold you accountable to what He spoke.

....
....
....

What steps of obedience or action steps are you going to take?

....
....
....

Acts 9:1–19

1. Time and Place—When and where did you meet with God?

....

....

....

2. Be Still and Worship (5–10 minutes)—Turn on worship music and ask God to help you connect to Him. Start by telling Him how wonderful He is and ask if there is any burden you need to release to Him. After you are finished, write down any impressions, thoughts, or themes you felt during your time of worship.

....

....

....

3. Read and Pray (10–15 minutes)—Read the following passage and use the SOAP method and the GOD SPA questions:

> "Meanwhile, Saul was still breathing out murderous threats against the Lord's disciples. He went to the high priest and asked him for letters to the synagogues in Damascus, so that if he found any there who belonged to the Way, whether men or women, he might take them as prisoners to Jerusalem. As he neared Damascus on his journey, suddenly a light from heaven flashed around him. He fell to the ground and heard a voice say to him, 'Saul, Saul, why do you persecute me?' 'Who are you, Lord?' Saul asked. 'I am Jesus, whom you are persecuting,' he replied. 'Now get up and go into the city, and you will be told what you must do.' The men traveling with Saul stood there speechless; they heard the sound but did not see anyone. Saul

got up from the ground, but when he opened his eyes he could see nothing. So they led him by the hand into Damascus. For three days he was blind, and did not eat or drink anything. In Damascus there was a disciple named Ananias. The Lord called to him in a vision, 'Ananias!' 'Yes, Lord,' he answered. The Lord told him, 'Go to the house of Judas on Straight Street and ask for a man from Tarsus named Saul, for he is praying. In a vision he has seen a man named Ananias come and place his hands on him to restore his sight.' 'Lord,' Ananias answered, 'I have heard many reports about this man and all the harm he has done to your holy people in Jerusalem. And he has come here with authority from the chief priests to arrest all who call on your name.' But the Lord said to Ananias, 'Go! This man is my chosen instrument to proclaim my name to the Gentiles and their kings and to the people of Israel. I will show him how much he must suffer for my name.' Then Ananias went to the house and entered it. Placing his hands on Saul, he said, 'Brother Saul, the Lord—Jesus, who appeared to you on the road as you were coming here—has sent me so that you may see again and be filled with the Holy Spirit.' Immediately, something like scales fell from Saul's eyes, and he could see again. He got up and was baptized, and after taking some food, he regained his strength." (Acts 9:1–19)

Observation—What stands out to you in this passage?

....
....
....
....
....
....
....
....

Application—How can you apply this passage to your life? (You may not have all of these answered for every passage, but it is helpful to ask the following questions). Is there a/an:

Growth Area?

....

....

....

Obedience Needed?

....

....

....

Direction to Follow?

....

....

....

Sin to Confess?

....

....

....

Promise to Claim?

....

....

....

Accountability?

....

....

....

Prayer—Spend a minute in prayer asking God to help you apply these truths to your life.

4. **Write and Listen** (10–15 minutes)—Write a letter to God. This can be in response to what He was saying to you through Scripture, or you can write Him about anything that is on your mind.

....
....
....
....
....
....
....
....
....
....
....
....
....
....
....

Listen for what God is saying to you. Write a letter to yourself from God with what you believe He is saying in response to you.

....
....
....
....
....
....
....

....

....

....

....

....

....

....

....

....

5. **Share and Obey** (After devo is completed)—With whom can you share what God spoke to you? If it is direction you received, it is wise to share this with the godly counsel in your life, and if it is revelation or insight, think about who would be encouraged to hear what God has been teaching you and who can hold you accountable to what He spoke.

....

....

....

What steps of obedience or action steps are you going to take?

....

....

....

1. **Time and Place**—When and where did you meet with God?

....

....

....

2. **Be Still and Worship** (5–10 minutes)—Turn on worship music and ask God to help you connect to Him. Start by telling Him how wonderful He is and ask if there is any burden you need to release to Him. After you are finished, write down any impressions, thoughts, or themes you felt during your time of worship.

....

....

....

3. **Read and Pray** (10–15 minutes)—Read the following passage and use the SOAP method and the GOD SPA questions:

> "For this reason, ever since I heard about your faith in the Lord Jesus and your love for all God's people, I have not stopped giving thanks for you, remembering you in my prayers. I keep asking that the God of our Lord Jesus Christ, the glorious Father, may give you the Spirit of wisdom and revelation, so that you may know him better. I pray that the eyes of your heart may be enlightened in order that you may know the hope to which He has called you, the riches of his glorious inheritance in His holy people, and His incomparably great power for us who believe. That power is the same as the mighty strength He exerted when He raised Christ from the dead and seated Him at his right hand in the heavenly realms, far above all rule

and authority, power and dominion, and every name that is invoked, not only in the present age but also in the one to come. And God placed all things under His feet and appointed him to be head over everything for the church, which is His body, the fullness of Him who fills everything in every way." (Ephesians 1:15–23)

Observation—What stands out to you in this passage?

....

....

....

Application—How can you apply this passage to your life? (You may not have all of these answered for every passage, but it is helpful to ask the following questions). Is there a/an:

Growth Area?

....

....

....

Obedience Needed?

....

....

....

Direction to Follow?

....

....

....

Sin to Confess?

....

....

....

Promise to Claim?

....

....

....

Accountability?

....

....

....

Prayer—Spend a minute in prayer asking God to help you apply these truths to your life.

4. **Write and Listen** (10–15 minutes)—Write a letter to God. This can be in response to what He was saying to you through Scripture, or you can write Him about anything that is on your mind.

....

....

....

....

....

....

....

....

....

....

....

....

....

....

....

....

....

Listen for what God is saying to you. Write a letter to yourself from God with what you believe He is saying in response to you.

....
....
....
....
....
....
....
....
....
....
....
....
....
....
....
....

5. **Share and Obey** (After devo is completed)—With whom can you share what God spoke to you? If it is direction you received, it is wise to share this with the godly counsel in your life, and if it is revelation or insight, think about who would be encouraged to hear what God has been teaching you and who can hold you accountable to what He spoke.

....
....
....

What steps of obedience or action steps are you going to take?

....
....
....

Deuteronomy 8:1–11

1. **Time and Place**—When and where did you meet with God?

....

....

....

2. **Be Still and Worship** (5–10 minutes)—Turn on worship music and ask God to help you connect to Him. Start by telling Him how wonderful He is and ask if there is any burden you need to release to Him. After you are finished, write down any impressions, thoughts, or themes you felt during your time of worship.

....

....

....

3. **Read and Pray** (10–15 minutes)—Read the following passage and use the SOAP method and the GOD SPA questions:

> "Be careful to follow every command I am giving you today, so that you may live and increase and may enter and possess the land the Lord promised on oath to your ancestors. Remember how the Lord your God led you all the way in the wilderness these forty years, to humble and test you in order to know what was in your heart, whether or not you would keep his commands. He humbled you, causing you to hunger and then feeding you with manna, which neither you nor your ancestors had known, to teach you that man does not live on bread alone but on every word that comes from the mouth of the Lord. Your clothes did not wear out and your feet did not swell during these forty years. Know then in your heart that as a man

disciplines his son, so the Lord your God disciplines you. Observe the commands of the Lord your God, walking in obedience to him and revering him. For the Lord your God is bringing you into a good land—a land with brooks, streams, and deep springs gushing out into the valleys and hills; a land with wheat and barley, vines and fig trees, pomegranates, olive oil and honey; a land where bread will not be scarce and you will lack nothing; a land where the rocks are iron and you can dig copper out of the hills. When you have eaten and are satisfied, praise the Lord your God for the good land He has given you. Be careful that you do not forget the Lord your God, failing to observe his commands, His laws and His decrees that I am giving you this day." (Deuteronomy 8:1–11)

Observation—What stands out to you in this passage?

....

....

....

....

....

Application—How can you apply this passage to your life? (You may not have all of these answered for every passage, but it is helpful to ask the following questions). Is there a/an:

Growth Area?

....

....

....

Obedience Needed?

....

....

....

Direction to Follow?

....

....

....

Sin to Confess?

....

....

....

Promise to Claim?

....

....

....

Accountability?

....

....

....

Prayer—Spend a minute in prayer asking God to help you apply these truths to your life.

4. **Write and Listen** (10–15 minutes)—Write a letter to God. This can be in response to what He was saying to you through Scripture, or you can write Him about anything that is on your mind.

....

....

....

....

....

....

....

....
....
....
....
....
....
....
....
....

Listen for what God is saying to you. Write a letter to yourself from God with what you believe He is saying in response to you.

....
....
....
....
....
....
....
....
....
....
....
....
....
....
....
....

5. **Share and Obey** (After devo is completed)—With whom can you share what God spoke to you? If it is direction you received, it is wise to share this with the godly counsel in your life, and if it is revelation or in-

sight, think about who would be encouraged to hear what God has been teaching you and who can hold you accountable to what He spoke.

....

....

....

What steps of obedience or action steps are you going to take?

....

....

....

Proverbs 3:1–6

1. **Time and Place**—When and where did you meet with God?

....

....

....

2. **Be Still and Worship** (5–10 minutes)—Turn on worship music and ask God to help you connect to Him. Start by telling Him how wonderful He is and ask if there is any burden you need to release to Him. After you are finished, write down any impressions, thoughts, or themes you felt during your time of worship.

....

....

....

3. **Read and Pray** (10–15 minutes)—Read the following passage and use the SOAP method and the GOD SPA questions:

> "My son, do not forget my teaching, but keep my commands in your heart, for they will prolong your life many years and bring you peace and prosperity. Let love and faithfulness never leave you; bind them around your neck, write them on the tablet of your heart. Then you will win favor and a good name in the sight of God and man. Trust in the Lord with all your heart and lean not on your own understanding; in all your ways submit to him, and he will make your paths straight." (Proverbs 3:1–6)

Observation—What stands out to you in this passage?

....

....

....

....

Application—How can you apply this passage to your life? (You may not have all of these answered for every passage, but it is helpful to ask the following questions.) Is there a/an:

Growth Area?

....

....

....

Obedience Needed?

....

....

....

Direction to Follow?

....

....

....

Sin to Confess?

....

....

....

Promise to Claim?

....

....

....

Accountability?

....

....

....

Prayer—Spend a minute in prayer asking God to help you apply these truths to your life.

4. **Write and Listen** (10–15 minutes)—Write a letter to God. This can be in response to what He was saying to you through Scripture, or you can write Him about anything that is on your mind.

....

....

....

....

....

....

....

....

....

....

....

....

....

....

....

....

....

....

....

....

Listen for what God is saying to you. Write a letter to yourself from God with what you believe He is saying in response to you.

....
....
....
....
....
....
....
....
....
....
....
....
....
....
....
....
....
....

5. **Share and Obey** (After devo is completed)—With whom can you share what God spoke to you? If it is direction you received, it is wise to share this with the godly counsel in your life, and if it is revelation or insight, think about who would be encouraged to hear what God has been teaching you and who can hold you accountable to what He spoke.

....
....
....

What steps of obedience or action steps are you going to take?

....
....
....

1. **Time and Place**—When and where did you meet with God?

....

....

....

2. **Be Still and Worship** (5–10 minutes)—Turn on worship music and ask God to help you connect to Him. Start by telling Him how wonderful He is and ask if there is any burden you need to release to Him. After you are finished, write down any impressions, thoughts, or themes you felt during your time of worship.

....

....

....

3. **Read and Pray** (10–15 minutes)—Read the following passage and use the SOAP method and the GOD SPA questions:

> "As the Father has loved me, so have I loved you. Now remain in my love. If you keep my commands, you will remain in my love, just as I have kept my Father's commands and remain in his love. I have told you this so that my joy may be in you and that your joy may be complete. My command is this: Love each other as I have loved you. Greater love has no one than this: to lay down one's life for one's friends. You are my friends if you do what I command. I no longer call you servants, because a servant does not know his master's business. Instead, I have called you friends, for everything that I learned from my Father I have made known to you. You did not choose me, but I chose you and appointed you so that you might go and bear

fruit—fruit that will last—and so that whatever you ask in my name the Father will give you. This is my command: Love each other." (John 15:9–17)

Observation—What stands out to you in this passage?

....

....

....

....

....

Application—How can you apply this passage to your life? (You may not have all of these answered for every passage, but it is helpful to ask the following questions.) Is there a/an:

Growth Area?

....

....

....

Obedience Needed?

....

....

....

Direction to Follow?

....

....

....

Sin to Confess?

....

....

....

Promise to Claim?

....

....

....

Accountability?

....

....

....

Prayer—Spend a minute in prayer asking God to help you apply these truths to your life.

4. **Write and Listen** (10–15 minutes)—Write a letter to God. This can be in response to what He was saying to you through Scripture, or you can write Him about anything that is on your mind.

....

....

....

....

....

....

....

....

....

....

....

....

....

....

Listen for what God is saying to you. Write a letter to yourself from God with what you believe He is saying in response to you.

....

....

....

....

....

....

....

....

....

....

....

....

....

....

....

....

5. **Share and Obey** (After devo is completed)—With whom can you share what God spoke to you? If it is direction you received, it is wise to share this with the godly counsel in your life, and if it is revelation or insight, think about who would be encouraged to hear what God has been teaching you and who can hold you accountable to what He spoke.

....

....

....

What steps of obedience or action steps are you going to take?

....

....

....

1 Samuel 3:1–11

1. Time and Place—When and where did you meet with God?

....

....

....

2. Be Still and Worship (5–10 minutes)—Turn on worship music and ask God to help you connect to Him. Start by telling Him how wonderful He is and ask if there is any burden you need to release to Him. After you are finished, write down any impressions, thoughts, or themes you felt during your time of worship.

....

....

....

3. Read and Pray (10–15 minutes)—Read the following passage and use the SOAP method and the GOD SPA questions:

"The boy Samuel ministered before the Lord under Eli. In those days the word of the Lord was rare; there were not many visions. One night Eli, whose eyes were becoming so weak that he could barely see, was lying down in his usual place. The lamp of God had not yet gone out, and Samuel was lying down in the house of the Lord, where the ark of God was. Then the Lord called Samuel. Samuel answered, 'Here I am.' And he ran to Eli and said, 'Here I am; you called me.' But Eli said, 'I did not call; go back and lie down.' So he went and lay down. Again the Lord called, 'Samuel!' And Samuel got up and went to Eli and said, 'Here I am; you called me.' 'My son,' Eli said, 'I did not call; go back and lie down.' Now Samuel did not yet know

the Lord: The word of the Lord had not yet been revealed to him. A third time the Lord called, 'Samuel!' And Samuel got up and went to Eli and said, 'Here I am; you called me.' Then Eli realized that the Lord was calling the boy. So Eli told Samuel, 'Go and lie down, and if he calls you, say, 'Speak, Lord, for your servant is listening.'" So Samuel went and lay down in his place. The Lord came and stood there, calling as at the other times, 'Samuel! Samuel!' Then Samuel said, 'Speak, for your servant is listening.' And the Lord said to Samuel: 'See, I am about to do something in Israel that will make the ears of everyone who hears about it tingle.'" (1 Samuel 3:1–11)

Observation—What stands out to you in this passage?

....

....

....

Application—How can you apply this passage to your life? (You may not have all of these answered for every passage, but it is helpful to ask the following questions.) Is there a/an:

Growth Area?

....

....

....

Obedience Needed?

....

....

....

Direction to Follow?

....

....

Sin to Confess?

....

....

....

Promise to Claim?

....

....

....

Accountability?

....

....

....

Prayer—Spend a minute in prayer asking God to help you apply these truths to your life.

4. **Write and Listen** (10–15 minutes)—Write a letter to God. This can be in response to what He was saying to you through Scripture or you can write Him about anything that is on your mind.

....

....

....

....

....

....

....

....

....

....

....

....

....

....

....

....

....

....

....

....

....

Listen for what God is saying to you. Write a letter to yourself from God with what you believe He is saying in response to you.

....

....

....

....

....

....

....

....

....

....

....

....

....

....

....

....

5. **Share and Obey** (After devo is completed)—With whom can you share what God spoke to you? If it is direction you received, it is wise to share this with the godly counsel in your life, and if it is revelation or in-

sight, think about who would be encouraged to hear what God has been teaching you and who can hold you accountable to what He spoke.

....

....

....

What steps of obedience or action steps are you going to take?

....

....

....

1. **Time and Place**—When and where did you meet with God?

....

....

....

2. **Be Still and Worship** (5–10 minutes)—Turn on worship music and ask God to help you connect to Him. Start by telling Him how wonderful He is and ask if there is any burden you need to release to Him. After you are finished, write down any impressions, thoughts, or themes you felt during your time of worship.

....

....

....

3. **Read and Pray** (10–15 minutes)—Read the following passage and use the SOAP method and the GOD SPA questions:

> "As Jesus and his disciples were on their way, he came to a village where a woman named Martha opened her home to him. She had a sister called Mary, who sat at the Lord's feet listening to what he said. But Martha was distracted by all the preparations that had to be made. She came to him and asked, 'Lord, don't you care that my sister has left me to do the work by myself? Tell her to help me!' 'Martha, Martha,' the Lord answered, 'you are worried and upset about many things, but few things are needed—or indeed only one. Mary has chosen what is better, and it will not be taken away from her.' " (Luke 10:38–42)

Observation—What stands out to you in this passage?

....

....

....

....

Application—How can you apply this passage to your life? (You may not have all of these answered for every passage, but it is helpful to ask the following questions.) Is there a/an:

Growth Area?

....

....

Obedience Needed?

....

....

....

Direction to Follow?

....

....

....

Sin to Confess?

....

....

....

Promise to Claim?

....

....

....

Accountability?

....
....
....

Prayer—Spend a minute in prayer asking God to help you apply these truths to your life.

4. **Write and Listen** (10–15 minutes)—Write a letter to God. This can be in response to what He was saying to you through Scripture, or you can write Him about anything that is on your mind.

....
....
....
....
....
....
....
....
....
....
....
....
....
....
....
....
....
....
....
....

Listen for what God is saying to you. Write a letter to yourself from God with what you believe He is saying in response to you.

....

....

....

....

....

....

....

....

....

....

....

....

....

....

....

....

5. **Share and Obey** (After devo is completed)—With whom can you share what God spoke to you? If it is direction you received, it is wise to share this with the godly counsel in your life, and if it is revelation or insight, think about who would be encouraged to hear what God has been teaching you and who can hold you accountable to what He spoke.

....

....

....

What steps of obedience or action steps are you going to take?

....

....

....

1. **Time and Place**—When and where did you meet with God?

....

....

....

2. **Be Still and Worship** (5–10 minutes)—Turn on worship music and ask God to help you connect to Him. Start by telling Him how wonderful He is and ask if there is any burden you need to release to Him. After you are finished, write down any impressions, thoughts, or themes you felt during your time of worship.

....

....

....

....

3. **Read and Pray** (10–15 minutes)—Read the following passage and use the SOAP method and the GOD SPA questions:

> "Blessed is the one who does not walk in step with the wicked or stand in the way that sinners take or sit in the company of mockers, but whose delight is in the law of the Lord, and who meditates on his law day and night. That person is like a tree planted by streams of water, which yields its fruit in season and whose leaf does not wither—whatever they do prospers. Not so the wicked! They are like chaff that the wind blows away. Therefore the wicked will not stand in the judgment, nor sinners in the assembly of the righteous. For the Lord watches over the way of the righteous, but the way of the wicked leads to destruction." (Psalm 1:1–6)

Observation—What stands out to you in this passage?

....

....

....

....

Application—How can you apply this passage to your life? (You may not have all of these answered for every passage, but it is helpful to ask the following questions.) Is there a/an:

Growth Area?

....

....

....

Obedience Needed?

....

....

....

Direction to Follow?

....

....

....

Sin to Confess?

....

....

....

Promise to Claim?

....

....

....

Accountability?

....

....

....

Prayer—Spend a minute in prayer asking God to help you apply these truths to your life.

4. **Write and Listen** (10–15 minutes)—Write a letter to God. This can be in response to what He was saying to you through Scripture, or you can write Him about anything that is on your mind.

....

....

....

....

....

....

....

....

....

....

....

....

....

....

....

....

....

....

....

....

Listen for what God is saying to you. Write a letter to yourself from God with what you believe He is saying in response to you.

....
....
....
....
....
....
....
....
....
....
....
....
....
....
....

5. **Share and Obey** (After devo is completed)—With whom can you share what God spoke to you? If it is direction you received, it is wise to share this with the godly counsel in your life, and if it is revelation or insight, think about who would be encouraged to hear what God has been teaching you and who can hold you accountable to what He spoke.

....
....
....

What steps of obedience or action steps are you going to take?

....
....
....

1. **Time and Place**—When and where did you meet with God?

....

....

....

2. **Be Still and Worship** (5–10 minutes)—Turn on worship music and ask God to help you connect to Him. Start by telling Him how wonderful He is and ask if there is any burden you need to release to Him. After you are finished, write down any impressions, thoughts, or themes you felt during your time of worship.

....

....

....

3. **Read and Pray** (10–15 minutes)—Read the following passage and use the SOAP method and the GOD SPA questions:

"Therefore I tell you, do not worry about your life, what you will eat or drink; or about your body, what you will wear. Is not life more than food, and the body more than clothes? Look at the birds of the air; they do not sow or reap or store away in barns, and yet your heavenly Father feeds them. Are you not much more valuable than they? Can any one of you by worrying add a single hour to your life? And why do you worry about clothes? See how the flowers of the field grow. They do not labor or spin. Yet I tell you that not even Solomon in all his splendor was dressed like one of these. If that is how God clothes the grass of the field, which is here today and tomorrow is thrown into the fire, will he not much more clothe you—you

of little faith? So do not worry, saying, 'What shall we eat?' or 'What shall we drink?' or 'What shall we wear?' For the pagans run after all these things, and your heavenly Father knows that you need them. But seek first his kingdom and his righteousness, and all these things will be given to you as well." (Matthew 6:25–33)

Observation—What stands out to you in this passage?

....

....

....

Application—How can you apply this passage to your life? (You may not have all of these answered for every passage, but it is helpful to ask the following questions.) Is there a/an:

Growth Area?

....

....

....

Obedience Needed?

....

....

....

Direction to Follow?

....

....

....

Sin to Confess?

....

....

....

Promise to Claim?

....

....

....

Accountability?

....

....

....

Prayer—Spend a minute in prayer asking God to help you apply these truths to your life.

4. **Write and Listen** (10–15 minutes)—Write a letter to God. This can be in response to what He was saying to you through Scripture, or you can write Him about anything that is on your mind.

....

....

....

....

....

....

....

....

....

....

....

....

....

....

....

....

Listen for what God is saying to you. Write a letter to yourself from God with what you believe He is saying in response to you.

....
....
....
....
....
....
....
....
....
....
....
....
....
....
....

5. **Share and Obey** (After devo is completed)—With whom can you share what God spoke to you? If it is direction you received, it is wise to share this with the godly counsel in your life, and if it is revelation or insight, think about who would be encouraged to hear what God has been teaching you and who can hold you accountable to what He spoke.

....
....
....

What steps of obedience or action steps are you going to take?

....
....
....

Esther 4:12–16

1. **Time and Place**—When and where did you meet with God?

....

....

....

2. **Be Still and Worship** (5–10 minutes)—Turn on worship music and ask God to help you connect to Him. Start by telling Him how wonderful He is and ask if there is any burden you need to release to Him. After you are finished, write down any impressions, thoughts, or themes you felt during your time of worship.

....

....

....

3. **Read and Pray** (10–15 minutes)—Read the following passage and use the SOAP method and the GOD SPA questions:

> "When Esther's words were reported to Mordecai, he sent back this answer: 'Do not think that because you are in the king's house you alone of all the Jews will escape. For if you remain silent at this time, relief and deliverance for the Jews will arise from another place, but you and your father's family will perish. And who knows but that you have come to your royal position for such a time as this?' Then Esther sent this reply to Mordecai: 'Go, gather together all the Jews who are in Susa, and fast for me. Do not eat or drink for three days, night or day. I and my attendants will fast as you do. When this is done, I will go to the king, even though it is against the law. And if I perish, I perish.'" (Esther 4:12–16)

Observation—What stands out to you in this passage?

....

....

....

....

Application—How can you apply this passage to your life? (You may not have all of these answered for every passage, but it is helpful to ask the following questions.) Is there a/an:

Growth Area?

....

....

....

Obedience Needed?

....

....

....

Direction to Follow?

....

....

....

Sin to Confess?

....

....

....

Promise to Claim?

....

....

....

Accountability?

....

....

....

Prayer—Spend a minute in prayer asking God to help you apply these truths to your life.

4. **Write and Listen** (10–15 minutes)—Write a letter to God. This can be in response to what He was saying to you through Scripture, or you can write Him about anything that is on your mind.

....

....

....

....

....

....

....

....

....

....

....

....

....

....

....

....

....

....

Listen for what God is saying to you. Write a letter to yourself from God with what you believe He is saying in response to you.

....
....
....
....
....
....
....
....
....
....
....
....
....
....
....
....

5. **Share and Obey** (After devo is completed)—With whom can you share what God spoke to you? If it is direction you received, it is wise to share this with the godly counsel in your life, and if it is revelation or insight, think about who would be encouraged to hear what God has been teaching you and who can hold you accountable to what He spoke.

....
....
....

What steps of obedience or action steps are you going to take?

....
....
....

Nehemiah 2:17–20

1. **Time and Place**—When and where did you meet with God?

....

....

....

2. **Be Still and Worship** (5–10 minutes)—Turn on worship music and ask God to help you connect to Him. Start by telling Him how wonderful He is and ask if there is any burden you need to release to Him. After you are finished, write down any impressions, thoughts, or themes you felt during your time of worship.

....

....

....

....

3. **Read and Pray** (10–15 minutes)—Read the following passage and use the SOAP method and the GOD SPA questions:

"Then Nehemiah said to them, 'You see the trouble we are in: Jerusalem lies in ruins, and its gates have been burned with fire. Come, let us rebuild the wall of Jerusalem, and we will no longer be in disgrace.' I also told them about the gracious hand of my God on me and what the king had said to me. They replied, 'Let us start rebuilding.' So they began this good work. But when Sanballat the Horonite, Tobiah the Ammonite official and Geshem the Arab heard about it, they mocked and ridiculed us. 'What is this you are doing?' they asked. 'Are you rebelling against the king?' I answered them by saying, 'The God of heaven will give us success. We his servants will start

rebuilding, but as for you, you have no share in Jerusalem or any claim or historic right to it.'" (Nehemiah 2:17–20)

Observation—What stands out to you in this passage?

....
....
....
....
....
....

Application—How can you apply this passage to your life? (You may not have all of these answered for every passage, but it is helpful to ask the following questions.) Is there a/an:

Growth Area?

....
....
....

Obedience Needed?

....
....
....

Direction to Follow?

....
....
....

Sin to Confess?

....
....
....

Promise to Claim?

....
....
....

Accountability?

....
....
....

Prayer—Spend a minute in prayer asking God to help you apply these truths to your life.

4. **Write and Listen** (10–15 minutes)—Write a letter to God. This can be in response to what He was saying to you through Scripture, or you can write Him about anything that is on your mind.

....
....
....
....
....
....
....
....
....
....
....
....
....
....
....

Listen for what God is saying to you. Write a letter to yourself from God with what you believe He is saying in response to you.

....
....
....
....
....
....
....
....
....
....
....
....
....
....

5. **Share and Obey** (After devo is completed)—With whom can you share what God spoke to you? If it is direction you received, it is wise to share this with the godly counsel in your life, and if it is revelation or insight, think about who would be encouraged to hear what God has been teaching you and who can hold you accountable to what He spoke.

....
....
....

What steps of obedience or action steps are you going to take?

....
....
....

1. **Time and Place**—When and where did you meet with God?

....

....

....

2. **Be Still and Worship** (5–10 minutes)—Turn on worship music and ask God to help you connect to Him. Start by telling Him how wonderful He is and ask if there is any burden you need to release to Him. After you are finished, write down any impressions, thoughts, or themes you felt during your time of worship.

....

....

....

3. **Read and Pray** (10–15 minutes)—Read the following passage and use the SOAP method and the GOD SPA questions:

> "That day when evening came, He said to His disciples, 'Let us go over to the other side.' Leaving the crowd behind, they took him along, just as he was, in the boat. There were also other boats with him. A furious squall came up, and the waves broke over the boat, so that it was nearly swamped. Jesus was in the stern, sleeping on a cushion. The disciples woke him and said to him, 'Teacher, don't you care if we drown?' He got up, rebuked the wind and said to the waves, 'Quiet! Be still!' Then the wind died down and it was completely calm. He said to his disciples, 'Why are you so afraid? Do you still have no faith?' They were terrified and asked each other, 'Who is this? Even the wind and the waves obey him!'" (Mark 4:35–41)

Observation—What stands out to you in this passage?

....

....

....

....

Application—How can you apply this passage to your life? (You may not have all of these answered for every passage, but it is helpful to ask the following questions). Is there a/an:

Growth Area?

....

....

....

Obedience Needed?

....

....

....

Direction to Follow?

....

....

....

Sin to Confess?

....

....

....

Promise to Claim?

....

....

....

Accountability?

....

....

....

Prayer—Spend a minute in prayer asking God to help you apply these truths to your life.

4. **Write and Listen** (10–15 minutes)—Write a letter to God. This can be in response to what He was saying to you through Scripture, or you can write Him about anything that is on your mind.

....

....

....

....

....

....

....

....

....

....

....

....

....

....

....

....

....

....

....

Listen for what God is saying to you. Write a letter to yourself from God with what you believe He is saying in response to you.

....
....
....
....
....
....
....
....
....
....
....
....
....
....
....

5. **Share and Obey** (After devo is completed)—With whom can you share what God spoke to you? If it is direction you received, it is wise to share this with the godly counsel in your life, and if it is revelation or insight, think about who would be encouraged to hear what God has been teaching you and who can hold you accountable to what He spoke.

....
....
....

What steps of obedience or action steps are you going to take?

....
....
....

1. **Time and Place**—When and where did you meet with God?

....

....

....

2. **Be Still and Worship** (5–10 minutes)—Turn on worship music and ask God to help you connect to Him. Start by telling Him how wonderful He is and ask if there is any burden you need to release to Him. After you are finished, write down any impressions, thoughts, or themes you felt during your time of worship.

....

....

....

3. **Read and Pray** (10–15 minutes)—Read the following passage and use the SOAP method and the GOD SPA questions:

"Now faith is confidence in what we hope for and assurance about what we do not see. This is what the ancients were commended for. By faith we understand that the universe was formed at God's command, so that what is seen was not made out of what was visible. By faith Abel brought God a better offering than Cain did. By faith he was commended as righteous, when God spoke well of his offerings. And by faith Abel still speaks, even though he is dead. By faith Enoch was taken from this life, so that he did not experience death: 'He could not be found, because God had taken him away.' For before he was taken, he was commended as one who pleased God. And without faith it is impossible to please God, because anyone who

comes to him must believe that he exists and that he rewards those who earnestly seek him." (Hebrews 11:1–6)

Observation—What stands out to you in this passage?

....
....
....

Application—How can you apply this passage to your life? (You may not have all of these answered for every passage, but it is helpful to ask the following questions.) Is there a/an:

Growth Area?

....
....
....

Obedience Needed?

....
....
....

Direction to Follow?

....
....
....

Sin to Confess?

....
....
....

Promise to Claim?

....
....

Accountability?

....

....

....

Prayer—Spend a minute in prayer asking God to help you apply these truths to your life.

4. **Write and Listen** (10–15 minutes)—Write a letter to God. This can be in response to what He was saying to you through Scripture, or you can write Him about anything that is on your mind.

....

....

....

....

....

....

....

....

....

....

....

....

....

....

....

....

....

....

Listen for what God is saying to you. Write a letter to yourself from God with what you believe He is saying in response to you.

....
....
....
....
....
....
....
....
....
....
....
....
....
....
....

5. **Share and Obey** (After devo is completed)—With whom can you share what God spoke to you? If it is direction you received, it is wise to share this with the godly counsel in your life, and if it is revelation or insight, think about who would be encouraged to hear what God has been teaching you and who can hold you accountable to what He spoke.

....
....
....

What steps of obedience or action steps are you going to take?

....
....
....

1. **Time and Place**—When and where did you meet with God?

....

....

....

2. **Be Still and Worship** (5–10 minutes)—Turn on worship music and ask God to help you connect to Him. Start by telling Him how wonderful He is and ask if there is any burden you need to release to Him. After you are finished, write down any impressions, thoughts, or themes you felt during your time of worship.

....

....

....

....

3. **Read and Pray** (10–15 minutes)—Read the following passage and use the SOAP method and the GOD SPA questions:

> "The Lord is my shepherd; I lack nothing. He makes me lie down in green pastures, He leads me beside quiet waters, He refreshes my soul. He guides me along the right paths for His name's sake. Even though I walk through the darkest valley, I will fear no evil, for you are with me; your rod and your staff, they comfort me. You prepare a table before me in the presence of my enemies. You anoint my head with oil; my cup overflows. Surely your goodness and love will follow me all the days of my life, and I will dwell in the house of the Lord forever." (Psalm 23:1–6)

Observation—What stands out to you in this passage?

....

....

....

....

Application—How can you apply this passage to your life? (You may not have all of these answered for every passage, but it is helpful to ask the following questions.) Is there a/an:

Growth Area?

....

....

....

Obedience Needed?

....

....

....

Direction to Follow?

....

....

....

Sin to Confess?

....

....

....

Promise to Claim?

....

....

....

Accountability?

....

....

....

Prayer—Spend a minute in prayer asking God to help you apply these truths to your life.

4. **Write and Listen** (10–15 minutes)—Write a letter to God. This can be in response to what He was saying to you through Scripture, or you can write Him about anything that is on your mind.

....

....

....

....

....

....

....

....

....

....

....

....

....

....

....

....

....

....

....

Listen for what God is saying to you. Write a letter to yourself from God with what you believe He is saying in response to you.

....
....
....
....
....
....
....
....
....
....
....
....
....

5. Share and Obey (After devo is completed)—With whom can you share what God spoke to you? If it is direction you received, it is wise to share this with the godly counsel in your life, and if it is revelation or insight, think about who would be encouraged to hear what God has been teaching you and who can hold you accountable to what He spoke.

....
....
....

What steps of obedience or action steps are you going to take?

....
....
....

Philippians 4:4–9

1. **Time and Place**—When and where did you meet with God?

....

....

....

2. **Be Still and Worship** (5–10 minutes)—Turn on worship music and ask God to help you connect to Him. Start by telling Him how wonderful He is and ask if there is any burden you need to release to Him. After you are finished, write down any impressions, thoughts, or themes you felt during your time of worship.

....

....

....

3. **Read and Pray** (10–15 minutes)—Read the following passage and use the SOAP method and the GOD SPA questions:

"Rejoice in the Lord always. I will say it again: Rejoice! Let your gentleness be evident to all. The Lord is near. Do not be anxious about anything, but in every situation, by prayer and petition, with thanksgiving, present your requests to God. And the peace of God, which transcends all understanding, will guard your hearts and your minds in Christ Jesus. Finally, brothers and sisters, whatever is true, whatever is noble, whatever is right, whatever is pure, whatever is lovely, whatever is admirable—if anything is excellent or praiseworthy—think about such things. Whatever you have learned or received or heard from me, or seen in me—put it into practice. And the God of peace will be with you." (Philippians 4:4–9)

Observation—What stands out to you in this passage?

....
....
....
....

Application—How can you apply this passage to your life? (You may not have all of these answered for every passage, but it is helpful to ask the following questions.) Is there a/an:

Growth Area?

....
....
....

Obedience Needed?

....
....
....

Direction to Follow?

....
....
....

Sin to Confess?

....
....
....

Promise to Claim?

....
....
....

Accountability?

....

....

....

Prayer—Spend a minute in prayer asking God to help you apply these truths to your life.

4. **Write and Listen** (10–15 minutes)—Write a letter to God. This can be in response to what He was saying to you through Scripture, or you can write Him about anything that is on your mind.

....

....

....

....

....

....

....

....

....

....

....

....

....

....

....

....

....

....

....

Listen for what God is saying to you. Write a letter to yourself from God with what you believe He is saying in response to you.

....
....
....
....
....
....
....
....
....
....
....
....
....
....
....
....

5. **Share and Obey** (After devo is completed)—With whom can you share what God spoke to you? If it is direction you received, it is wise to share this with the godly counsel in your life, and if it is revelation or insight, think about who would be encouraged to hear what God has been teaching you and who can hold you accountable to what He spoke.

....
....
....

What steps of obedience or action steps are you going to take?

....
....
....

1. **Time and Place**—When and where did you meet with God?

....

....

....

2. **Be Still and Worship** (5–10 minutes)—Turn on worship music and ask God to help you connect to Him. Start by telling Him how wonderful He is and ask if there is any burden you need to release to Him. After you are finished, write down any impressions, thoughts, or themes you felt during your time of worship.

....

....

....

3. **Read and Pray** (10–15 minutes)—Read the following passage and use the SOAP method and the GOD SPA questions:

"In the year that King Uzziah died, I saw the Lord, high and exalted, seated on a throne; and the train of his robe filled the temple. Above him were seraphim, each with six wings: With two wings they covered their faces, with two they covered their feet, and with two they were flying. And they were calling to one another: 'Holy, holy, holy is the Lord Almighty; the whole earth is full of His glory.' At the sound of their voices the doorposts and thresholds shook and the temple was filled with smoke. 'Woe to me!' I cried. 'I am ruined! For I am a man of unclean lips, and I live among a people of unclean lips, and my eyes have seen the King, the Lord Almighty.' Then one of the seraphim flew to me with a live coal in his hand, which he had

taken with tongs from the altar. With it he touched my mouth and said, 'See, this has touched your lips; your guilt is taken away and your sin atoned for.' Then I heard the voice of the Lord saying, 'Whom shall I send? And who will go for us?' And I said, 'Here am I. Send me!'" (Isaiah 6:1–8)

Observation—What stands out to you in this passage?

....

....

....

....

Application—How can you apply this passage to your life? (You may not have all of these answered for every passage, but it is helpful to ask the following questions.) Is there a/an:

Growth Area?

....

....

....

Obedience Needed?

....

....

....

Direction to Follow?

....

....

....

Sin to Confess?

....

....

....

Promise to Claim?

....

....

....

Accountability?

....

....

....

Prayer—Spend a minute in prayer asking God to help you apply these truths to your life.

4. **Write and Listen** (10–15 minutes)—Write a letter to God. This can be in response to what He was saying to you through Scripture, or you can write Him about anything that is on your mind.

....

....

....

....

....

....

....

....

....

....

....

....

....

....

....

Listen for what God is saying to you. Write a letter to yourself from God with what you believe He is saying in response to you.

....
....
....
....
....
....
....
....
....
....
....
....
....
....
....
....

5. **Share and Obey** (After devo is completed)—With whom can you share what God spoke to you? If it is direction you received, it is wise to share this with the godly counsel in your life, and if it is revelation or insight, think about who would be encouraged to hear what God has been teaching you and who can hold you accountable to what He spoke.

....
....
....

What steps of obedience or action steps are you going to take?

....
....
....

John 21:4–14

1. **Time and Place**—When and where did you meet with God?

....

....

....

2. **Be Still and Worship** (5–10 minutes)—Turn on worship music and ask God to help you connect to Him. Start by telling Him how wonderful He is and ask if there is any burden you need to release to Him. After you are finished, write down any impressions, thoughts, or themes you felt during your time of worship.

....

....

....

3. **Read and Pray** (10–15 minutes)—Read the following passage and use the SOAP method and the GOD SPA questions:

> "Early in the morning, Jesus stood on the shore, but the disciples did not realize that it was Jesus. He called out to them, 'Friends, haven't you any fish?' 'No,' they answered. He said, 'Throw your net on the right side of the boat and you will find some.' When they did, they were unable to haul the net in because of the large number of fish. Then the disciple whom Jesus loved said to Peter, 'It is the Lord!' As soon as Simon Peter heard him say, 'It is the Lord,' he wrapped his outer garment around him (for he had taken it off) and jumped into the water. The other disciples followed in the boat, towing the net full of fish, for they were not far from shore, about a hundred yards. When they landed, they saw a fire of burning coals there with

fish on it, and some bread. Jesus said to them, 'Bring some of the fish you have just caught.' So Simon Peter climbed back into the boat and dragged the net ashore. It was full of large fish, but even with so many the net was not torn. Jesus said to them, 'Come and have breakfast.' None of the disciples dared ask him, 'Who are you?' They knew it was the Lord. Jesus came, took the bread and gave it to them, and did the same with the fish. This was now the third time Jesus appeared to his disciples after he was raised from the dead." (John 21:4–14)

Observation—What stands out to you in this passage?

....
....
....
....

Application—How can you apply this passage to your life? (You may not have all of these answered for every passage, but it is helpful to ask the following questions.) Is there a/an:

Growth Area?

....
....
....

Obedience Needed?

....
....
....

Direction to Follow?

....
....
....

Sin to Confess?

....

....

....

Promise to Claim?

....

....

....

Accountability?

....

....

....

Prayer—Spend a minute in prayer asking God to help you apply these truths to your life.

4. **Write and Listen** (10–15 minutes)—Write a letter to God. This can be in response to what He was saying to you through Scripture, or you can write Him about anything that is on your mind.

....

....

....

....

....

....

....

....

....

....

....

....

Listen for what God is saying to you. Write a letter to yourself from God with what you believe He is saying in response to you.

....

....

....

....

....

....

....

....

....

....

....

....

....

....

....

....

5. **Share and Obey** (After devo is completed)—With whom can you share what God spoke to you? If it is direction you received, it is wise to share this with the godly counsel in your life, and if it is revelation or insight, think about who would be encouraged to hear what God has been teaching you and who can hold you accountable to what He spoke.

....

....

....

What steps of obedience or action steps are you going to take?

....

....

....

1. **Time and Place**—When and where did you meet with God?

....

....

....

2. **Be Still and Worship** (5–10 minutes)—Turn on worship music and ask God to help you connect to Him. Start by telling Him how wonderful He is and ask if there is any burden you need to release to Him. After you are finished, write down any impressions, thoughts, or themes you felt during your time of worship.

....

....

....

....

3. **Read and Pray** (10–15 minutes)—Read the following passage and use the SOAP method and the GOD SPA questions:

"When Joseph's brothers saw that their father was dead, they said, 'What if Joseph holds a grudge against us and pays us back for all the wrongs we did to him?' So they sent word to Joseph, saying, 'Your father left these instructions before he died: 'This is what you are to say to Joseph: I ask you to forgive your brothers the sins and the wrongs they committed in treating you so badly.' Now please forgive the sins of the servants of the God of your father.' When their message came to him, Joseph wept. His brothers then came and threw themselves down before him. 'We are your slaves,' they said. But Joseph said to them, 'Don't be afraid. Am I in the place of God? You intended to harm me,

but God intended it for good to accomplish what is now being done, the saving of many lives. So then, don't be afraid. I will provide for you and your children.' And he reassured them and spoke kindly to them." (Genesis 50:15–21)

Observation—What stands out to you in this passage?

....

....

....

....

Application—How can you apply this passage to your life? (You may not have all of these answered for every passage, but it is helpful to ask the following questions.) Is there a/an:

Growth Area?

....

....

....

Obedience Needed?

....

....

....

Direction to Follow?

....

....

....

Sin to Confess?

....

....

....

Promise to Claim?

....
....
....

Accountability?

....
....
....

Prayer—Spend a minute in prayer asking God to help you apply these truths to your life.

4. **Write and Listen** (10–15 minutes)—Write a letter to God. This can be in response to what He was saying to you through Scripture or you can write Him about anything that is on your mind.

....
....
....
....
....
....
....
....
....
....
....
....
....
....
....
....
....

Listen for what God is saying to you. Write a letter to yourself from God with what you believe He is saying in response to you.

....
....
....
....
....
....
....
....
....
....
....
....
....
....

5. **Share and Obey** (After devo is completed)—With whom can you share what God spoke to you? If it is direction you received, it is wise to share this with the godly counsel in your life, and if it is revelation or insight, think about who would be encouraged to hear what God has been teaching you and who can hold you accountable to what He spoke.

....
....
....

What steps of obedience or action steps are you going to take?

....
....
....

Romans 12:1–10

1. **Time and Place**—When and where did you meet with God?

....

....

....

2. **Be Still and Worship** (5–10 minutes)—Turn on worship music and ask God to help you connect to Him. Start by telling Him how wonderful He is and ask if there is any burden you need to release to Him. After you are finished, write down any impressions, thoughts, or themes you felt during your time of worship.

....

....

....

3. **Read and Pray** (10–15 minutes)—Read the following passage and use the SOAP method and the GOD SPA questions:

> "Therefore, I urge you, brothers and sisters, in view of God's mercy, to offer your bodies as a living sacrifice, holy and pleasing to God—this is your true and proper worship. Do not conform to the pattern of this world, but be transformed by the renewing of your mind. Then you will be able to test and approve what God's will is—his good, pleasing and perfect will. For by the grace given me I say to every one of you: Do not think of yourself more highly than you ought, but rather think of yourself with sober judgment, in accordance with the faith God has distributed to each of you. For just as each of us has one body with many members, and these members do not all have the same function, so in Christ we, though many, form

one body, and each member belongs to all the others. We have different gifts, according to the grace given to each of us. If your gift is prophesying, then prophesy in accordance with your faith; if it is serving, then serve; if it is teaching, then teach; if it is to encourage, then give encouragement; if it is giving, then give generously; if it is to lead, do it diligently; if it is to show mercy, do it cheerfully. Love must be sincere. Hate what is evil; cling to what is good. Be devoted to one another in love. Honor one another above yourselves." (Romans 12:1–10)

Observation—What stands out to you in this passage?

....

....

....

....

Application—How can you apply this passage to your life? (You may not have all of these answered for every passage, but it is helpful to ask the following questions.) Is there a/an:

Growth Area?

....

....

....

Obedience Needed?

....

....

....

Direction to Follow?

....

....

....

Sin to Confess?

....

....

....

Promise to Claim?

....

....

....

Accountability?

....

....

....

Prayer—Spend a minute in prayer asking God to help you apply these truths to your life.

4. **Write and Listen** (10–15 minutes)—Write a letter to God. This can be in response to what He was saying to you through Scripture, or you can write Him about anything that is on your mind.

....

....

....

....

....

....

....

....

....

....

....

....

....

....

Listen for what God is saying to you. Write a letter to yourself from God with what you believe He is saying in response to you.

....

....

....

....

....

....

....

....

....

....

....

....

....

....

5. **Share and Obey** (After devo is completed)—With whom can you share what God spoke to you? If it is direction you received, it is wise to share this with the godly counsel in your life, and if it is revelation or insight, think about who would be encouraged to hear what God has been teaching you and who can hold you accountable to what He spoke.

....

....

....

What steps of obedience or action steps are you going to take?

....

....

....

1. **Time and Place**—When and where did you meet with God?

....

....

....

2. **Be Still and Worship** (5–10 minutes)—Turn on worship music and ask God to help you connect to Him. Start by telling Him how wonderful He is and ask if there is any burden you need to release to Him. After you are finished, write down any impressions, thoughts, or themes you felt during your time of worship.

....

....

....

3. **Read and Pray** (10–15 minutes)—Read the following passage and use the SOAP method and the GOD SPA questions:

> "The hand of the LORD was on me, and he brought me out by the Spirit of the LORD and set me in the middle of a valley; it was full of bones. He led me back and forth among them, and I saw a great many bones on the floor of the valley, bones that were very dry. He asked me, 'Son of man, can these bones live?' I said, 'Sovereign LORD, you alone know.' Then he said to me, 'Prophesy to these bones and say to them, 'Dry bones, hear the word of the LORD! This is what the Sovereign LORD says to these bones: I will make breath enter you, and you will come to life. I will attach tendons to you and make flesh come upon you and cover you with skin; I will put breath in you, and you will come to life. Then you will know that I am the LORD." So I prophesied

as I was commanded. And as I was prophesying, there was a noise, a rattling sound, and the bones came together, bone to bone. I looked, and tendons and flesh appeared on them and skin covered them, but there was no breath in them. Then he said to me, 'Prophesy to the breath; prophesy, son of man, and say to it, 'This is what the Sovereign LORD says: Come, breath, from the four winds and breathe into these slain, that they may live.'' So I prophesied as he commanded me, and breath entered them; they came to life and stood up on their feet—a vast army. Then he said to me: 'Son of man, these bones are the people of Israel. They say, 'Our bones are dried up and our hope is gone; we are cut off.' Therefore prophesy and say to them: 'This is what the Sovereign LORD says: My people, I am going to open your graves and bring you up from them; I will bring you back to the land of Israel. Then you, my people, will know that I am the LORD, when I open your graves and bring you up from them. I will put my Spirit in you and you will live, and I will settle you in your own land. Then you will know that I the LORD have spoken, and I have done it, declares the LORD.'"
(Ezekiel 37:1–14)

Observation—What stands out to you in this passage?

....

....

....

Application—How can you apply this passage to your life? (You may not have all of these answered for every passage, but it is helpful to ask the following questions.) Is there a/an:

Growth Area?

....

....

....

Obedience Needed?

....
....
....

Direction to Follow?

....
....
....

Sin to Confess?

....
....
....

Promise to Claim?

....
....
....

Accountability?

....
....
....

Prayer—Spend a minute in prayer asking God to help you apply these truths to your life.

4. **Write and Listen** (10–15 minutes)—Write a letter to God. This can be in response to what He was saying to you through Scripture, or you can write Him about anything that is on your mind.

....
....

....
....
....
....
....
....
....
....
....
....
....
....
....
....

Listen for what God is saying to you. Write a letter to yourself from God with what you believe He is saying in response to you.

....
....
....
....
....
....
....
....
....
....
....
....
....
....
....
....

5. **Share and Obey** (After devo is completed)—With whom can you share what God spoke to you? If it is direction you received, it is wise to share this with the godly counsel in your life, and if it is revelation or insight, think about who would be encouraged to hear what God has been teaching you and who can hold you accountable to what He spoke.

....

....

....

What steps of obedience or action steps are you going to take?

....

....

....

2 Corinthians 4:7–18

1. **Time and Place**—When and where did you meet with God?

....

....

....

2. **Be Still and Worship** (5–10 minutes)—Turn on worship music and ask God to help you connect to Him. Start by telling Him how wonderful He is and ask if there is any burden you need to release to Him. After you are finished, write down any impressions, thoughts, or themes you felt during your time of worship.

....

....

....

3. **Read and Pray** (10–15 minutes)—Read the following passage and use the SOAP method and the GOD SPA questions:

"But we have this treasure in jars of clay to show that this all-surpassing power is from God and not from us. We are hard pressed on every side, but not crushed; perplexed, but not in despair; persecuted, but not abandoned; struck down, but not destroyed. We always carry around in our body the death of Jesus, so that the life of Jesus may also be revealed in our body. For we who are alive are always being given over to death for Jesus' sake, so that his life may also be revealed in our mortal body. So then, death is at work in us, but life is at work in you. It is written: 'I believed; therefore I have spoken.' Since we have that same spirit of faith, we also believe and therefore speak, because we know that the one who raised the Lord Jesus from

the dead will also raise us with Jesus and present us with you to himself. All this is for your benefit, so that the grace that is reaching more and more people may cause thanksgiving to overflow to the glory of God. Therefore we do not lose heart. Though outwardly we are wasting away, yet inwardly we are being renewed day by day. For our light and momentary troubles are achieving for us an eternal glory that far outweighs them all. So we fix our eyes not on what is seen, but on what is unseen, since what is seen is temporary, but what is unseen is eternal." (2 Corinthians 4:7–18)

Observation—What stands out to you in this passage?

....

....

....

Application—How can you apply this passage to your life? (You may not have all of these answered for every passage, but it is helpful to ask the following questions.) Is there a/an:

Growth Area?

....

....

....

Obedience Needed?

....

....

....

Direction to Follow?

....

....

....

Sin to Confess?

....

....

....

Promise to Claim?

....

....

....

Accountability?

....

....

....

Prayer—Spend a minute in prayer asking God to help you apply these truths to your life.

4. **Write and Listen** (10–15 minutes)—Write a letter to God. This can be in response to what He was saying to you through Scripture, or you can write Him about anything that is on your mind.

....

....

....

....

....

....

....

....

....

....

....

....

Listen for what God is saying to you. Write a letter to yourself from God with what you believe He is saying in response to you.

....
....
....
....
....
....
....
....
....
....
....
....
....
....
....
....
....

5. **Share and Obey** (After devo is completed)—With whom can you share what God spoke to you? If it is direction you received, it is wise to share this with the godly counsel in your life, and if it is revelation or insight, think about who would be encouraged to hear what God has been teaching you and who can hold you accountable to what He spoke.

....
....
....

What steps of obedience or action steps are you going to take?

....
....
....

Matthew 20:1–16

1. **Time and Place**—When and where did you meet with God?

....
....
....

2. **Be Still and Worship** (5–10 minutes)—Turn on worship music and ask God to help you connect to Him. Start by telling Him how wonderful He is and ask if there is any burden you need to release to Him. After you are finished, write down any impressions, thoughts, or themes you felt during your time of worship.

....
....
....

3. **Read and Pray** (10–15 minutes)—Read the following passage and use the SOAP method and the GOD SPA questions:

"For the kingdom of heaven is like a landowner who went out early in the morning to hire workers for his vineyard. He agreed to pay them a denarius for the day and sent them into his vineyard. About nine in the morning he went out and saw others standing in the marketplace doing nothing. He told them, 'You also go and work in my vineyard, and I will pay you whatever is right.' So they went. He went out again about noon and about three in the afternoon and did the same thing. About five in the afternoon he went out and found still others standing around. He asked them, 'Why have you been standing here all day long doing nothing?' 'Because no one has hired us,' they answered. He said to them, 'You also go and work in my vineyard.' When

evening came, the owner of the vineyard said to his foreman, 'Call the workers and pay them their wages, beginning with the last ones hired and going on to the first.' The workers who were hired about five in the afternoon came and each received a denarius. So when those came who were hired first, they expected to receive more. But each one of them also received a denarius. When they received it, they began to grumble against the landowner. 'These who were hired last worked only one hour,' they said, 'and you have made them equal to us who have borne the burden of the work and the heat of the day.' But he answered one of them, 'I am not being unfair to you, friend. Didn't you agree to work for a denarius? Take your pay and go. I want to give the one who was hired last the same as I gave you. Don't I have the right to do what I want with my own money? Or are you envious because I am generous?' So the last will be first, and the first will be last." (Matthew 20:1–16)

Observation—What stands out to you in this passage?

....
....
....
....
....
....
....

Application—How can you apply this passage to your life? (You may not have all of these answered for every passage, but it is helpful to ask the following questions.) Is there a/an:

Growth Area?

....
....
....

Obedience Needed?

....

....

....

Direction to Follow?

....

....

....

Sin to Confess?

....

....

....

Promise to Claim?

....

....

....

Accountability?

....

....

....

Prayer—Spend a minute in prayer asking God to help you apply these truths to your life.

4. **Write and Listen** (10–15 minutes)—Write a letter to God. This can be in response to what He was saying to you through Scripture, or you can write Him about anything that is on your mind.

....

....

....
....
....
....
....
....
....
....
....
....
....
....
....
....

Listen for what God is saying to you. Write a letter to yourself from God with what you believe He is saying in response to you.

....
....
....
....
....
....
....
....
....
....
....
....
....
....
....
....

5. **Share and Obey** (After devo is completed)—With whom can you share what God spoke to you? If it is direction you received, it is wise to share this with the godly counsel in your life, and if it is revelation or insight, think about who would be encouraged to hear what God has been teaching you and who can hold you accountable to what He spoke.

....

....

....

What steps of obedience or action steps are you going to take?

....

....

....

1. **Time and Place**—When and where did you meet with God?

....

....

....

2. **Be Still and Worship** (5–10 minutes)—Turn on worship music and ask God to help you connect to Him. Start by telling Him how wonderful He is and ask if there is any burden you need to release to Him. After you are finished, write down any impressions, thoughts, or themes you felt during your time of worship.

....

....

....

3. **Read and Pray** (10–15 minutes)—Read the following passage and use the SOAP method and the GOD SPA questions:

> "Elijah went before the people and said, 'How long will you waver between two opinions? If the LORD is God, follow him; but if Baal is God, follow him.' But the people said nothing. Then Elijah said to them, 'I am the only one of the LORD's prophets left, but Baal has four hundred and fifty prophets. Get two bulls for us. Let Baal's prophets choose one for themselves, and let them cut it into pieces and put it on the wood but not set fire to it. I will prepare the other bull and put it on the wood but not set fire to it. Then you call on the name of your god, and I will call on the name of the LORD. The god who answers by fire—he is God.' Then all the people said, 'What you say is good.' Elijah said to the prophets of Baal, 'Choose one of the

bulls and prepare it first, since there are so many of you. Call on the name of your god, but do not light the fire.' So they took the bull given them and prepared it. Then they called on the name of Baal from morning till noon. 'Baal, answer us!' they shouted. But there was no response; no one answered. And they danced around the altar they had made. At noon Elijah began to taunt them. 'Shout louder!' he said. 'Surely he is a god! Perhaps he is deep in thought, or busy, or traveling. Maybe he is sleeping and must be awakened.' So they shouted louder and slashed themselves with swords and spears, as was their custom, until their blood flowed. Midday passed, and they continued their frantic prophesying until the time for the evening sacrifice. But there was no response, no one answered, no one paid attention. Then Elijah said to all the people, 'Come here to me.' They came to him, and he repaired the altar of the LORD, which had been torn down. Elijah took twelve stones, one for each of the tribes descended from Jacob, to whom the word of the LORD had come, saying, 'Your name shall be Israel.' With the stones he built an altar in the name of the LORD, and he dug a trench around it large enough to hold two seahs of seed. He arranged the wood, cut the bull into pieces and laid it on the wood. Then he said to them, 'Fill four large jars with water and pour it on the offering and on the wood.' 'Do it again,' he said, and they did it again. 'Do it a third time," he ordered, and they did it the third time. The water ran down around the altar and even filled the trench. At the time of sacrifice, the prophet Elijah stepped forward and prayed: 'LORD, the God of Abraham, Isaac and Israel, let it be known today that you are God in Israel and that I am your servant and have done all these things at your command. Answer me, LORD, answer me, so these people will know that you, LORD, are God, and that you are turning their hearts back again.' Then the fire of the LORD fell and burned up the sacrifice, the wood, the stones and the soil, and also licked up the water

in the trench. When all the people saw this, they fell prostrate and cried, 'The Lord—he is God! The Lord—he is God!'" (I Kings 18:21–39)

Observation—What stands out to you in this passage?

....

....

....

....

....

Application—How can you apply this passage to your life? (You may not have all of these answered for every passage, but it is helpful to ask the following questions.) Is there a/an:

Growth Area?

....

....

....

Obedience Needed?

....

....

....

Direction to Follow?

....

....

....

Sin to Confess?

....

....

....

Promise to Claim?

....

....

....

Accountability?

....

....

....

Prayer—Spend a minute in prayer asking God to help you apply these truths to your life.

4. **Write and Listen** (10–15 minutes)—Write a letter to God. This can be in response to what He was saying to you through Scripture, or you can write Him about anything that is on your mind.

....

....

....

....

....

....

....

....

....

....

....

....

....

....

Listen for what God is saying to you. Write a letter to yourself from God with what you believe He is saying in response to you.

....
....
....
....
....
....
....
....
....
....
....
....
....
....
....
....
....

5. **Share and Obey** (After devo is completed)—With whom can you share what God spoke to you? If it is direction you received, it is wise to share this with the godly counsel in your life, and if it is revelation or insight, think about who would be encouraged to hear what God has been teaching you and who can hold you accountable to what He spoke.

....
....
....

What steps of obedience or action steps are you going to take?

....
....
....

John 13:1–16

1. **Time and Place**—When and where did you meet with God?

....

....

....

2. **Be Still and Worship** (5–10 minutes)—Turn on worship music and ask God to help you connect to Him. Start by telling Him how wonderful He is and ask if there is any burden you need to release to Him. After you are finished, write down any impressions, thoughts, or themes you felt during your time of worship.

....

....

....

3. **Read and Pray** (10–15 minutes)—Read the following passage and use the SOAP method and the GOD SPA questions:

"It was just before the Passover Festival. Jesus knew that the hour had come for him to leave this world and go to the Father. Having loved his own who were in the world, he loved them to the end. The evening meal was in progress, and the devil had already prompted Judas, the son of Simon Iscariot, to betray Jesus. Jesus knew that the Father had put all things under his power, and that he had come from God and was returning to God; so he got up from the meal, took off his outer clothing, and wrapped a towel around his waist. After that, he poured water into a basin and began to wash his disciples' feet, drying them with the towel that was wrapped around him. He came to Simon Peter, who said to him, 'Lord, are you going to wash my

feet?' Jesus replied, 'You do not realize now what I am doing, but later you will understand.' 'No,' said Peter, 'you shall never wash my feet.' Jesus answered, 'Unless I wash you, you have no part with me.' 'Then, Lord,' Simon Peter replied, 'not just my feet but my hands and my head as well!' Jesus answered, 'Those who have had a bath need only to wash their feet; their whole body is clean. And you are clean, though not every one of you.' For he knew who was going to betray him, and that was why he said not every one was clean. When he had finished washing their feet, he put on his clothes and returned to his place. 'Do you understand what I have done for you?' he asked them. 'You call me "Teacher" and "Lord," and rightly so, for that is what I am. Now that I, your Lord and Teacher, have washed your feet, you also should wash one another's feet. I have set you an example that you should do as I have done for you. Very truly I tell you, no servant is greater than his master, nor is a messenger greater than the one who sent him.'" (John 13:1–16)

Observation—What stands out to you in this passage?

....
....
....
....
....
....

Application—How can you apply this passage to your life? (You may not have all of these answered for every passage, but it is helpful to ask the following questions.) Is there a/an:

Growth Area?

....
....
....

Obedience Needed?

....
....
....

Direction to Follow?

....
....
....

Sin to Confess?

....
....
....

Promise to Claim?

....
....
....

Accountability?

....
....
....

Prayer—Spend a minute in prayer asking God to help you apply these truths to your life.

4. **Write and Listen** (10–15 minutes)—Write a letter to God. This can be in response to what He was saying to you through Scripture, or you can write Him about anything that is on your mind.

....
....
....

Listen for what God is saying to you. Write a letter to yourself from God with what you believe He is saying in response to you.

5. **Share and Obey** (After devo is completed)—With whom can you share what God spoke to you? If it is direction you received, it is wise to share this with the godly counsel in your life, and if it is revelation or insight, think about who would be encouraged to hear what God has been teaching you and who can hold you accountable to what He spoke.

....
....
....

What steps of obedience or action steps are you going to take?

....
....
....

Daniel 3:13–29

1. Time and Place—When and where did you meet with God?

....

....

....

2. Be Still and Worship (5–10 minutes)—Turn on worship music and ask God to help you connect to Him. Start by telling Him how wonderful He is and ask if there is any burden you need to release to Him. After you are finished, write down any impressions, thoughts, or themes you felt during your time of worship.

....

....

....

3. Read and Pray (10–15 minutes)—Read the following passage and use the SOAP method and the GOD SPA questions:

"Furious with rage, Nebuchadnezzar summoned Shadrach, Meshach and Abednego. So these men were brought before the king, and Nebuchadnezzar said to them, 'Is it true, Shadrach, Meshach and Abednego, that you do not serve my gods or worship the image of gold I have set up? Now when you hear the sound of the horn, flute, zither, lyre, harp, pipe and all kinds of music, if you are ready to fall down and worship the image I made, very good. But if you do not worship it, you will be thrown immediately into a blazing furnace. Then what god will be able to rescue you from my hand?' Shadrach, Meshach and Abednego replied to him, 'King Nebuchadnezzar, we do not need to defend ourselves before you in this matter. If we

are thrown into the blazing furnace, the God we serve is able to deliver us from it, and he will deliver us from Your Majesty's hand. But even if he does not, we want you to know, Your Majesty, that we will not serve your gods or worship the image of gold you have set up.' Then Nebuchadnezzar was furious with Shadrach, Meshach and Abednego, and his attitude toward them changed. He ordered the furnace heated seven times hotter than usual and commanded some of the strongest soldiers in his army to tie up Shadrach, Meshach and Abednego and throw them into the blazing furnace. So these men, wearing their robes, trousers, turbans and other clothes, were bound and thrown into the blazing furnace. The king's command was so urgent and the furnace so hot that the flames of the fire killed the soldiers who took up Shadrach, Meshach and Abednego, and these three men, firmly tied, fell into the blazing furnace. Then King Nebuchadnezzar leaped to his feet in amazement and asked his advisers, 'Weren't there three men that we tied up and threw into the fire?' They replied, 'Certainly, Your Majesty.' He said, 'Look! I see four men walking around in the fire, unbound and unharmed, and the fourth looks like a son of the gods.' Nebuchadnezzar then approached the opening of the blazing furnace and shouted, 'Shadrach, Meshach and Abednego, servants of the Most High God, come out! Come here!' So Shadrach, Meshach and Abednego came out of the fire, and the satraps, prefects, governors and royal advisers crowded around them. They saw that the fire had not harmed their bodies, nor was a hair of their heads singed; their robes were not scorched, and there was no smell of fire on them. Then Nebuchadnezzar said, 'Praise be to the God of Shadrach, Meshach and Abednego, who has sent his angel and rescued his servants! They trusted in him and defied the king's command and were willing to give up their lives rather than serve or worship any god except their own God. Therefore I decree that the people

of any nation or language who say anything against the God of Shadrach, Meshach and Abednego be cut into pieces and their houses be turned into piles of rubble, for no other god can save in this way.'" (Daniel 3:13–29)

Observation—What stands out to you in this passage?

....
....
....
....
....

Application—How can you apply this passage to your life? (You may not have all of these answered for every passage, but it is helpful to ask the following questions.) Is there a/an:

Growth Area?

....
....
....

Obedience Needed?

....
....
....

Direction to Follow?

....
....
....

Sin to Confess?

....
....
....

Promise to Claim?

....

....

....

Accountability?

....

....

....

Prayer—Spend a minute in prayer asking God to help you apply these truths to your life.

4. **Write and Listen** (10–15 minutes)—Write a letter to God. This can be in response to what He was saying to you through Scripture, or you can write Him about anything that is on your mind.

....

....

....

....

....

....

....

....

....

....

....

....

....

....

....

....

....

....

Listen for what God is saying to you. Write a letter to yourself from God with what you believe He is saying in response to you.

....
....
....
....
....
....
....
....
....
....
....
....
....
....
....
....
....

5. **Share and Obey** (After devo is completed)—With whom can you share what God spoke to you? If it is direction you received, it is wise to share this with the godly counsel in your life, and if it is revelation or insight, think about who would be encouraged to hear what God has been teaching you and who can hold you accountable to what He spoke.

....
....
....

What steps of obedience or action steps are you going to take?

....
....
....

1. **Time and Place**—When and where did you meet with God?

....

....

....

2. **Be Still and Worship** (5–10 minutes)—Turn on worship music and ask God to help you connect to Him. Start by telling Him how wonderful He is and ask if there is any burden you need to release to Him. After you are finished, write down any impressions, thoughts, or themes you felt during your time of worship.

....

....

....

3. **Read and Pray** (10–15 minutes)—Read the following passage and use the SOAP method and the GOD SPA questions:

> "Finally Pilate handed him over to them to be crucified. So the soldiers took charge of Jesus. Carrying his own cross, he went out to the place of the Skull (which in Aramaic is called Golgotha). There they crucified him, and with him two others—one on each side and Jesus in the middle. Pilate had a notice prepared and fastened to the cross. It read: JESUS OF NAZARETH, THE KING OF THE JEWS. Many of the Jews read this sign, for the place where Jesus was crucified was near the city, and the sign was written in Aramaic, Latin and Greek. The chief priests of the Jews protested to Pilate, 'Do not write 'The King of the Jews,' but that this man claimed to be king of the Jews.' Pilate answered, 'What I have written, I have written.' When the sol-

diers crucified Jesus, they took his clothes, dividing them into four shares, one for each of them, with the undergarment remaining. This garment was seamless, woven in one piece from top to bottom. 'Let's not tear it,' they said to one another. 'Let's decide by lot who will get it.' This happened that the scripture might be fulfilled that said, 'They divided my clothes among them and cast lots for my garment.' So this is what the soldiers did. Near the cross of Jesus stood his mother, his mother's sister, Mary the wife of Clopas, and Mary Magdalene. When Jesus saw his mother there, and the disciple whom he loved standing nearby, he said to her, 'Woman, here is your son,' and to the disciple, 'Here is your mother.' From that time on, this disciple took her into his home. Later, knowing that everything had now been finished, and so that Scripture would be fulfilled, Jesus said, 'I am thirsty.' A jar of wine vinegar was there, so they soaked a sponge in it, put the sponge on a stalk of the hyssop plant, and lifted it to Jesus' lips. When he had received the drink, Jesus said, 'It is finished.' With that, he bowed his head and gave up his spirit." (John 19:16–30)

Observation—What stands out to you in this passage?

....
....
....
....

Application—How can you apply this passage to your life? (You may not have all of these answered for every passage, but it is helpful to ask the following questions.) Is there a/an:

Growth Area?

....
....
....

Obedience Needed?

....

....

....

Direction to Follow?

....

....

....

Sin to Confess?

....

....

....

Promise to Claim?

....

....

....

Accountability?

....

....

....

Prayer—Spend a minute in prayer asking God to help you apply these truths to your life.

4. **Write and Listen** (10–15 minutes)—Write a letter to God. This can be in response to what He was saying to you through Scripture, or you can write Him about anything that is on your mind.

....

....

....

....

....

....

....

....

....

....

....

....

....

....

....

....

....

Listen for what God is saying to you. Write a letter to yourself from God with what you believe He is saying in response to you.

....

....

....

....

....

....

....

....

....

....

....

....

....

....

....

5. **Share and Obey** (After devo is completed)—With whom can you share what God spoke to you? If it is direction you received, it is wise to share this with the godly counsel in your life, and if it is revelation or insight, think about who would be encouraged to hear what God has been teaching you and who can hold you accountable to what He spoke.

....

....

....

What steps of obedience or action steps are you going to take?

....

....

....

1. **Time and Place**—When and where did you meet with God?

....

....

....

2. **Be Still and Worship** (5–10 minutes)—Turn on worship music and ask God to help you connect to Him. Start by telling Him how wonderful He is and ask if there is any burden you need to release to Him. After you are finished, write down any impressions, thoughts, or themes you felt during your time of worship.

....

....

....

3. **Read and Pray** (10–15 minutes)—Read the following passage and use the SOAP method and the GOD SPA questions:

"The LORD said to Samuel, 'How long will you mourn for Saul, since I have rejected him as king over Israel? Fill your horn with oil and be on your way; I am sending you to Jesse of Bethlehem. I have chosen one of his sons to be king.' But Samuel said, 'How can I go? If Saul hears about it, he will kill me.' The LORD said, 'Take a heifer with you and say, 'I have come to sacrifice to the LORD.' Invite Jesse to the sacrifice, and I will show you what to do. You are to anoint for me the one I indicate.' Samuel did what the LORD said. When he arrived at Bethlehem, the elders of the town trembled when they met him. They asked, 'Do you come in peace?' Samuel replied, 'Yes, in peace; I have come to sacrifice to the LORD. Consecrate yourselves and come to the

sacrifice with me.' Then he consecrated Jesse and his sons and invited them to the sacrifice. When they arrived, Samuel saw Eliab and thought, 'Surely the LORD's anointed stands here before the LORD.' But the LORD said to Samuel, 'Do not consider his appearance or his height, for I have rejected him. The LORD does not look at the things people look at. People look at the outward appearance, but the LORD looks at the heart.' Then Jesse called Abinadab and had him pass in front of Samuel. But Samuel said, 'The LORD has not chosen this one either.' Jesse then had Shammah pass by, but Samuel said, 'Nor has the LORD chosen this one.' Jesse had seven of his sons pass before Samuel, but Samuel said to him, 'The LORD has not chosen these.' So he asked Jesse, 'Are these all the sons you have?' 'There is still the youngest,' Jesse answered. 'He is tending the sheep.' Samuel said, 'Send for him; we will not sit down until he arrives.' So he sent for him and had him brought in. He was glowing with health and had a fine appearance and handsome features. Then the LORD said, 'Rise and anoint him; this is the one.' So Samuel took the horn of oil and anointed him in the presence of his brothers, and from that day on the Spirit of the LORD came powerfully upon David. Samuel then went to Ramah." (I Samuel 16:1–13)

Observation—What stands out to you in this passage?

....

....

....

Application—How can you apply this passage to your life? (You may not have all of these answered for every passage, but it is helpful to ask the following questions.) Is there a/an:

Growth Area?

....

....

Obedience Needed?

....
....
....

Direction to Follow?

....
....
....

Sin to Confess?

....
....
....

Promise to Claim?

....
....
....

Accountability?

....
....
....

Prayer—Spend a minute in prayer asking God to help you apply these truths to your life.

4. **Write and Listen** (10–15 minutes)—Write a letter to God. This can be in response to what He was saying to you through Scripture, or you can write Him about anything that is on your mind.

....
....
....

....
....
....
....
....
....
....
....
....
....
....
....
....

Listen for what God is saying to you. Write a letter to yourself from God with what you believe He is saying in response to you.

....
....
....
....
....
....
....
....
....
....
....
....
....
....
....
....

5. **Share and Obey** (After devo is completed)—With whom can you share what God spoke to you? If it is direction you received, it is wise to share this with the godly counsel in your life, and if it is revelation or insight, think about who would be encouraged to hear what God has been teaching you and who can hold you accountable to what He spoke.

....
....
....

What steps of obedience or action steps are you going to take?

....
....
....

Matthew 28:1–20

1. **Time and Place**—When and where did you meet with God?

....

....

....

2. **Be Still and Worship** (5–10 minutes)—Turn on worship music and ask God to help you connect to Him. Start by telling Him how wonderful He is and ask if there is any burden you need to release to Him. After you are finished, write down any impressions, thoughts, or themes you felt during your time of worship.

....

....

....

3. **Read and Pray** (10–15 minutes)—Read the following passage and use the SOAP method and the GOD SPA questions:

"After the Sabbath, at dawn on the first day of the week, Mary Magdalene and the other Mary went to look at the tomb. There was a violent earthquake, for an angel of the Lord came down from heaven and, going to the tomb, rolled back the stone and sat on it. His appearance was like lightning, and his clothes were white as snow. The guards were so afraid of him that they shook and became like dead men. The angel said to the women, 'Do not be afraid, for I know that you are looking for Jesus, who was crucified. He is not here; he has risen, just as he said. Come and see the place where he lay. Then go quickly and tell his disciples: 'He has risen from the dead and is going ahead of you into Galilee. There you will see him.' Now I have

told you.' So the women hurried away from the tomb, afraid yet filled with joy, and ran to tell his disciples. Suddenly Jesus met them. 'Greetings,' he said. They came to him, clasped his feet and worshiped him. Then Jesus said to them, 'Do not be afraid. Go and tell my brothers to go to Galilee; there they will see me.' While the women were on their way, some of the guards went into the city and reported to the chief priests everything that had happened. When the chief priests had met with the elders and devised a plan, they gave the soldiers a large sum of money, telling them, 'You are to say, "His disciples came during the night and stole him away while we were asleep." If this report gets to the governor, we will satisfy him and keep you out of trouble.' So the soldiers took the money and did as they were instructed. And this story has been widely circulated among the Jews to this very day. Then the eleven disciples went to Galilee, to the mountain where Jesus had told them to go. When they saw him, they worshiped him; but some doubted. Then Jesus came to them and said, 'All authority in heaven and on earth has been given to me. Therefore go and make disciples of all nations, baptizing them in the name of the Father and of the Son and of the Holy Spirit, and teaching them to obey everything I have commanded you. And surely I am with you always, to the very end of the age.'" (Matthew 28:1–20)

Observation—What stands out to you in this passage?

....
....
....
....
....
....
....
....

Application—How can you apply this passage to your life? (You may not have all of these answered for every passage, but it is helpful to ask the following questions). Is there a/an:

Growth Area?

....

....

....

Obedience Needed?

....

....

....

Direction to Follow?

....

....

....

Sin to Confess?

....

....

....

Promise to Claim?

....

....

....

Accountability?

....

....

....

Prayer—Spend a minute in prayer asking God to help you apply these truths to your life.

4. **Write and Listen** (10–15 minutes)—Write a letter to God. This can be in response to what He was saying to you through Scripture, or you can write Him about anything that is on your mind.

....
....
....
....
....
....
....
....
....
....
....
....
....
....
....

Listen for what God is saying to you. Write a letter to yourself from God with what you believe He is saying in response to you.

....
....
....
....
....
....
....

....
....
....
....
....
....
....
....
....

5. **Share and Obey** (After devo is completed)—With whom can you share what God spoke to you? If it is direction you received, it is wise to share this with the godly counsel in your life, and if it is revelation or insight, think about who would be encouraged to hear what God has been teaching you and who can hold you accountable to what He spoke.

....
....
....

What steps of obedience or action steps are you going to take?

....
....
....

1. **Time and Place**—When and where did you meet with God?

....

....

....

2. **Be Still and Worship** (5–10 minutes)—Turn on worship music and ask God to help you connect to Him. Start by telling Him how wonderful He is and ask if there is any burden you need to release to Him. After you are finished, write down any impressions, thoughts, or themes you felt during your time of worship.

....

....

....

3. **Read and Pray** (10–15 minutes)—Read the following passage and use the SOAP method and the GOD SPA questions:

"David asked, 'Is there anyone still left of the house of Saul to whom I can show kindness for Jonathan's sake?' Now there was a servant of Saul's household named Ziba. They summoned him to appear before David, and the king said to him, 'Are you Ziba?' 'At your service,' he replied. The king asked, 'Is there no one still alive from the house of Saul to whom I can show God's kindness?' Ziba answered the king, 'There is still a son of Jonathan; he is lame in both feet.' 'Where is he?' the king asked. Ziba answered, 'He is at the house of Makir son of Ammiel in Lo Debar.' So King David had him brought from Lo Debar, from the house of Makir son of Ammiel. When Mephibosheth son of Jonathan, the son of Saul, came to David, he

bowed down to pay him honor. David said, 'Mephibosheth!' 'At your service,' he replied. 'Don't be afraid,' David said to him, 'for I will surely show you kindness for the sake of your father Jonathan. I will restore to you all the land that belonged to your grandfather Saul, and you will always eat at my table.' Mephibosheth bowed down and said, 'What is your servant, that you should notice a dead dog like me?' Then the king summoned Ziba, Saul's steward, and said to him, 'I have given your master's grandson everything that belonged to Saul and his family. You and your sons and your servants are to farm the land for him and bring in the crops, so that your master's grandson may be provided for. And Mephibosheth, grandson of your master, will always eat at my table.' (Now Ziba had fifteen sons and twenty servants.) Then Ziba said to the king, 'Your servant will do whatever my lord the king commands his servant to do.' So Mephibosheth ate at David's table like one of the king's sons. Mephibosheth had a young son named Mika, and all the members of Ziba's household were servants of Mephibosheth. And Mephibosheth lived in Jerusalem, because he always ate at the king's table; he was lame in both feet." (2 Samuel 9:1–13)

Observation—What stands out to you in this passage?

....

....

....

Application—How can you apply this passage to your life? (You may not have all of these answered for every passage, but it is helpful to ask the following questions). Is there a/an:

Growth Area?

....

....

....

Obedience Needed?

....

....

....

Direction to Follow?

....

....

....

Sin to Confess?

....

....

....

Promise to Claim?

....

....

....

Accountability?

....

....

....

Prayer—Spend a minute in prayer asking God to help you apply these truths to your life.

4. **Write and Listen** (10–15 minutes)—Write a letter to God. This can be in response to what He was saying to you through Scripture or you can write Him about anything that is on your mind.

....

....

....

....

....

....

....

....

....

....

....

....

....

....

....

Listen for what God is saying to you. Write a letter to yourself from God with what you believe He is saying in response to you.

....

....

....

....

....

....

....

....

....

....

....

....

....

....

....

....

5. **Share and Obey** (After devo is completed)—With whom can you share what God spoke to you? If it is direction you received, it is wise to share this with the godly counsel in your life, and if it is revelation or insight, think about who would be encouraged to hear what God has been teaching you and who can hold you accountable to what He spoke.

....

....

....

What steps of obedience or action steps are you going to take?

....

....

....

1. **Time and Place**—When and where did you meet with God?

....

....

....

2. **Be Still and Worship** (5–10 minutes)—Turn on worship music and ask God to help you connect to Him. Start by telling Him how wonderful He is and ask if there is any burden you need to release to Him. After you are finished, write down any impressions, thoughts, or themes you felt during your time of worship.

....

....

....

3. **Read and Pray** (10–15 minutes)—Read the following passage and use the SOAP method and the GOD SPA questions:

"Then I saw 'a new heaven and a new earth,' for the first heaven and the first earth had passed away, and there was no longer any sea. I saw the Holy City, the new Jerusalem, coming down out of heaven from God, prepared as a bride beautifully dressed for her husband. And I heard a loud voice from the throne saying, 'Look! God's dwelling place is now among the people, and he will dwell with them. They will be his people, and God himself will be with them and be their God. He will wipe every tear from their eyes. There will be no more death or mourning or crying or pain, for the old order of things has passed away.' He who was seated on the throne said, 'I am making everything new!' Then he said, 'Write this down, for these words are trust-

worthy and true.' He said to me: 'It is done. I am the Alpha and the Omega, the Beginning and the End. To the thirsty I will give water without cost from the spring of the water of life. Those who are victorious will inherit all this, and I will be their God and they will be my children.'" (Revelation 21:1–7)

Observation—What stands out to you in this passage?

....

....

....

....

Application—How can you apply this passage to your life? (You may not have all of these answered for every passage, but it is helpful to ask the following questions.) Is there a/an:

Growth Area?

....

....

....

Obedience Needed?

....

....

....

Direction to Follow?

....

....

....

Sin to Confess?

....

....

....

Promise to Claim?

....

....

....

Accountability?

....

....

....

Prayer—Spend a minute in prayer asking God to help you apply these truths to your life.

4. **Write and Listen** (10–15 minutes)—Write a letter to God. This can be in response to what He was saying to you through Scripture, or you can write Him about anything that is on your mind.

....

....

....

....

....

....

....

....

....

....

....

....

....

....

....

....

Listen for what God is saying to you. Write a letter to yourself from God with what you believe He is saying in response to you.

....
....
....
....
....
....
....
....
....
....
....
....
....
....
....
....
....

5. **Share and Obey** (After devo is completed)—With whom can you share what God spoke to you? If it is direction you received, it is wise to share this with the godly counsel in your life, and if it is revelation or insight, think about who would be encouraged to hear what God has been teaching you and who can hold you accountable to what He spoke.

....
....
....

What steps of obedience or action steps are you going to take?

....
....
....

Acknowledgments

I would first and foremost like to thank **Jesus**. In the past twenty years of walking with You, I have learned there is no more worthwhile pursuit than knowing You and following Your voice. I am who I am because of You.

I would also like to thank:

Taryn—From the first time I met you and you told me that you wanted to "do something great for God," I knew you were the one I wanted with me on this journey. You have helped me become a better man, a better leader, and a better father. After fourteen years of marriage, I am even more in love with you, and I believe we are about to walk into our best season as we continue to follow God's voice together.

Isaac, Josiah, Asher, and Karis—I pray that you, too, will walk in this adventure of learning to hear and follow God's voice. You are my favorite legacy, and I can't wait to see what God does through each of your lives as you say yes to Him. I love you so much!

My parents—Dad, I watched you kneel beside your bed every night modeling a life of prayer, and, Mom, your love for God and for me helped me find Him. I would not be who I am today without both of your influences or the godly legacy you passed down to me.

My grandfather—I watched you study your Bible, while I studied your life, and you made me want to know the God that you knew. You taught me about hearing the voice of God and in many ways inspired the journey that led to this book. I can't wait to see you again.

Julie Reams—Thank you for all your help with every step of the journey toward my first book becoming published. You became my Baruch

(Jeremiah 36:32) as my scribe and editor, but, most important, as my friend. Your friendship is such a gift to Taryn and me.

Lisa Stilwell and the team at Howard Books—Thank you for believing in this message and for helping expand its reach. I appreciate your invaluable partnership.

Cassie Hanjian—Thank you for being an amazing literary agent and a champion for this message. I appreciate all your wisdom and help with the editing and publishing process.

DC Metro Launch Team—Thanks for following the voice of the Lord to embark upon the adventure of planting DC Metro Church with Taryn and me. We appreciate your support and belief in the vision before it was a reality more than you know.

DC Metro staff and family—We would not be where we are today if you had not chosen to invest your lives in this vision of building a God-first culture throughout the D.C. metro area. We are thankful for each of you, and we are excited to follow God's voice with you!

DC Metro Lead Team—It is an honor to do life and ministry with each of you. Leading the church with you has become a fun and fulfilling adventure. We are definitely better together.

Notes

Part One: Contact

1. "Americans Feel Connected to Jesus," Barna Group, published April 25, 2010, www.barna.org/barna-update/culture/364-americans-feel-connected-to-jesus#.Va_CtIr3anN.

2. Amos 3:7 (New King James Version).

3. Frank C. Laubach, *Channels of Spiritual Power* (New York: Fleming H. Revell Co., 1954), 92.

4. Exodus 29:42 (New Living Translation).

5. Lauren Morello, et al., "Obama Plays Scientific Favourites," *Nature*, April 11, 2013, www.nature.com/news/obama-plays-scientific-favourites-1.12787.

6. Albert Einstein quote, accessed April 7, 2016, www.quotes.net/quote/9306.

Part Two: The Practical Science of Hearing from God

Chapter One: Questions

1. Sylvia Earle quote, accessed October 20, 2014, www.brainyquote.com/quotes/authors/s/sylvia_earle.html.

2. Thomas Berger quote, retrieved October 20, 2014, www.brainyquote.com/quotes/authors/t/thomas_berger.html.

3. Philip Yancey, *Reaching for the Invisible God: What Can We Expect to Find?* (Grand Rapids, MI: Zondervan Publishing Company, 2000).

4. Timothy Keller quote, www.thegospelcoalition.org/article/20-quotes-from-tim-kellers-new-book-on-prayer.

5. Gerhard Freidrich, ed., *Theological Dictionary of the New Testament. vol. 5* (Grand Rapids: Wm. B. Eerdmans Publishing Company, 1967), 774–75.

6. Thoralf Gilbrant, ed., *The New Testament Greek-English Dictionary* (Springfield: The Complete Bible Library Co., 1986), 630.

7. Ibid., 385.

Chapter Two: Research

1. Albert Szent-Gyorgyi quote, http://thinkexist.com/quotes/albert_szent-gyorgyi/.

2. Carl Sagan quote, http://thinkexist.com/quotation/somewhere-something_incredible_is_waiting_to_be/154069.html.

3. 2 Timothy 2:15 (King James Version).

4. Ibid.

5. A. W. Tozer, *The Pursuit of God* (Harrisburg, PA: Christian Publications, 1948), 10.

6. Devotions & Journaling, www.enewhope.org/nextsteps/journaling/.

Chapter Three: Constructing and Testing the Hypothesis

1. Enrico Fermi quote, retrieved October 29, 2014, www.brainyquote.com/quotes/authors/e/enrico_fermi.html.

2. Proverbs 12:15 (New King James Version).

3. Proverbs 11:14 (New King James Version).

4. Peter Haas, Q&A, http://substancechurch.com/wp-content/uploads/2016/03/QA-ChurchSize2016.pdf.

5. *Forrest Gump*, directed by Robert Zemeckis, 1994, Paramount Pictures.

6. Larry Crabb, *The Safest Place on Earth.* (Nashville: Thomas Nelson Publishing, 1999), 22.

7. C. S. Lewis, *Letters to Malcolm: Chiefly on Prayer.* (New York: Harcourt, Brace & World, 1964), 93.

8. C. S. Lewis quote, www.goodreads.com/quotes/183419-in-friendship-we-think-we-have-chosen-our-peers-in-reality.

Chapter Four: Analysis and Conclusion

1. Milton Friedman quote, www.brainyquote.com/quotes/authors/m/milton_friedman.html#DQzdzAc8qgiLPLMf.99.

2. Thomas Edison quote, https://www.fi.edu/history-resources/edisons-light-bulb.

3. Joyce Bedi, "Thomas Edison's Inventive Life," published April 18, 2004, http://invention.si.edu/thomas-edisons-inventive-life.

4. "Edison's Lightbulb," www.fi.edu/history-resources/edisons-lightbulb.

5. Ibid.

6. William Barclay, *The New Daily Study Bible* (Louisville, KY: Westminster John Knox Press, 2004).

7. International Standard Bible Encyclopedia, www.studylight.org/encyclopedias/isb/.

8. Colossians 3:15 (New King James Version).

Chapter Five: Communicating Your Results

1. Revelation 19:10 (New King James Version).

Part Three: The Experiment— a 40-Day Guide to Hearing God's Voice

1. Psalm 32:8 (New King James Version).

2. 1 Kings 19:12 (King James Version).

NOTES | 303

About the Author

As Founding Pastor of DC Metro Church, Dr. David Stine is known for how he uses his practical biblical teaching, his visionary leadership, and his heart to impact the D.C. metropolitan area. David's authenticity and his ability to communicate the truth of God's Word in a humorous, dynamic, and revelatory manner helps people understand the Bible and how to apply its teachings to their everyday lives. David is passionate about people coming to know Christ, getting planted in God's house, and becoming transformational leaders who work together to build a God-first culture throughout the D.C. metro area and beyond.

Shortly after coming to Christ in college, David knew there was a call on his life to full-time ministry and sensed God leading him to seminary at Regent University, where he earned a Master of Practical Theology and a Doctorate of Ministry in Leadership. David met his future wife, Taryn, at Louisiana State University where they both majored in business and were involved in a campus ministry together. After graduation, they were advancing in their respective careers, but the deepest desire of their hearts was to do something great for God together. Today they are parents to four growing children and are loving their call to full-time ministry at DC Metro Church. They believe nothing compares to the joy of experiencing the transformation in people's lives as they choose the God-first life.

Contact the Author

If you have any comments or would like to share any way God has encouraged you or helped you grow in hearing His voice through reading this book, we would love to hear from you. You can contact David Stine at david@davidstine.com or by visiting davidstine.com/contact.

READING GROUP GUIDE

HEARING FROM
GOD

DAVID STINE

Study Guide Questions

Use these study guide questions to further personalize your study on *Hearing from God*. These questions can also be used to facilitate discussion in a small group, Bible study, or classroom environment.

1. We are all in different places in our journey in hearing from God. Where would you say that you are in learning to recognize His voice, His guidance, His direction? What helps you to recognize God's voice in your life?

2. What are the biggest hindrances in your life to having a regular devotional time with God, and what can you do to overcome these over the next twenty-one days?

3. Has God's voice guided you in any of the different ways that His voice can be heard? In the book, I shared six different ways that God's voice can be heard. They include: 1) Strong recurring thought; 2) Idea with genuine excitement; 3) Deep calming peace; 4) Inner warning, caution, or check; 5) Supernatural knowing; 6) Open/closed door. Of these six, which ways has God's voice guided you?

4. God's voice did not always come in dramatic audible manifestations throughout the Bible, but, instead, He was often heard as a still small voice. Why do you think this is how God frequently speaks?

5. In the event that our life gets off course, God is faithful in helping us quickly get back on track as long as we surrender to Him. Have you ever experienced this before?

6. How has God guided you through His Word? Can you think of a particular instance that He has spoken to you in His Word?

7. What makes you feel closer to God when studying His Word?

8. What is challenging for you about studying God's Word?

9. How has God's Word encouraged, directed, or corrected you recently?

10. How has God guided you through others? List some of the people that God has used most significantly in your life to guide you. Next to each person that you list, note how they have helped you.

11. Oftentimes God does not just put people into our lives to help us—He puts people in our lives for us to help them in His plan for their

lives. Using the same list from question 10, note next to each person how you can be an encouragement in her or his life.

12. In the book, I talk about having at least three **SAFE** (**S**upportive, **A**ccountable, **F**un, **E**mpowering), close Christian friends. Who is currently playing this role in your life? If you don't have three people yet, what are some ways you can be intentional in trying to find and develop these types of relationships?

13. How can you navigate relationships when you have a difference of opinion with someone who is a close friend or someone who is playing the role of godly counsel in your life?

14. Do you have any friendships or close relationships that have been through seasons of hurt, offense, or disagreement? Did you eventually reconcile with these people? How can you determine which relationships are worth fighting to keep and which relationships need to transition to a less central role in your life?

15. How can you keep your friendships healthy, growing, and encouraging so that you can be a conduit for God to speak through and encourage others through godly counsel?

16. We all struggle with peace from time to time. Do you feel like His peace is something that you struggle to have in your own life on a regular basis? What causes you to go without God's peace in your life most often?

17. How can you continue to position yourself for growth and hearing God's voice more clearly in the future?